D0898755

SHIVERS VII

edited by Richard Chizmar

SHIVERS VII

edited by Richard Chizmar

CEMETERY DANCE PUBLICATIONS

Baltimore
❖ 2013 ❖

Contents

The Departed

Clive Barker

It was not only painters who were connoisseurs of light, Hermione had come to learn in the three days since her death; so too were those obliged to shun it. She was a member of that fretful clan now— a phantom in the world of flesh—and if she hoped to linger here for long she would have to avoid the sun's gift as scrupulously as a celibate avoided sin, and for much the same reason. It tainted, corrupted, and finally drove the soul into the embrace of extinction.

She wasn't so unhappy to be dead; life had been no bowl of cherries. She had failed at love, failed at marriage, failed at friendship, failed at motherhood. That last stung the sharpest. If she could have plunged back into life to change one thing she would have left the broken romances in pieces and gone to her six-year-old son Finn to say: trust your dreams, and take the world lightly, for it means nothing, even in the losing. She had shared these ruminations with one person only. His name was Rice; an ethereal nomad like herself who had died wasted and crazed from the plague but was now in death returned to corpulence and wit. Together they had spent that third day behind the blinds of his shunned apartment, listening to the babble of the street and exchanging tidbits. Towards evening, conversation turned to the subject of light.

"I don't see why the sun hurts us and the moon doesn't," Hermione reasoned. "The moon's reflected sunlight, isn't it?"

"Don't be so logical," Rice replied, "or so damn *serious*."

"And the stars are little suns. Why doesn't starlight hurt us?"

"I never liked looking at the stars," Rice replied. "They always made me feel lonely. Especially towards the end. I'd look up and see all that empty immensity and..." He caught himself in mid-sentence. "Damn you, woman, listen to me! We're going to have to get out of here and *party.*"

She drifted to the window.

"Down there?" she said.

"Down there."

"Will they see us?"

"Not if we go naked."

She glanced round at him. He was starting to unbutton his shirt.

"I can see you perfectly well," she told him.

"But you're dead, darling. The living have a lot more trouble." He tugged off his shirt and joined her at the window. "Shall we dare the dusk?" He asked her, and without waiting for a reply, raised the blind. There was just enough power in the light to give them both a pleasant buzz.

"I could get addicted to this," Hermione said, taking off her dress and letting the remnants of the day graze her breasts and belly.

"Now you're talking," said Rice. "Shall we take the air?"

All Hallows' Eve was a day away, a night away, and every shop along Main Street carried some sign of the season. A flight of paper witches here; a cardboard skeleton there.

"Contemptible," Rice remarked as they passed a nest of rubber bats. "We should protest."

"It's just a little fun," Hermione said.

"It's our holiday, darling. The Feast of the Dead. I feel like…like Jesus at a Sunday sermon. How dare they *simplify* me this way?" He slammed his phantom fists against the glass. It shook, and the remote din of his blow reached the ears of a passing family, all of whom looked towards the rattling window, saw nothing, and—trusting their eyes—moved on down the street.

Hermione gazed after them.

"I want to go and see Finn," she said.

"Not wise," Rice replied.

"Screw wise," she said. "I want to see him."

Rice already knew better than to attempt persuasion, so up the hill they went, towards her sister Elaine's house, where she assumed the boy had lodged since her passing.

"There's something you should know," Rice said as they climbed. "About being dead."

"Go on."

"It's difficult to explain. But it's no accident we feel safe under the moon. We're *like* the moon. Reflecting the light of something living; something that loves us. Does that make any sense?"

"Not much."

"Then it's probably the truth."

She stopped her ascent and turned to him. "Is this meant as a *warning* of some kind?" she asked.

"Would it matter if it were?"

"Not much."

He grinned. "I was the same. A warning was always an invitation."

"End of discussion?"

"End of discussion."

There were lamps burning in every room of Elaine's house, as if to keep the night and all it concealed at bay.

How sad, Hermione thought, to live in fear of shadows. But then didn't the day now hold as many terrors for her as night did for Elaine? Finally, it seemed, after thirty-one years of troubled sisterhood, the mirrors they had always held up to each other—fogged until this moment—were clear. Regret touched her, that she had not better known this lonely woman whom she had so resented for her lack of empathy.

"Stay here," she told Rice. "I want to see them on my own."

Rice shook his head. "I'm not missing this," he replied, and followed her up the path, then across the lawn towards the dining room window.

From inside came not two voices but three: a woman, a boy, and a man whose timbre was so recognizable it stopped Hermione in her invisible tracks.

"Thomas," she said.

"Your ex?" Rice murmured.

She nodded. "I hadn't expected…"

"You'd have preferred him not to come and mourn you?"

"That doesn't sound like mourning to me," she replied. Nor did it. The closer to the window they trod, the more merriment they heard. Thomas was cracking jokes, and Finn and Elaine were lapping up his performance.

"He's such a *clown!*" Hermione said. "Just listen to him."

They had reached the sill now, and peered in. It was worse than she'd expected. Thom had Finn on his knee, his arms wrapped around the child. He was whispering something in the boy's ear, and as he did so a grin appeared on Finn's face.

Hermione could not remember ever being seized by such contrary feelings. She was glad not to find her sweet Finn weeping—tears did not belong on that guileless face. But did he have to be quite so content; quite so forgetful of her passing? And as to Thom the clown, how could he so quickly have found his way back into his son's affections, having been an absentee father for five years? What bribes had he used to win back Finn's favor, master of empty promises that he was?

"Can we go trick-or-treating tomorrow night?" The boy was asking.

"Sure we can, partner," Thomas replied. "We'll get you a mask and a cape and—"

"You too," Finn replied. "You have to come too."

"Anything you want…"

"Son of a bitch," Hermione said.

"…from now on…"

"He never even *wrote* to the boy while I was alive."

"…anything you want."

"Maybe he's feeling guilty," Rice suggested.

"Guilty?" She hissed, clawing at the glass, longing to have her fingers at Thomas's lying throat. "He doesn't know the meaning of the word."

Her voice had risen in pitch and volume, and Elaine—who had always been so insensitive to nuance—seemed to hear its echo. She rose from the table, turning her troubled gaze towards the window.

"Come away," Rice said, taking hold of Hermione's arm. "Or this is going to end badly."

"I don't care," she said.

Her sister was crossing to the window now, and Thomas was sliding Finn off his knee, rising as he did so, a question on his lips.

"There's somebody…watching us," Elaine murmured. There was fear in her voice.

Thomas came to her side; slipped his arm around her waist.

Hermione expelled what she thought was a shuddering sigh, but at the sound of it the window shattered, a hail of glass driving man, woman and child back from the sill.

"*Away!*" Rice demanded, and this time she conceded; went with him, across the lawn, out into the street, through the benighted town and finally home to the cold apartment where she could weep out the rage and frustration she felt.

Her tears had not dried by dawn; nor even by noon. She wept for too many reasons, and for nothing at all. For Finn, for Thomas, for the fear in her sister's eyes; and for the terrible absence of sense in everything. At last, however, her unhappiness found a salve.

"I want to touch him one last time," she told Rice.

"Finn?"

"Of course Finn."

"You'll scare the bejeezus out of him."

"He'll never know it's me."

She had a plan. If she was invisible when naked, then she would clothe every part of herself, and put on a mask, and find him in the streets, playing trick-or-treat. She would smooth his fine hair with her palm, or lay her fingers on his lips, then be gone, forever, out of the twin states of living death and Idaho.

"I'm warning you," she told Rice, "you shouldn't come."

"Thanks for the invitation," he replied a little ruefully. "I accept."

His clothes had been boxed and awaited removal. They untaped the boxes, and dressed in motley. The cardboard they tore up and shaped into crude masks—horns for her, elfin ears for him. By the time they were ready for the streets All Hallows' Eve had settled on the town.

It was Hermione who led the way back towards Elaine's house, but she set a leisurely pace. Inevitable meetings did not have to be hurried to; and she was quite certain she would encounter Finn if she simply let instinct lead her.

There were children at every corner, dressed for the business of the night. Ghouls, zombies and fiends every one; freed to be cruel by mask and darkness, as she was freed to be loving, one last time, and then away.

"Here he comes," she heard Rice say, but she'd already recognized Finn's jaunty step.

"You distract Thom," she told Rice.

"My pleasure," came the reply, and the revenant was away from her side in an instant. Thom saw him coming, and sensed something awry. He reached to snatch hold of Finn, but Rice pitched himself against the solid body, his ether forceful enough to throw Thom to the ground.

He let out a ripe curse, and rising the next instant, snatched hold of his assailant. He might have landed a blow but that he caught sight of Hermione as she closed on Finn, and instead turned and snatched at her mask.

It came away in his hands, and the sight of her face drew from him a shout of horror. He retreated a step; then another.

"Jesus... Jesus..." he said.

She advanced upon him, Rice's warning ringing in her head. "What do you see?" she demanded.

By way of reply he heaved up his dinner in the gutter.

"He sees decay," Rice said. "He sees rot."

"Mom?"

She heard Finn's voice behind her; felt his little hand tug at her sleeve. "Mom, is that you?"

Now it was she who let out a cry of distress; she who trembled.

"Mom?" he said again.

She wanted so much to turn; to touch his hair, his cheek; to kiss him goodbye. But Thom had seen rot in her. Perhaps the child would see the same, or worse.

"Turn round," he begged.

"I...can't...Finn."

"Please."

And before she could stop herself, she was turning, her hands dropping from her face.

The boy squinted. Then he smiled.

"You're so *bright*," he said.

"I am?"

She seemed to see her radiance in his eyes; touching his cheeks, his lips, his brow as lovingly as any hand. So this was what it felt like to be a moon, she thought; to reflect a living light. It was a fine condition.

"Finn..."

Thom was summoning the boy to his side.

"He's frightened of you," Finn explained.

"I know. I'd better go."

The boy nodded gravely.

"Will you explain to him?" She asked Finn. "Tell him what you saw?"

Again, the boy nodded. "I won't forget," he said.

That was all she needed; more than all. She left him with his father, and Rice led her away, through darkened alleyways and empty parking lots to the edge of town. They discarded their costumes as they went. By the time they reached the freeway, they were once more naked and invisible.

"Maybe we'll wander awhile," Rice suggested. "Go down south."

"Sure," she replied. "Why not?"

"Key West for Christmas. New Orleans for Mardi Gras. And maybe next year we'll come back here. See how things are going."

She shook her head. "Finn belongs to Thom now," she said. "He belongs to life."

"And who do we belong to?" Rice asked, a little sadly.

She looked up. "You know damn well," she said, and pointed to the moon.

Red Rover, Red Rover

Norman Partridge

Everyone says the lake is haunted, but the boys have been looking all summer and they haven't seen one ghost.

Until now.

Of course, it's not a ghost in the conventional sense of the word, though the boys can't understand that yet. Right now it's just a man. The boys are in the cattails, trying to catch a couple frogs when they first notice him standing there with a canvas bag in one hand on a little scab of beach across the lake.

"Hey," Jason says. "What do you suppose he's got in the bag?"

"I don't know," Bill says.

"I know you don't *know*, numbnuts. I just asked what you *suppose* he's got."

"Pipe down! The guy's gonna hear you if you don't. He's probably some kind of nut, like that bum who hangs out in Miller's Woods. He hears you, he'll probably be over here in a minute shaking us down for pocket change."

"He doesn't look like a nut," Jason says.

Bill snorts a laugh. "That's what you think, genius."

Both boys give the stranger the eye. They're best friends. Jason's the bigger of the two. He just turned eleven a couple days ago—August 1, 1969 to be exact—but he could pass for thirteen easy. Bill gave Jason a board game called Clue for his birthday. They've been playing it for a week, solving murder mysteries while the old black-and-white TV in Jason's living room drones on in the background and Jason's kid sister Molly begs them to play Candy Land with her. That's a laugh. Bill and Jason don't care anything about Candy Land. They ignore Molly completely. She says, "All you care about is Colonel Mustard in the library with the candlestick and Professor Plum in the kitchen with a rope. That's a *stupid* game. Everybody just kills everybody else!"

Bill and Jason don't see it that way. They're pretty good at Clue. They figure they're ace detectives—that's why they're here at the lake in the first place, to see what's up with all the ghost stories going around the neighborhood. And now there's a stranger here, and they want to find out something about him. It's like another mystery they have to solve, and they'll solve it together. Like I told you, they're best friends.

Keeping his head down so he won't be noticed, Bill peeks through the cattail curtain. The sun is setting behind the trees, and it's hard to see the stranger on the other side of the lake when you're staring into the sun that way.

So Bill can't see the mystery man's features very well, but there's other stuff he *can* see that tells him something about the guy. Like the fact that he's clean-shaven and his clothes look neat and new. The man is wearing the kind of stuff Bill always thinks of as "Dad's day off" clothes: khaki pants and a plaid short-sleeve shirt and some kind of loafers... probably Hush Puppies, Bill figures, because every dad he knows owns a pair of Hush Puppies—

"Hey, look what he's doing!" Jason says.

With one hand, Bill shades his eyes against the sun for a better look. The man's holding the canvas bag by the knotted end, pivoting in a circle as he swings the bag, taking little Hush Puppie steps as he turns 'round and 'round and 'round.

"Jesus Chrysler!" Jason says. "This guy's a human tilt-a-whirl!"

For once, Jason's right. Bill can see that. The man must be getting dizzy. He misses a step, nearly trips. He's close to the water's edge now, out of tree-shadow and into setting sunlight, and the stark brightness catches his sunglasses and Bill thinks he can see the man smiling for a second and he thinks: *Yeah, he's gotta be a nut, smiling like that, spinning 'round and 'round and 'round in his Hush Puppies like that.*

The man lets go of the bag. It sails out over the lake... and the man watches it... and Bill watches it... and Jason watches it....

It's completely quiet. Just for a second. And then there's a big splash as the bag hits the water. The mystery man just stands there watching. He's not smiling now.

And the bag starts to sink. And the canvas ripples. There's something inside the bag, thrashing around.

Something that barks, then squeals.

"It's a dog!" Jason says. "That creep put a dog in that bag! He's gonna drown it!"

"Shut up!" Bill says. "You keep yelling, he's gonna hear you for sure!"

Bill looks across the lake to confirm his suspicions, but the mystery man isn't there anymore. In the couple of seconds Bill spent staring at the canvas bag floating out there in the lake, the guy has vanished.

Bill stares across the lake for a couple more seconds, just to be sure the stranger's really gone. Nothing moves over there on that little scab of a beach. There's nothing under the trees but shadows.

"Hey," Jason says. "How'd he disappear so fast?"

Bill doesn't answer.

He peels off his T-shirt and tosses it on the shore behind him.

He dives through the cattails, hits the water, and starts swimming.

Bill is a good swimmer.

And fast.

It's a hot day. Been hot for a week now. Pushing a hundred degrees every day, and no breeze at all, and about six kinds of miserable if you're not eating an ice-cream cone or sitting cool and cozy in an air-conditioned movie theater. So the water feels pretty good to our friend Bill.

Or it should. After all, the water's cold, like that August sun up there in the sky doesn't bother it at all. Cold enough to raise gooseflesh on your skin. October cold. You'd think more kids would be at the lake on a day like this, because it isn't that far from town. It's just a mile or so off a country road which is a mile or so from the tract-house neighborhood where Bill and Jason both live.

Yeah. You'd think more kids would be here today, relaxing in the shade beneath the old oak trees, taking a cool dip in the heat of the late afternoon. But no one comes to the lake much anymore.

To tell the truth, it was never really good for swimming anyway. First off there are the cattails, which rim most of the lake. They're like some kind of wall, and the little scab of a beach where Bill and Jason spotted the stranger is one of the few places where you can actually wade straight out into the water if you want to.

You do that, you find out PDQ that the lake bottom is slimy muck. Kind of stuff that sucks at your feet like it wants to gobble 'em up while you wade through it. You get out a little further, to a place where it's actually deep enough to swim, you run into clots of water lilies. They blanket big sections of the glassy surface and they're cold and slimy and they make Bill think of dead fish floating belly up. He can't stand them.

So the lake's no good for swimming. Oh, maybe kids might try it once in a while. Maybe they'd come here and swim across the lake... but only on a dare. And as far as dares go, it'd have to be a double-dog after that little girl drowned last year.

It's her ghost that kids have been talking about all summer. Some say they've seen her walking along the country road at night in wet cutoffs and a T-shirt, trying to find her way home. Others—mostly older kids, teenagers who visit the lake to drink beer—say they've heard her voice soughing through the cattails with the evening breeze. Sometimes Bill believes those stories and sometimes he doesn't. Either way they scare him, and like any good detective he wants to know the truth. That's why he and Jason came to the lake today with sleeping bags, canteens, and knapsacks packed with dinner. They'd planned to camp out tonight and find out for themselves if there's really a ghost or not.

One thing's for sure—if there is a ghost, Bill and Jason are bound to recognize her, because the drowned girl was in their class. Her name was Cheryl Ann Rose. She took a dare from her friends last summer, tried to swim across the lake on a hot August afternoon. Liza Rycott said Cheryl Ann was doing fine until she hit one of those clots of water lilies. She went under and that was the last they saw of her. Took the cops three days to find Cheryl Ann's body down there in that cold black water, down there in the mud with only a blanket of water lilies to keep her warm—

No. Bill's not going to think about Cheryl Ann. He can't afford to do that now. Because he's closing in on the bag. If he starts thinking about Cheryl Ann, he's going to start thinking that every plant that brushes his foot is her ghostly hand, trying to pull him under.

So he thinks about the bag instead, and that's all he thinks about. As he raises his head for a breath he can see that the bag is mostly underwater, but the knotted end and a couple three inches of canvas still break above the surface. The material isn't entirely saturated with water yet, and since the bag's still floating there's got to be a pocket of air trapped inside. Bill's thinking that if there's an air pocket in there, the dog might still be okay.

Just then the bag bobs in the water. Movement. That means the dog's still alive. At least right now it is... and right now Bill's just ten feet away.

He raises his head for another breath, then keeps on stroking. Behind him he hears Jason splashing along in his wake. Jason's not much of a swimmer—he's a big kid, already has a set of shoulders that tell you he'll end up playing football in high school.

If he lives that long, Bill thinks. And just that quick he shakes the idea out of his head. Because he's really not thinking of Jason at all. He's really thinking of Cheryl Ann Rose.

He won't do that now.

Not when he's so close.

Not when he's *right there*.

Bill grabs the bag and starts treading water. The bag's not very big at all. He rolls onto his back, pulls the bag up on his belly and holds it there with his hands. He glances at Jason behind him, just to be sure his friend is okay. Once he's certain of that, he starts kicking toward shore, doing a modified backstroke.

He kicks through clutches of spidery plants that scrape at him from the mucky bottom, and he doesn't think of the drowned girl's hands once. Instead he tells himself that he's going to keep kicking until he hits that little scab of beach on the other side of the lake.

Bill feels other legs kicking, too.
They're kicking against his chest.
The dog in the bag. It's still alive.
Bill hears it whimper. The poor thing must be terrified.
He swims on, advancing through the cold dark water.
He doesn't make a sound.

Bill's been on shore for a couple minutes, the open bag at his feet, when Jason comes slogging out of the water onto the little beach.

"All right!" Jason says. "The dog's okay!"

Bill doesn't say anything. Jason's right, of course. The rust-colored terrier is fine. The runty pooch barks and wags its nub of a tail. It's soaked straight through, shivering on little chopstick legs while it trots around in shadows cast by a couple of old oak trees. But Bill isn't looking at the dog. He's looking at the canvas bag—

"Hey, Bill, are you okay?"

Bill doesn't answer, because he's got the pocket knife he used to open the bag in one hand, but in his other hand he clutches a tangle of colored ribbon that had sealed the bag.

He hadn't noticed the ribbon when he first grabbed the bag out there in the lake. He'd been too intent on getting the dog to shore safely. But he notices it now, because a good detective has to be observant. There are two intertwined strands of ribbon, royal purple and dark valentine red, the kind of stuff you get at the five-and-dime when you want to wrap up a present. The ends of the ribbon have been scored with a pair of scissors or a knife, making curlicues that wrap around Bill's fingers. He can't imagine why someone who wanted to drown a dog would use gift ribbon to close up the bag, or why they'd score that ribbon with curlicues. He can't imagine why the man who threw the dog in the lake would do that, but the fact that he did scares Bill, even though he really can't explain why.

Jason sweeps the mutt into his arms. The pooch nuzzles under his chin with its nose, then licks his cheek, and Jason can't help but laugh while he scratches the dog behind one ragged ear.

"Hey," Jason says. "This mutt's got a tag."

And he's right. There's a leather collar around the dog's neck, with a silver tag dangling from it. Jason sets the dog on the ground. Bill kneels, takes the tag in his hand, and reads one side:

MY NAME IS:
RED ROVER

And then the other:

I BELONG TO:
CHERYL ANN ROSE
(707) 641-8734

Bill swallows hard. He lets go of the tag. Red Rover barks happily, wags that nub of a tail and nuzzles Bill's hand, then barks again.

Bill stares down at the wet mutt. He's Cheryl Ann Rose's dog. Cheryl Ann drowned in the lake last summer. She drowned, and it took the cops three days to find her down there in that cold black water, down there in the mud with only a blanket of water lilies to keep her warm. And now someone has brought her dog here, brought him here to drown in a canvas bag wrapped with gift ribbons of royal purple and dark valentine red, brought him here like a present for a dead little girl—

It all starts to make sense to Bill. Like Colonel Mustard in the library with the candlestick, like Professor Plum in the kitchen with a rope...

The dog cocks his head toward the shadows and growls.

Bill reaches down and grabs Red Rover's collar.

He hears the footsteps before he sees the man step from the shadows.

Hush Puppies... khaki pants... a plaid short-sleeve shirt... and sunglasses.

The same man who threw the dog into the lake.

Cheryl Ann Rose's father.

Dad's day off...

Bill can see the whole picture now.

Mr. Rose... at the lake... with the canvas bag...

Mr. Rose steps onto the gritty beach. Bill holds tight to Red Rover's collar. The little mutt barks at Mr. Rose, but the man only smiles.

Mr. Rose stares at Bill from behind his sunglasses.

"Give me that dog," he says.

"W-we can't do that," Jason says, his voice shaking like it's a loose part he's ready to cough up and spit out.

Mr. Rose laughs. "You can and you will. That dog belongs to my daughter. Her name's Cheryl Ann, and the dog's name is Red Rover. Just look at the tag if you don't believe me."

Mr. Rose stares at the boys like he's just explained something only a moron would have trouble understanding. He stands there at the edge of the woods, his arms crossed, waiting for an answer. Jason doesn't say anything, just shoots a worried glance Bill's way. Bill doesn't know what to say, either. He's never talked to a crazy person before.

And he's sure that's exactly what Mr. Rose is. A crazy person. Forget the man's neat appearance. Forget the "Dad's day off" wardrobe. Mr. Rose is crazy. Anyone can see that.

Even Red Rover.

Mr. Rose takes a step forward, and the little dog barks louder, baring his teeth.

Mr. Rose sighs. "I'm glad someone here will talk to me, but that's enough from you, Rover. I already heard you bark. After all, that's why I came back to check on you."

Cheryl Ann's father smiles some more, but Bill's having none of it. "We saw you throw this dog in the lake," he says plainly, because he can't see any point in sugarcoating what happened. "We can't let you have it back."

"You boys are making a mistake."

"No," Jason says, and his voice doesn't quaver at all this time. "You made the mistake, mister. You tried to drown your dog. And we saw you do it."

"Red Rover is not my dog. I've already explained that to you. He belongs to my daughter, Cheryl Ann."

"It doesn't really matter who he belongs to," Bill says. "As far as we're concerned this dog is our responsibility now, and we're going to take care of him."

Mr. Rose shakes his head. "You boys have to listen to me," he says. "I know it sounds strange. I didn't believe the stories about my daughter when I first heard them myself. I didn't believe them until I came out here to the lake a few months ago, on the anniversary of Cheryl Ann's death. That's when I found out that the stories were true. I heard my daughter's voice, heard it as plain as you're hearing my voice right now. I heard her calling for Red Rover. She had a special way of calling him. *Red Rover, Red Rover, won't you come over...*"

"Look," Bill says. "We're sorry about Cheryl Ann, but—"

"I don't care if you boys are sorry or not," Mr. Rose says, his voice rising. "All I care about is my daughter. She wants her dog back. She loves that little guy so much, and she's all alone now. She needs Red Rover. You boys can understand that, can't you? You wouldn't want my daughter to be all alone out here, would you?"

Mr. Rose waits for an answer, but he doesn't get one.

A moment later he wipes a hand over one cheek, just below his sunglasses.

The boys can't believe it. Mr. Rose has started to cry.

Bill doesn't know what to say to that. Neither does Jason. He bends down and picks up Red Rover and cradles him under one arm. Then he turns his back on Mr. Rose and starts walking. Mr. Rose doesn't make a move. After a minute, Bill follows Jason. They start along a dirt trail that traces the edge of the lake. The trail that leads back to town begins where Mr. Rose is standing, but they can't take that one yet. First they have to go back to the other side of the lake, to the spot where they were looking for frogs. That's where they left their camping stuff and, more importantly, their shoes. It's a mile from the lake back to the country road that leads to town, another mile from there to their neighborhood. They'll never make it that far barefoot.

They walk fast. It's rough going, though. The path is rocky, and they have to watch their step. While they walk, Bill keeps glancing over his shoulder, watching Mr. Rose, all alone on that little scab of a beach.

It's dusk now, and soon it will be dark.

Mr. Rose just stands there, not doing a thing.

Bill steps on a sharp rock and winces. He looks down. He'd better watch where he's going. There are lots of rocks on this part of the path. If he remembers right, there are a few broken beer bottles, too.

Right now, a hunk of broken glass in his foot is the last thing he needs.

What happens next, Bill doesn't need, either.

The next time he looks over his shoulder, he sees Mr. Rose coming after them.

And he's running.

Bill yells a warning, and Jason turns to look.

"Jesus Chrysler!" he yells. He turns to run, the dog still cradled in his arms. Bill's right behind him, picking up steam. A couple more steps and Bill's shot past him. Rover's clawing Jason's chest, trying to break free, but Jason holds on, trying to keep his eyes on the dog and the trail at the same time. The rocks are killing his feet. Jason hates going barefoot and never does it. Bill's always teasing him, saying that for a guy who wants to join the U. S. Marines someday he sure has tender baby feet—

Jason sees the broken beer bottle a second too late, just in time to hear a thick shard crunch under his right foot. The pain explodes up his ankle, turns his knee to jelly, and drops him as surely as if he'd been hit by a hammer. He lays there on the path, and he's still got Rover in his arms—he'd pulled the dog to his chest like it was a football when he fell—but he can't hold on and the terrier scrambles away and charges up the path toward Bill, who doesn't even know that his friend has fallen.

Jason looks in the other direction and sees Mr. Rose running up the path, coming straight for him.

"Bill," Jason shouts. "Hold up!"

Bill breaks stride. Stops and turns. Red Rover shoots past him like a rocket, and Bill swears.

Jason gets up as quick as he can. He tries putting weight on his cut foot, but suddenly it's like his foot has grown a mouth, and it lets go with a scream of bloodcurdling proportions.

Jason grimaces. Gotta be he's sliced up pretty good, but that's the least of his worries. Mr. Rose is still coming down the path, running hard. Jason stands there, waiting, trying to brace himself. There's not much else he can do.

He closes his eyes, just for a second.

He hears Mr. Rose's footsteps in front of him.

And Bill's footsteps coming from behind.

He takes a deep breath.

He opens his eyes.

Bill watches as Mr. Rose barrels into Jason. The big kid doesn't stand much of a chance. He's unsteady on his feet to begin with, like he twisted his ankle or something, and he starts to go down as soon as Cheryl Ann's father hits him.

At least Jason manages to grab Mr. Rose and take him down, too. They roll off the trail, into the water, and they end up in a tangle of cattails. Mr. Rose comes out on top. He's screaming now, but Bill can't make out a word the man's saying.

Bill tries to run faster, tries to hurry. He's so intent on helping his friend that he almost steps on a busted beer bottle. He jumps it and doesn't even break stride but he's still about twenty feet away from Jason and Mr. Rose and he's dancing over rocks, but he can't miss all of them, and the ones he steps on punch his heels like nasty little fists and—

Just that fast, Bill stops cold.

It's the look on Mr. Rose's face that stops him. The man's smiling, his thin lips framing gritted teeth. He's got Jason pinned in the cattails, and he's holding the boy's head underwater, and Jason's exhalations are bubbling to the surface.

"You boys *shouldn't* have given me an argument," Mr. Rose says, looking at Bill. "You *should* have given me that dog while you still had the chance."

Jason's arms thrash in the muddy water, but Mr. Rose holds him firm.

Bill's heart pounds in his chest.

He snatches up a rock.

It's about the size of a golf ball.

He lets fly.

Bill has never heard a sound like it. It's awful. Like a cleaver hitting a rack of beef ribs, only worse.

Bill doesn't see where the rock goes after it hits Mr. Rose in the forehead. He expects the man to fall over, the way bad guys do on television. But Mr. Rose just stares at him from behind his sunglasses, and pretty soon Bill wonders if the rock missed the man entirely.

No, he tells himself. *I know the rock hit him. I heard the sound.*

The same way Mr. Rose hears his daughter calling in the night? asks a voice in Bill's head.

No! I heard it hit him! I know I did!

And just that quick Bill knows he's right, because just that quick he sees blood gushing from Mr. Rose's forehead. Red streaks spill down the lenses of the man's sunglasses. Blood washes down his nose and drips off his chin. But Mr. Rose doesn't cry out, and he doesn't wipe away the blood.

He releases Jason, and Bill's friend crawls out of the muddy water coughing and gasping for air.

Mr. Rose stands up and wades out of the cattails. He climbs onto the path. And now he's coming towards Bill. And he's still smiling. And he pushes his sunglasses high on his nose, as if nothing has happened at all.

Bill backs off. He sees Jason gagging by the side of the lake. His friend is in no condition to help him stop Mr. Rose. So Bill dips down fast and picks up another rock. The lenses of Mr. Rose's sunglasses are painted with blood. Bill doesn't even know if the man can see him anymore. All he knows is that Cheryl Ann's father is coming for him.

Mr. Rose's Hush Puppies crunch over the same broken beer bottle that cut Jason's foot. He opens his mouth. He's still smiling. His teeth are red with dripping blood.

"Red Rover," Mr. Rose says. "Red Rover. Won't you... come..."

Mr. Rose doesn't finish the sentence.

He finally falls.

He falls hard.

The boys move away from Mr. Rose as fast as they can. When they're about fifty feet down the trail, Jason has to take a break. He hobbles over to a big rock by the lake's edge, splashes water on his foot and washes the cut, which is already caked with dirt from the path. Once he gets it clean the cut doesn't look as bad as it feels, but it's bleeding pretty steadily.

Bill climbs up on the rock and tries to spot the place where Mr. Rose collapsed, but he can't see the injured man—or the section of path where he fell—over the cattails.

"Don't worry," Jason says. "You knocked him cold. He's not gonna move for a while."

Bill nods, but he's just not sure. All he knows is that he wants to get away from the lake as quickly as possible. First, he needs to get Jason to a doctor. His friend probably needs stitches in his foot. Then he needs to call the cops and tell them about Mr. Rose.

Before Bill can do any of that stuff, he and Jason have to get their shoes. They follow the trail back to the spot where they set up camp. That takes a while. Jason's hobbling pretty bad. He practically has to hop down the trail. But Jason doesn't complain, and he seems a little better once he gets his shoes and socks on. They're PF Flyers. They're almost new, and they're white, but Bill knows they won't be white for long. At least not the right shoe, because it's Jason's right foot that's bleeding, and they've got a good walk ahead of them.

There's a trail that cuts over the hills behind the lake and connects to the country road that leads back to town. It's a little longer than the trail that runs along the shore, but neither boy wants to take that one. It would mean passing Mr. Rose, and they don't want to take that chance.

The boys leave their camping stuff behind. They're just about at the trailhead when they remember the dog. They haven't seen Red Rover since Mr. Rose jumped Jason.

"We can't just leave him here," Bill says. "What if Mr. Rose gets hold of Red Rover before we can call the cops?"

"I don't think the dog would go near that nut," Jason says. "Besides, it's getting dark. I don't want to be around here at night."

"What's the matter?" Bill says. "Are you scared you'll see Cheryl Ann's *ghost?*"

Jason stops dead in his tracks. After everything that's happened, he's completely forgotten about the little girl's ghost. He looks at his friend. All of a sudden Bill's got a goofy grin on his face, like he finally figured out the biggest joke of all. Bill starts laughing, and so does Jason. The whole thing *does* seem pretty funny. After all, they came out here to see if they could spot a ghost, an ectoplasmic will o' the wisp, a good old-fashioned spook. They sure didn't see anything like that.

"I don't even believe in ghosts anymore," Jason says. "But I *do* believe in Mr. Rose."

"Yeah," Bill says. "I guess I believe in him, too."

"Besides, I figure Red Rover can take care of himself. He's probably long gone, anyhow. Let's you and me get out of here."

They start walking. Jason has a tough time of it. He can't move very fast, even when he leans on Bill's shoulder, but he doesn't give up. He won't *cry uncle*, no matter what.

A grove of eucalyptus trees separates the lake from the hill. Powdery gravel crunches under the boys' feet as they follow an inclined path into shadows that smell clean and crisp.

At the edge of the trees, Jason stops for a break. Already, his right PF Flyer is getting red on one side, but that isn't what's bothering him. "Maybe we should at least try to call the little mutt," he says. "That wouldn't hurt, would it?"

"No," Bill says. "That wouldn't hurt at all."

Both boys turn toward the lake. The sun's gone now. The evening sky is streaked with royal purple and dark valentine red.

It's twilight.

Bill opens his mouth to call the dog. He doesn't even get a word out before he spots Red Rover running down the path, coming toward them like a bullet.

Below, Mr. Rose's voice cuts through the cattails like a scythe. "Red Rover... Red Rover... won't you come over?"

"He's close," Jason says.

"Yeah," Bill says, staring through the eucalyptus grove at the trail that leads to the hill. "Think you can run?"

Jason glances down at his bloodstained tennis shoe. He shakes his head. Then he looks toward the lake trail, watching for Mr. Rose.

"If we can't outrun him, then we'll have to hide," Bill says. "Maybe we can find a good spot in the woods—"

"Maybe we don't have to," Jason says. Because he's seen something that Bill missed. There's a blackberry thicket at the juncture of the lake and hill trails. A deer run cuts into the blackberries. Both Bill and Jason have spent time in there during the last three picking seasons, only to emerge with scratched arms and snagged T-shirts and lips purple with the sweetest berries you ever tasted. Which is another way of saying that the blackberry thicket isn't exactly easy going, but it *is* a great place to hide.

Bill and Jason disappear into the thicket.

Red Rover follows the boys.

It's dark now.

No more royal purple or dark valentine red in the sky. Bill, Jason, and Red Rover are nested in a blackberry burrow that some animal—or some bum—must have abandoned. They stare up through a crosshatched roof of blackberry brambles, and the only thing they see that isn't black is a ripe melon slice of moon.

The moon doesn't provide much light, but it's enough to reveal tangled vine shadows on Bill and Jason's faces, enough to expose the terror in Red Rover's gleaming eyes each time Mr. Rose calls his name.

So far the little terrier has been quiet. Just as quiet as the boys. So far...

But Mr. Rose is coming closer now.

"Red Rover... Red Rover... won't you come over?'

The dog whines and Bill pulls him to his chest. Mr. Rose's voice cuts through the blackberries the same way it cut through the cattails—high and keening, like a scythe. Forget Carol Ann's ghost. Her dad's voice is all it takes to frighten Bill more than he's ever been frightened in his life.

Bill closes his eyes, but there's no escape. He pictures Mr. Rose wandering around out there beneath the slivered moon, his face a mask of drying blood, his eyes hidden behind those blood-splattered sunglasses even in the dark of the night.

"Red Rover... Red Rover... won't you come over..."

Bill's eyes flash open. The dog whines. Bill grabs Red Rover's muzzle. The little mutt's shaking, his heart thudding against the crook of Bill's elbow. The boy holds Red Rover tight and doesn't let go, but he can't stop the dog from whining.

"That mutt's gonna give us away," Jason says.

Bill knows that Jason is right, but there's nothing he can do about it. Jason can't run on his sliced-up foot. Bill can't leave his friend behind. He can't leave the dog, either. So all they can do is sit tight and hope that Mr. Rose doesn't find them.

"Red Rover... Red Rover..."

The dog squirms away from Bill.

Red Rover barks.

Not far from the burrow, Mr. Rose laughs.

"That's a good doggy," he says.

Ten or fifteen feet away, something hits the blackberry vines. Bill figures that Mr. Rose probably has a broken branch or something. He's literally beating the bushes, trying to flush them out.

"Red Rover!" Mr. Rose says. "C'mon, boy! Cheryl Ann's waiting for you! You want to see her, don't you?"

Red Rover whines again, and Bill's hand tightens around the dog's muzzle. Bill doesn't feel like a detective anymore. He doesn't want to solve any mysteries. In the dark under a melon slice of moon, he's suddenly scared of everything, because everything he imagines seems thoroughly plausible and undisputedly real. Mr. Rose. Cheryl Ann's ghost. His own shadow, hidden somewhere in a dark pocket of night. All of it boils up in his brain in a hundred wild imaginings, each one real enough to hurt him, each one real enough to *kill* him if he just sits there waiting—

Mr. Rose calls again. The branch hits another tangle of blackberry vines. Every fiber of Bill's being tells him that he should run, get out of here as fast as he can, run as fast as his legs will carry him and never look back... but he can't do that. Not with Jason the way he is... and not with the dog trembling in his arms.

So he doesn't move a muscle and he peers through the vines, watching the deer run for a sign of Mr. Rose. Shadows creep out there in the night, and one of them might be Cheryl Ann's father gripping a twisted branch in his hands, but Bill can't be sure.

"Red Rover... Red Rover..."

This time, the voice comes from behind. Bill turns and stares at the back of the burrow, but the only thing he sees through the brambles is that ripe melon slice of a moon, and all he can think of is a scythe because that's what Mr. Rose's voice sounds like. He's coming for them. He's gonna *get* them. Kill them, just like they're a couple of characters in Clue. And the cops'll come out and find their bodies, the same way they found Cheryl Ann's body. *It was Mr. Rose in the blackberry thicket with a scythe,* they'll say, but none of it will matter because Bill and Jason will be dead—

Again, the cutting voice, but this time different words.

"I see you!"

Red Rover explodes from Bill's arms. Toward the back of the burrow, a shadow darts through the brambles. It brushes Bill's head, tries to grab a handful of hair, but Bill pulls away and rolls toward the burrow's entrance where he bumps up against Red Rover, who's barking his little head off.

"Let's go!" Jason says, and he shoots out of the burrow, so scared he's hardly limping at all.

Red Rover follows.

So does Bill.

Bill figures it's just dumb luck that gets them out of the blackberries before Mr. Rose. Must have been that he was on another path that snaked around the backside of the burrow when he tried to grab Bill through the brambles. That path didn't connect up with the deer run, so they managed to give Cheryl Ann's dad the slip.

They take the lake trail. Bill and Jason and Red Rover. Soon they're about halfway to the little scab of a beach. Bill can smell the lake, hear frogs croaking out in the cattails. He also hears Mr. Rose swearing as he thrashes around back there in the blackberry thicket, trying to find a way out.

Let him swear, Bill thinks. He almost wants to laugh. His arms are scratched and his T-shirt is torn courtesy of his stay in the blackberries, but suddenly he's not afraid anymore. Not of Mr. Rose. Not of the lake, with its cold black water and blankets of water lilies. Not of Cheryl Ann Rose's ghost—

And now Bill does laugh. If he's learned anything tonight, it's that he shouldn't be afraid of ghosts. No. It's the living he should fear. The rest of it's just make-believe. The rest of it's not real.

Mr. Rose is real. Bill understands that now. The real ghosts are men like Cheryl Ann's father. Men who can never bury their dead little girls. Men who are forever haunted by tragedy and tortured by regret and—

Up ahead, Jason trips and goes down hard. Bill sees a dark mound in the moonlight. There must be a big rock in the middle of the trail.

Only Bill doesn't remember there being a rock in this place. He stops short of the mound. Red Rover heels at his side. Jason's already getting up, dusting himself off.

Together, they look down. Neither one of them says a word, because there on the ground, exactly where he fell after being hit in the head by the rock that Bill threw, lies Mr. Rose.

He's as still as the grave.

He doesn't move a muscle.

His lips don't part for a breath or a word.

Not even when his voice rings out from the blackberry thicket, cutting through the night like a scythe.

"Red Rover... Red Rover... won't you come over?"

"Oh, God," Jason says as he gapes at the dead man. "Oh... Jesus!"

And then another voice rises in the distance. It comes from the lake, soughing through the cattails like a cool evening breeze.

It's a voice that once belonged to a little girl.

"Red Rover... Red Rover... won't you come over?"

The little dog whines, shivering in the moonlight as the voices join in a duet.

"Red Rover... Red Rover..."

The boys stare down at the dead man.

Mr. Rose doesn't move at all.

But he comes for them just the same.

Breakbone

Bill Pronzini

The dashboard clock read 7:30 when I pulled into the truck stop west of Tucumcari, New Mexico—and there he was, sitting on a bench outside the café. It was a hot July evening and I'd been on the road for nine hours and nearly seven hundred miles, but after dinner I figured I could make another hundred or more before I packed it in for the day. Pushing it because of the job with Burnside Chemicals but mainly because Karen was waiting in L.A. I hadn't seen her in two weeks and I was hungry for her and she would be for me, too.

Right now it was food I was hungry for; I hadn't eaten since an early breakfast. I filled the Audi's tank and then pulled over into one of the parking slots near the café. On the walk from there to the entrance I had to pass by the guy sitting slumped on the bench.

He was the biggest man I'd ever seen outside a basketball arena. Close to seven feet tall, lean but not skinny; huge hands like a couple of fur-backed catcher's mitts, the fingers gnarled and scarred from manual labor. Wearing a sweat-stained shirt, dusty Levi's, and old, heavily scuffed boots. He was bent forward with the hands hanging down between his knees, his chin tipped toward his chest, his gaze on the small, battered duffel between his feet. He had a kind of heavy, bland face, and he looked hot and tired and forlorn, like a kid nobody wanted to have anything to do with. But he wasn't a kid, exactly. Late twenties, I thought, a few years younger than me.

I went past him by a couple of steps, then stopped and turned back. There was just something about him. That forlorn look, I guess. Karen says I'm a sucker for strays, the lost and lonely in human and animal kingdoms both. I don't deny it. Better that kind of person than the one who doesn't give a damn.

"Sorry to bother you," I said, "but are you okay?"

He looked up. He had big, sad eyes, the irises the color of milk chocolate. "Hot," he said. His voice was soft, a little dull.

"Sure is that. Why don't you go inside? Sign there says it's air-conditioned."

"Can't. Run out of money from my last job."

"That's too bad. You live around here?"

"No. Just passing."

"How about your car? Got enough gas?"

"Don't have a car," he said.

"How'd you get here, then? Hitchhike?"

"Walked."

"Walked? From where?"

"Town back there."

"All the way from Tucumcari? That's a lot of hot miles."

"Wouldn't nobody give me a ride." He added in melancholy tones, "Won't hardly ever."

"Man, you must be exhausted. When did you eat last?"

"Yesterday sometime."

Exhausted and starving. "Lot of people stop here," I said. "Have you asked any of them? I mean…you know."

"Don't believe in it. Begging."

I hesitated, but I just couldn't walk away from a man in his condition. "How about a helping hand from a fellow traveler?"

"Huh?"

"Come on," I said. "I'll treat you to a cold drink and a sandwich."

He blinked. "Do that for me? Why?"

"Why not? You're hungry and so am I."

"Nobody ever bought me nothing before."

"First time for everything," I said. "How about it?"

"Okay."

I watched him unfold from the bench. God, he was big—almost twice my size. He towered over me; it was like looking up at a beanstalk giant, only one of the gentle type. We went into the café. The place was crowded, but there was one empty booth at the far wall. Heads turned and faces stared as the giant and I walked over to the booth and sat down. A few of them kept right on staring. He didn't seem to notice.

A waitress brought over menus and some ice water. The big guy emptied his glass in one long slurp. She couldn't help staring, either, her eyes round and her forehead washboarded as if he was some kind of sideshow freak. I didn't open the menu; neither did he. He waited for me to order—a cheeseburger with fries and a large lemonade—and then said he'd have the same.

"My name's Jack," I said when the waitress moved away. "Jack Tobin. What's yours?"

"Breakbone."

It was my turn to blink. "How's that again?"

"Breakbone. That's what they call me."

"That's some name."

"Not my real one. Kind of a nickname. On account of how big I am. And my hands—they're real strong."

"I believe it. Do me a favor—don't shake with me."

"Okay. Can I have your water?"

"Help yourself."

One long swallow emptied my glass, too.

"So where are you headed, uh, Breakbone?" I asked him.

"Nowhere in partic'lar. Moving around, different places."

"Looking for work?"

"Looking," he said.

"What kind of work do you do?"

"Don't matter. Any kind I can get."

"Where's your home, if you don't mind my asking?"

"Ain't got one."

"I mean originally. What part of the country?"

"Midwest." He didn't seem to want to talk about it, so I got off the subject.

"California's where I'm going," I said. "Moving out there from Pennsylvania. I've got a good job waiting for me, much better than my old one and lucky to get it. I'm a research chemist."

"Uh-huh."

"My girl's waiting, too. She's been in L.A. two weeks now, setting up housekeeping for us. We're getting married as soon as I settle into the new job—September, probably."

"I never had a girl," Breakbone said.

"That's too bad. Every guy should have a girl. Unless he's gay, of course."

"I ain't gay."

"I didn't mean to imply that you were," I said quickly, even though he didn't sound annoyed or angry. "I'm sorry you never had a girl. One of these days maybe you will."

"Naw," he said. "They don't like me. I'm too big."

"Lot of big girls out there that like big men."

"Not me."

I let it go. Trying to hold a conversation with him wasn't easy. His mind seemed to work in a slow and not quite linear fashion. Not that it mattered to me, but I wondered if he was mildly retarded.

We didn't have much more to say to each other. The food came and he wolfed his, finishing everything on his plate before mine was half empty. Poor bastard, I thought. Probably the first decent meal, if you could call a greasy burger decent, he'd had in a long time. I was glad I'd decided to treat him to it.

I paid the bill and we went back out into what was left of the day's heat. He stood looking past the gas pumps to Interstate 40 with that forlorn expression back on his face.

"What're you going to do now?" I asked him.

"Dunno. Ranches around here ain't hiring this time of year. Not me, anyways. Got a better chance of finding something in a town."

"It's a long way to the nearest one."

"Don't matter. I'm used to walking, sleeping out."

I was still feeling sorry for him. "Well, look, Breakbone, I'll give you a ride as far as Santa Rosa if you want. I'd stake you to a night's lodging, too, but I'm short on funds right now. Enough for another meal's the best I can do."

He gave me a long, solemn look. "Do all that for me, too?"

"The original good Samaritan, that's me. How about that ride?"

"Sure. Okay."

We got into the Audi. He was so tall that he had to sit scrunched down with his duffel on the floor mat and his knees up against the dashboard, and at that the top of his head scraped the headliner. He didn't have anything to say once we were underway. That was all right with me. Having to hold a conversation while I'm driving, particularly after an already long day behind the wheel, tends to distract me, even out in the middle of nowhere.

This was high desert country, pretty desolate, mostly flat with a few rolling hills and mesas in the background. Horse and cattle country, though how cattle could survive on the sparse grass was beyond me. Most of the terrain seemed to be barren except for patches of cactus and yucca and stunted juniper trees.

Traffic was light. We'd gone about ten miles and were making good time when an interchange appeared ahead. As we neared it, I noticed a guy with a backpack sitting on the grassy verge between the entrance ramp and the highway on this side. Another hitchhiker. It's against the law to troll for rides on an interstate, but there's always somebody ready and willing to defy laws and take chances.

Breakbone was looking out the side window at the hitchhiker as we rolled on past. He said suddenly, "Stop the car."

"What? No way. I don't pick up hitchers—"

"Stop the car."

"—and even if I did, there's not enough room in back—"

His body turned and one of his huge hands clamped down in a tight squeeze on my right knee. "Stop the car!"

It was like being caught in the iron jaws of a scoop shovel. I felt cartilage grind; pain shot all the way up into my groin. Reflex made me jam my left foot down so hard on the brake I nearly lost control of the car. The rear end fishtailed, wobbling, the skidding tires smoked and must have laid fifty feet of rubber before I managed to straighten out and then maneuver the Audi off onto the side of the highway. No other car had been close; if one had been....

"Jesus Christ," I said, "what's the idea? You nearly caused an accident."

He wasn't listening to me. He had the passenger door open and was looking back, gesturing. In the rearview mirror I saw the hitchhiker running toward us, his backpack clutched against his chest.

Young guy, nineteen or twenty; short and thin, with a long mop of blond hair and a heat-blotched face.

Breakbone got out and opened the rear door. The kid came to an abrupt stop, staring up at him. "Wow," he said.

"Get in," Breakbone said. "There's enough room."

"Hey, thanks, thanks a lot." The kid squeezed himself into what little space there was on the rear seat, holding the backpack on his lap. "Man, that air-conditioning feels good," he said. Then, to me through a friendly grin, "Thanks to you, too, mister. I didn't think anybody was going to stop and I'd have to spent the night out there."

"I almost didn't."

"Yeah, I saw. You sure made up your mind in a hurry."

"Didn't I, though."

Breakbone was filling up the passenger seat again. He said, "Okay. Let's go."

I wanted to say something more to him in protest; my knee and leg were still smarting. But with the kid already in the car now, it didn't seem to be worth making an issue of it. Over and done with and no real harm done. I put the car in gear and pulled back onto the highway.

We went a mile or so in silence. Then the kid said, "All this stuff back here. You guys moving somewhere?"

"Just me," I said. "California."

"I'm going to Phoenix. Well, Tempe. Arizona State University. I'm a student there. I don't suppose you could take me that far? Or at least as far as Flagstaff if you're staying on Forty?"

"Well...."

"I understand if you can't. I'm grateful for any ride I can get, as far as I can get. My name's Rob, by the way."

"Jack."

Breakbone didn't offer his nickname.

It got quiet again. I could feel an edginess growing in me. It wasn't the same having Breakbone along now, after that knee-squeezing business. I didn't want him in the car anymore. Once we got to the outskirts of Santa Rosa, I'd stop and let him out. The kid, Rob, seemed to be all right; I *could* take him as far as Phoenix because my route plan was to swing down through there and pick up Interstate

10 into L.A. But I didn't want him with me, either—no more company at all after Santa Rosa. Why had Breakbone forced me to stop for him? Compassion for a fellow traveler, I supposed, like I'd had compassion for him.

The quiet kept playing on my nerves. I turned on the radio, thinking: Music, news, call-in show—anything. The station I was tuned to was playing a song by Willie Nelson. Breakbone immediately reached over and turned it off.

"What'd you do that for?"

"Don't like the radio playing."

"Well, I do."

"So do I," the kid said. "Jazz is my thing, though. None of that country stuff."

"Leave it off, Jack," Breakbone said.

I didn't argue with him. I wanted to, it was my car, dammit, but I didn't.

There was something about the way he was sitting there, so damn big and Sphinx silent, those massive hands bulked together in his lap.

The miles piled up, fifteen or so. Dusk had settled; I switched the headlights on. How many more miles to L.A. and Karen? Only about eight-fifty now. And maybe another hundred closer before I called it a day. I could be with her sometime tomorrow night if I got an early start in the morning and drove straight through. I was even more eager to see her now. And it wasn't just sex. It was her—her smile, her voice, the way she laughed, everything about her. I'd been in love before, but never the way I was in love with Karen....

Twilight was rapidly fading into darkness, the shadows long and clotted on the empty desert landscape. Night came down fast out here. It'd be full dark in another few minutes.

Another mile clicked off on the odometer. And then Breakbone put an end to the silence. "That exit up there, Jack," he said. "Take it."

I peered ahead. The exit, according to the sign, was to a secondary road that led to a couple of far-off towns I'd never heard of. There were no services there, just the off-ramp and sign and a crossroad stretching both ways across the desert flats.

"What for?"

"Take it."

"Now listen—"

His big hairy paw dropped on my knee again, the stone-hard fingers digging in. Not with any pressure, not yet. "Take it."

I slowed and took it.

"What's going on?" Rob said from the back seat. He sounded sleepy; he must have been dozing.

"Turn right," Breakbone said.

Don't do it, I thought. But I didn't even hesitate at the stop sign, just swung onto the secondary road heading east. "Where is it you want to go?"

"Keep driving."

A mile, two miles. Full dark now, no moon, the black sky pricked with stars that seemed paler and more remote than usual. Up ahead, the headlights picked out the opening to a side road that branched off to the left. We'd almost reached it when Breakbone said, "Turn in that road."

I still couldn't make myself defy him. We rattled over a cattle guard. The narrow track was unpaved, dusty, rutted—some sort of backcountry ranch road. We bounced along at less than twenty through a grove of yucca trees. I didn't dare go any faster.

"Hey," Rob said, "what's the idea?" He sounded scared, as scared as I was now. "You guys thinking of robbing me or what? You won't get much, I'm only carrying a few dollars...."

"Shut up."

The kid shut up.

Pretty soon Breakbone said, "Far enough, Jack. Stop the car."

I stopped.

"Shut off the engine."

As soon as I did that, he reached over and yanked the keys out of the ignition.

"Now the headlights."

Everything went black when I clicked the switch, the yucca trees blotting out all but a faint glimmer of starshine. It gave me a sudden feeling of suffocation, as if I'd been trapped inside a box. I heard Rob making moaning noises and fumbling at the door handle, trying to get away. Then the dome light came on, but not because the kid had gotten his door open; it was Breakbone climbing out through the passenger door. He yanked the back one open, hauled the kid out with one of his huge paws. Rob fought him, yelling, but he couldn't break loose. It was like a small animal trying to fight a behemoth.

Breakbone picked him up under one arm as if he weighed nothing at all, grabbed the backpack with his other hand. "Stay here, Jack," he said to me. "Don't go nowhere." Then he kicked both doors shut, closing me into the black box again, and went stomping off into the darkness outside.

I just sat there, numb. I couldn't wrap my mind around what was going on.

Things like this didn't happen in my world, they just didn't happen—

Then it got worse, much worse.

Then the screaming started.

Horrible screams like nothing I'd ever heard before, shrill with pain and terror, so loud that they penetrated and echoed inside the box. On and on, on and on, as if the night itself was being ripped apart. I jammed the heels of my hands over my ears, but I could still hear them. They were like knifepoints jabbed into my eardrums.

I couldn't stand it in there, surrounded by the noise; couldn't breathe. I flung myself out of the car and stumbled around and away from it, trying to escape the screams. But I lost my bearings among the yuccas and went the wrong way, toward them instead—far enough to hear the other sounds that came before each of the shrieks. Meaty thwacking sounds. Crunching, snapping sounds.

I swung around, staggered back to the car. I knew I ought to run, hide, but my legs wouldn't work anymore. All I could do was lean against the front fender with my hands back over my ears.

It was a long time before the screaming stopped. And then I heard him coming back, shuffling over the parched ground—alone. He was just a giant looming shape until he reached the car and opened the passenger door and the dome light came on again. Then I saw the blood. It was smeared on his hands and on his pantlegs where he'd wiped them, spattered on forearms and across the front of his shirt. Even more terrible was the way he was grinning. Like a death's head mask. Like a skull.

I turned aside and puked up my dinner. When the convulsions stopped I sagged against the fender again, weak, shaking, my knees like pudding. He was watching me. Not grinning any more, his face without expression of any kind.

"You killed him." Somebody else's voice, not mine.

"Yeah. Busted all his bones."

"A kid, a stranger. *Why?*"

"I like it. It's fun."

Fun. Jesus!

"Tell you a secret," he said. "Nobody give me my nickname, like I told you before. I give it to myself after the first time I done it."

I couldn't look any more at those hands, the scars and gnarled joints that hadn't come from manual labor, the blood glistening like black worms in the spill from the dome light. I said to the darkness, "You going to kill me now?"

"Kill you? Naw, I wouldn't do that. I like you, Jack, you been real nice to me. We're friends. I never had a friend before."

Friends....

"You got a blanket or something in the car?"

"What?"

"So I don't get blood all over the seat."

"Trunk."

He went back there, rummaged around, came back with the picnic blanket Karen had bought for us. "Okay," he said then. "Let's go."

I groped around to the driver's side. He squeezed in next to me, the blanket wrapped around him, and let me have the keys, but it was a little while before I was steady enough to drive. I still couldn't think, didn't want to think. Finally I started the engine, turned the car around, headed back down the road with the headlights boring holes in the night.

When we neared the intersection with the county road, I heard myself say, "What now?"

"Find some place I can wash up, change clothes."

"Then what?"

"Keep on going. Drive all night, maybe. Get us another car, bigger one, then go wherever we feel like. Big country. Ain't hardly seen much of it yet."

It took a few seconds for his meaning to sink in. "No! *No!* My girl, my job...."

"They don't matter no more. Just you and me, Jack, from now on."

Bloodstained fingers snaked out of the blanket, closed around my knee again. The feel of them made my flesh crawl.

"We'll have fun together," he said. "Lots of fun."

The Storybook Forest

Norman Prentiss

It wasn't a girls' ride any longer.

The giant teacups had lost their glossy white sheen, and the flowery trim had faded beneath new designs of chipped paint and cracked fiberglass. Craig aimed his flashlight over the nearest rim: dead leaves and broken branches settled into a wet muck at the bottom of the cup. The circular bench was broken in three places.

"Reading the tea leaves?" Eddie said, peering over his shoulder.

"Yeah. They tell me it's time to trash this place." Craig smacked the side of the cup with his palm. He expected a hollow thump, but it was firm and flat, like hitting a piece of drywall. They must have reinforced the frame with bent iron, poured concrete into the hollow fiberglass. Safer that way.

"This one's better," Skates yelled from the edge closest to the moonlit castle. He was climbing into one of the cups, his long legs straddling over the rim instead of using the rounded doorway opposite the teacup handle. His foot caught on the rim and he almost fell inside headfirst—not because he was drunk, yet, but because Skates was basically lanky and uncoordinated. His nickname altered his last name of Slate, and reflected his ambitions more than any success with the skateboard. He was mostly a wipe-out kind of guy.

Craig headed over, Eddie following like he usually did. Craig kicked a broken bottle out of their path, and it clanked against a pile of rusted beer cans. They obviously weren't the first who'd trespassed into Storybook Forest for a bit of underage drinking.

Skates set his six-pack of Bud on the flat round steering wheel at the center of the cup, then put his wide-bottom flashlight next to it, letting the beam shine up like a weak spotlight. "C'mon in. Got our own coffee table." He wrapped his T-shirt around a bottle cap, twisted it off, then took a loud swig.

The metal chain was still fastened across the doorway. Back when the park was open, vinyl padding covered the chain—white, if Craig remembered properly, sewn with pink thread to match pink roses painted on the cup. He brushed along the chain, brittle like sand beneath his fingertips, then found the hook-latch. He squeezed the release to open it, and the latch broke in his hand.

He must have cried out—startled, or maybe a sliver of rust lanced into his thumb or beneath his fingernail—because Eddie said, "Careful you don't get tetanus." That was Eddie, always giving advice after it was too late.

The chain clanked to the side of the cut-out doorway. Craig rubbed his thumb and forefinger together. "What is tetanus, any-way? Do you even know?"

That would quiet him for a few minutes.

The bottom wasn't as mucked up as in the other cups, and the bench around the inside perimeter was still intact. Craig stepped over Skates' legs and sat across from him, leaving space for Eddie. Each cup was designed to hold two parents and a couple of kids. They had plenty of room.

"Some ride," Eddie said. He clinked his quart bottle of Colt 45 on the center wheel. Eddie never shared, never pitched in with Skates' six-pack. His glass bottle always looked the same, with a heavily rubbed label. He probably filled the bottle with diet soda.

"This was the *only* ride," Craig said. "Guy who built the place wanted a different kind of amusement park. The idea was for kids to walk through these fake little houses, as if they were Goldilocks or Hansel and Gretel or something." Craig remembered how it pissed him off as a kid: they got to go to King's Dominion *once* when he was growing up—with its dizzying Tilt-a-Whirl, water slides, and the Rebel Yell coaster that his parents wouldn't let him ride. *Maybe when you're older,* but they never went back.

Instead, his family went to Storybook Forest for a half-day every summer.

"My sister loved it here," he said. "Hallie thought the place taught her how to read. How to love books, I guess."

"Yuck," Skates said, and Eddie punched him in the shoulder. "What's that for?"

"'Cause you're a douche." Eddie took a sip from his Colt 45. A faint hiss like carbonation came from the bottle. He screwed the cap back on, like he always did after each sip.

Skates started laughing. Nothing was *that* funny, and for a moment Craig wondered if maybe he should punch the guy too. Then Skates grabbed at the steering wheel. "Oh man, how fast did this thing go? I bet you had to hold on for dear life!"

All three of them were laughing now, a kind of pre-drunk high where stupid stuff managed to hit you the right way. "God, Craig, your mom must have been terrified."

"Stop it. You're killing me." Craig lifted a bottle from his half of the carton, popped it open.

"I mean, with this thing spinning and shit. It spins, right?" He held the wheel again, this time grunting.

"Put your weight into it," Eddie said.

"Yeah, it spins. It's gotta." He had that same determined look on his face like when he attempted a triple Ollie or tried to jump his board over the curb. He usually failed.

"Let me." Eddie grabbed the wheel too, and there was some confusion over clockwise or *counter-clockwise, you idiot,* and still nothing happened. Then Skates grunted like grinding metal, or that movie sound a pirate ship makes when the deck lurches.

The teacup didn't spin, though. It tilted up off its saucer at a steep angle, as if some invisible giant lifted it to take a drink.

The big flashlight rattled off the wheel and onto the ground. Craig saved the carton, though he spilled his half-empty bottle in the process. He remained inside the cup, one leg balanced against the steering post. Skates had been in the end that arced into the air, and he'd kind of leaped out, arms and legs wide, and actually cleared the guardrail surrounding the entire ride—probably his most impressive aerial stunt ever, if he'd actually planned it, and if he hadn't tripped on his ass after he landed. Wipe-out.

Eddie was outside the dip, like he'd been poured out of the cup onto the metal platform. His foot was caught under the cup's rim.

"Careful," he said. Craig stepped down to help him, and the shift in weight curled the rim tighter against Eddie's ankle. Where the flashlight had fallen, its beam illuminated Eddie's expression: he smiled and winced at the same time, his face round and white in the glow, like Tweedledum.

"Don't think that was supposed to happen." Skates dusted off the seat of his trousers and straddled back over the guardrail. "Somebody musta hit the reject button."

"Quit joking around and get this offa me." It was Eddie's teacher voice, since he liked to imagine himself as the guy who kept everybody else in line. But how often is a teacher flat on the ground, stuck under a giant cup? In that position, it would be wise not to get bossy with the students.

Craig was used to this tone, so it didn't bother him. The most important thing was to help his friend. Besides, they could tease him mercilessly later.

"Roll it *counter*-clockwise," Tweedle-Eddie said. "To the left. *My* left, not yours. Toward the castle."

Maybe it was too much clarification, like they were both stupid. Skates got called stupid often enough, and had the grades to back it up. He wasn't that strong either, but he was tall—which sometimes gave him leverage.

Craig knelt down, pushing against the cup to roll it to the left—per teacher's instructions—and it felt smooth, like Skates was working with him, but also like the cup was moving on its own. It may have been like guiding a planchette around a Ouija board, where the slider seems to move by magic, but maybe somebody's fingers are pushing that thing on purpose. To make the board tell the guy something he needs to hear.

He pushed, Skates pushed near the top—*leverage*—and the cup didn't so much roll to the left as it just kept tipping. Off the saucer, and over Eddie.

It sounded like a car crash. A heavy dent into the hollow metal platform, an echoing scrape against the matching saucer.

Eddie was silent.

Then, not so silent. High pitched complaints about how he landed, the rim barely missing his head, and his body cramped and curled around the steering post. Threats also, explaining what he might do to his friends once they got him out of there.

If he was really going to do those things, they'd be foolish to let him out.

Easier decided than done, anyway. When the ride had been operational, the main platform circled slowly, like a merry-go-round. There were a dozen or so cup-and-saucer compartments on the dilapidated ride, all attached to this metal platform. Their cup—the one they'd upended over their friend—had landed snug into the platform space between its vacated saucer and two other saucers. It was pinned in place at three separate points. The notched doorway had landed at an inconvenient angle, the opening mostly blocked by a saucer lip. Only a half-moon slot was visible, not big enough even for skinny Skates to limbo through. For Eddie, it was out of the question.

Skates retrieved his flashlight and shined it into the blocked opening. Eddie's face slid into the light, a prisoner looking out from his dungeon. A cloud of breath came from his mouth like angry smoke. He blinked, then shifted back into darkness. "Done looking?"

Skates shrugged and set the flashlight on the ground. He gripped the lid of the opening and tested it. "Heavier than I thought. Help me, Craig."

They couldn't lift it, and couldn't shift the cup to clear the opening. Eddie's fingers suddenly appeared in the opening, an extra pair of hands that for some reason Craig hadn't been expecting. They didn't help.

"We need something," Skates finally said, out of breath. "A crowbar or a log or something."

Craig shouted into the dark opening. "You'll be all right here?" As if Eddie had a choice.

"Leave me a flashlight."

"Mine's broken," Craig said. "We need the other one for searching and stuff."

Eddie sighed. He mentioned calling an ambulance or the police, then at once realized how stupid the idea was. What a humiliation it would be, caught trespassing in a kiddie park, and trapped under an upended, paint-flecked, fiberglass teacup.

Skates patted the side of the cup. "We won't be long."

"You better not be."

Trouble was, the place really was a forest. Suburban property was plentiful when park designers conceived the idea for Storybook Forest, so they spread their attractions over a large area. Little kids would walk along park paths, discovering one presumably magical attraction after another. Hallie used to run from Jack Spratt's pumpkin house to find the giant shoe around the next corner. Dad would read the placard for her, until she learned how to read it herself: "There was an old woman who lived in a shoe. She had so many children, she didn't know what to do."

So Craig and Skates had a lot of ground to cover—especially since they didn't exactly know what they were looking for.

They found the house for the three little pigs. Not a brick one, which would be too much like an ordinary house, but the one made of straw. A fiberglass wolf used to huff and puff outside the door; his feet remained, legs snapped off at the ankles, and a few other broken pieces stomped into the ground. Once upon a time, the straw was simulated with bright yellow paint, brown now and making it more like a house of wet, dirty rope. The place seemed menacing in a way unintended in the park's heyday. It was smaller than a real house. Instead of sharp corners, the angles were rounded and out of alignment—a whimsical effect on sunny days when the house was fresh, but now it looked as if the place was melting. The windows were smashed. Craig imagined innocent children reaching across the empty frames, their soft wrists tearing over jagged glass.

The windows were too small to climb through. Craig shined a light inside, revealing plump, upright pigs that had been target practice for beer bottles. Ears and snouts were broken off, little pig hooves shattered into sharp claws. Judging from the smell, they'd also been pissed on.

If vandals could have stepped inside, the pigs would likely have been torn to pieces, like the wolf.

"Chinny chin chin," Skates said. He pushed his finger against the tip of his nose, turning it into a snout.

"Let's try another house." They followed the curve of the cracked blacktop path. Signposts had long-since disappeared, but a few joined shadows in the clearing identified the route: these were silhouettes of the remaining gingerbread children, baked to death in the witch's oven. The doomed children always seemed blissfully happy, hands linked and dancing in a circle. Mom and Dad bought cookies from the snack booth, and Craig and his sister sat at a bench beside the victim circle, biting off cookie arms and legs, and not at all feeling like cannibals.

"Long past its expiration date," Skates said. The house itself had grown horribly unappetizing. Giant gumdrop trim looked moldy, and gingerbread shingles were stale and drizzled with grime. The ice cream chimney was cracked down the side of the cone; a vanilla dip at the top was brown and lumpy, like a huge scoop of vomited oatmeal.

Inside was a single room, a large metal cauldron at the center and overflowing with garbage.

"Look at her feet!" Skates pointed and laughed at the brick oven. The witch's legs were painted dangling at the back of the open oven, presumably because Hansel and Gretel had just pushed her inside. "And check out the cage." A sign beside a grid of iron bars said, *Next Victims.* Skates laughed some more.

And that was what was wrong with Storybook Forest. It made you laugh. Happy little stories for happy little kids. There was no lock on the cage. You could climb inside, wrap your tiny hands around the metal bars, and know all along you'd never get cooked by the witch.

Craig hated the treachery of it all. The smiling storybook world where nothing bad ever happened. "They sanitized all the stories. I wanted stuff to be scary, like the thrill-rides at King's Dominion, and it always disappointed me."

Skates pulled at one of the metal bars. It didn't budge from its concrete moorings.

"You know," Craig said, "the real versions of the nursery stories are pretty gruesome. The wolf eats Little Red Riding Hood's grandma—the woodsman has to carve her out of his stomach. And Cinderella wasn't like the Disney cartoon. The stepsisters cut off parts of their feet so the glass slipper would fit."

"That's kinda cool."

"I dragged us here tonight—pushed for it, even, when Eddie tried to talk us out of it—because I thought for once the forest actually might be scary. We'd break in late at night, and the place would be falling apart and maybe dangerous. Haunted. But it's not. It's just sad."

"I bet Eddie's pretty scared right now. He probably crapped himself when that cup fell on him."

Craig wouldn't laugh with him. "You didn't do that on purpose, did you?"

"No. Did *you?*"

"I mean, you said you didn't realize how heavy it was."

"I said no." Skates attempted a serious expression, but it still came across like a smirk. He got in trouble for that a lot at school.

"All right," Craig said. "Let's keep looking around."

Outside, Craig cupped his hands over his mouth and yelled into the air. "We're still here. We'll get you out soon."

No answer. Might have been too far away, and the sound didn't carry well. Just as likely, Eddie was giving them the silent treatment.

Skates did a two-fingered whistle, then made a few hoot-owl noises.

"Cut it out," Craig said. "He's probably sulking."

Still no signposts, but he registered where they were headed. In the midst of the overgrown forest a giant shoe loomed, a front door carved out of its heel. He remembered the windows in the sides and up the tall back of the shoe—like a tower, the old woman leaning out the top window to wave at her many children, some of them scrambling over bright blue laces, and she'd waved at him and Hallie, too.

She still waved, but she was headless. The filthy shoe looked like something a homeless giant had worn through, then discarded.

The door was open, but when Skates ducked inside he couldn't get far. Craig pushed in after him. A spiral staircase had fallen over, along with all the upstairs exhibits. A few small body parts were visible: several of the old woman's children had been crushed in the collapsing rubble.

Skates pulled at a plank that looked intact. It broke at his touch. The wood was rotten.

Craig recalled Hallie's sing-song recitation of the rhyme—*so many children she didn't know what to do.* How many children were there, really?

"This is a terrible rhyme," he told Skates.

"Dude, it's a lame-ass park all around."

"That not what I mean. The rhyme—I think it's about being poor. This woman's got all these kids, and she's freaking *old,* and doesn't have a husband or a job. They're living in a shoe, for Christ's sake. Real life, they'd be starving to death."

Skates kicked at another board. A tiny fiberglass hand holding a lollipop rolled off the pile. "What a shithole."

"Hallie actually cried when they closed this place down. But I guess she cried about a lot of things."

"Can't compete with that, can you?"

"Nope. Hallie always got her way."

"I'm sorry man."

"That's okay." Craig closed his eyes for a second, blacking out the flashlight beam and the trash and the pile of collapsed rubble. Everything but the memories. "I wish I'd never come here."

"We'll be out soon enough," Skates said. He set the flashlight on the floor, planted one foot at the bottom of the heap, and grunted and pulled at a curled metal bar. It was part of the broken banister, about five feet long once he'd extracted it. "This'll work like a big crowbar, don't you think?"

Outside, Skates whistled and did the hoot-owl a few more times. As they retraced their steps back to the teacup ride, he dragged the metal bar on the path behind him, a dragon's claw scraping at the blacktop. Craig held the flashlight, which began to dim; he flicked the power off now and then, to conserve the battery. Slivers of moonlight through the trees made it easy enough to see, as long as they stayed on the path.

"How about this," Skates said. "We get back there, pry the cup off him, and it's like one of those ghost stories where at the end the guy's hair has turned white from fear. Imagine Eddie with white hair. And he's lost his voice from being so scared, that's why he doesn't answer. He'll never talk again."

"We should be so lucky."

"Could be, you know, some serial killer followed us into the park. Waited for us to split up, like dumb kids do in horror movies. He'd go after the weaker kid first, the one who's alone and can't get away."

"And we'd be next."

"Sure. We're probably walking into a trap." Skates practically had to shout to be heard over the scrape of the metal bar. Now he lifted the bar and switched to a whisper: "We get there, and it's totally silent. The cup's been lifted and you point the light inside and nobody's there. But there's all these splashes of fresh blood."

"You're enjoying this a little too much."

"Or try this: We get there, and that dumb cup's still upside down, and Eddie's still sulking and saying nothing, and we creep closer and we hear…*chewing.* Teeth tearing at flesh, chomping on bone."

"Okay, you're really starting to spook me a bit." He wasn't really, but Craig figured that was the only way to get him to stop.

"One more. We get there, and Eddie *does* talk, says something like, 'Give me a hand.' The voice is a little hoarse, though, and I think maybe he's been crying like a baby, so I reach in through the opening. A hand closes over mine, and… it's *not* Eddie. It's not even human."

The punchline to his story echoed in the forest; the flashlight was off, the moon had gone behind a cloud, the trees were thicker overhead. "Good one," Craig said, not intending a compliment. His friend laughed, like someone who had lost his mind.

Ridiculous. Skates was joking around. Eddie was angry, but he was fine. After all, this was the Storybook Forest. Nothing terrible ever happened here.

Clouds drifted away from the moon. In the distance, the facade of a castle appeared through the trees, a sign they'd nearly reached the site of the teacup ride. One of the turrets was split down the side—painted Plexiglas instead of stone. Branches hatched thick shadows across the castle's decayed surface. From this angle, it really did look haunted.

They hurried up the path, hoping to rescue whatever was left of their friend.

Simple

Al Sarrantonio

Two boys.
   Two girls.
   Dusk.
   Halloween.

The rising moon hung sharp-edged and near-full behind a gauzy blanket of clouds. Sidewalks rose and sank, up one gentle hill, down another, their cracks sprouting brown, dry grass. The wind, picking up winter-to-come's chill, rattled the trees, making them shed—brown red yellow leaves which nestled against the gutters and rustled like there were living things beneath.
   Two girls.
   Two boys.
   The town of Orangefield.

"I say he don't exist!" insisted Excalibur, whose real name was Jim Gates. "I say it's all hooey!" A night spent as an actual sword, made of stiff cardboard wrapped in aluminum foil with a face cut out the center had made him cranky and bold.
   "Hell," said his male companion, Gil, dressed like a simple cowboy, his brimming candy bag weighing him down, "you weren't even born here! You just moved in! What do you know?" He frowned. "And your Great Uncle Riley was one of his *victims*!" The weight

of the treasure bag finally became too much for him, and he put it down with an "Oooof!"

The girls, twins named Marcey and Carsey, remained silent, wide-eyed. Their own bags were on the ground already—it had been a profitable evening.

"I gotta be home—" Carsey said, as the silence lengthened, but Marcey gave her a dirty look, twitching her cat girl whiskers.

"No we don't," Marcey countered, her whiskers twitching again, one side of them falling off.

"Hey, we're all ten years old, right?" Gil said, trying to stand tall, though he was the shortest of them, even with his cowboy hat on.

Jim narrowed his eyes. "What did you have in mind?"

Gil looked at the ground, but Marcey said, almost a shout, "Let's go find 'im!"

Carsey's eyes grew real wide, and she looked like she wanted to cry.

Then Gil looked up, and suddenly he smiled, and the rest smiled too, even Carsey, in a sad way.

And Excalibur, for a brief moment, shined with an almost blinding light as the Moon broke through the clouds and looked coldly down at the four of them.

They hid their candy in Ranier Park, between two big rocks with another across the top that made a cave. Gil swore it would be safe there, and when Jim protested he said, "You're new here. Trust me."

Jim looked back longingly at the small dark cave mouth as they walked away, but once again Gil repeated, "Trust me."

Ten minutes later found them in the empty pumpkin patches of Schwartz's farm. The ground was rutted, filled with rows of twisting dead pumpkin vines, already waiting for the winter to freeze them stiff and turn the furrows to brown icy ditches.

But here at the end of October the ground was still soft, the vines in the moonlight looked like twisting fingers.

"This is creepy," Carsey said.

"This is where they first saw the Pumpkin Boy," Gil countered. "It's *supposed* to be creepy."

"We're not looking for the Pumpkin Boy," Marcey remarked.

"I don't believe that one, either," Jim said, his jaw hurting from bumping against the lower cardboard cutout of his huge mask.

Finally he made them stop while he yanked the top of the costume off, shredding aluminum foil and hitting the bottom of his jaw again as he pulled the massive mask off.

"Ow!"

"I'd say 'ow' too if I had a face like that," Gil said, laughing.

"I meant to tell you earlier how dumb your cowboy outfit was," Jim said, recovering.

The two girls laughed, a simultaneous giggle, half an octave apart.

Jim threw down the ruined sword, which settled into a furrow, in a nest of vines and they walked on.

"And that's the valley where the Pumpkin Boy snatched little Jody Wendt," Gil announced, as they stood on the top of a steep slope which led down to a patch of woods near a thin, bubbling creek.

"Now that one I *know* was hooey," Jim snapped. "That Pumpkin Boy thing was just a machine some loony made."

Down below, in the middle of the thin spot of woods, something glowed, silver and orange.

"You don't think…" Marcey said.

"They say you can still see him, some Halloweens," Gil answered, his voice suddenly soft.

"Good thing we're not going that way," Jim said, trying to sound tough, but he too was rooted to the spot as something peeked out of the woods and then was gone.

"I thought I saw…" Carsey squeaked.

"A pumpkin head?" Gil said, and there was no mockery in his voice.

Carsey nodded, but then there was a hoot and a laugh from down below and three older children emerged from the woods, two wearing realistic animal masks, fox and hound, and the other with a pumpkin head, which he removed, laughing again.

"So much for the Pumpkin Boy!" Jim hooted.

Gil reminded him: "But that's not who we're looking for."

Carsey looked back as they left, and something else, more ethereal, glowed in the woods down below.

They followed the line of the slope, until it gradually disappeared underfoot, leading them down gently to the level of the valley. Ahead of them was a deeper wood, darker, thick with trees. There were stout elms and stately oaks, and the forest floor was covered with fallen acorns.

The moon had climbed above the thin clouds.

The wind was sharper, colder.

"When did we have to be home?" Marcey asked, suddenly hopeful. "What time is it? I think we should go now."

"You were the one said we didn't have to be home," Carsey replied.

"You sure we hid that candy where the big kids won't find it?" Jim said.

"The candy's fine," Gil snapped. "And no one's going home yet."

Carsey looked like she wanted to cry.

"I don't want to do this," she said.

Gil shot her a look, and Marcey hissed, "Be quiet."

Carsey began, "But–"

"*Be quiet!*"

Jim looked at the three of them. "What's wrong with you guys?"

Gil smiled tightly. "Nothing."

"Are we going in or not?"

The others stood still.

"Why don't you go in first?" Gil offered. He gave a weak smile. "Since it's all hooey."

Jim shrugged. "Fine."

He took a step forward into the woods.

The wind suddenly died, and it became very quiet. He could not see the path before him, only the darker edges of nearby trees.

There came a rustling in the dark ahead of him, swallowed by an almost palpable silence, and then nothing.

He turned around, expecting to find his new friends behind him, but they had stepped away from the woods.

"Marcey? Carsey? Gil?" he called.

"We've…decided to go home," Gil said.

"You can't go home," Jim answered.

Gil's smile was even weaker than his last one, and then he looked at the ground. "What are you going to do, threaten us with your sword?"

"Go home, then," Jim said.

The three of them suddenly turned and ran.

"See you!" Gil called back, and it sounded like a choked sob.

Marcey and Carsey's crying echoed and faded.

Jim turned back toward the woods, and something just inside the dark, something that looked like a gently flapping cape topped with a white oval of a face cut by a thin red slash of mouth, said, "Come in."

Back in Ranier Park, at the mouth of the cave, four fat bags of trick-or-treat loot sat amidst three trick-or-treaters.

No one said anything until Gil, fumbling with the handles of his own bag, looked up from the fourth bag and said, "I don't want any of it."

"Me either," echoed Carsey. "Maybe we can give it to charity or something."

"Maybe there's a hospital that could use it," Marcey offered. "For the kids who couldn't go trick-or-treating this year."

"Maybe we could put it in a box and send it to India, to poor kids there."

Gil shook his head. "I don't think they have Halloween in India."

"Maybe we could—" Marcey began, but her sister cut her off.

"He should have known better."

The three of them nodded.

Gil added, "He should have especially known, being Riley Gate's kin and all."

Again all three of them nodded their heads.

Marcey said, "Too bad he was the new kid in school. I kind of liked him. Too bad it couldn't have been Larry Jarvis. I can't stand him."

"Me neither," Gil said. "But Larry Jarvis knows."

"Of course he does," Carsey said. "We all know. The only ones who don't know are the new ones."

Again there was a silence, this one longer.

"I wish it hadn't been our turn," Gil whispered, looking at the floor.

Marcey said, "Everybody gets a turn. That's just the way it is. When you're nine, or ten, or eleven, it gets to be your turn. You don't have a choice."

Carsey began to sniffle. "I liked him."

"Me too."

"And me too."

"Too bad."

The three of them nodded.

Gil sounded like he was talking to himself, justifying. "And that's just the way we keep things…simple."

"Simple," Marcey parroted.

Carsey nodded, drying her sniffles.

"And you don't mess with Samhain," Gil added.

"No you don't."

"*Everybody* knows that."

"It's all he asks for. One a year. To keep things…simple."

They all nodded.

The longest silence of the evening. Marcey sat staring at the extra bursting bag of candy.

"I suppose it wouldn't hurt if we just took a little."

She reached out, scooped some Double Bubble from the very apex of the bulging bag.

Carsey nodded, plucking a Mars bar whose end peeked above the upper level.

"It would be a shame to let it go to waste."

"A sin, even," Gil said, shoving his palm into the brimming horde and removing a handful, which he stuffed in a jacket pocket.

"After all, we don't have a big box. And I don't even know where India is."

Soon the bag was empty.

Born Dead

Lisa Tuttle

Florida McAfee was about the last person I would have imagined getting pregnant by accident, or, to be honest, in any other way, for although she was beautiful—even when she was over sixty her tall, willowy figure, large lustrous eyes and high cheekbones attracted admiring looks—there was something *noli me tangere* about her, and while she had dated an impressive variety of men over the years, she hadn't married or lived with any of them.

I assumed she preferred to live alone, that it had been a positive choice, rather than it being something that had just happened while she'd been so busy with her career. If she'd wanted a family, I reasoned, surely she could have managed that emotional juggling act with the same skill she'd brought to establishing an internationally famous clothing brand.

She was my heroine. Her example declared it was possible for a woman to become rich and powerful entirely by her own efforts, and without compromising her beliefs. I needed to believe she was single and childless by choice, not because her kind of success was incompatible with family life. Not every woman wanted children—I still wasn't sure myself—and if marriage was really so wonderful, why did so many of them end in divorce?

I'd been working for her for seven years—not directly, but climbing the corporate ladder in a way that had attracted her notice, until I was the head of division, London-based in theory but actually spending most of my life in other parts of the world. It was fun, exciting, rewarding, exhausting, all those good things, and as much as I was enjoying myself, I knew it couldn't last forever.

Crunch-time was coming, and I was going to have to make decisions that would affect the rest of my life.

By many standards I was successful—I made good money, I liked my job, what I did made a difference—but I was not yet where I wanted to be. If I was to make my youthful dreams come true I had to cut loose and start up my own business. It would be risky, and lots more hard work, but neither of those things scared me. I even had an idea that I knew I could turn into a marketable business plan, and the time seemed right to launch it.

But even as I was aware of the opportunities opening up in the business world, I saw the entrance to another world shrinking. I was well into my thirties, young and fit in terms of work, many productive years ahead of me, but the window to motherhood—maybe even to marriage—was narrowing by the day, and if I didn't do something about it soon it would close, and I would end up by myself. Maybe that suited Florida, but it gave me a chill to think of growing old alone. And it was looking more likely by the day: I might have been too busy to care, but the simple fact was that I hadn't had so much as a date in nearly a year. More and more, the men I met through work were married—recently, happily, smugly, sporting their new, gold rings. Not that they were better, smarter, or luckier than me, but they had been quicker off the mark, realizing what they wanted, and going after it. It had taken me so long to notice that life's dance-floor was almost filled with couples, and I was going to have to put some serious effort into finding a partner, if that's what I really wanted.

The obvious thing to do, if I was serious about wanting to meet someone, was to go out more, to places where that might happen. Join a club, try something different, spend less time working…

Exactly the opposite, in fact, of what was required for my start-up. For that, I needed to concentrate on wooing investors, a different pool from potential husbands.

The thought of putting my business plans on hold made me even more uneasy. What if somebody else took my idea and ran with it? Things can change awfully fast, and if you drop out for a couple of years, nobody holds your place. You have to start all over again. And if I came back from my sabbatical a bride, people would wonder how soon I'd get pregnant, and how I'd manage to divide my attention between home and business. Of course it wasn't fair, since a man getting married proved how solid and dependable and *bankable* he was, but there was no sense whining about that.

Florida always took a mentoring interest in her employees, especially the most ambitious, workaholic females. Her latest invitation to lunch arrived in the midst of my soul-searching, and while I didn't want to let her know I might be leaving her employ, I had hopes that she'd provide the answer.

I'd made some vague remark about the difficulty of balancing outside work with child-care when she suddenly asked me if I'd ever been pregnant.

"No," I said. "But I'm keeping my options open. I'm on the pill."

"So was I." She gave me a long, measuring look before going on. "I thought it was making me bloated. And when I stopped, and didn't get a period, I thought it was just my body re-adjusting." She looked down and toyed with her salad. "It never once occurred to me that I might be pregnant."

I felt shocked, and a little queasy, wondering why she'd decided to confide in me, but said nothing.

"I was nearly forty," she went on. "So, the fact that I'd put on a little weight, that I wasn't having periods, that I felt strange... I put it down to the menopause. I didn't go to a doctor; why should I? No one else noticed anything odd. Something about the way the baby was lying meant I never looked pregnant."

"When did you realize?"

"After I gave birth."

This was so unexpected, I could do nothing but gape.

"I know, it sounds mad," she said calmly, taking a tiny bite of her salad. "But I never guessed. I had been feeling constipated for several days, and then one evening, just as I got home, I started getting pains, low in my belly. I thought it must have been something I ate. The pain came and went through the night, but it wasn't until the baby actually came out of me that I realized. And by the time I understood I was pregnant—well, I wasn't anymore."

She fell silent, looking weary, and for the first time I saw her as an old woman.

"So what did you do then?"

"Well, I picked him up, I cuddled him… I thought how strange he looked. It still seemed unreal to me, what had happened. I got a knife to cut the cord—I didn't sterilize it; how could I, on my own, holding a baby, still attached to me…it was a clean knife, from the kitchen, and I just had to hope it was clean enough. I guess it was. I couldn't think what to do with the cord, or the other stuff—placenta—it seemed wrong to just stuff it all in the bin, but that's what I did. I cleaned up as best I could, although there was a spot on the carpet I never could get out—I finally had to get new carpet laid—and then I ran a bath…"

Impatient with all this detail, the pointless obsession with carpeting, I interrupted: "But what about the baby?"

"Oh, I took him into the bath with me, of course. I got him all nice and clean, and then I used a hand towel, the softest one I had, to dry him. I wished I had some clothes for him, but of course I didn't, why would I, when I'd never expected…? I thought I could make a nappy out of a square of cloth, but the tea towels were too rough, and I only had a few silk scarves, and they weren't the right shape. I thought about cutting up a pashmina, which was certainly soft enough, but one was black and the other pink…" She met my gaze and made an ironic mouth. "Of course, it was absurd, but people do often focus on irrelevant details when they've had a shock. I thought about going out to buy something, but I was so tired, and it was so late at night… In the end, I just cleared out a drawer, and lined it with both pashminas, and laid him down in that, just pulling the edge of the pink one up to his chin. He looked so sweet lying there, so peaceful, I could almost believe he was asleep."

I felt a sickening pang as I understood. "He wasn't? He died? Or…he was born dead?"

"He never made a sound, never opened his eyes. Never took a breath."

I wondered, with an odd, internal lurch, half excitement, half fear, if I was hearing the confession of an old crime.

"What did you do?"

She gave the tiniest shrug, as if to say I should have known. "I went to bed. I slept, so deeply that in the morning it all seemed like a dream. I was still tired when the alarm went, too tired to think, really. I got dressed and went to work as usual."

"But the baby?"

She shot me a look that said I wasn't paying attention. " I told you, I put him in a drawer."

I'd been imagining that drawer pulled out. I shut my mouth and nodded.

The waiter arrived to ask if everything was all right. Florida indicated that he should take away her largely untouched salad, and, having lost my appetite, I did the same.

"Would you like something else?"

"Just coffee, thank you."

When we were alone again, she continued her story. "Two days later, I flew to New York. We were in the middle of negotiations, hoping to establish the brand in America, and so, for the next few months, I was hardly at home at all, rarely for more than a few nights. It was one of those nights, or early mornings, when I was so jet-lagged I hardly knew what time it was, and so wired on the excitement of building my own company into a global brand that I didn't care, that I happened to notice that small, dark patch on my bedroom carpet, and suddenly all the details rushed back, and I broke out in a cold sweat.

"I opened the drawer and there was my baby, looking just as sweet and peaceful as the day he was born, and yet...not exactly. Even before I picked him up I could see signs of change."

My stomach clenched as I anticipated the gory details to come, and wondered about the smell. But she surprised me again.

"He was bigger, plumper than when I'd last seen him, almost too big for the drawer. When I lifted him out, I could tell that he'd gained weight. I held him close and kissed him, and although his skin was cool to the touch, and he didn't breathe, he had that wonderful new baby smell. You know what I mean?"

"He was alive? After—how long since you left him there? A month?"

"Closer to three. No, he was still dead."

"But you said that he'd grown, put on weight—that's impossible." She had to be winding me up, but I couldn't imagine why, and it was totally out of character for the woman I knew.

The waiter arrived with our coffee, and she waited until he'd gone away again to say, quietly, intently, "I know it's impossible, but it happened. I still can't explain it except to call it a miracle."

I thought that was no explanation at all. "So what did you do?"

"There was a twenty-four hour Asda or something not far away, so I went there and bought a cot and some clothes. After the end of the year, when I had more time at home, I redecorated the guest room for him. It was all right for a tiny baby to share my room, but he would need his own space as he was growing up."

"You mean, he kept growing?"

"Yes. Just like a live baby."

Maybe one thing was no more or less impossible than the other, but I was shocked. "You mean, he didn't *stay* a baby? He grew into a little boy?"

"And then a bigger one."

"Did you tell anyone?"

"Of course not."

"Why not? If it really happened?"

"You don't believe me." She looked amused. "Of course not. What sane person would believe such an outrageous tale? Does that answer your question?"

"You could have taken him to a doctor."

Her expression hardened. "Take my dead boy to a doctor? Why?"

"To find out the reason—"

She shook her head at me. "There is no reason, or not one that science can accept. If I turned up with a dead body of an unknown man, what do you suppose would happen?"

I shrugged as if I didn't know, but of course, I knew as well as she did that she'd have fallen under suspicion of murder, whether the body was that of a baby, or a young man.

"At the very least, they'd take him away from me. And if I told the truth, they'd lock me up. And bury David. Even if someone believed me, and decided to *observe* him for a few weeks, and saw he wasn't an ordinary corpse—what would be gained by that? We'd be a public freak-show. I don't want that. Not for David, not for me. I thank my lucky stars that I've always been able to take care of him, that I have enough money." She stopped abruptly and took a drink of coffee.

David. It was a nice name, I thought, Biblical, not exactly unusual, but kind of old-fashioned; I had the idea that it meant 'beloved.' It made the subject of Florida's story much more real to me, and I found myself wondering if other babies, born dead, had the potential to continue to grow, if Florida wasn't the first this had happened to, only the first to notice…

I caught myself, shocked by how easily I was sliding into belief. Was this some kind of weird test?

"And you've never told *anyone?*"

She had a pretty good poker face, did Florida, but that was a game I played, too. I saw something in her expression respond to my question; just the quickest, tiniest flicker, but when she assured me that she'd never told anyone but me, I knew she was lying. And as that occurred to me, I realized that nothing else she'd told me had felt like a lie. At the very least, *she* believed

"So why are you telling me, now?"

She put down her cup and folded her hands together in front of her. "I think you know I've always been impressed by your performance. You are a positive asset to the company, and I should be very sorry to lose you, if…well, I can understand if you are considering moving on, striking out on your own."

I sat very still. I hadn't said a word to *anyone* about my plans. How could she know what I was thinking?

She grimaced. "Maybe I'm projecting. You see, you rather remind me of myself at your age, and although my situation was quite different, if I were you, I'd be thinking that now was the time to aim higher, and that would have to mean striking out on my own.

"I'm nearly seventy," she said. "And although I'm not eager to retire, I can't keep working at the same pace. I know I will have to hand over to someone else."

She didn't say "That could be you," but she paused, and my mouth went dry with excitement and apprehension.

She went on, "Then there's David's welfare to consider. What happens to him when I die? I've made plenty of money, but he has special needs. I can't put the money into a trust for him, or even open a bank account for him because, as far as the outside world is concerned, *he doesn't exist.*"

She sighed. "If there were only someone I could trust to look after him when I'm gone… It wouldn't be difficult. He's so undemanding. Of course, if the two were tied in together—unofficially, of course—the running of the business, caring for my son—I've always known that I couldn't pass it on to him, but as long as he benefits from my success, I'd be happy." She gave me a look I'd never expected or imagined to see from my boss, the famously powerful, self-sufficient Florida McAfee, a look that was anxious and hopeful and almost pleading.

I said, "I'd like to meet this son of yours."

We both made calls to reschedule our afternoons. It took her longer than me, not because she had more scheduled, but because her personal assistant was still very new to the job, and needed to be talked through it all. The woman who'd worked for her in that capacity for over a decade had left a few months earlier, to start a new life in Australia after coming into an unexpected inheritance or winning some lottery—I wasn't sure of the exact details, just that she was now rich and somewhere far away.

When we were done, Florida's driver took us to her house in Holland Park. The journey passed without conversation; she was busy with her iPhone, and I was too nervous to speak. This was a first for me, and I'd never heard of anyone being invited to her home. When she entertained, she rented some appropriate venue, a nightclub in central London or a villa in Italy.

The house was smaller than I'd expected, just an ordinary house on a quiet street. After entering, she took me straight upstairs.

The room behind the locked door was small, no bigger than my own walk-in wardrobe, kitted out like a home office with built-in shelves, desk and filing cabinet. But this was only a front: as she explained, "I was afraid that I might get a cleaner for whom a locked door was just too tempting to resist. And the more difficult I made the lock, the more likely it would seem there was something worth stealing, worth gossiping about, and attracting the attention of burglars."

She pulled out a book in the middle of the third shelf down, revealing an electronic keypad. She keyed in a number and the bookshelf-wall opened to reveal a bedroom.

There was a window, on the back wall, curtains open, letting in the soft light of late afternoon. If a burglar had looked in, he'd see a few things worth stealing, although they were no more than the electronic goodies any reasonably well-off young man might own: the sleek laptop, the iPod in a Bose docking system. But if he saw those things, he'd also see their owner, stretched out, fully clothed, on top of the bed, as if asleep. It would take a little while, or a much closer inspection, to recognize the sleeper as a dead man.

"David," said Florida, in a peculiarly gentle voice I'd never heard her use before. "Darling, I've brought someone to meet you. I've told you about her. It's Leslie…you remember, I've told you about the clever girl I put in charge of R&D?"

Part of me wanted to turn and run like hell. And if I had, I have no doubt there would have been a handsome severance package in my near future, and maybe that would have been just the spur I needed to get out and start up my own company, although it's likely there would have been some sort of non-competition clause to encourage me to go to New Zealand or Canada, or at least far enough from London so Florida wouldn't have to see my face again.

But I was curious. I had to see him for myself, had to confront Florida's secret. I would have to stare down at his closed, handsome face, and touch his cool skin; hold his unresponsive hand in mine; spend time with him, trying to know him, to figure out who he was and what was meant by his existence.

Later, in the weeks and months to come, Florida answered my questions as best she could, as she described her attempts to be a good mother to a child who could not respond, but she could never explain the mystery of their relationship to my satisfaction. Unlike David, I kept asking for more.

But she didn't mind. My questions, my refusal to go away, confirmed that she'd been right in her choice, and that both her business and her son would be safe with me. Just as, in the past, she'd bought him new clothes when he outgrew the old ones, bought him toys and games and books and music, trying to give him what every boy should have, redecorating his room every few years so that it better reflected his age, and filling it with all the latest things, all the treasures she had purchased, as if they were offerings left in the tomb of a young prince, now she had brought him her final gift, me.

Reader, I married him.

The Baby Store

Ed Gorman

"You know how sorry we all are, Kevin," Miles Green said, sliding his arm around Kevin McKay's shoulder and taking his right hand for a manly shake. "It's going to be rough and we know it. So any time you need some time away, take it. No questions asked. You know?"

"I really appreciate it, Miles. And so does Jen. Everybody here has just been so helpful to us."

Miles smiled. "If you're not careful, you're going to give us lawyers a good reputation, Kevin." He checked the top of his left hand where the holo was embedded. "Time for me to head out for LA. The rocket leaves in three hours."

The Miles incident had occurred at the top of the day, just as Kevin had been about to settle himself into his desk chair for the first time in two months. The firm of Green, Hannigan & Stortz had been generous indeed with one of its youngest and most aggressive lawyers.

By day's end Kevin had been consoled by fourteen different members of the staff, from the paralegals to the executive secretaries to the firm's reigning asshole, Frank Hannigan himself.

Hannigan said: "I know Miles told you to take all the time you need. But if you want my advice, Kevin, you'll get back in the game and start kicking some ass. And not just for the sake of your bonus this December. But for your mental health. You're a gladiator the same as I am. The battle is what keeps you sane." Hannigan frequently spoke in ways this embarrassing.

As Kevin was leaving the office, he heard a brief burst of applause coming from one of the conference rooms. As he passed the open door, David Stortz waved him in. "C'mon in and celebrate with us, Kevin. My son just graduated at the top of his class at his prep school."

Reluctant as he was to listen to even ten minutes of Stortz's bragging, Kevin stepped into the room and took a seat.

Stortz, a balding enthusiastic man with dark eyes that never smiled, said, "This is quite a week for this firm, I'd say. Phil's son jumped from second grade to fourth after taking a special test. Irene's daughter wrote a paper on George Gershwin that's going to be published. And now my boy is at the top of his class."

The people Stortz had cited were sitting around the conference table, pleased to be congratulated by one of the firm's founders.

No one seemed to understand that inviting Kevin in to hear people bragging on their children was a bit insensitive given what had happened to him and his wife. But then nothing ever seemed to deter the lawyers here from bragging on their kids.

More than winning cases, more than accruing wealth, more than performing as talking heads on the vidd networks, the greatest pleasure for these men and women came from congratulating themselves on how well they'd designed their children at Generations or what the populist press disdainfully called "The Baby Store." Of course it wasn't just this law firm. Designer children had become status symbols for the upper classes. An attractive, bright child obviously destined to become an important citizen was now the most important possession you could boast of.

These parents were unfazed by the media criticism that insisted that the wealthy and powerful were creating a master race by genetically engineering their progeny. After all, as Miles had once said, "You design the child yourself. And it's no sure thing. Every once in a while somebody designs a dud."

Kevin was able to leave before the liquor appeared. It would be a long one. Six fathers and mothers bragging on their children took some time.

"May I help you, Sir?"

Only up close did the woman show even vague evidence of her actual age. The plastic surgery, probably multiple surgeries in fact, had been masterful. In her emerald-colored, form-fitting dress, with her perfectly fraudulent red hair, she looked both erotic and efficient.

"Just looking, really."

"Some very nice ones. And feel free to read their biographies. Some of them are pretty amazing."

"I don't have much time today. I think I'll just look at the holos."

"Fine." A smile that would have seduced a eunuch. "I'll just let you look. If there's anything you need, just let me know."

He spent equal time with male and female holos. They were all so perfect they began to lose individuality after a time. As Stortz said, people did, of course, design duds. The looks didn't turn out quite right; the intelligence wasn't impressive or even, sometimes, adequate; and then there were personality flaws, sometimes profound. Most of these problems resulted from parents who wouldn't listen to the advice of the scientists and programmers. But their arrogance could be tragic.

Given what had happened, he settled on looking at the girls. These were finished products, used to guide the buyer in creating their own girls. He was particularly taken with a dark-haired girl of sixteen whose fetching face was as imposing as the amused intelligence that played in her blue-eyed gaze. Yes, good looks—and intelligence. Requisites for a leadership role later on.

He doted on the girl, imagining the kind of boasting you could do in a session like the one he'd just left. Even up against the likes of Stortz and the others, this girl would undoubtedly triumph. Whoever had designed her obviously had known exactly what they were doing.

But then it was time to catch the bullet train home. Soft summer suburban night awaited. He just hoped Jen was free of her depression, at least for a few hours.

He was never sure how to characterize the sounds she made—
"crying" was too little but then "sobbing" was probably too much.
He usually settled for "weeping."

She was weeping when he got home that night. He went upstairs
immediately to knock softly on the door of the master bedroom. "Is
there anything I can do, honey?" he asked as he'd asked every night
since the death of their five-year-old son three months ago.

"Just please leave me alone, Kevin," she said between choked
tears. "Just please leave me alone." Even given the loss they'd suffered,
could this tragedy alone fuel so many endless days of bitter sobbing
sorrow?

Dinner alone. By now he was used to it. An hour or so in front
of the vidd with a few drinks. And then bringing her a tray of food.
Otherwise she wouldn't eat. He'd come to think of all this reasonably
enough as The Ritual.

After eating—she'd lost fifteen pounds from an already thin
lovely body—Jen usually went into the bathroom and showered for
bed. Afterward was when they talked.

"Somebody at the office told me about a very good doctor. Very
good with depression."

"Please, Kevin. No more shrinks. I couldn't take another one."

"I wish you'd take the meds."

"The headaches they give me are worse than the depression."

Sometimes he wondered if she wasn't purposely punishing herself. Maybe her depression was her way of dealing with what she'd
saw as her negligence in the death of Kevin, Jr.

"You know the doctor said he'd never heard of anybody getting
headaches from this particular med."

"That's what I mean about doctors. They say things like that
all the time? *They* don't take the drugs. *We* do. We're their guinea
pigs. And when we complain about something, they tell us we're just
imagining it."

And so on.

The best part of the night was when she lay in his arms in the
darkness, responding finally to his patience and kindness, trusting
him once more as she had always trusted him in their young marriage. Sometimes they made love; sometimes the day-long siege of

depression and tears had left her too shattered to do much more than lie next to him.

Tonight he was afraid. He didn't know if he should tell her what he'd done or not. He certainly didn't want to set her off. But maybe the idea would appeal to her. Maybe she was ready now to talk about the rest of their lives. Maybe a talk like this was exactly what she needed to hear to make her forget—

He'd tell her about his impulsive visit to the Baby Store and—

But then he smiled to himself for there, her regal blonde head on his shoulder, came the soft sweet sounds of her child-like snoring.

❊

In the next few weeks he visited the Baby Store three times after work. On the second visit he asked if he could visit with one of the consultants. He kept assuring the doctor that he was only asking questions while he waited for his train. The doctor kept assuring him in turn that he understood that quite well.

On the third visit, his words seeming to come unbidden, Kevin explained how our-five-year-old Kevin, Jr. had drowned in the small lake that ran very near the front porch of their summer cottage and how Jen blamed herself for it. She'd been on the phone when he walked into the water. Kevin had been in the backyard dealing with some particularly aggravating gopher holes.

The doctor, a middle-aged man with kind blue eyes, said, "It's especially traumatic when you lose a child you designed yourself. It's a double loss."

"I guess I hadn't thought of that. You're right. And we spent so much time making sure he'd be just right."

The doctor, whose name was Carmody, spoke gently. "I know why you're coming here, Kevin. And I think you've got the right idea. But what you're worried about is convincing your wife."

Kevin smiled. "You're a mind reader, too."

"Oh, no. It's just that I've been through this process with a number of people over the years. Something unfortunate happens to the child they've designed and they're not sure if they can deal with designing another one."

"That's right. That's exactly right."

"Usually the man is the one who suggests it. The woman is too lost in her grief. And he knows that she won't like the idea at all. Not at first. And her feeling is perfectly natural. You'll both feel guilty about designing another child. Kevin, Jr. is dead and here you are going on with your lives—and replacing him."

"I'm already feeling guilty. But I think that's what we both need. A new child. While we're still in our early thirties. With our lives still ahead of us."

Dr. Carmody nodded. "But it won't be easy. She'll resist. She'll probably even get very angry. And she'll feel even more isolated than she does now. She'll think you don't understand her mourning at all."

"So maybe I shouldn't suggest it?"

"Not at all, Kevin. All I'm saying is that you should prepare yourself for some very heated discussions. Very heated."

"I don't know how you could even *think* about another child now," Jen said at dinner that night. "We loved him so much. It's not like buying a new pair of shoes or something."

"Honey, all I said was that it's something to think about. You're so sad all the time—"

"And you aren't?"

"I guess I don't have *time* to be sad most of the time. I'm always rushing around with work and—" He knew he'd said the wrong insensitive thing. He eased his hand across the candlelit dinner that the caterers had prepared so nicely. He'd wanted the right mood to even raise the subject. He knew that convincing her was somewhere in the future. "Why do you think I don't sleep well? I'm thinking about Kevin, Jr."

By the look in her blue eyes he could see that he'd rescued himself. And what he'd said hadn't been untrue. He couldn't sleep well these nights. And a good deal of the time during those uneasy hours, he thought of his son, his dead son.

"I don't even want to talk about it now," she said. "Or think about it." Her smile surprised him. One of the old Jen smiles, so girlishly erotic. "Tonight I want us to drink all three bottles of wine and just be silly. It's been a while since we've been silly."

He slid his hand over hers, touching it with great reverence. His one and only love. He missed her. The old her. "Well, if you want silly, Madame, you've come to the right guy. Nobody's sillier than I am."

And they toasted his silliness. In fact, before they managed to stagger into bed and have some of that old-time sex of theirs, they'd toasted a good many things. And every one of them had been silly. Very, very silly.

Then came the day when he got home from work and found Jen's personal holo filled with images of children from the Baby Store. Jen often forgot to turn the holo to FADE when she was done with it. His first inclination was to rush up the stairs to the exercise room and congratulate her for beginning to show interest in designing another child. But then he realized it would be better to let her interest grow at its own pace.

He was disappointed that she didn't mention the holo that night at dinner. But the fact that she'd come down to dinner at all told him that old Jen hadn't been lost to him after all. The old Jen was slowly returning to the shining presence he loved so much.

She didn't mention anything about the holo—or subsequent viewings of the Baby Store holos—for the next eight evening meals. And when she brought it up the reference was oblique: "Sometimes it's so quiet here during the day. Bad quiet, I mean, not good quiet."

It had rarely been quiet when Kevin, Jr. had been alive.

Dr. Carmody said, "I think a little nudge might be appropriate here, Mr. McKay."

"What kind of nudge, Dr. Carmody?"

"Oh, nothing confrontational. Nothing like that. In fact, something pleasant. I had a patient who was having a difficult time getting her husband to come in. They'd only recently come into some money and her husband still had some of his old attitudes about designer babies from the days when he'd been so well off. But she surprised him. Invited him to his favorite restaurant, which just happened to be near her, and after the meal she just happened to steer him in our direction—and four days later, he came in and signed the papers and started creating not one but two children. Twins."

"Well, one of Jen's favorite restaurants is near here, too. We go there for our anniversary every year."

"When's your next anniversary?"

"Two weeks from tomorrow."

Dr. Carmody smiled his Dr. Carmody smile. "That's not very far off, is it?"

She was late getting into the city and for a frantic half hour Kevin was afraid that Jen had known that this would be more than an anniversary dinner. He couldn't contact her on her comm, either. Maybe she'd decided not to meet him. Maybe she was in the bedroom, weeping as she once had. He stood on their street corner lost in the chill April dusk and the shadow crowds racing to the trains and the freeways.

And then, golden and beaming, tossing off an explanation for her tardiness that was both reasonable and reassuring—then she was in his arms and they were walking like new lovers to the restaurant where their reserved table waited for them.

After her second glass of wine, she said, "After dinner, let's go for a walk. I don't get down here very often. And I still love to window shop."

The center of the city gleamed in the midst of darkness, an entity constantly reinventing itself, taller, faster, more seductive in every respect, the streets patrolled by android security officers. The androids were without mercy.

The store windows Jen stopped at were alive with quickly changing holos of haute couture. He was happy to see her interested in her appearance again. She even talked about making one of her shopping trips.

He made sure that they kept moving in the direction of the Baby Store. As they turned a corner, entering the block the store was on, she said, "I think I've got a surprise coming up."

"A surprise?"

She leaned into him affectionately, tightening her grip on his arm. She laughed. "You've been steering us in a certain direction since we left the restaurant."

"I have?"

"We're going to the Baby Store as you've always called it."

"We are?"

But of course they were.

A small staff kept the three-story building open during the night-time hours. As Kevin had arranged, Dr. Carmody had stayed late. He greeted them in the lobby and led them back to his office.

"Happy Anniversary to both of you," he said.

"Thank you, Dr. Carmody. I guess I knew in the back of my mind we'd end up here tonight. Sometimes I can sort of read my husband's mind."

"I hope you're not disappointed, Mrs. McKay."

She shrugged in that sweet young-girl way she had. "No, maybe Kevin's right. Maybe this is what I need."

"We'll certainly do our best," Carmody said.

And so they began.

Coffee cleared their minds and numerous holos of designed girls—that was the only thing Jen knew for sure; a girl this time—sharpened their imaginations. They began to form a picture of the infant Jen would carry. And what this infant would look like at various stages of her life. And what kind of intellectual acumen the child would have. In a world as competitive as this one, superior beauty without superior intelligence was nothing.

Dr. Carmody had left them alone in front of the enormous holo console. They were so infatuated with the prospect of a new child that they became infatuated with each other, friendly kisses giving way to passionate ones; a breast touched, long lovely fingers caught behind Kevin's neck pulling him closer, "Maybe the wine hasn't worn off after all," Kevin said.

After forty-five minutes they stopped looking at holos and began talking seriously about the child they'd come to create. Hair color, eye color, body type, features—classic or more contemporary? What sort of interests it would have. The level of intelligence—some parents went too far. The children had serious emotional problems later on.

Kevin asked Dr. Carmody to join them.

"Did you like any of the holos you saw?"

"They were all very impressive, Dr.," Kevin said. "In fact they were all so good it got kind of confusing after a while. But I think we've started to have a pretty good idea of what we're looking for."

"Well, we're certainly ready to proceed with the process any time you are," Dr. Carmody said, his perfectly-modulated vidd-caster voice never more persuasive. "We just need to look over our standard agreement and get to work."

"I'm sure that won't be any problem," Kevin said. But as he spoke he noticed that Jen no longer seemed happy. The tension of the past four months had tightened her face and given her eyes a somewhat frantic look.

Dr. Carmody had become aware of her sudden change, too. He glanced at Kevin, inclined his head vaguely toward Jen. He obviously expected Kevin to deal with this situation. It wasn't the doctor's place to do so.

But as Kevin started to put his hand on her arm, she stood up with enough force to make herself unsteady. Kevin tried to slide his arm around her waist to support her but she pulled away from him. She was suddenly, violently crying. "I can't do this. It's not fair to our boy. It's not fair!"

And then before either man could quite respond effectively, Jen rushed to the door, opened it and disappeared.

Kevin started to run after her. Dr. Carmody stopped him. "Just remember. She's been through a lot, Kevin. Don't force her into this until she's really ready. Obviously she's having some difficulty with the process. There's no rush with this."

Kevin, scarcely listening, rushed out the door after his wife. She was much faster than he'd imagined. She wasn't in the hall nor, when he reached the lobby, was she there. He hurried outside.

The sidewalk was crowded with people his own age, of his own status. Drink and drugs lent them the kind of happiness you usually saw only on vidd commercials.

He didn't see Jen at first. Luckily he glimpsed her turning the far corner. He ran. People made wary room for him. Somebody running in a crowd like this instinctively made them nervous. A running man meant danger.

There was no time for apologies, no time for gently moving people aside. When he reached the corner, his clothes were disheveled and his face damp with sweat. He couldn't find her. He felt sick, scared. She was in such a damned vulnerable state. He didn't like to think of what going to the Baby Store might have triggered in her.

He quit running, falling against a street lamp to gather his breath. He got the sort of cold, disapproving glances that derelicts invited. While he was getting his breath back, he smelled the nearby river. The cold early spring smell of it. He wasn't sure why but he felt summoned by the stark aroma of it.

In a half-dazed state, he began moving toward the water, the bridge that ran north-south coming in view as soon as he neared the end of the block.

She stood alone, staring down at the black, choppy water that was freezing. Though he knew it was probably best to leave her alone for a while, his need to hold her was so overpowering that he found himself walking toward her without quite realizing it until he was close enough to touch the sleeve of her coat.

She didn't acknowledge him in any way, simply continued staring into the water. Down river the lights from two tug-boats could be seen, like the eyes of enormous water creatures moving through the night. In the further distance a foghorn sounded.

He leaned against the railing just the way she did. He remained silent. He smelled her perfume, her hair. God he loved her.

When she spoke, her voice was faint. "I killed our son."

"Honey, we've been over this and over this. You were on the phone and he didn't stay on the porch like you told him. He went into the lake despite everything we'd warned him about."

She still didn't look at him. "I lied. I ran out the door in time to save him. I could have dived in and brought him back to shore. But I didn't. I *wanted* him to drown, Kevin, because I was ashamed of him. All the women I know—they were always bragging about their sons and daughters. But Kevin Jr.—we did something wrong when we created him. He just wasn't very smart. He would never have amounted to much. And so I let him drown. I stood there and let him drown while you were in the backyard."

He'd always felt that her grief was more complicated than the accidental death of their son. And now he knew that his guess had been correct. In addition to loss, she was dealing with a kind of guilt he couldn't imagine.

"You just thought I was in the backyard."

For the first time she turned and looked at him, her face in shadow. "But you *were* in the backyard."

"True. But only for a while. I heard him scream, too, I ran around to the side of the house. I was going to save him. That was all I thought about. But then I stopped myself. I started thinking—you know how in just a few seconds you can have so many different thoughts—I started thinking the same things you did. I loved him but we'd created a child who just couldn't compete. Who'd *never* be able to compete."

She clutched his arm. "Are you lying to me, Kevin?"

"No. I'm telling you the truth. And I'm telling you that we're both equally guilty—and that we're not guilty at all. We made a terrible mistake. We didn't listen to our counselor. We designed our son badly. It wasn't his fault and it wasn't ours. I mean we had the best of intentions."

"But we let him die."

"Yes, we did. And you know what? We did him a favor. We'd already seen how mediocre his school work was. What kind of future would he have had? He wouldn't have had any kind of enjoyable life." He drew her close to him. "But now we have another chance, Jen. And this time we'll listen to our counselor. Dr. Carmody will help us. We'll create the kind of child we can be proud of. And when Stortz and everybody at the office starts bragging about *their* kids, I'll finally be able to brag about mine."

She fell against him. This time joy laced her sobbing. He could almost psychically share the exuberance she felt knowing that he was as much to blame for Kevin, Jr.'s death as she was. There was such a thing as the saving lie and he was happy to relieve her of at least some of her guilt.

A numbing wind swept up from the river. She shuddered against him.

"We need some coffee," he said. He slid his arm around her shoulders and together they started walking back toward the center of the city.

"We never did decide if we want our daughter to be blonde or brunette," he said.

"Or a redhead," she said. "I've got an aunt with beautiful red hair."

An image of an ethereal red-haired girl came into his mind. One who inspired lust and myth in equal parts. That was the kind of daughter they'd create. He couldn't wait to see the envy on Stortz's face when the daughter was fifteen or so. The envy would be something to exult about for weeks.

A Lonely Town in Alaska

Darren Speegle

"What's your name?" said the woman through the open passenger window of the weathered Jeep Cherokee.

"Hunter," said the man at the wheel.

"Hunter? That's a bit obvious, isn't it?"

"Not if you're from my generation."

"Your generation? How old could you be?" she said. "Thirty?"

"Actually, I'm forty-seven. Call it living well."

"Yeah? What do you do, bathe in the blood of infants or something?"

"Why? Are you an infant?"

She hesitated a moment, searching his face, and then, seeming to trust what she saw, said, "Not after the journey I'm returning from."

"Well, get in and tell me about it."

Again the hesitation. Again the look that said, *He's one of us... whoever the hell* we *are*. She had that air about her. That of the lonely spirit.

"Where are you headed?" she asked.

"Hooking up with the Alaska Highway eventually."

"You must have just gotten off the ferry."

"Do I have the look of the lower forty-eight states, is that it?"

"Where else would you be coming from? Road ends not three miles beyond the terminal." She smiled, and he thought, *She herself has a trustworthy face. Clear and open without being naïve.* He wondered if it was a universal Alaskan trait.

"Yes, I remember that now. When I look at a map I tend to look in the direction I want to go. Never backwards."

"Wise man," she said, idly fiddling with the strap of her backpack. "The Alaska Highway, huh? To get there, I suppose you know, you have to go through Chi Bay." Now the shadow lingered a little longer, bringing out lines in her face that had previously been invisible.

"And?"

"And nothing. I'm going there myself."

"Well hop in. I could use somebody to point me around. I plan to spend the night there before heading on in the morning."

"My backpack?" she said, pulling the strap forward with her thumb.

"Of course. Let's put it in back."

When that was done and she'd settled into the seat beside him, he put the Jeep in gear and glanced through the side view mirror before pulling onto the road.

"I tell you there's nothing back there, man," his passenger said. "The kids party at this camping spot at the end of the road, but that's on weekends. If you were the only vehicle off the ferry, you're the only one this side of Chi Bay. You might catch a cop out here pretending to be busy, but that's about it on a Monday afternoon. People in Chi Bay don't wander much. And the kids, well, they go in packs."

"So where are you coming from then? I didn't see you on the ferry."

She pointed over her shoulder with her thumb. "The trail."

"Judging by the size of your backpack, you've been at it awhile."

"Since Grant's Cove."

"And how far's that?" He tried to remember another town on the map. Considering his way with maps, he wasn't surprised when he came up blank.

"Thirty some miles. A few nights under the stars. I'm used to it. Spent the last year and a half backpacking around Europe."

"Yeah? I've spent some time abroad myself. What is it the Germans call it? *Wanderlust*? But this is Alaska. A whole other animal."

"That it is. But you came at the right time of year. This is your best month in Southeast Alaska. It's why I decided to return home in May. It can still be a little cool at night. But at least you get a break, if you're lucky anyway, from the otherwise constant precipitation."

"Chi Bay's home then?" Hunter said.

"I guess you could call it that. I prefer Juneau where I went to college, but this is the area I grew up in. Honestly I don't really know why I've come back. I ran away at sixteen, haven't seen the place since."

He nodded, watching the road and wondering if she saw the empathy on his face. He said, "I've given you my name, but you haven't given me yours."

"Huntress," she said. And smiled that clear smile of hers.

"First name or last name?"

"Middle."

"Ah."

"Okay, enough with that. Call me Von. My parents called me Vera. My foster parents insisted on using my full name, Veronica. I like Von."

The road was narrow, cutting through fir woodlands when it wasn't hugging the rocky beach. He was driving through forest now, the path before him a shadowy tunnel through the dense trees. Where the sunlight filtering through the canopy drew designs, there was possibility, a sort of hope amid the muddle.

A little vignette by Hemingway came to him. An example from a college writing course of a short story of perfect brevity. *For sale: Baby shoes, never worn.* Nothing muddled in its spare words.

"Your parents…"

"They died. When I was fifteen. They hiked up Harrow Mountain to one of the Forest Service's remote cabins for the weekend. They never hiked back down."

"That was here in Chi Bay?"

Von looked at him oddly. "Funny you put it that way. *Here* in Chi Bay. There's not a hint of the town in sight."

"The sign at the terminal said Chi Bay Ferry Terminal. These are the outskirts, right?"

"Yes, but…it's the way you said it. Like the place already had you. Chi Bay—not the town itself but the area—has that kind of effect on strangers. I remember my father talking about it once. He did these backcountry tours and was always coming home with little stories for my mother. Odd remarks the tourists and out-of-towners had made. He said the strangers were more at home in Chi Bay than the residents. They were, quote, 'in touch' with the same loneliness that alienated the locals." She paused, then looking at the road ahead said, "He'd know about alienation. He was a master at it."

Unsure how to respond to that, Hunter pursued the less personal point. "Do you get a lot of strangers?" Though Von had set the precedent, the word "strangers" felt awkward off his tongue. Visitors would have seemed the better description.

"*I* don't get anything. Remember, I'm a stranger too."

He detected the suggestion of something in her voice, though he could not have named what. Maybe the clarity about her was an illusion. Maybe there was a muddled quality here after all.

The road in front of him curved to the left, and the sea was visible again. The slate beach strewn with boulders. A bald eagle perched on a lip of one of those boulders, watching the vehicle pass.

People in Chi Bay don't wander much.

He had the sudden compulsion to ask her how her parents had died. *What is it about your Chi Bay, Von, that inspires these expressions of yours? You seem disturbed in your homecoming. Haunted.* But he refrained. For maybe it was the tragedy itself that had seeped into the environment. Again he empathized with her. His own parents, who to his knowledge had yet to be covered in earth, were nonetheless as dead to him as if he'd committed the act with his own hand. And maybe he had. Maybe they were the infants that had kept him young. Certainly they had never grown up enough to raise two children. Ask his twin Hannah, who'd made sure no one could question whether or not the earth had come shoveling down on her. Leaving behind an example of brevity to rival Hemingway's own. Its very words: *You want a note? Fuck you.*

A house came into view. An impressive A-frame set in a crook along the shoreline. Its seaward-facing façade boasted windows from floor to rafter. A handsome hand-carved wooden bear stood on two legs in the yard, its maw open wide. To the left of the house a trailer on which rested an expensive-looking motorboat was parked. A Hummer sat inside a carport. The next house, nestled among the trees on the opposite side of the road, was much more modest. In its gravel drive was a battered Toyota pickup. Its bear was a porcupine, one of those knick-knacks for brushing off shoes. It rested by a front door whose aged paint was flaking away in leprous patches. Hunter wondered which situation Von had come from. Had her people been affluent or had they struggled as his own parents had? Struggled without really struggling as they partied themselves to oblivion every night of every week into infinity. What did a backcountry tour guide earn for a living? Enough to estrange himself from his child, apparently. Always enough for that.

Von spoke, and in a faraway voice, and Hunter wasn't sure as she returned to the subject whether it was one he'd really wanted to tackle after all.

"Aren't you going to ask me about my parents? Aren't you interested in knowing how an expert on strangers could be a stranger to his own daughter? Easy. You see her as a nuisance, a thing to be swatted away for her familiarity, for the mistake she was."

Which said to Hunter that strangers were actually not the less personal point.

"My mother, though, she was acceptable to him," his passenger went on. "Because she helped him with his work. Once upon a time she'd been something of a local celebrity, a poet 'in touch'—yes, there's that expression again—with dark and mysterious Chi Bay. It's what drew him to her, I'm sure. He was already involved in his work when he met her. You see, he was what you might call an occultist. Eventually they both were. I don't doubt it's what delivered them to their end."

Hunter looked at her, wondering just why she was opening herself up to him like this. Was that the way it was with strangers and wanderers who'd mutually acknowledged the fact? Was there a brotherhood? Stranger yet that the conversation had taken this turn; that the word "occultist" had been thrown out there as though it was an everyday word. And yet somehow it was not so strange. Hadn't there been something peculiar about this whole encounter from the beginning? The way she'd turned and simply stared at him when she'd heard the Jeep round the bend? The way he'd almost automatically applied pressure to the brakes then pulled up beside her as though it was the most natural thing in the world to offer a ride to someone who was clearly not hitchhiking, judging by the nature of the bundle she carried, bedroll and tent attached. How strong she must be beneath her khakis, he'd thought at the time, to carry such weight. And now…to know she'd hauled her load across thirty some miles in "a few nights under the stars." Where'd she get the strength for the other? The demons surrounding her homecoming?

"No, Hunter, in case you're wondering," she said. "I do not spill my life to every stranger I meet. You just happen to be here when needed. Do you think that's the right word? 'Happen?'"

"Strangely, no," he said. Meaning it.

"Do you believe in fate?"

"Today I 'happen' to."

She smiled, and yes, it was the clearest thing in the world.

More houses appeared, a mixture of modest and not so modest as she went on, in a less faraway voice now, with her sharing. "I did my thesis at Southeast Alaska on the Chi-Ikuk, the native Alaskan tribe the town was named for. The instructor allowed me to change my subject matter before failing me for what she referred to as 'pure and inappropriate fantasy.' I knew it wasn't fantasy because I'd taken my material from my father's own notes, and my father, well, he was obsessed with accuracy when it came to this his one passion in life. So in a way I suppose you could call him a historian, though that's not to replace the term occultist. Chi Bay has been a breeding ground for the sort of material he immersed himself in for longer than it's been Chi Bay." She paused, gesturing ahead. "And here the devil is now. Welcome, my stranger Hunter, to one lonely town in Alaska."

As the view opened up before them, the trees falling back to allow for the tableau of town and bay, Chi Bay was as one might have expected of a seaside Alaskan village. While more worn by the elements, it reminded Hunter vaguely of some of the towns he'd seen in Maine during his wanderings. Its dwellings were mainly scattered along the base of a mountain, with a few along the near waterfront, while the commercial and municipal buildings were clustered near a bridge that crossed to an island running generally parallel to the mainland. Between the two the wider bay funneled into a channel at whose mouth were harbored an array of boats, a newer-looking marina standing in the foreground. Rolling his window down, Hunter partook of the air of the place. As expected, it had its own charm, the brine a pleasant assault on the senses in spite of the underlying odor of fish.

"That delicious taste in your mouth is from the fishery," Von said, pointing to the left at a long aluminum structure. "The ancient building beside it, the one that's on stilts, is the cannery. Like the mine on the far side of town, it's just an attraction now. Fluffed up with the brown historic signs for the cruise ship tourism we got over a few summers before the locals decided they'd had enough of being overrun by gawkers. This back in the late nineties when I was still devising a way out of this place."

"You're telling your age," Hunter smiled.

"What's to hide? I'm twenty-nine, and aging as fast as you are de-aging. That's what you're doing, isn't it? You've reached a plateau and now you're aging backward and I'm the truth you missed on your way up the hill. The truth that age itself is an illusion. That there are still places on this earth like Chi Bay."

She looked at him as if expecting an answer. Since he had none, he went with the thought that failed at obscuring his own questions. "Are you sure you're not the poet in the family?"

"I don't have a dark enough soul for that task."

"You do paint a picture though."

"It's easy when you're a Chi-ite. But where was I? Oh yes, the tourism. The natives weren't as happy about dropping the cruise ship traffic as the rest of the town. They didn't like losing all that business. They didn't have much ground to stand on, though, considering that the death toll among our eager visitors had reached a half dozen over those summers. You can warn an outsider only so many times to stay on the trail, lose the perfume and loud deodorants in bear-populated areas—which is everywhere—and treat this particular Alaskan town with a modicum of respect. Chi Bay is not Juneau or Ketchikan or Haines or any other place you can name. It's built on a fault, so to speak, and that fault tends to yawn open when it's hungry."

Hunter stopped at one of two visible traffic lights on this side of town, eyes drawn to the sparse afternoon foot traffic along the street while his mind tried to make sense of what was being generated by this special clarity of Von's.

"If the townsfolk seem zombies to you," she said, "it's because they are. Oh, there's no shortage of hospitality, or that pretense anyway, but you'll find a blankness in the eyes of Chi Bay residents that you'll not find elsewhere. It's the only substitute, in the end, for the terror."

"Terror?" he said, emphasizing each syllable.

"Sound extreme? I guess it would to an outsider." She smiled mirthlessly as she added, "An outsider coming home again."

As he looked around at this ageless town of hers he found himself feeling precisely that way. Like an outsider coming home again. He'd have thought a little conversation with the locals, some immersing in the culture would have been required to validate her father's observation. But no, just being here did the trick. And not necessarily as pertained to the town itself, but rather, as Von had suggested, the environment in which the town's props had been erected. There was a nostalgic flavor to being surrounded by the stage pieces, certainly. But there was a deeper something involved, an older, almost primal something. While many places he'd visited had inspired a certain bittersweetness, an indefinable yearning, a sense of filling up while emptying out, this was something different, something more. A strange wind blew in Chi Bay; there was no denying its delicate caress.

As they approached the next light, Von interrupted his philosophizing. "Turn left here."

"Where are we going?" he said, pleased with the fact that, wherever it was, it was on the waterfront side.

"The hotel. You okay money-wise? The Red Bear's a little on the expensive side, but it's the most charming of your choices. Another one of those historic sites if you go for that sort of thing."

"Sounds nice. But what about yourself? Do you have a place to stay?" Oddly, he didn't feel awkward asking.

"I'll be staying there as well. While I'm not hurting on the money end, I wouldn't mind sharing the expense of a room."

How natural, in fact, that what had started a quarter-mile from the ferry terminal should come to this. And without the sexual tension that might have accompanied such an encounter. Indeed, while she was attractive, and had the "natural" qualities he was attracted to in a woman, he hadn't thought of her in that way until now. Of course, offering to share the expense of a room with someone was not the same as inviting that someone into bed with you—whatever one preferred to read in that open, clear face of hers.

"Sure," he said, hoping it didn't sound too casual.

When the uncertainty in his voice didn't make it by her, he found it natural, also, to laugh along with her.

The room smelled of cedar from its rough-cut beams. Its furnishings were plush in an upscale hunting lodge sort of a way. The floor was carpeted in a rich maroon, and a fireplace stood between the two high-posted wooden beds. They hadn't had to ask for the room type, it had been the only one available, saving them any discomfort (which he doubted at this point) an option might have caused. When Hunter had asked Von where the hotel got its guests with no tourists around, she'd told him Chi Bay appealed to a certain breed of out-of-towners. Her words: "With Alaskans being the secretive lot they are, you won't find the town in any docudramas. But Chi Bay has its faithful."

"Occultists like your father?" he'd said.

"More like tornado chasers. Though they'd never admit, even to one another, what they're up to."

"And just what are they up to?"

"I think brandy's the appropriate drink for this place, don't you? Or better yet, a good red wine. We'll get a couple bottles while we're out."

Evening had settled and they were preparing to go out now. She looked refreshed after a shower and a two-hour nap. Not in the least bit tired after sleeping much of the way on the ferry, Hunter had followed his shower with a stroll along the waterfront promenade, stopping in at one of the drinkeries for a couple beers while letting Von rest her joints and muscles from the day's hike. As she'd remarked, the locals were very hospitable, but equally detached. There had been no mixing among them, though the joint had been relatively busy. But Hunter hadn't been there to appraise them, only to relax with his Alaska Ambers and enjoy the view of the bay and snow-capped mountains beyond. It was everything he'd imagined it would be, his first sit-down view from Alaskan shores. Haines, beautiful in its own right, had just been a stop where everyone who'd driven or walked aboard in Bellingham, Washington had offloaded except himself. But the view from the Chi Bay waterfront, it was the kind of experience he'd subsisted on these past several years, first in Europe, then South America, then during this revisiting of the homeland. Lonely and beautiful and soul-satisfying. For at least those choice moments in time.

"You ready?" Von asked him as she stuck a pin in the knot she'd made of her long, honey-brown hair. She looked in the mirror, fussing with the knot a bit, then with a dissatisfied twist of her lips pulled the pin and let her hair down again.

"Hey, I rather liked it like that," Hunter said.

"Is that so."

"Yeah. It went well with the turtleneck. Gave you a certain sophisticated look."

"In spite of the lack of effort that went into it?"

"Less effort goes into leaving it down."

"Are you a woman?"

"No."

"Then shut up."

He smiled. The fact was, she didn't need to be a botherer when it came to her appearance. Nor, he suspected, did she ever put more time into it than he'd watched her do this evening. Deeply tanned, with a smooth, clear complexion, she'd put on very little make-up, and then only around the eyes, with a sparing tastefulness. The jade-colored turtleneck, the jade earrings, the fashionable if wrinkly jeans…granted, she was working out of a backpack, but she'd spent about as much time selecting these as it had taken him to wash the shaving cream off his face. Hell, *he* had been the one to run his outfit by the other.

She was really rather lovely, he'd decided. And appearance only a part of it.

"Are you going to stare at me or answer the question?" she said with a girl's grin.

No use letting *her* know how he felt. "I've been ready, Von. I'm a man."

She stuck her tongue out at him. "I'll give you the benefit of the doubt and assume there's not a double meaning there."

He felt himself blush, a rarity for him. "So where are we going?"

"As I've told you, it's a surprise."

"Well, I hope they have food there. I'm starved."

"I should have thought that obvious. When a small-town Alaskan says she's going out in her small town, she means she's going out to eat and, if she's in the mood, have a few drinks. Where the hell else is there to go? The club? The symphony?"

"I get your point. So are we walking or driving?"

"Driving."

"After you," he said with a gentlemanly sweep of his arm.

Of all the places she might have taken him—okay, of all the *few* places she might have taken him—he'd never have guessed *here*. He'd known it would be outdoors after a trip to Wal-Mart ("You have a *Wal*-Mart?" he'd voiced in amazement as the store came into view) to pick up a tablecloth, a block of sharp cheddar cheese, a half dozen slices of semi-fresh deli ham, a loaf of semi-fresh bakery bread, and a basket of semi-edible-looking strawberries ("Fresh produce in Chi Bay?" she'd said. "Forget it."). At her insistence they'd split both that bill and the bill for the wine, which, along with a pair of red wine glasses and a corkscrew, they'd picked up at a legitimate dealer at a cost that had made him glad for her sharing spirit. But picnic materials invoke images of pretty parks and sandy beaches, not the sort of place to which she took him. Not in a million years would he have expected an abandoned turn-of-the-century gold mine, even with its brief mention of earlier.

Thankfully, the only accessible part of the hundred-plus-year-old setup was *outside* the mountain, and it a skeleton of what it had once been. The mine was accessed by an offshoot of the road out of town. The main road, according to Von, continued on in a curve around the mountain, passing through a tunnel and a few residential areas before settling into its long, lonely pursuit of the fabled Alaska Highway. A foot trail led to the site from the spot at the end of the road where they parked, following the edge of a length of wetlands active with ducks and other waterfowl before entering a body of trees which Von identified for him as Western Hemlocks. Ten minutes along, the path, by way of a dilapidated wooden bridge, crossed a stream carrying the melt of the winter snows to the sea. A short distance beyond, the trees opened up and the mine, in phantom shapes, presented itself.

The picnic spot was inside the larger and most intact of three concrete buildings standing in close proximity to each other. In the building's main room a concrete platform that must have been a work table of some sort provided a handy surface on which to place the tablecloth. As they laid out their gourmet spread, a light wind blew through the holes where the windows and doors had once been. The beach was easily visible from the room, the high tide line some forty or fifty yards from the building. The waves coming in now were far from that line, lapping softly at the lonely posts left behind by a collapsed pier; a bright half-moon, visible through a gaping vacancy in the ruined roof, highlighting the gentle crests that occasionally formed. In the foreground rusty metal chutes extended from the next building, some broken and lying in the silt, others connecting to an unidentifiable apparatus that stood silhouetted in the dusk. More of these chutes extended in the opposite direction toward the mountain, where other, smaller structures lay in ruin. The generous moonlight contributed to the overall industrial phantasmagoria, and Hunter, taking it all in, found the surprise the location had brought along with it giving way to a sort of adolescent thrill.

He told Von she'd done well with her spooky site.

"Naturally," she said.

They sat on the platform, the food and wine between them. "You've been here before, I take it," he said as he picked up the Buck pocketknife she'd had the foresight to take from her backpack, and began cutting slices of cheese and bread.

"Once. With my parents," she said as she worked on uncorking one of the wine bottles. "They didn't like having their nuisance along when communing with the spirits. This is one of those sites, according to my father's notes, where the energy surrounding Chi Bay is concentrated. Not because of what happened here, but because of what caused what happened here. Meaning the energy is older than any tragedy."

He paused before asking the question. He'd known, hadn't he, that there was something? As opposed as Von was to her father's occultism, she herself was fascinated with that aspect of Chi Bay—if indeed there was such an aspect outside of the mind. But no, Hunter knew this to be rigid thinking. And a reversal at that, as he'd already allowed for the strange wind that blew around here. A man's skepticism had to yield sometimes to his subtler senses. And the subtler senses required no proof beyond the vibrations they picked up.

And yet, mustn't there also be some allowance for words? For expression? For the tenor and inflection of the voice? The nuances of the face and body? For the subtle power of suggestion? Von was certainly persuasive, and all the more so because of her innocence. That established, it seemed to him that the empirical should also be trusted. Not without reason did a person grow increasingly more skeptical, more reasonable in their thinking as they aged, the fancifulness of youth dissipating with hard experience. Von could talk all she wanted of his aging backwards, but the imagination does not revert after the plateau; it merely deteriorates. They were two different things. A person could dream, for example, of misspent youth, but a person could not dream the dreams of misspent youth; they were gone forever. Yet not without leaving a man susceptible to language, to the particular thrums of the vocal cords.

But Von, having poured them each a glass of wine to go with the food, was now answering his unspoken question, and he had to tune in lest he miss something that might make this debate with himself irrelevant.

"Tragedy is nothing new to Chi Bay. Examples of this force we're talking about were happening as far back as the days of the town's settlement. Maybe before that, who knows. It's not like there's a dependable record. Far from it. It's as though everything that had to do with the natives, the Chi-Ikuk specifically, was expunged. Why I link the tribe, which I presume you've gathered is extinct, with the tragedies of Chi Bay, I can't say exactly. Nor could my father, whose research was far more extensive than mine. For him it was life. For me, a thesis. A way of coming to terms with my parents' deaths. But that's a separate chapter. We're talking about what happened here at the mine, not up on Harrow Mountain."

She paused, taking a bite of the bread and cheese and washing it down with wine. Hunter added a piece of ham to his bread and looked through the doorway across the slate beach to a tidal pond where a swan floated contentedly.

"That's a trumpeter," Von said, noticing the direction of his gaze. "Not only big, but a mean rascal if it feels threatened. If young are around, stay clear." She took another swallow of wine before using the swan as a segue back to the subject. "The Ikuk believed any living thing, human, swan, what have you, was subject to the energy of this place, and that the result could appear in any number of manifestations, all of them bad. Madness. Murder. Suicide. Or in this particular case, disappearances. The mine employed dozens of people in its day, and had yet to reach its peak before it was unexpectedly shut down. It's output, already hefty, was growing every year, putting it on pace to give the Treadwell operation in Juneau a run for its money. Everybody was happy. As happy as a bunch of zombies can be anyway. The town was prospering as business flourished. It was almost enough to make folks forget that tragedy, to one degree or another, *always* strikes again in Chi Bay. And so it did. One fall morning the wives kissed their husbands goodbye for the day, and the husbands went to their various posts at work. When lunchtime came around and the wives who expected their men home for a bite found the food getting cold, they thought little of it. Their husbands had been late for lunch before. When mid-afternoon rolled around and still no sign of their husbands, a few of the wives, still not overly concerned, went to the mining offices to inquire."

She paused again, motioning for the wine, which had remained idle in his hand as he listened to her story, though he'd already guessed its end. Perhaps seeing this in his face, she decided to quit with the fluff and build-up and proceed straight there, drinking directly from the wine bottle as she did so.

"That's right, Hunter. The Devil's Triangle for the whole goddamn crew. Clerks, supervisors, miners, everyone. Poof. Gone. The only ones saved were those sick, or on their off-day, or on a later shift—security guards, evening bookkeepers, etcetera. At best, ten percent of the work force. The other ninety simply vanished without a trace. And I mean *no* trace. Multiple investigations turned up nada. Absolutely zero."

Thirsty suddenly, Hunter reached over for the bottle and followed her example by partaking directly from the bottle. It felt good going down his throat. Cool, wet. His preference was white wine, chilled, but right now this seemed similar. Had his throat gone dry because of the story, or was it the flickers of movement he'd detected in the trees outside the windows while she spoke? As though the two could be separated.

"It's the breeze," Von said.

"What?"

"I remember the movement in the trees too. If I were the dramatic type, I'd tell you yes, the tales have it right, their ghosts linger."

"But?"

"But nothing. I'm not the dramatic type."

No, you spin your threads more delicately, he thought.

They were quiet for a while, letting their thoughts drift as they finished off the slices of bread and cheese he'd cut, waving off the rest in favor of the wine. As he emptied the first bottle, she opened the second. The glasses sat forgotten, lonely in their emptiness. The breeze off the water now had a perceptible nip to it. It felt good to Hunter. A sort of counterpoint to the warm embrace of the wine.

"So what about your parents?" he finally said. The words seeming as much an affront to the peaceful quiet as the voice that uttered them.

She sat near the corner of the platform, farthest from the door. The window across from her was the natural place for the eyes to stray, which they did as she spoke, seeming to look through the trees into that not-so-distant place that is less a refuge than a reference point for the drifty soul. "It makes me lonely thinking about them. Because that's how it was living with them. Can you imagine existing as an outsider within your own family? Knowing their entire focus is elsewhere? On something that is not even tangible?"

"Actually I can," he said in a softer voice than he'd intended.

When she looked at him, lines of inquiry, of attempted com-
prehension, creasing her brow, he felt the urge to look away, or to
explain himself, or to simply vanish as the miners had. But he owed
her more than that, as fate had predicated when it brought their like
souls together. "Go on," he said, in an even softer voice.

"My parents' is a short chapter really. Shorter than the miners'.
There were no spouses to miss them, only a lonely child. And she
left nothing for their ghosts to cling to, to find purchase in. Even the
wind can't remember them. I hiked up that mountain three times
after the first time looking for glimmers, but there simply are none.
And yet my parents haunt me still. In my sleep. In my daydreams.
Funny I never see the act. The act of their bodies being shredded.
They are always whole, as whole as was possible for them. They're
poring over books, notes, oblivious to the moth that has flittered into
the room until its shadow disturbs one of the pages. Then they're
fierce, especially him. This is when he's most whole. The fury brings
him there. It ignites in his eyes, eyes grown almost totally black from
the layers and layers of text imprinted on them. The fire itself is
black, and the moth wonders if he, if both of them, aren't the very
embodiment of the force that holds Chi Bay in its clutch. Not in
the same way as the ones that went mad, the ones that turned on
their loved ones, on themselves. Nor like the lost ones, the ones who
retained only the most basic outline of their former selves. I'm talking about the *very* embodiment, the thing itself as they hurled their
fury at this moth that would dare flitter its shadow across their work.
And my mother, somehow it was even more terrible in her because
it was less formed. Her flames fed off the central fire, which was his,
only his, and came from the furnace of his heart and his bowels. He
wanted to be in touch and oh was he, Hunter. Oh, was he…"

A fire of her own seemed to die in her eyes as she let her words ta-
per away, shivering suddenly though the nip on the breeze remained
slight, certainly no match for the wine's warmth. As Hunter removed
his jacket, placing it over her shoulders, her gaze seemed to remain
halfway in, halfway out of that place of reference, the ghosts among
the trees reflected in them. But only momentarily as Hunter faced
her, holding her shoulders and searching her face for answers that he
had never been able to find. Then she was looking at him, focusing in

on him. Her hand came up to touch his hand on her shoulder. Her trembling lips found his mouth, and they were lost in the desperateness of it for a few moments before one of them managed to pull away from the other.

As they separated, Hunter saw that tears had formed in her eyes. She let them fall as he watched, saying, "They were ripped to shreds, Hunter. Beaten, *torn* to death. Though the authorities never found the weapon used, they thought it must have been a hooked instrument, an instrument that could be used with a pulling action as well as for bludgeoning. A fireplace poker—just like the family that died up there years before them. Only this time there was no evidence to show who had done the deed. No body in the lake outside the cabin. No father and husband to blame for killing his child and wife before walking out on the frozen surface of Harrow Lake and chopping open a hole in the ice with the murder weapon and then dropping the tool and himself into the crack for the police to find later. But what difference would the details make? My father killed his wife as surely as if he'd wielded the poker. He killed his child in much the same way, with swings and thrusts and yanks; he just took a little more time at it, stretching the deed out over the years of her shadowy little life. And you know what a year is to a child, Hunter? It's an eon. But fuck, where's the wine? Hunter, you drink, and then kiss me. Let me taste it on your lips. It's warm. It's life. I came back down the mountain that first time, but that's not life. I came back down, but even blood, that's not life—"

He kissed her, the wine spilling from his mouth and trickling down their chins. "I know," he said around their hunger, their need. "I had a sister...Hannah...I helped her. I loved her and I helped her do it. Our parents, they had forgotten her. They had forgotten both of us. Hannah was strong. I tried to be strong with her. We did it with Demerol. My mother's opiate of choice. Demerol and tequila. Three shots for Hannah, three shots for me, one pill for Hannah. Three shots for Hannah, three shots for me, *two* pills for Hannah. I lost myself for a while after. There was this piece of property in Florida. An expanding company wanted it and I sold it to them for a cool two million dollars. Thing is, it wasn't mine to sell. It was my father's.

Hunter senior. A poor replacement for a fireplace poker, yeah, but it made things easier on me…the forgetting. The endless forgetting."

He was speaking in her ear now, and she was kissing his neck, clinging to him, digging her fingernails into his back. "I live for places now, Von. Landscapes. Scenery. Open spaces. Places that sing rather than suffocate, that broaden rather than constrict, that are apathetic in a pleasing rather than a crushing way. Sure, it's still props, but there's less poison in it. I admit I laugh at myself sometimes for this church I've found, but I attend anyway. While there is an Alaska Highway out there, Alaskas and Canadas and places of sweeping, unpolluted beauty, I attend. Did I tell you I was on my way to Canada? Do you want to join me, Von? Where else is there to go really?"

"Nowhere," she said, releasing him finally. "Nowhere."

She drank more wine, passed the half-empty bottle to him, and then suddenly seized his arm. "Did you see me, Hunter? When I told you about it, did you see me coming—"

But her attention was drawn to something beyond him, through the door of the building. He turned and saw what she saw, the swan making its slow, awkward way up the beach in their direction.

"It's only the swan," she said, eyes lingering there for a moment.

"Did I see what, Von?" Hunter had to know.

"Don't you know?" she said, letting the bird go. Looking into his eyes.

"What, Von? What should I have seen?"

"Me coming down the mountain that first time. Fireplace poker resting on my shoulder. I put it in my pack before I reached the trailhead, but it hung out so I wrapped the end in a rag. The rag I brought to clean myself with. No matter, our house was the third one you came to as you walked along the road from the trailhead. It was dark by then anyway, and no car passed. I remember thinking that meant something. Nothing to do with justice; it was more like I was being told I had a calling. A light, that's what it was. A warm light a little moth could fly to. But it didn't last. The light gradually flickered out as I sat naked by the fireplace and watched all traces of the thing disappear, knowing no one would remember the smoke, not in the late fall, not in the season for such things. Watching my clothes turn to ash and the caked blood on the poker burn away, I lost the connection with the force that has driven so many of us, us Chi-ites. I don't know if I bored it or if maybe it understood that my pain would be worse if I were simply left alone. In any case I—"

Again her attention was diverted. This time her eyes catching fire.

Nothing to compare to the eyes of the swan though as it descended through the door, throwing its wings wide, casting shadow over the whole room in spite of the moonlight from above. Eyes black as the pit of the soul as they devoured these homecomers then spat them back out again, blazed then disappeared in the madness of the beast's retreating wings. The shock of it leaving them breathless, holes of themselves, until Von, in a moth's whisper, uttered, "Can you see me now, Hunter? Can you see me fluttering down that mountain?"

Zombie Dreams

Tim Waggoner

Jared ran.

Sweat pouring off his body, heart pounding in his chest, lungs heaving, each breath a sharp knife in his side. Branches whipped his face, hands, and chest, scratching, cutting, bruising. He'd left the trail behind and the ground was uneven here, covered with underbrush that snagged his pants legs and threatened to trip him. But he couldn't let himself stumble, couldn't allow himself to fall. For if he did, *they* would get him for sure. And once *they* got him, it would be all over.

Something hit a tree to his right, splitting off a chunk of bark and spinning it away. A second later Jared heard the crack of a rifle. He knew he shouldn't turn, couldn't afford to slow down for even a second, but he couldn't help himself. Instinct forced his head around even though he knew damn well who—or what—pursued him. The movement threw him off balance, his legs twisted, and he crashed to the ground, flattening underbrush and knocking the wind out of him. His mouth gaped like a fish out of water as he tried to suck in air and re-inflate his lungs. He attempted to get up, but sharp pain lanced through his left ankle, and he feared it was twisted, or worse, broken. Still gasping for breath, he put his weight on his right foot, hoping that it wouldn't betray him too, and pushed himself up. His right ankle held, and he managed to stand once more. His lungs ached and felt heavy as lead, but they had enough air in them now that he thought he could start moving again. But before he could take a step, another chunk of bark was blasted from a tree, and another rifle shot echoed through the woods. It was too late; they'd caught up with him.

There were three of them, all male, all wearing dirty jeans, soiled flannel shirts, and ball caps mottled with old sweat stains. John Deere, Nascar, and Cincinnati Reds. Two of them carried guns—a double-barreled shotgun and a rifle, respectively—while the third held an axe, the rusty head covered with dried blood and bits of hair. They shared one more horrid similarity: they were all dead. Their flesh was grayish-green tinged with black where it had begun to rot. Dry yellowed eyes were wide and bulging, black mucus running from the corners as if fluid were building up behind the eyes, threatening to pop them out of their sockets any moment. Their lips were cracked and leathery, stretched into grins far wider than they could've managed in life, teeth brown, tongues nothing but lifeless lumps of gray meat.

Jared didn't know how it was possible for these things to chase him, let alone catch him. They took in no oxygen, their hearts pumped no blood, their muscles were dry and tight as jerky. They shouldn't be able to move at all, let alone keep up with a living man. Jared might not have been the fittest forty-one-year-old man in the world, and he carried twenty pounds too much around his middle, but he was *alive*, goddamnit, while these fucking things weren't. They should've been shuffling, jerking, stiff-limbed marionettes manipulated by a puppeteer with severe arthritis. But the hunters moved with a swiftness equal to, if not greater, than his own.

A German phrase whispered through his mind, one that he'd heard or read before, though he couldn't recall where.

Die Toten reiten schnell.

The Dead travel fast.

The gray-skinned hunters just stood looking at him with their bulging eyes and too-wide grins for several moments. And then finally the one with the John Deere cap raised his shotgun and aimed it at Jared's forehead. A rotting finger tightened on the trigger, and Jared tensed for the impact to come, knowing there was no way even a dead man could miss at this range.

Thunder crashed and Jared screamed.

"God, hon, you look like death warmed over."

"Not funny," Jared mumbled. He pulled out a chair and flopped into it. He leaned his elbows on the dining table and propped up his chin with his hands. Peter and Heather were too busy shoveling Kix into their mouths to pay their dad any attention. He glanced at the grandfather clock in the corner and saw that it was 7:20. No wonder the kids were eating so fast; the bus would be here any minute. Michelle came in from the kitchen carrying a mug of steaming coffee. As she set it on a coaster in front of Jared, he said, "I knew there was a reason I married you."

His wife grinned. "You mean beside the fact that I'm a total hottie?"

That got the kids' attention. They both looked up, but while Peter smirked, Heather—who was two years younger and had just started fourth grade—scrunched up her face.

"Mom, that's gross!" she said.

Michelle laughed. "Since when did we start raising the world's youngest prude?"

"Mo-om!"

Jared doubted Heather knew what a *prude* was, but she sounded mortally offended just the same.

Normally Jared would've been amused by the domestic banter, but not this morning, not after the night he'd had. He ran his fingers through sweat, sleep-matted hair. "Didn't the alarm go off?"

Michelle sat down next to him. She didn't have any food or coffee in front of her, but then she was both an early riser and a light eater, especially in the morning. She'd doubtless already nibbled on something before he'd gotten up.

"It did, and it kept buzzing for five minutes before I turned it off. From what I could tell, you hadn't moved a muscle. Bad dreams again?"

"You could say that." Though the coffee was still way too hot for him, he took a sip anyway, instantly regretting it when he scalded his tongue. Though everyone else was dressed and ready for the day, he still wore the briefs and T-shirt he'd slept in, he needed a shave, and his mouth tasted sour and sticky, as if a small rodent had crawled inside sometime during the night and died in there. Usually, he was ready to go to work by this time. Of all the days to be late…

He took another scorching sip of coffee. "I gotta hit the shower."

As he started to get up, Michelle said, "Aren't you going to eat something?" She worked as a dietitian for a nursing home, and though she was good about not nagging him too much about his eating habits, she didn't ignore them entirely.

"I'll grab something on my way out the door." He picked up his coffee and started shuffling away from the dining table. "I've got that presentation today."

Michelle started to say something more, but a loud horn sounded outside.

"There's the bus! C'mon guys!"

Jared waved to his children as they jumped up from the dining table and hurried into the living room to grab their backpacks. They didn't wave back. He trudged down the hallway toward the master bedroom, hearing the front door open, Michelle saying goodbye to the kids, the door closing again. By the time he'd gotten a towel and washcloth out of the linen closet in their bathroom, Michelle had joined him.

"Want to tell me about it?" She leaned back against the bathroom counter, arms folded, gazing at him with slightly narrowed eyes. She might've been a dietitian, but she'd always been interested in psychology and fancied herself something of an amateur psychoanalyst. As far as Jared was concerned, it was one of her less-endearing qualities.

"Not much to tell, really." He turned on the water in the shower, leaving it colder than he usually liked in the hope it would help him wake up faster. He then took off his clothes, stepped into the shower stall, and slid the door closed. He hoped Michelle might take the hint and leave, but she remained leaning against the counter.

"You haven't slept well all week."

Jared picked up the soap and began lathering up. "Don't make it out to be a bigger deal than it is, Shell. I've been working on these budget cuts for the last several weeks, and while I think I've done a good job, I don't know how the rest of the department is going to react to them. Especially Ned." Ned was his immediate supervisor and the man who'd first tasked Jared with coming up with budget cuts. Almost certainly so Ned wouldn't have to do them himself. "We're going to have to eliminate some personnel, and Ned hates that."

"You mean he hates looking responsible for it," Michelle countered.

"Yeah." Jared rinsed the soap off his body, then reached for his shampoo. "One way or another, he'll make sure I'm the bad guy." He began working thick blue goo into his wet hair. "I'm really not looking forward to today."

"Look at it this way: by the time you get home tonight, it'll all be over. Maybe then you'll be able to get a decent night's sleep."

As Jared scrubbed his scalp, he thought of the three dead hunters grinning at him, heard the sound of a rifle blast cutting through the woods.

"I sure hope so."

Michelle had already left for the nursing home by the time Jared pulled his Nissan Maxima out of the garage. It was late July, and the interior of the car was stuffy, the air thick and humid. Breathing it made him think of how he'd had the wind knocked out of him when he'd fallen in his dream, and he turned the AC to high. He reached for the remote attached to the visor and thumbed the button to close the garage door. He then backed into the cul-de-sac, braked, put his car in drive, and started forward. He glanced at his house as he drove away—a large Tudor with perfect landscaping and a neatly trimmed and edged lawn. On days like today, it helped to remind himself why he worked, and this house, along with the picturesque strand of woods it sat next to, was a big part of the reason. Michelle had been right. Today might not be a whole lot of fun, but he'd have his family, this house, and their woods to come home to. It was a good life he had, and today he was going to earn it all over again.

As he drove down his street, he saw Dale Baxter out watering his front lawn, ever-faithful border collie Zoe sitting next to him. Dale was a retiree and a widower, and roamed about the neighborhood always looking for someone to talk to and ease his loneliness. Jared felt sorry for the old guy, but not so sorry that he didn't run inside whenever he saw Dale walking down the sidewalk with Zoe. Jared had learned from experience that if Dale caught you, he'd bend your ear for the better part of an hour, if not longer.

Dale waved as Jared drove by, and though Jared wanted to ignore him—for he was certain Dale was outside right now only to wave at whoever was leaving for work or school—he waved anyway. As if she recognized his car, Zoe barked once and wagged her tail. Jared had always liked dogs, though since Michelle was allergic they'd never had any pets. He smiled as he continued driving. Maybe Zoe's greeting was a good omen and today wouldn't turn out to be so bad after all.

Jared was stopped at an intersection, waiting for the light to change, when the smooth jazz station he'd been listening to cut out. Not particularly a patient man, he began pushing pre-set channel-select buttons, searching for another station. But they were silent as well, and he'd begun to fear the radio was broken when he pushed the last button. At first there was nothing, but then he heard soft moaning punctuated with occasional grunting. What the hell was this? Some kind of rock song with simulated sex noises, like those Donna Summers disco hits when he'd been a kid? But there wasn't a sensual quality to these sounds. They were mournful, bestial, mindless... Then a new noise was added to the mix, a wet tearing followed by what sounded like chewing. Jared imagined someone sinking teeth into raw meat, ripping away ragged crimson mouthfuls, jaws working rhythmically as blood trickled over the lips. The image was nauseating, and yet on some level, it was appetizing as well. His stomach gurgled, but whether in discomfort or hunger, he couldn't tell. Michelle had been right. He should've eaten breakfast.

A car horn blared, startling him. Jared looked up and saw the light was green, and the car ahead of him was already through the intersection. He glanced at the rearview mirror, at the same time raising his hand in an apologetic wave to the person behind him. A woman at the wheel of a dark blue BMW was shouting at him, her face contorted with anger, and he was glad he couldn't hear what she was saying. He started to take his foot off the brake, intending to stomp on the accelerator and get through the intersection before the light changed. But in the rearview mirror, he saw the face of the woman begin to transform. Her skin took on a grayish cast, and her blond hair became waxy and coarse as straw. Her left eye deflated like a balloon losing air and subsided into the socket. A flap of skin peeled away from her right cheek all the way down to her jaw, revealing bone and teeth.

Jared gripped his steering wheel tighter as he stared at the thing reflected in his mirror. It looked just like the undead hunters in his dream, same ghastly pallor, same dead eyes…er, *eye*. The woman was still yelling, the motion jiggling her flap of cheek-skin. Bloody spittle flew from her mouth, stippling the inside of her windshield. She flipped him the bird with a skeletal finger, and jammed her other hand into the center of her steering wheel and let out a long blast on her car horn. When the horn's noise died away, the woman was normal again, left eye restored, cheek unmarred and intact, skin pink and healthy.

Jared looked at the light and saw it was yellow. He stepped on the gas, his tires squealed, and he fishtailed through the intersection. The light turned red before he was halfway through, leaving the woman in the BMW stuck behind him. She honked once more, but Jared refused to look in his rearview mirror this time. The radio was playing smooth jazz again—a David Sanborn tune, he thought—but he stabbed his finger at the power button and turned the radio off anyway. He drove the rest of the way to work in silence, telling himself that there was no need to be stressed, it would all be over soon.

"Today's the big day, eh?"

Jared had been running through his PowerPoint presentation for the fifth time that morning, tweaking a little here and there. He made one last change before looking over the top of his monitor and seeing Malcolm Posner standing at the entrance to his cubical.

Malcolm was nine years Jared's junior, though sometimes he acted much younger than that.

"Guess so," Jared said.

"Nervous?"

Malcolm was a good enough guy, but he was one of the prime distributors of office gossip, and Jared knew he was fishing for information.

"A little," Jared said, knowing that Malcolm would never buy it if he denied being nervous at all, but not wanting to give the office weasel any more ammunition than he had to. "But that's good, right? Gives you a little extra energy when you present."

Malcolm shrugged, clearly disappointed with Jared's less-than-forthcoming response. "If you say so. Nice suit. Is it new?"

Jared had bought it earlier in the month just for today, though he had worn it to the office on one previous occasion, so it wouldn't *look* like he'd bought it special for today's presentation. "Not *that* new. I've had it for a while. Still, it's the nicest one I own, so I figured today would be a good time to wear it."

The suit was navy blue, and Jared wore a white shirt and a maroon tie along with it. He'd found the suit at a closeout sale at the Right Look in the mall, but he'd never tell Malcolm that.

"Can't argue with that." Malcolm paused, as if waiting to see what, if anything, Jared might add. But when Jared just kept looking at Malcolm silently, the younger man said, "Well, I'd better get back to it. Good luck today."

"Thanks," Jared said as Malcolm departed. Jared wondered what the *it* was that Malcolm intended to get back to. Whatever it was, Jared bet it wasn't work.

He ran through his presentation one more time, nearly nodding off as he reached the last slide. He needed another cup of coffee. The last thing he wanted was to be yawning and fighting to stay awake during his presentation. He got up from his desk, walked out of his cubicle, and headed for the break room. His limbs felt heavy, as if they were weary and trying to drag him down into sleep with them. *Later,* he thought, almost as if he were trying to placate his body. *I can take a nap after I get home.*

The break room wasn't much—just a couple snack and beverage vending machines and a half dozen round white tables with black plastic chairs. There was a microwave oven on the counter for those who brought their lunch and wished to heat it up. No refrigerator, though, so there was a limit to what you could bring from home. The break room was often empty throughout the day, but three other people were there at the moment, two women and one man, all sitting at the same table. They held 16 oz. plastic soft-drink bottles in their hands, and they looked up as Jared came in, staring at him with empty expressionless gazes. Jared smiled and nodded to them, though he didn't know any of them well, couldn't even remember their names. But none of them acknowledged his gesture. They just continued looking at him.

Jared felt a nervous, crawly-tingly feeling in his stomach, but he did his best to ignore his three rude co-workers as he stepped over to the vending machines. He wasn't really all that hungry, but coffee—especially the thick tarry stuff that came out of the machine here—had a tendency to upset his stomach, so he thought it best that he nibble on something. Besides, nervous as he was, he doubted he'd eat any lunch before this afternoon's meeting, so he'd better put something in his stomach now.

He scanned the snack machine offerings, expecting to see chips, cookies, candy bars, granola bars, and chewing gum. But today the machine contained a very different selection: severed ears, fingers, toes, noses, tongues, eyes, lips, nipples… At first he thought it was some sort of grotesque joke, that the body parts were merely rubber novelties, the kind of thing you could buy anywhere around Halloween. But the texture and color of the skin was too realistic, and the blood smeared on the end where each part had once been connected to a body looked like the real thing too. Jared glanced to the right of the snack machine at the cold beverage dispenser. Instead of colas, lemon-lime drinks, or bottled water, this machine offered plastic bottles filled with blood (both white and red cells), plasma, spinal fluid, urine, pus, and bone marrow.

Unable to believe what he was seeing, Jared backed away from the vending machines. He turned and started for the doorway, but he stopped when he saw the trio sitting at the round table still staring at him. In unison they raised plastic bottles to their lips and drank deeply, various bodily fluids dribbling from the corners of their mouths.

A branch only inches from Jared's head exploded in a shower of splinters, a number of which became embedded in his cheek, barely missing his eye. It felt like dozens of fiery needles had been inserted into his flesh, and he could feel warmth as beads of blood began to well forth from the tiny wounds.

John Deere lowered his shotgun, and his undead companions shook with silent laughter. Jared understood that the hunter hadn't missed; the son-of-a-bitch was toying with him. Even so, Jared had an opportunity, and he was determined not to waste it. He turned and started running through the woods once more, ignoring the pain that shot through his twisted ankle with every step. This time, he wove between trees, hoping their thick trunks would shield him from the hunters' guns. His tactic seemed to be working when he heard two more shots—the boom of John Deere's second barrel and the crack of Nascar's rifle—but neither hit him.

Jared was running downhill now and picking up speed. His surroundings became a blur as he plunged through the woods, knocking aside tree branches, crushing undergrowth beneath his clumsy feet, birds and small animals fleeing to get out of his path. He heard the stream before he saw the gurgling, rushing water, and he knew it was flowing high as a result of last week's rains. Normally the stream was so narrow that even a pot-bellied middle-aged man like himself could jump over it, but now... Still, he felt a surge of hope. The stream was not far from his home. The edge of the woods was maybe twenty, thirty yards on the other side, and his house lay just across an open field, perhaps an acre-and-a-half beyond that. Once he made it home, everything would be okay. He'd be safe, because that's what home was, right? The place where you were safe. Home-free.

The bank sloped sharply down to the swollen stream here, but though he tried to slow down, momentum and his injured ankle got the better of him. He lost his balance and tumbled headfirst toward the water. He managed to get his hands out in front of him in time to catch himself as he hit muddy-brown water that was surprisingly cold for late July. Water sprayed against the side of his face as the stream rushed around him, and he closed his eyes, though his mouth stayed open, treating him to a taste of grainy silt. His chest and waist were soaked, but his legs—which still remained on the bank—were dry. As he pulled himself to his feet, he looked down at the muddy wet stains on his suit jacket and pants, and though he was running for his life and knew it was absurd to think about his clothes right now, he couldn't help feeling a wave of disappointment. He'd just gotten this suit a couple weeks ago, and now it was probably ruined.

Jared heard a sound behind him, and he whirled around to see the three undead hunters standing at the top of the bank. John Deere raised his shotgun to his shoulder, took aim, and let loose with both barrels this time. As the shot tore through Jared's clothing and into his skin, he knew that a few mud stains were the least of his worries now.

Jared jerked awake and sat upright in his chair. He saw the PowerPoint presentation playing automatically on his computer screen, but at first he didn't know what it was. But then his mind cleared and he realized what had happened. He'd been so exhausted that he'd fallen asleep at his desk. How long…

He glanced at the time display in the lower right-hand corner of the screen. 1:06 p.m. He'd slept through lunch hour and was now officially six minutes late for what might well turn out to be the most important meeting in his life. He yanked the disk containing his presentation out of the computer without bothering to close the PowerPoint program, leaped out of his chair, and ran from his cubicle. He hurried past the other cubes, ignoring the curious stares and knowing snickers from his fellow wage-slaves, and headed down the hall toward the meeting room. Ordinarily he would've stopped off in the men's room to check his hair, straighten his tie, and make sure his shirt was tucked in. But it was too late to worry about the niceties of personal grooming. Maybe too late to worry about a lot of things.

He walked the last few yards to the meeting room, both so that no one would hear him running and to give himself a chance to catch his breath. He took a last deep breath and then entered. The lights had already been turned off for his presentation and the room was dark. He couldn't see much more than their silhouettes, but he knew they were all there—Donna from Human Resources, Robert from Accounting, a half-dozen more...including Malcolm, who no doubt was doing a piss-poor job of trying to conceal a smirk. And sitting at the head of the oval table and undoubtedly scowling in the dark was Ned Wilkerson, AKA the Boss.

Jared tried to sound calm and relaxed as he spoke. "Sorry I'm late everybody." He didn't bother to offer an excuse. Not only did Ned frown on them, no matter how legitimate they might be, Jared didn't have the mental energy to think up a good lie just then.

The presentation screen had already been erected in a corner of the room, and the laptop and projection unit on the table were on and running. Jared walked over to the computer and inserted the disk with his presentation. He opened it, and the words *New Challenges, New Opportunities* appeared on the screen.

"If no one has any questions, I'll go ahead and start," Jared said.

"You don't mind if we snack while you talk, do you?" Donna asked. "I worked right through lunch today, and I'm starving."

"Me, too," Robert said. "But Ned wouldn't let us touch anything until you got here."

Because the lights were off, not to mention how nervous he was, Jared hadn't noticed what sort of food was on the table. Ned always made sure there were snacks of some kind, though. Often, it was the only way to guarantee attendance at the meetings—especially the most boring ones. It was never anything elaborate, just finger food, but Jared's co-workers had gotten so used to having it at every meeting that he sometimes thought they'd go on strike if they didn't get it.

"Sure, don't let me stop you."

Shadowy hands reached toward a large serving bowl, snatched fistfuls of goodies, and deposited the food on smaller plates. Then Jared's co-workers pulled their snacks over in front of them and began to feed. They tore into their food with more gusto than usual, and Jared wondered if they'd *all* skipped lunch.

He cleared his throat and started talking.

"As you all know, the downturn in the economy has hit our industry hard in the last six months, necessitating that we take a clear-eyed, rational look at our current budgetary needs, and decide what we need to do to keep our company strong and healthy as we move forward."

He paused for a moment to gauge everyone's mood, so he'd have a better idea how to proceed. Should he be serious and somber, encouraging and guardedly optimistic, or continue with light-hearted fatalism? But all he could hear was the sound of his co-workers chewing, several of them moaning softly just like…on…his…radio.

Trembling, he walked over to the wall, fumbled for the switch, and turned on the lights. He already knew what he would see: everyone would be gnawing on fingers, toes, ears, and other parts from the vending machine in the break room. But he was wrong. Because of the importance of today's meeting, Ned had pulled out all the stops and ordered some truly *special* food.

A glistening mound of organs sat inside a chrome serving bowl in the center of the table. Loops of intestine, livers, kidneys, gall bladders, spleens, hearts…Jared's co-workers were stuffing the soft wet delicacies into blood-rimmed mouths, gore and bits of meat splattering onto the table as they feasted. One by one they stopped chewing and looked at Jared—faces grayish-green, dead eyes wide and staring—as if they'd only just realized that he'd stopped speaking and had turned on the lights.

Ned—bald, bespectacled, looking like a rotting version of the husband in the *American Gothic* painting, only in modern dress—mumbled through a mouthful of pancreas. "Somefing wong?"

"Don't ssstop," Donna said, spraying a tiny jet of blood as she pronounced the S. "It was jussst getting good."

"We're looking forward to hearing your ideas about the budget," Robert said, a coil of intestine drooping from one corner of his mouth.

Ned grinned, displaying blood-slick teeth with shreds of pancreas caught between. "Especially the *cuts*."

Everyone laughed. Jared turned and fled.

✳

Everything would be fine once he reached home. Fine-and-fucking dandy.

Jared drove well over the speed limit, wove in and out of traffic, ran stop signs and stoplights, and had more near-collisions than in the entire twenty-five years since he'd received his license. His tires shrieked as he whipped the Maxima into his cul-de-sac, and he nearly lost it right there, almost spun into the front yard of the dentist that lived on the corner. He managed to maintain control out of sheer desperation, and he zoomed down the street, the Maxima's engine roaring and juddering as if it were about to explode. *Hold on, just a little more…*

He saw Dale sitting on the sidewalk in front of his house, Zoe's savaged corpse splayed on his lap. The old man's gray-green face was smeared with the dog's blood, and he waved one of her chewed-up legs at Jared as he passed.

"Home, home, home, home, home…" Jared repeated the word as if it were both a calming mantra and a protective charm. He was almost there, almost *home*-free.

He pulled into his driveway, not bothering to open the garage door. He slammed on the brakes, leaving skid marks on the concrete as the Maxima slid toward the garage, but the front bumper only tapped the door before the car finally came to a stop. Jared turned off the engine without bothering to put the vehicle in park, and then threw open the driver's side door. He left the keys in the ignition as he got out, not caring that the car might roll back into the street, not caring that someone might come along—maybe Dale with his bloody mouth and half-eaten dog leg—and decide to take the Maxima for a spin. All that mattered was that he'd made it: he was home.

As he started toward the front door, he heard a gunshot echo through the woods, followed closely by a scream of pain. He then heard someone thrashing through the brush, yelling, "Help! Help me!" in a desperate, terrified voice.

Jared wanted to ignore the pleas for help, wanted nothing more than to go inside his house, lock the door, and never come out again. But he turned in the direction of the trees, and walked away from his car, his driveway, and his beloved home, toward a figure in a mud-stained blue suit emerging from the woods. As they drew near one another, Jared could see the man was drenched with sweat, one side of his face bleeding from dozens of tiny wounds, his paunchy stomach bleeding from a single large one. One Jared fell into the arms of the other, looked up into his own eyes, and in a hoarse voice whispered, "Run…"

Jared released his other self, and the wounded doppelgänger slumped to the ground, dead or close to it. Jared looked up and wasn't surprised to see the three undead hunters come striding out of the woods, grinning their too-wide grins, weapons held at the ready. Nascar stopped, lifted his rifle, and squeezed off a shot. The bullet slammed into Jared's shoulder, nearly knocking him off his feet. The wound blazed with fiery pain, and he pressed his hand to it, finding the navy blue cloth of his suit already moist with blood. He turned and started running toward his backyard as Nascar fired another round. This one missed, though, and Jared kept on going. He didn't look back to see if the hunters followed. Of course they did.

He nearly laughed with joyous relief as he entered his backyard and saw the old oak tree with the tire swing, the green turtle sand-box with the lid slightly askew, the inflatable wading pool filled with water. But then he realized: his family was home, and he had come bringing Death in his wake. He started to turn, intending to run back across the field at an angle, hopefully make it into the woods once more before the hunters could finish him off. He didn't care about his own survival now. All he cared about was luring the three grinning killers away from his family. But before he could take a step, he saw that the water in the pool was tinted a faint red.

Despite the afternoon heat, Jared shivered with cold as he walked over to the edge of the pool and saw what was left of Peter's body floating there. He heard the back screen door open and shut, and he looked up to see Michelle walking toward him, carrying Heather's head by the hair. She brought the head up to her mouth and took a bite out of it, as if she were eating an apple. She chewed as she continued toward him, swallowing as she stopped.

"What's wrong, sweetheart? You don't look so—"

A rusty axe blade hissed through the air and buried itself deep within Michelle's skull. She dropped Heather's head as blood jetted out of her own, and the hunter in the Reds cap yanked the axe free and struck her again. Michelle's body jerked and spasmed as the damaged brain inside her split skull misfired one last time, and then her body fell to the ground.

Jared looked at the man in the Reds cap. He stared at Michelle's corpse, axe handle held tight, blood dripping from its blade and pattering onto the grass. He was breathing hard, and lines of sweat ran down his face…a face that was no longer that of a dead man. Jared turned to look at John Deere and Nascar and saw that they too appeared to be perfectly normal, *living* men.

Then he looked down at his own grayish-green hands.

"End of the line, motherfucker," Nascar said, and pointed his rifle barrel at Jared's forehead. "Game's over."

Jared looked up just in time to witness the muzzle flash with his dry, dead eyes.

"You ever wonder what goes through their heads?"

"What the hell are you talking about?"

"You know how they say that when it's your time, your life flashes before your eyes? I just wonder what goes through their heads at the end. I mean, sometimes they just look so surprised, you know?"

"I'll tell ya what goes through their heads—a fucking bullet, that's what."

The three men laughed as they walked away from the Tudor house and returned to the hunt. But despite their laughter, the men were hardly enjoying themselves. What they did was hard, bloody work, and it wore on a man after a while. But they couldn't afford to rest, for there were a lot more deaders out there that needed to be put down, a hell of lot. The only thing that made it possible for them—and all the others like them—

to keep going day after day was the knowledge that what they were killing wasn't human. Oh, sure, they'd been human *once*, but not anymore.

Not anymore.

Echoes

Don D'Ammassa

I had expected the cell to be squalid, but I hadn't anticipated just how unpleasant the conditions of my incarceration would be. Under ordinary circumstances I would be outraged at the indignity, but given the alternative, I can only view this as a mildly painful inoculation to ward off what might have been a much more serious malady.

The first time I experienced the echo, it was so transient that I imagine most people would have dismissed the phenomenon as just a trick of the light or a blurring of the vision. Fortunately, unlike most people, I'm acutely aware of conditions in my immediate surroundings at all times. I've never understood how someone could believe that there is a distinct line of demarcation between their body and their physical location. After all, the body is just the immediate, portable environment that contains the essential us. If I cut my hair or bleed or even if I were to lose a limb, that wouldn't diminish who I am. We don't have absolute control over our own bodies, any more than we do over the rest of our environment. I wouldn't be able to grow back that missing limb, and if someone should choose to stab me or if the police locked me up, they'd be demonstrating that at least in some respects they have as much control over my body as I do myself.

But I'm straying from my point here. The incident occurred just a I passed my first anniversary at Eblis Manufacturing, where I sat in a cubicle for eight hours a day and processed inventory transactions, filled in spreadsheets, prepared materials requisitions, and pretty much spent all my time pushing paper, or more properly, pushing pixels around the screen since most of my work was at a computer terminal. There were two other people in the same office, Dorothy Gingrich, who looked old enough to have learned the fundamentals of her job in ancient Rome, and Hector Racina, a quiet, lumpish young man who spoke very labored English. Both of them kept to themselves, which suited me just fine, and I don't think we'd exchanged more than a dozen words a week in the entire year that I'd been there.

Nor was Mr. Horty, my nominal superior, any more voluble. Once I had assured him that I understood the essentials of my job, he seemed content to let me fill in the gaps on my own, and from that point forward treated me—and my co-workers—as though we were simply pieces of office equipment with no personalities or opinions. His attitude suited me perfectly, as it apparently did Dorothy and Hector.

But one day I received an email telling me that my annual review was to be held at 2:00 PM the following Monday and that I should report to Mr. Horty's office at that time. It was annoying, certainly, since I knew perfectly well that I was performing above the level which was expected of me. I had the lowest error rate in the department and the highest productivity level, and several of my suggestions to the software support staff had been implemented. I'd even received a commendation (by email) from Mr. Horty for my observations about the redundancies in the scrap reporting system.

The meeting started well. Horty waved me to a chair without looking up from the file folder spread open on his desk, presumably my personnel records. I was hoping for nothing more than a brisk "well done" or perhaps a "thank you for your efforts" or, if Horty was feeling particularly expansive, "you're an important asset in this department". But Horty was apparently in a rare mood of conviviality.

He called me Mr. Vardoger instead of Vincent, and the first thing he asked was how I liked working at Eblis.

"I've found it rewarding and professionally satisfying."

Then he wanted to know if I had any complaints.

"None whatsoever." Actually, the air conditioner was too loud and it blew directly down into my cubicle, Hector had a distracting habit of tapping his pencil against the side of his coffee cup, the lighting was not optimal, and the rest rooms could have been better maintained, but I wanted to help Horty along and get this interview done as quickly as possible.

"Do you have any suggestions to make about how we could improve things around here?"

"I've sent along a few ideas."

His eyes glanced up from the folder and met mine for the first time. "Yes, I see that noted here. How about your co-workers? Any conflicts there?"

"No, sir."

His eyes drifted away, contemplating something on the wall behind me, or perhaps in another place altogether. "Where do you see yourself two years from now, Mr. Vardoger?"

I was momentarily confused by his question, but realized he meant this on a metaphorical rather than physical level. "I have no plans to look for another job, Mr. Horty. As I said, I'm quite happy here at Eblis."

"Yes, but in what capacity?" He sounded mildly, unaccountably annoyed. "You're a young man, hard working and bright. You surely don't want to sit at a desk processing transfer slips and receiving logs for the rest of your life."

Well, actually, that seemed perfectly agreeable to me, but I could tell that Horty was looking for a different answer. "I'd be willing to serve in whatever capacity I'm suited for."

His eyes flashed and I had the strangest feeling that he was seeing me for the very first time. "So you don't want my job eventually?"

The prospect made me distinctly uncomfortable. It is difficult enough to be responsible for the actions of one's own body without having to worry about those of others as well. "I don't think I'm cut out for a supervisory position, sir."

He resumed his contemplation of my file and our eyes never met again during the course of the interview, which seemed to go on interminably. Every suggestion that I'd offered was mentioned and faintly praised, and Horty made a check mark in the file after each. I thought we were just about finished when he shifted position in his chair and moved on to what he termed "opportunities for improvement" in my performance.

It was all that I could do to sit in my seat while he made totally inappropriate or trivial suggestions. I should take the training course for our new order entry software, even though I would never have any reason to use it. I had made six transaction errors during the past quarter, out of over fifteen thousand entries, much better than Hector or Dorothy had ever managed to achieve. I needed to make a stronger effort to interact with my co-workers in order to develop team spirit and improve morale. There were a few other things, so inconsequential that I would be embarrassed to even note them here.

At last it was over. Horty said "thank you for your time" without looking up. I hesitated, then stood up, tempted to say something rash about how unfair and arrogant it was to turn what should have been a rewarding experience into an exercise in humiliation but thought better of it. As I stood, out of the corner of my eye and for just a second, I thought that I saw myself still sitting in the chair, leaning forward with a hint of aggressiveness, but as I half turned back, that secondary figure stood and turned and melted into me and my vision was completely normal.

I finished the day in a quiet rage, well below my usual productivity level, and I just barely caught myself before I made a significant transaction error.

The second time it happened, I was tempted to dismiss the phenomenon as the product of an overactive imagination. Fortunately, unlike most people, my imagination is firmly under control and I never allow it to interfere with my perceptions of the world. I am not a hypochondriac; if I seek medical help it is always because of an actual illness. Although I have a deep love of books, I do not read fiction; I have never understood why one would want to immerse oneself in another person's artificial reality. I rarely dream and do not confuse the lingering after effects with the waking world. I do not believe in ghosts, flying saucers, an omniscient god, conspiracy theories, the assertions of politicians, or any other fantasies. My beliefs and perceptions are thoroughly grounded in reality.

I was certain that what I saw was neither a mirage nor a delusion. Besides, I wasn't the only one who witnessed the event.

It was on a Saturday and I was running a few errands in downtown Managansett. I hadn't slept well the night before and was drowsy, so I decided to stop and have a cup of coffee. It was moderately crowded and I had to wait in line while four other people were served, but eventually I faced a young lady with her hair tied back who asked me "What can I get for you?" except she slurred it all into one word.

"A tall French roast, black." And then I watched as she filled a cup from an urn clearly marked "Decaf."

"That'll be two dollars," she said, another single word.

"I beg your pardon. I asked for regular. That's decaf."

She looked at me as though I'd grown a set of horns. "You don't want it?"

"I want a tall French roast, black. Not decaf." My voice, I assure you, was perfectly even and inoffensive.

"Why didn't you say so then?" But she set it aside and took a fresh cup as she turned away. And filled it with decaf again.

I'm not bellicose by nature. If anything, I'm too self-effacing. Most mornings I would have meekly accepted what she offered and quietly decided never to do business there again. But I was tired, grouchy, and the memory of my humiliation at the hands of Mr. Horty had still not completely faded.

"Young lady, I asked for a regular coffee, not a decaf. If you can't serve your customers properly, I suggest you find someone who can." And I turned on my heel and stalked away, while the three people standing in line behind me turned their faces away, pretending not to have seen or heard what had just happened. I trust they had better luck with their own purchases.

But that wasn't the end of it.

Leaving my car in the coffee shop's parking lot, I walked across the street to the post office and purchased some stamps. When I emerged, I could see a small crowd gathered in front of the coffee shop, and as I crossed back to retrieve my car, I could hear someone shouting angrily. I had just reached the sidewalk when I noticed the young woman who'd so badly served me coming in my direction, waving her arms, her expression furious.

"You son of a bitch!" was the first thing I could actually distinguish, each word distinct this time. As she approached, I also noticed something altered in her appearance. The hair on one side of her head was plastered down against her skull and there was a dark smear over the same shoulder and the front of her uniform. I couldn't understand this or why she would have reacted so strongly to my earlier comment, or waited so long to display her rage, and I stood frozen, trying to interpret the situation so that I could understand it.

Had it not been for one of the other customers, an older man with a completely bald head wearing a sweat suit, I really believe she might have physically assaulted me. She was only two steps away when he caught her by the arm. "Miss, it wasn't him. I saw the guy run the other way, up toward Cannell Street."

She allowed herself to be stopped, but glared at me with undiminished fury. "I saw him! This is the guy!"

"No, it's not," said the man quietly. "They're dressed the same way and they look alike, but it wasn't him."

For a few seconds, my fate hung in the balance, and even when she turned and stalked back toward the coffee shop, her body language said she didn't believe what she'd been told.

"What was that all about?" I asked.

The bald man shrugged. "Some guy who looked just like you threw a cup of coffee in her face, then ran off." He looked at me closely. "You don't have a twin brother, do you? He sure looked a lot like you."

The incident troubled and excited me.

I own my own home, a little cottage on Vernon Street just a half mile from downtown Managansett. It was a pretty little place, in reasonably good repair, in an attractive neighborhood. On one side was an undeveloped triangular lot, too small and awkwardly shaped to build on, and that afforded me a welcome degree of privacy. On the other side, unfortunately, was the proverbial neighbor from hell.

Ted Kramer was a teamster currently in the second year of idleness following a road accident that left him, theoretically, disabled. He had a tall stockade fence around his backyard, but I knew for a fact that he'd recently built himself a patio, laying the concrete and doing the brickwork himself, and I wondered how long it would take the insurance company to catch up to him. There were two large apple trees on the side of his property that bordered my yard, and some of the branches extended well past the fence. It was a nuisance cleaning up the dropped, rotting apples before I could cut the grass, but even worse were the hordes of insects that were drawn to the fruit. I had broached the subject of trimming the branches back shortly after moving in, and Kramer had responded with an obscenity-laden warning not to touch his trees. Although I had the law on my side, I had decided not to make things even more unpleasant by carrying through with my plan.

My consideration had not been reciprocated. The Kramers had frequent parties which were invariably loud and raucous, went on until all hours, and left a mess of debris that blew down the street and into my privet hedge. Sometimes his guests parked in front of my house, and on two occasions they'd blocked my car in the driveway. Kramer also had a pair of dogs which he frequently let loose and they left pungent evidence of their visits on my lawn and woke me up howling in the night. Agnes Kramer was no better than her husband, an overweight slattern whose hair seemed to be perpetually in curlers and who went out for the mail wearing a tattered bathrobe. She played the radio loudly (country and western) while sitting on the new patio in the evenings when they didn't have guests—and sometimes when they did. I hadn't spoken to either of them since the first month of our acquaintance and sincerely hoped not to do so ever again. Actually, I hoped that lightning would strike their house, or that the earth would open up and swallow it into a sinkhole, or that they'd drive off in their pickup truck one morning and just never come back.

It was late in the week following the coffee shop incident. I'd just come home from work to find the street in front of my house covered with damp, wet leaves and pine needles. The Kramers had raked their yard into the street, then run the sprinklers, which eventually washed much of the waste material down into the shallow depression in front of my property. Fuming, I got out of my car, started for the house, and promptly stepped into a particularly unpleasant dog mess. As I was scraping it off my shoe, I heard my neighbor's screen door slam and a moment later Merle Haggard's voice carried over the fence.

I rarely drink alcohol; I don't like the way it interferes with my perceptions. But I had half a bottle of brandy in a kitchen cupboard and I poured myself a small glass, rationalizing that it was to calm my nerves. I had barely sipped it when the doorbell rang and, before I could possibly have reached it, rang again. When I opened it at last, I was startled to find Ted Kramer standing on my doorstep. It was the first time to my knowledge that he had ever ventured onto my property, preferring to send his four legged emissaries instead.

He was wearing a torn, sleeveless tee shirt and had a can of beer in one hand. I felt almost physically repelled by him even before I saw the expression on his face, which made me take an involuntary step backward.

"Hey, Vardoger, I want to talk to you."

"I'm just on my way out," I lied. "What do we have to talk about?"

He pushed his way past me into my house, a violation of my physical environment that I found so offensive that it overwhelmed my nascent alarm. "Seems like you've got plenty of time to talk when it suits you."

I had no idea what he was getting at and told him so. If anything, this seemed to make him even angrier. Kramer was a big man, topping six feet easily, broad shouldered, running more than a bit to paunch but certainly not soft. He stepped toward me and I retreated again, determined to keep a small circle of my own space. "Someone's been calling the insurance people, telling them I'm cheating them out of money."

I'd fantasized about doing that very thing, of course, but I'd never followed through. "Well, it wasn't me. Would you please leave now?"

"Who the hell else would know I dug out the garden Monday afternoon? Someone would have to climb up and spy over the fence to see that, and the Nelsons next door are out on Cape Cod for the week."

"Then maybe someone came into their yard and watched you," I said with a trembling voice. "It certainly wasn't me. I would have been at work, remember?" But that wasn't true. I'd taken Monday morning off to have my teeth cleaned. I was still at the house until 10:30, but I hadn't spied on the Kramers and I hadn't called anyone.

My quasi-lie seemed to have penetrated, however, because Kramer looked less certain of himself, though no less upset. "You just better watch your step, neighbor," he said belligerently. To my great relief, he started toward the door. "I don't like busybodies and I don't like snitches. You keep your eyes off my property and your hands out of my business, you understand?"

I closed the door the moment he was outside. But I didn't slam it, as much as I wanted to.

Instead I experienced a burst of quiet rage more intense than I'd ever felt before in my entire life. I stormed from room to room, as if trying to reach a place where my memories of the conversation couldn't find me, but they always did. At times I talked aloud, berating myself for not standing up to Kramer, rehearsing what I should have said one moment and raging incoherently the next. I'm not sure how long this went on before I returned to the kitchen and the brandy, but some time after that I had another reason to complain. The bottle was empty and I was still conscious. It all seemed unfair.

I knew what I wanted to do. I wanted to go next door, tear up the Kramer's garden, cut down their apple trees, strangle the dogs, slash the tires on their truck, and then burn down the house. If the Kramers were trapped inside, so much the better. Eventually the brandy caught up to me and I fell asleep on the couch, staring at the blank screen of the television.

Wailing sirens wakened me.

Initially I was disoriented by the sound, by the darkness, by the fact that I was not wearing pajamas and lying in bed. There were flashing lights close by, very close, and the sirens abruptly stopped, but the echoes seemed to be trapped inside my head and I kept hearing them for quite a while afterwards. When I tried to stand, I nearly fell. My head ached, my stomach rumbled, and one of my legs was all pins and needles. I waited until the room slowed to minimal rotation, then carefully walked to the bathroom and vomited efficiently and refreshingly into the toilet.

I'm not sure how long it was before I took interest in the outside world again. It might have been an hour or more because I fell asleep with my forehead pressed against the white porcelain of the toilet. When I next opened my eyes, it was just before three in the morning. There were still flashing lights outside and voices talking loudly, and at irregular intervals the crackle of a police radio. I washed my face, checked my appearance in the bathroom mirror, then walked to the front door and stepped outside. It must have rained earlier in the evening because the grass was wet and the lights reflected oddly.

The Kramers' house was a smoldering ruin. Two hoses were still playing on the ashes but it was clear that the fire was effectively out. I blinked, wondering if I was dreaming, and glanced toward the apple trees, half expecting to find that they'd been cut down. They hadn't. I came as close as the firemen would allow, joining several other neighbors, all of whom were talking in hushed tones. The Kramers' pickup truck was still there and its tires were flat, melted rather than slashed. There were three police cars and an ambulance, which had driven up onto the lawn and was now parked in the garden, the front wheels in the marigolds, the rear mashing down daffodils. The back of the ambulance was open and there were two stretchers on the ground nearby. No one seemed to be in a hurry.

Edith Neal, an elderly widow and chief neighborhood gossip from up the block, saw me and broke away from the group she was with. We weren't exactly friends because she'd spread some nasty stories about me a while back, but we pretended to be sociable when we met. "Isn't it terrible, Mr. Vardoger?"

"I'm not sure what happened, Edith. I was asleep."

She looked at me oddly. "How could you sleep through all of this, Mr. Vardoger?"

"I took some pills," I lied. "I have insomnia. Are the Kramers all right?" I tried to sound sincerely interested.

Edith shook her head. "Gone, the both of them. They just brought the bodies out a few minutes ago."

It was the next day before I heard the rest. The fire had started in the kitchen and speculation was that one of the Kramers had left a burner lit on the gas stove and that a stray breeze had blown a curtain into the flame. They had probably been overcome by smoke and died without ever waking.

Edith made a point of stopping by to tell me the details. "I wonder why the dogs didn't raise a ruckus when the fire started. They were both sleeping in the house at the time. Something doesn't sound right to me. Those dogs barked if a fly flew in through a window or a car passed on the street. I say they were already dead when the fire started, and that means it wasn't an accident."

But the police apparently weren't seriously bothered by the inconsistency. I wouldn't have been either except for one thing. When I went back inside, I took off my shoes so that I wouldn't track water into the house. They'd been dry when I went out, of course, or I would have found evidence on the carpet or in the bathroom. There was no question at all in my mind; I hadn't set fire to the Kramers' house while sleepwalking or in a drunken stupor. I hadn't left the house at all.

But my umbrella was sitting in the hall closet, and it was still damp.

The next few days were uneventful, but the following week – this past week – has been a complete disaster. One of the apple trees was damaged in the fire, and during a windy rainstorm the trunk split, depositing the bulk of the tree on my property. A call to the police was not helpful; the Kramers had no known relatives and the disposition of their estate—and responsibility for its liabilities—was unresolved. That same evening, another of my neighbors came home late, drunk, and sideswiped my car, which I'd parked in the street to avoid having it scratched by the fallen tree's grasping branches. I called a local tree service, who removed the debris on Thursday, but they carelessly damaged my lilacs in the process. Friday morning, Mr. Horty called me into his office and told me that because of low sales, they were being forced to reduce expenses, and even though my performance was outstanding, Hector and Dorothy had seniority so I was the one who would have to go. Arriving home, I found my front window broken with a note from still another neighbor saying his son had been playing baseball in the street and they would, of course, pay for the damage.

Earlier this evening I changed into a sweatshirt and jeans and sat in the front room with a fresh bottle of brandy, a full one this time, but even though I drank steadily, I remained conscious and reasonably sober, my fury burning off the effects of the alcohol. It was just after midnight when I felt a bit strange and hastened to the bathroom, assuming that I was about to become sick. The strangeness, however, passed within a few seconds and with no obvious resolution. Just to be safe, I remained in the bathroom, leaning against the side of the shower, trying not to be consumed by my thoughts. By my anger.

I wanted to smash Mr. Horty's face with a blunt object. I wanted to throttle Mrs. Neal for the unkind gossip she'd circulated when I first moved to Managansett. I wanted to throw the Wilson boy through a window like a baseball, beat Oliver Begley to death for having hit my car, and disembowel the ignorant lout who'd mangled my shrubbery.

The front door closed.

I always lock up when I'm in the house. It seems to me a rudimentary precaution. Nevertheless, I was quite sure of what I'd just heard and, under normal circumstances, I would immediately have started to consider concealing myself from whatever intruder had picked my lock or in whatever other manner gained entry. But the past week had drained all of the emotion out of me, and the brandy probably added another layer of indifference, so instead I boldly opened the door and stepped out to confront my mysterious visitor.

But there was no one there. As I mentioned, I live in a small cottage. There is no place that anyone could have been hiding. I was alone in the house. But the door had definitely closed. I walked across the room and discovered that it was not locked. My hand lifted and I almost turned the knob to secure it, but a flicker of motion out of the corner of my eye distracted me and instead I crossed to the front window and looked out onto the front lawn.

There were several people there, or rather, there were several of the same person there. He was wearing a sweatshirt and jeans and he looked a lot like me. He, they, could have been my twins, and they were all moving away from the house, dispersing now on their various missions.

I thought about Mr. Horty and Mrs. Neal and Petey Wilson and Oliver Begley and the landscaper whose name I didn't know and it occurred to me that I should warn them, but frankly there probably wasn't time to convince them that I wasn't nuts, and even more frankly, I felt a surge of fierce glee at the thought of what was coming to them, of what they had coming to them, and instead I climbed into my car and drove downtown and parked in front of Terry's Bar & Grille. The clientele there were notoriously unruly and it was not at all difficult to entice one of the older men into starting a fight. He was uncoordinated and clumsy and I managed to avoid any serious harm while prolonging things until the bartender had successfully summoned the police.

And now I'm sitting in this cell, only a few feet from my erstwhile combatant, and the officer who arrested me told me that I was in big trouble and maybe he's right.

But at least I have an alibi.

Bone by Bone

Scott Nicholson

The evening air of the Appalachian farmhouse tasted of old news-print, or maybe the dry rot of a diary's pages smeared with October yellow.

Not yellow like mustard, or the bleeding yolk of a sunny-side fried egg, or the skin of a summer squash. This was the yellow of sulfuric dust, a noxious meringue. Each breath came at a cost. Roger Main had survived hundreds of thousands of breaths, but now they dragged their slow way into his lungs as if propelled by tiny hooked claws.

Blame the cigarettes. That's what any rational man would do. He'd clung to his unfiltered Pall Malls the way a drowning man clung to an anchor chain. They were an affectation, the prop of the intellectual. But "intellectual" was an inside joke; despite publishing in the Journal of Parapsychology, hooking up with some generous grants through the Rhine Research Center, and writing a few boo articles in the popular press each Halloween, Roger was about as smart-ass as a suicide bomber.

Smart-ass enough to take on the Rominger Place and its run-of-the-mill legend. The assignment had looked like a sucker's bet on paper. Spend a night, vomit 1,000 words for the Horror Hood webzine, and pocket enough to cover two months of booze and smokes. Horror Hood was the latest start-up, the kind of website that featured blinking pumpkins, bloody eyeballs, and swollen female breasts. Funded by a 22-year-old heir to a motel chain known for its low rates and illegal employees, Horror Hood aimed for the same sort of experience—don't look too closely at the sheets and check out before the rodents get hungry.

All in all, Roger would rather brave the Rominger Place than one of the publisher's motels. The Rominger homestead was deep in the Blue Ridge Mountains of Tennessee, a day's mule ride from the North Carolina border. Down the end of a long dirt road, tucked at the bottom of a hill, the two-story farmhouse leaned a little to the left, tin roof rusted and buckled. Most of the ripple-glass windows had been shattered, and the outbuildings were nothing more than collapsed heaps of rotted logs. As Roger stood on the sagging porch, he couldn't resist the urge to knock on the front door.

"Anybody home?" he called. His professional rule of thumb was not to enter if any ghosts ever answered, but so far he was batting a thousand and figured it would stay that way. However, like most abandoned, isolated houses, the Rominger Place looked like the perfect hangout for bums, illegal immigrants, or meth cooks, any of whom could be dangerous.

The door had no handle, only a black, fist-sized hole that oozed cool air and darkness. He kicked it open. "Nobody here but us chickens," he shouted.

The foyer was mostly bare, sporting only a vinyl sofa of that era when olive green was considered stylish. Only one cushion remained and it was gutted, spilling ocher foam. A mattress leaned against the wall by the brick fireplace, blotched with stains that must have leached from the bodies of diseased travelers. Apparently some of America's great unwanted knew about this place, though they obviously hadn't found it to their liking enough for an extended stay. No tin cans, whiskey bottles, or wads of toilet paper marked any recent tenancy.

Maybe the ghosts had scared them away. Roger smiled at the notion, wrinkling his nose against the sick air. Even the dust was fulsome, hanging like a thick growth on every surface. Odd that the local teens hadn't made the place a party mecca. Scaring the pants off a girl was a tried-and-true approach, despite the horror-movie mandate that all unmarried fornicators must die.

As Roger explored the house, he tried to visualize the crimes that had occurred here: a crazed and jealous husband, name of Hollis Rominger, had killed his wife Maude sometime after the turn of the nineteenth century. Maude's absence initially had been reported by a member of her church sewing circle, but a search revealed nothing. Rumors flew that she'd hopped a train to Norfolk to meet up with a sailor back from the Spanish-American War, that she'd gotten pregnant, that she had been sent off to an asylum due to a bout of melancholia. Hollis remained steadfast in both his sorrow and his denial of wrongdoing.

Until, that was, one of the sheriff's deputies saw a message scratched in flour on the kitchen wall of the old farmhouse. "Well," the flour had spelled, in what had been described as an uneven hand. This disturbed the investigators, mostly because the Rominger Place was fed by a spring, through a steel pipe that sent a steady trickle into the kitchen sink. And, of course (at this point in reading the historical account in a staple-bound book in the Stamey County Public Library, Main had stifled a deep yawn), a neighbor had come along who had a reputation as a witchwoman, prone to giving out herbs and muttering folk spells. The old woman dredged up a childhood memory of a long shaft behind the barn, of horses tugging ropes, sweaty men digging, stinky black mud drying in the sun.

The well was located with the help of a terrier, a breed of dog known to explore tunnels and ditch-pipes for rats. The hole had been covered with rotted boards and rusty tin, overgrown with honeysuckle vines that had been recently disturbed. A thoroughly hacked Maude was found in the well, her flesh already turning to cheese despite the cool liquid depths thirty feet below ground level. Hollis Rominger paid for his crime by dancing at the end of a short length of coiled hemp, and that should have been that.

Except—and this was the part of the case that first excited Roger Main—two other small bodies had been found in the well, both reduced to skeletons but obviously thrown into the common grave years apart.

Why hadn't a flour-dusted finger spelled out their location? Main had wondered. *And why wasn't Hollis charged with those crimes as well? Because humans, even the most twisted of the species, were creatures of habit. If Hollis "went to the well" once, why not over and over again?*

The $2,000 question. And, while the story he fed Horror Hood might be just as cheesy as the site's graphic design, the mystery stimulated him enough to be standing in the kitchen, where kudzu and

Virginia creeper vines oozed through the walls. The counters had long ago collapsed, but the pipe still carried water, though there was no sink. The clear stream spouting from the pipe splashed into a ditch carved by decades, running under the house and adding to the rot trapped in the boards.

"Guess I'm on my own for dinner," he said, switching on his battery-powered lantern in the darkening room. He wasn't sure when he'd begun talking aloud during his adventures. He'd cultivated the public persona of an eccentric, the weirdo who would explore where no sane paranormal enthusiast would follow. He eschewed the EMF recorders and infrared cameras the serious investigators used to "prove" supernatural activity. To Roger, it was like trying to prove a negative—as with God, you couldn't prove something that didn't exist.

But what would he prove here anyway? Even if he encountered something otherworldly, he'd have only his senses and his memory, and both of those had repeatedly proven faulty. The best hope was to turn in a suspenseful, provocative article and clear the check before the publisher folded. With the laptop, he should be finished by dawn.

He set up shop in what must have been the sitting room, where a blackened brick fireplace stood. He propped his lantern so the light rose to the ceiling and bathed the room in honey-edged shadows. Lacking a desk, he leaned against the wall and propped the portable computer across his knees. He was warming up for the lead, something along the lines of, "In the haunted hillbilly country...," when the sound descended the stairs.

It was nothing more than the Blue Ridge wind pouring unfettered through the numerous holes in the plank siding. And, naturally, as it curled under the eaves and slid along the tin roofing, it would shift into a high, keening moan.

Causing it to resemble a crying infant.

"Hell, yeah," Roger said. "I can use that. Stephen King got nothing on me, the squirrel-eyed son of a bitch. Next thing you know, the stairs will start creaking, making it sound like Old Man Rominger is walking down from the attic."

A wooden rapping followed in the ensuing silence, but it didn't come from above. The front door.

Roger had heard no car engine and the headlights would have swept over the windows. Perfect. A polite bum, just what he needed to round out the story.

He opened the door with a grin fixed on his face, not sure whether he was going to invite the bum in or not. A man in a brown uniform stood at the edge of the porch. The light leaking from the sitting room gleamed off the man's badge.

"Sheriff's Department," the man said, stating the obvious in a neutral voice. "Got a report of trespassing."

"The property's not posted," Roger said, struggling to remain neutral himself. Aside from a high school pot bust and a close encounter on a "domestic-violence-type situation," Roger had little experience with cops, either as enforcers or protectors. But having one walk up out of nowhere in the middle of the night had put him off his game.

Again came the steady voice: "You're not a Rominger, are you?"

Roger debated a bluff, and then realized his photo ID bore his real name. Besides, his license plate numbers were easy enough to trace. "No, I got permission from the family to stay here."

The deputy stepped forward so his face was in the light. A long flashlight was shoved in his belt. A beard covered his chin and neck, which was odd, since the only unshaven cops Roger had ever seen were undercover drug agents on television. The man's eyes were the color of frozen steel and seemed not to blink. "Well, I'm a Rominger. I don't recall anybody asking for permission to stay here."

"Wonderful," Roger said, affecting a cheerful manner. "Maybe you can help me with my history project."

The eyes narrowed but became no less intense. "You from the university?"

Appalachian State University was just over the ridge, though in the next county and state, and was noted for its regional collection. Roger had checked its online resources but had found nothing except what was already recorded in newspaper accounts. However, the granite-faced cop might give a little more leeway to an egghead who probably had lawyer friends. "Sure," Roger said. "My contact was supposed to get clearance from the family. I'm working on a book."

"Something along the lines of 'Murder in the Mountains,' probably," the cop said in his slow, easy, but troubling voice.

"All I want to publish is the truth."

"I been around long enough to know the truth is like a snake in dry well. You leave it alone, and it does you and the snake just fine. But when you poke around, one of you ends up snakebit."

Roger noted the "dry well" metaphor and wondered how he could work it into the story. "There's a lot of wisdom in that, Deputy Rominger, but—"

"I ain't a Rominger. I married into the family."

"Sure, Deputy, but unless I'm breaking some sort of law—"

"There's the law of the land and then there's the law of the Rominger Place."

Roger almost grinned at the man's Will Rogers homilies, but those metallic eyes spoke of a grim earnestness. "Speaking of wells, do you mind showing me where the bodies were found? The faster I finish my business here, the faster I'll be on my way."

The deputy flicked on his flashlight and played it up the stairs, briefly defeating the gloom. "You hear something?"

This time, Roger did grin. That was the corniest trick in the book. Trying to scare off the stranger with spook stories. "Sounded like maybe a fingernail scratching on the wall."

"Wonder what words she wrote this time."

Roger figured "she" must mean Maude, who was believed to have written that afterlife message in the flour. The redemption story was older than Christ. Such myths appealed to people's sense of justice. This whole gig was starting to shape up as a tired episode of "The Ghost Whisperer."

"How do you know it was Maude that did the writing?" Roger asked. "Has she ever written anything besides 'Well,' or does she just write the same thing over and over?" Roger could relate to that, because some of the most successful paranormal writers, as well as those pimping horror fiction, did little more than repeat the same weary tale. Roger had no respect for the hackwork that passed muster in the juvenile world of giggly spooks and jiggly boobs, but he also understood his chosen genre was one of the few where his own limited talents were acceptable.

"Maude's gone on to her eternal reward," the deputy said. "Her spiritual suffering ended the day her account was squared."

Roger couldn't help casting a glance up the dark stairwell. "So who is doing the writing?"

"Want to go up and see, or would you rather see the well?"

For the first time in his skeptical ghost-hunting career, he was glad for company. The deputy, though a bit melodramatic, was stoic and calm, bearing the look of one who could deal with "situations," as they were known in cop vernacular.

"Let's try the well," Roger said. "Might be dangerous for me to go stumbling out there in the dark by myself. Better to have a tour guide who knows the territory."

The deputy blinked and raised one corner of his mouth in a gesture that might have been a smile. "Got an extra flashlight?"

Roger nodded. He'd packed a high-powered pen light as a back-up. He fished it out of his pocket as the deputy drew out his own flashlight as if it were a battle-ax.

"Follow me," the deputy said.

Roger let himself be led off the porch, around the house, and down a weedy trail between leaning outbuildings. A sallow slice of moon hung in the sky, dimmed by a gray wreath of clouds. Despite the October chill, crickets worked the night air and dead leaves rattled against bone-dry fence posts. Roger realized one sound was missing: most cops let their car engines idle while making a call, in case an emergency required a fast response.

The deputy's flashlight beam bounced ahead, throwing a pumpkin-colored pall on the weedy farmyard. Roger's own light did little to penetrate the black wool of darkness, but it gave him a measure of comfort. He was about to call Deputy Rominger, and then remembered he wasn't a Rominger. On reflection, Roger realized the officer wore no brass nameplate above his shirt pocket, nor insignia of any kind besides the badge.

A killer. Exactly the kind of crap those best-selling horror writers would dream up. Creep dresses as a cop, pretends to make a welfare check, gets the victim's guard down, then performs a Hannibal Lecter on his ass. Then—insert creepy synthesizer riff—blame it on the Curse of the Rominger Place!

The idea was so outlandish that Roger was thinking of a way to work it into his article—"The Mysterious Stranger who showed up at the crack of midnight"—when the deputy drew to a halt.

"Here it is."

Roger stayed close to the deputy, expecting to find a band of yellow tape blowing in the wind, a remnant of a crime scene investigation, though Maude's death had been investigated long before the era of modern forensics. Instead, a rusty sheet of tin lay on the ground, covered by brown weeds and red briars.

"Too cold for rattlesnakes," the deputy said, booting the piece of tin to the side. The kick revealed a wedge of blackness deeper than the night, and a moist, fetid aroma arose from the crevice. Another kick and the gap grew wide enough to hold a man.

"How deep is it?" Roger asked.

"Depends," the deputy said, and Roger expected him to add some somber witticism like "What's the bottom of a human soul?" but instead he said, "In the melt, the water rises and it's about twenty feet down. Right now, in the dry times, I'd guess thirty feet."

Roger thought that wasn't so deep for a murdering hole. Of course, Maude had been chopped up like a slutty extra banging the director of a low-budget slasher flick, so she had been dead long before her meat hit the water. The children, on the other hand—

"What about the two other skeletons?" Roger asked, for the first time realizing how isolated the Rominger Place was. Too far from the liquor store for bums, too squalid for hippie hikers. Even with their flashlights fixed on the well, which swallowed the beams as if thirsting, no porch lights were visible against the surrounding hills.

"They were fished out long ago," the deputy said. "A smart fellow like you would have read up on that."

The deputy stressed the word "smart" with the same subtle sneer he'd used in questioning Roger's interest in the house and its history.

"No charges were ever filed, and their identities were never verified."

"According to the newspapers and court records."

Roger tilted his light up, sending eerie shadows crawling along the deputy's face. "But you know something that wasn't put down in the report, huh? A family secret, maybe?"

"Family secrets stay in the family, even if it's a married secret," the deputy said. "But, no, it's nothing like that."

"Okay, how much do you want? I know our fine public servants never get adequately rewarded for all the risks and hardships they endure. I'm willing to compensate—"

The eyes didn't flinch, and seemed to absorb the light in the same manner as the well. "Bribing an officer is a felony in this state."

"No, sir, you misunderstood. I meant, after you go off duty. Personal, not professional." Despite the autumn breeze and the cool, sinuous draft rising from the well, sweat ringed Roger's scalp.

"I don't go off duty," the deputy said, motioning toward the opening with the flashlight. "You want a look or not?"

Roger gulped, glanced at the man's packed side holster, and nodded. He'd come this far, and no doubt he'd find enough adjectives to wring out his Horror Hood article, despite the deputy's reticence. *Just one look, for the sake of first-person narrative.*

He knelt, half expecting a shove from behind as he played his thin beam into the inky hollow. The deputy drew closer, shining his own light over Roger's shoulder. Despite the deputy's assurance about reptilian hibernation, Roger thought he heard the faint scraping of scaly skin over stone.

"See 'em?" the deputy said, in an almost reverent tone.

Roger saw nothing but blackness, the glint of moist rocks, twin dots of light reflecting from the water far below. "No, I—"

And then he did see them. Two tiny skeletons with mossy bones half submerged. As he tried to steady his shaking light, the dark water rippled. A stalk of white bones lifted, water dripping from the cracked and bent calcite. The second form also rose from the water, shaking water like a gaunt dog in a storm.

Then they were climbing, reaching with brittle fingers, skulls tilted back and staring upward with eyes blacker than the Devil's bowels.

Roger drew back, dropping his light, and the clatter echoed for a couple of seconds before a distant splash marked its watery grave.

He fell against the deputy's knees, scrambling, and the deputy put a boot down on the fingers of his writing hand.

"Got a good mind to kick you in there with them," the deputy said. "Like he did with Maude."

"Please," Roger said, summoning enough strength to rip his hand free and roll away in the crisp weeds, briars tearing at his clothes. From the hole arose a high-pitched wail, the cries of lost and frightened children. The sound grew louder, with less reverberation, marking their progress up the slimy sides of the well. Roger imagined those thin, sharp phalanges probing for chinks, jaws hinged open and grinning, eyeholes fixed on the lesser darkness that beckoned from above.

"Hollis got his peace, too," the deputy said. "Can you imagine being married to a woman who called these things up night after night? A lonesome, heart-broke woman who couldn't bear children of her own? Somebody who maybe got a little crazy in the head?"

Panting, Roger scrambled along the trail, heedless of the rusted barbwire tugging his flesh, the branches slapping at his face.

The deputy was right behind him, marching, taunting. "You want answers, Mr. Smart University Man, or do you want me to lay the tin back over the well and close it off?"

Roger, unable to regain his legs, flopped against a rotted shed. "Close it! For God's sake, close it!"

The deputy stomped away. Metallic thunder boomed, the tin stomped into place with a sure, heavy boot. Roger could barely hear it over the hammer of his own pulse in his ears, the windstorm of his own breath. Then the flashlight beam was on his face.

"You maybe want to go see what's wrote on the walls?"

Roger squinted against the force of the light and shook his head.

"Maude didn't leave that message. Hollis did. And he didn't write just 'Well.' The witchwoman got that part wrong, because the flour had sifted down a little bit and smeared the words."

Words?

"It really said, 'All is well.' Like Maude had finally paid for her sins."

"How do you know?" The flashlight burned his eyes, and Roger could no longer be sure a man stood behind its all-consuming brilliance.

"Romingers don't take kindly to trespassing."

"Please, deputy, just let me get my gear and—"

"You won't be doing no writing here. Not about this place."

"No, sir, of course not. But the laptop is valuable and I left—"

"I can move that piece of tin if you want. I don't know how fast the twins are, but they ain't got nothing but time."

Roger raised a palm to ward off the glare. He thought he heard a rattling thump of rusty sheet metal. "Okay, I'm gone. I'll keep your secret."

"Ain't my secret. Now it's yours."

Roger rose, wiping at a bloody scratch on his cheek. His car was a couple hundred feet away. He could make it in the dark, assuming he was pointed in the right direction. Turn the key, put the Rominger Place and its strange guardian in the rearview mirror, find a clean, well-lighted hotel, get out the telephone note pad and an ink pen—

For the first time, he'd be able to spin an unbelievable tale without lying.

"Your kind has been through here before," the deputy said. "All of them came to the same deal. And all of them lived to not tell, if you catch my drift."

Roger longed to put distance between himself and the well, and now he hurried on aching, limp legs, as if balanced on the extended slant of the flashlight's beam. He was still undecided on how much he'd give to Horror Hood, but his asking price had just tripled. He sprinted past the open doorway of the house, his lantern inside painting a yellow rectangle against the warped boards. He was nearly to the car—

No sheriff's cruiser on the overgrown road—

when the flashlight beam switched on, fifty feet in front of him.

"Some stories don't got no end, Mr. Main. Don't you forget that."

He'd not given the officer his name.

By the time he'd slid behind the wheel and fumbled with his keys, dropping them twice like they always did in horror movies, the light had bobbed closer. The engine caught and he pumped the gas, yanking the transmission into gear. He navigated toward the swelling circle of light that blocked him from the highway.

The light might have been the tip of a great cigarette, a monstrous out-of-season firefly, or a portal to hell. Whatever its nature, he would ram through it. Twigs scratched the chassis, or maybe it was small bones. The air tasted yellow again, the light piercing, and Roger wondered if crime scene tape would mark off the tire tracks leading away from the corpse of an officer killed in the line of duty.

But he went toward the light (just like those phony mediums suggested to fictional lost spirits on television), then through it, and there was no thud of meat against the bumper, no grunt of pain, no spray of blood on the windshield.

The wheels spun in the mud and weeds, and he fishtailed away, giving one last glance in the mirror, half expecting the deputy to be sitting in the back seat like a legendary hitchhiker.

Only darkness stared back.

It continued staring all the way to the Tennessee line.

Sleeping with the Bower Birds

Kaaron Warren

Flowering trees reached over either side of the driveway, forming a tunnel Serena felt nervous to walk through. She heard the high buzz of bees and a chorus of birds, and hoped they wouldn't be attracted to her. The clothes she wore belonged to the store and her boss would make her pay for them if they got shat on.

Next to the driveway, the front lawn stretched green and manicured.

There stood a naked marble woman, posed with a hand resting over her pubic bone. The other arm was lifted, holding a bowl; here, birds fluttered in the water. Serena, thankful of the excuse to put her heavy bags down, touched the cold marble, admiring the lifelike pose.

Stones in diminishing sizes lined the path across the lawn to the front door, and she walked up the steps wondering if she'd brought the right selection of clothing. In the store, mother and daughter, Rachel and Ava, had seemed shy, unsure of themselves. Rachel was tiny and could wear almost anything, as long as it was adjusted to her height. Ava was much larger, but clothing was made for her size these days. It was the coloring; she was pale. And she lacked confidence, so any new clothes had to build on that, not make her feel more self-conscious. So nothing showing cleavage, nothing too tight. Serena's boss had left the selection up to her. "I can't deal with any woman fatter than size ten," her boss had said.

Serena hefted her bags again, hoping they'd like what she brought.

"You came!" Rachel said, throwing open the front door. "Let's go round the back. Ava's in the granny flat. Well, she calls it the den. We call it the granny flat." She stepped out, strained her head towards the driveway. "Where'd you park?"

Serena stammered, not wanting to admit she'd come by public transport. She was trying to appear professional, as if she did this for a living.

"What, d'you come by bus? Don't worry, my brother'll give you a lift home." She led the way down the driveway and around the back, through an ornate gate that seemed to sigh as she opened it. The granny flat looked half the size of the house itself. "Ava!"

The girl opened the door sullenly, as if she was expecting the dentist rather than a woman bringing bags of clothes for her. She was about the same age as Serena and they'd bonded in the store over the awful muzak playing.

Inside, the granny flat was neat but dull, and far smaller than it had appeared on the outside. It was stuffy and warm. *Thick walls and plenty of insulation,* Serena thought.

"I'll leave you to it," Rachel said. "I'll bring us all back some champers in a while, how about that?", egging her daughter on as if this was some treat, something she'd looked forward to.

Ava lifted her shoulders and didn't let them drop again.

Serena straightened the nest-like bed and laid out the clothing she'd brought. "Let's pull your hair back, cos it can be easier to see a style that way," she said, thinking that the lank, greasy hair might dirty the samples.

She handed Ava a dress with three-quarter sleeves, tapered hem and a square neckline. "I've got a good feeling about this one. I wasn't sure about the color, so I brought a few, but let's start with the dark brown."

Ava took it reluctantly and stood with it draping on the floor.

"I'll wait outside," Serena said, and tugged open the sticky glass door.

She wasn't sure how long it would take, or if the girl would have the confidence to call her when she was ready. She stood, arms crossed, stamping her feet to keep warm.

The back garden was small but beautifully designed. She saw four more naked female statues, each one more graphic than the last. Someone had draped an old dress over one of them and she wondered if this was humor or prurience. Who sculpted these? They were very good; anatomically correct, and the women's faces beautiful; slack with desire. She walked amongst them, touching the cold marble, enjoying the art.

She pulled up sharp when she realized there was an aviary running along the back fence. She hadn't seen it behind the statues and the long trails of tomato plants, cactus pots and calendula flowers. There was movement inside but she couldn't see the birds, so stepped up to the wire cage.

She didn't notice the man until she heard him breathing. Wheezing.

He crouched on a stack of concrete blocks, his knees under his chin, his long, thin arms wrapped around his shins. His hair stood straight up and had feathers stuck in it. His face was unevenly shaved and seemed bruised. He didn't look at her and she wondered if he'd even seen her. He ducked his head and tilted it as if listening to something she couldn't hear.

She stepped carefully away.

Ava opened the granny flat door and stood in the doorway.

"Oh, look!" Rachel said. She held a tray of drinks and carried a packet of potato chips under her arm. "Look at her!" Rachel's long, brightly-painted fingernails were like talons. She scratched a red spot on her cheek. "You look gorgeous!"

Ava smiled. "I actually look okay," she said.

"Let's try some more stuff on," Serena said, taking a glass of champagne. "I've got these amazing pants, and some tops that will look fantastic on you." She had a feeling she was going to sell the lot. The boutique owner would be thrilled.

Serena and Rachel waited outside with their champagne as Ava tried on the next outfit. The man had turned his head, though his body remained still. He looked at them with wide eyes.

"That's my brother-in-law, Finch. He loves birds."

"Is his name really Finch?"

"He's my ex-husband Jay's brother. Their father was obsessed with birds. Geddit, Jay and Finch? He was a real shit. It's why I forgave Jay a lot. Why we lasted as long as we did. Total arsehole." She spoke between sips of champagne, drinking it like a bird swallowing nectar.

"Your ex or the father?" Serena said, curious. Her family had rare divorces and there were no obsessions. None spoken of.

"Funny! Both of them. Two arseholes in one family. Finch's all right, though. Harmless." He turned back to the aviary, resting one hand on the wire. Two jet black birds with bright gold peaks hopped around, pecking.

"What sort of birds are they?"

"Bower birds. You should see. They make the most amazing nests."

Bowers, Serena thought but didn't say.

"Regent Bower Birds," Finch said.

Rachel rolled her eyes.

"I'll give you a feather next time they drop one. You could pin it on your dress."

Inside the aviary was another naked woman statue, this one with her hands on her hips, her back arched, her throat exposed, her chin sharp, beak-like. A bird sat on her shoulder, hopping up and down.

"They're a bit crazy cos they're locked up," Rachel said.

"They're not crazy! They get to build a new one whenever they want!" Finch said. He pointed.

There were two birds and two bowers. One ran deep, to the back wall and into darkness, the other rose over a log and was built up against the left hand wall. It glinted in the sunlight that shone briefly. Serena saw glass, mirrors, silver paper, scraps of metal and tiny balls. "It's beautiful!" She said.

Finch nodded. "They get better as they get older. These guys are both getting on. They've had like twenty wives each."

"Wives!" Rachel snorted. "Those birds are as sleazy as Jay. Come on, let's check on Ava."

Ava had showered; her hair was wet but clean, her face shining. She'd only rejected a couple of the items, things Serena had thrown in as a contrast. Serena was pleased with herself. Rachel whistled in appreciation.

"You should try some of this stuff on," Ava said. "I want to see what it looks like on a skinny person."

"I'm not skinny and you're not fat," Serena said, looking at Rachel for back up.

"She could drop a dress size. Easy. Look at me; it's genetic, you know." Rachel was far too skinny, almost bird-like, Serena thought. Like a skinny little starved sparrow.

Ava twitched. Serena said, "Dress sizes vary so much, don't you think? My mother is really big, but then she only wears trakkie daks and truly awful T-shirts so who the hell knows what size she is?"

"Where did you get your style from? What's the secret?"

"A little bird told me not to tell," Serena said. They all laughed, tiny peck peck snickers, and Ava put her arm around Serena.

"You're cool. We like you."

"We do! You should stay," Rachel said.

"I probably should get going." Serena wanted to stay but she was here on business. She wasn't here to make friends. Her boss had told her, *don't get personal with them. Don't get caught up. They'll be asking for freebies if you do.*

"I'll get my brother to give you a lift home," Rachel said. Serena looked out at Finch, still squatting near the glinting bowers. "No, not him! My actual brother, Luke. Chalk and cheese!"

Luke came out carrying keys. Serena caught her breath. He was broad, strong, tanned. Aquiline. He smelled good. Clean. Expensive scent but not a lot of it.

"He's a catch," Rachel whispered. "Don't worry about it. He's got women all over him but he's a nice guy. Don't worry about it."

Luke drove casually, confidently. She liked a man who drove like that.

"So you sell clothes? I used to own a clothes shop. I love fashion. But my girlfriend kicked me out and took the lot. I couldn't even bring stuff down for Rach and Ava."

"That's a shame. So do you still deal with clothes?"

"Nahh, I'm a builder by trade. Built that place, my sister's place. I'll show you around next time. I've done some shit hot stuff there."

"I don't know if I'll come back. Ava's picked heaps of clothes."

"You can come back to visit me then." He winked. "Rache's a lot older than me, don't worry! And don't worry about Finch, either. He's a fucking lunatic, but I'll be getting him out soon."

Serena hated being dropped at her plain, unadorned, quiet house, so clearly a family home. She didn't want him to know she still lived with her parents. He drove her to the door, kissed her cheek, gave her his card and said, "Call me."

She went back a month later, after texting with Ava, sharing music and jokes.

There was a high bamboo fence built in front of the house and she wondered if Luke had done it alone, bare-chested, or if Finch had helped him.

She walked through the driveway bower and around the back to see Finch. She could hear him cheep cheeping and wondered if they'd talk back today.

She arrived to find him leaving the cage, feathers and twigs in his hair, the mark of same on his cheek. There was a tiny bone over his ear. She pointed.

"They love bones. Human bones the best, but not the big ones. Hand bones. Toe bones. They love those. Ear bones. They can make a beautiful bower out of those. That's why they're called ghost birds. That and the mimicry." He tilted his head from side to side, his mouth opening and shutting. "Usually they mimic other songs, but in captivity they mimic human voices." He put his finger on his lips.

Silence.

"They're clearer at dawn," he said. "And you have to know what to listen for." He crouched. She realized that his elbows were in his crotch and looked away.

As the light dropped, Serena thought she saw movement in the cage, fluttering. "Did you get more birds? It seems busy in there."

He gave a "huh" of surprise. "Why, do you see more?"

She squinted. "No…I thought I did."

"After you spend a night with ghost birds, nothing is ever the same," he said.

The bower birds sat each in the mouth of their bower. Each had added items since she was last there: hair ties, plastic bag scraps,

Christmas tinsel. She'd read about the tricks they used, the visual manipulation they played with, to make their bowers look bigger and more impressive than they actually were. Lining up stones from smallest to largest, so it appeared to be a grand walkway. Tricky in such a small space, but she imagined these creations in all their magnificence out in the open.

She wondered how lonely they felt, sitting there with their beautiful homes, waiting for females who never arrived.

"Don't they get frustrated?"

He pressed his elbows harder into his crotch. "I bring 'em ladies every now and then. Borrow them from a mate. He gets the babies but he gives me one when these ones die. He takes the ladies away when it's all done. They have to make their own nest."

"Just like Rachel's ex," Serena said, making the family joke.

"Jay's nested happily with his second wife," Finch said, casting a guilty look at the house. "They just didn't get on."

Rachel called out, "Come in if you're coming in! Dinner's on!"

"I'm not hungry," Finch said, cheeping it like a bird, but he reached into his pocket and pulled out a packet of sunflower seeds.

"Not hungry," she heard, an echo, one clear note.

"What was that?"

"Huh!" Finch said again. He stood up; skinny legs, jeans too short. She mostly saw him squatting and was surprised again at how tall he was.

Fragile.

"He can learn to sound like you if you want him to. Pick a sentence and say it to him."

"What sort of thing?"

"Doesn't have to be profound." He smiled, his cheeks lifting up to show his rough yellow teeth.

"Polly want a cracker?"

"Not that!" But he laughed with her. "Something you'd like to be remembered for."

"I know." She leaned into the cage and spoke breathily, imagining herself Coco Chanel. "I don't do fashion. I am fashion."

"Say it again," he whispered. "Sometimes they need to hear it twice."

"I don't do fashion. I am fashion."

The bird turned his head at her, his beak opening and closing. He squawked a few times as if practicing, then repeated the words.

"He sounded like me!"

Finch ducked gently, then reached in with a piece of apple; they came to him, all of them hacking at it till he dropped it.

"What did they learn from you? What do you want to be remembered for?"

"I can't think of anything," he said, and Serena thought that was the saddest thing she'd heard in a while.

"Come inside," Ava said, tugging at Serena's arm. "Finch is okay. Leave her alone, Finch." Ava wore the pants and shirt Serena had chosen for her; she seemed to walk with more confidence, and she'd had her hair cut. They could hear Rachel singing inside, her trilling, wordless song.

It was dark and Serena scraped her arm against the outstretched finger of one of the statues.

"Watch it!" Luke. Serena's heart beat faster. He had an armful of building supplies, she thought; shining things he'd make stuff with. "That's how Finch likes 'em," Luke said as they climbed the steps and went inside. "All cold, unmoving. Like my ex-girlfriend."

"Don't go there," Rachel said. "Not again. Can we not have the jokes this time?"

"She's got no sense of humor, I swear," Luke said.

Dinner was something cooked in a pot. Serena couldn't quite identify it. At home, each food item stayed separate on the plate, perhaps joined by some sauce or gravy. Everyone digging in, elbows out, her sister eating with her fingers, the only thin, beautiful part of her. Barely a word spoken unless it was something about the TV that blared in front of them. None except Serena concerned about the quantity of the food, all of them shoveling it in as if it made no difference to their size at all. Serena felt like an outsider amongst them, an imposter, a cuckoo. Here, they sat at the table and ate carefully measured portions. Ava ate quickly, then said, "I'm going to stay at Dad's tonight."

"But Serena's here!"

"I know! She can keep you company. Dad's got a new game he wants to show me. And he's closer to school. And he's got a big house. And I don't feel as if I'm in a bird feeder there. And there are no shitty birds there, either."

"See, this is what I've been talking about," Luke said, "Finch is Jay's brother, yet we're the ones who have to put up with him. Shitty birds," Luke said. Ava laughed.

"First, this isn't your house to have an opinion on. Second, that arsehole pays rent for him to be here." Rachel held out one fine leg. "Look at these shoes! This is what *I'm* talking about."

They were beautiful, hugging her foot with soft, mauve leather. Rachel was so well-dressed. Serena had long known the women she admired the most, the women she considered the most intelligent, were the well-groomed ones. Even her boss, who was small-minded and bitchy, she admired for her dress-sense.

"Touch them. Go on. Put your finger on the toe."

The feel of them made Serena coo. "They are lovely."

"Paid for by him." She tilted her head. "He's alright, anyway. Harmless." She screeched out for Finch at the back step, wanting him at the table to eat the leftovers.

Even inside, Finch sat in a crouch. Rachel had made him take his shoes off at the door to stop him tracking bird shit through the house and he perched on his chair at the table, watching them.

"Can we watch the bird doco?" he said. He flapped his arms as if they were wings.

Luke laughed. "That's all you watch! How about a bit of footy? Soccer? Or we could send the girls out and watch something with a bit more action."

He stood up, his crotch pressed up against the back of his chair. His jeans were tight, a size too small, and his stomach squeezed out over the waistband. Finch shook his head and shuffled outside.

"Dad's here," Ava said. At the front door, she whispered to Serena, "Thank you. Seriously. You being here gives me the tiniest breathing space."

Serena couldn't imagine wanting to escape them.

Everything about the family fascinated her. There was music everywhere. Rachel singing or humming, Luke's radio playing if he was at home, Ava playing her own music in the granny flat, Finch tweeting and peeping, trying to get his birds to talk. She wanted to save Ava from her body-judgmental mother, help give her the confidence to wear what she wanted to wear. She wanted to fuck Luke, regardless of how sleazy or manipulative he was. She wanted him just once, just to have a man like that once, before settling for a nice guy, or a series of nice guys. He was the opposite of all she'd been led to believe she deserved, but there was nothing to it. It'd be shallow, and quick.

And she knew it probably wouldn't happen.

"Hey, I haven't shown you my cupboards," Luke said.

He showed off the house he'd built. Mirrors, special cupboards, equipment carefully concealed. Serena tried to stay interested, but mostly she wanted to look inside the cupboards, see what was inside this family, find their secrets. In the bathroom, she saw expensive lotions for men, six or seven all lined up neatly. The walls were straw colored and he said, "Don't worry about those, I'll paint 'em soon. Shitty color, that one."

Afterwards, they sat on the veranda and drank. Luke drank whiskey, glass after glass, and, in the moonlight and the glow of the candles Rachel lit, Serena could see him becoming redder and shinier. Finch joined them, sitting on the step and drinking apple cider, sculling can after can and stacking them in a tower on the lower step.

Rachel drank white wine in a beaker.

Serena drank white also, in a long, fine champagne glass. In the conversational breaks, she could hear the gentle murmur of the birds (two of them? Mimicking more?) and a soft tapping she eventually realized were the wind chimes above her head.

Made of bones.

"Finch's rejects!" Luke said. "All the bones the birds don't want!"

Finch laughed at that, a cheep cheep chuckle that made her want to laugh out loud.

"I designed them. Designed plenty in the house. I shoulda been a fashion designer," Luke said. "I woulda made beautiful clothes."

"So why didn't you?"

"Mum always said it was stupid. Dumb idea for a man."

"Our mum was so unsupportive. Always telling both of us we were useless, no matter what we did. I wanted to be a model but she always told me no fucking way. She always said I was too fat and no amount of feathering up could make me look better."

Luke nodded. "She told her to get a job in an office where it didn't matter what she looked like so long as she had clean clothes on."

"And neat."

"Yeah, neat."

"That's why I'm so keen for Ava to have good dress sense. That's why you're doing such a good job, bringing her all these fabulous clothes."

"You still could be a designer," Serena said. She didn't know what to say to Rachel, who was well past modeling age. "You could start a company." She wondered if she could be their buyer. If they'd ask her. Lots of late nights. Getting some take away in. And he'd take his shirt off if he got hot and she'd be laughing at him, making fun of him in a teasing way but really wanting to run her fingers over him, to see how that made her feel. "I'm always fiddling with designs. I've got all sorts of stuff to play with."

"I bet you have," he said. He'd encircled her. Enclosed her.

His phone rang. He checked the screen. "This one I'll take." He winked at Serena, which broke her heart; it meant she was like a sister. Or niece.

He picked up his keys. "I'm out," he said, kissing his sister on the cheek, Serena full on the mouth. His lips were soft, slightly salty, with a hint of lime. She wanted to press up against him, to see his bedroom, what color his sheets were.

"I can drop you home on the way," Luke said.

Serena spent her first night there a week later.

Rachel called her with an emergency: Ava asked out for dinner with a group of people from school and nothing at all to wear for it. They stayed up late talking, trying things on, and Serena hoped that Luke would come home soon. That she could flutter inside for a glass of something, even a cup of tea, and he'd tell her about his night. The back of the house glowed with the lights he'd installed;

butterfly lights in many colors that blinked and illuminated the tiny pot plants he'd lined the walls with.

"You should crash here," Ava said, and the idea of getting home made her so tired, Serena agreed. Home would be quiet and dull, her parents gently snoring, her sister watching TV in the dark with a lap full of chocolate, the dog snuffling in his crotch.

Sheathed in a sleeping bag, Ava watched a movie on her laptop. Serena checked her messages and played on her phone until they were tired.

"I feel like a 12 year old on a sleepover," Serena said, and they both got the giggles.

It was a quiet night. As she tried to doze off, Serena thought she could hear chattering.

"Is that your mum talking? And Luke?"

"It's only the birds. Finch reckons they talk to each other."

"It sounds like heaps of them, though."

"There are only two," Ava said.

"Sounds like more. Where does Finch sleep, anyway? Out there, with them?"

"Sometimes, I think. Make sure the blind is closed properly. Door locked. I've caught him staring in before. He gives me the total creeps. That's another reason I spend a lot of time over at Dad's. He's kinda gross."

"He's weird. Obsessed. He does love those birds. I guess he's guarding them. Scared someone's going to steal them."

"Or listen to them properly. Sometimes I wonder if they're trying to tell me something but he keeps them quiet."

The birds woke Serena early. Stretching, she stepped outside, not wanting to lie in bed, nor wake up Ava.

Finch was already up, looking dirty, unkempt. He was demolishing the bunkers, the birds fluttering about, helping him, she imagined. He said, "That's the way, that's the way."

"They hate an old house," he said as Serena stood next to him, rubbing her eyes. "They peck at me sometimes if I leave it too long." He swept out the cage, scooping up debris into a large garbage bag. Shards, tiny bones, broken things, some of it crushed to dust.

"It doesn't actually smell that bad," Serena said. She fingered through the basket full of new things he'd collected for his birds. Glass, mirrors, hair (hers, she thought, or at least some of it) and bones. Bits of chain.

Once the cage was clean, the bars stripped, he carefully spread the new treasures on the ground. The birds squawked. Serena heard them saying, "It's good, it's good," but she laughed at her own imagination. Finch wore a crown of tinsel, but they didn't pluck from it. He ducked his head from side to side.

Finch squatted on his concrete blocks. Serena dragged a chair over and sat there for a while. She went inside for coffee (she could smell it brewing and Rachel loved to crow over her coffee), came and sat outside with it, watching the artist birds create.

"I love this. Isn't it pure magic?" Finch said.

It seemed to her there was a flurry of them, many birds all fluttering and building. She squeezed her eyes but it didn't help. It was the mirrors, all the mirrors and the glass, making it appear there were many birds in there, not just two.

Finch opened up a plastic bag and tipped the contents inside. Bones. They clunked onto the floor of the aviary and sat there in a pile. The birds inspected, squawking and leaping excitedly.

"They like bones the best. They know the ones that are people bones."

"They're not."

"They might be. Hospitals chuck out bones all the time. All those fingers chopped off. The toes. Stuff like that."

"Stuff like that! What else is like that?" Serena laughed.

Ava joined them. "Mum says breakfast."

"Not hungry," Finch said, and Serena wasn't either, but she went inside out of politeness. Really, she wanted to watch the birds building. Listen to them. "Fuck off useless" she thought she heard "fuck off fuck off useless" and she laughed at herself.

There were more new shoes inside. "Try 'em!" Rachel said. "I don't mind. Aren't they gorgeous?"

They were beautiful. Like a second skin.

"Poor old Finch. Don't be too nice to him. He's got no idea about parameters." Luke leaned against the kitchen bench, eating what looked like a dozen Weet-Bix.

"Why don't you get him a girlfriend?"

"Him? He's too skinny. Women hate skinny men." Finch was very thin. Fine-boned. He ate little. Only Luke ate a lot, making up for all of them. "He never eats. It's weird. My ex always had me on a diet. I hated it."

He looked out the window at Finch. "Look at him. He's never going to attract a gaggle of girls." He had beautifully manicured hands. Rachel did them for him.

After that, Serena stayed often. With Ava spending a lot of time at her father's, the granny flat was usually empty. Serena worked there on her days off, sewing and designing. She brought her boxes of baubles, sequins and buttons, her threads, her tiny jewels. Finch watched her unpacking, blinking at the glint, wanting them for his birds.

Their house was a closer bus route into the boutique, and she liked being around them. Liked the self-indulgence that existed, that all of them did exactly what they wanted to do. There was no sense of sacrifice, none of "doing the right thing." They simply did whatever they wanted.

Luke worked on the house. Finch found him treasures; a picture frame, a strip of beautiful wallpaper, a series of painted rocks. Things to make the place look amazing. They wove ivy through the bamboo fence and painted beautiful designs along the top. He gave Serena a string of beads he'd found, each one hand painted.

At night, especially if Ava was at her father's, Serena heard the birds more and more clearly. Some nights she heard ten or more different voices, all talking against each other.

One night, they were so loud she pulled on a jumper and went out there.

Finch sat in his position in the dark.

"Can you hear them?" he whispered. She nodded. "Listen."

Don't Luke don't, she heard. *Don't luke don't luke don't luke don't.*

She grasped Finch's shoulder. He flinched then relaxed. "Who's that? Who are they mimicking?"

He gave a headshake.

"Come on."

"It's her." He motioned his head, ducked it down. Whispered, "His ex."

don't luke don't luke don't luke don't luke.

Finch smiled and she wondered if he was playing with her, somehow putting these words out there. He was very good if that was the case; his lips weren't moving.

The bird said, "You're fuckin' kidding me, Luke."

"She talked exactly like that. She was a total slapper," Finch said. His voice was harsh; she hadn't heard him speak like that before.

Later, thinking it was something to talk about, hoping to make him sad and needy, Serena asked Luke about it. She understood Finch was joking with her; she wanted Luke to know it was happening.

"Fucking Finch. He thinks it's funny. What, did you think I killed her?" He touched her thigh, his hand warm, soft, slightly rough. "She's on Facebook, you can check her out. Half the time she's bitching about me, other half she's talking about how pissed she was." There was nothing sad, nothing needy. He swept his hair back with one hand, grabbed his keys. "Be back soon," he told Rachel. "Bringing someone home for a drink, we can sit and watch your fuckhead of a brother-in-law so she can see the contrast."

"Ask her if she's got a sister for Finch," Rachel said, and the two of them laughed.

Serena found the branch of a large flowering tree sitting on the ground and hated to see it go to waste. Finch took it from her, his mouth opening and shutting, mimicking words with no sound coming out.

He opened the cage and laid the branch down, then they watched as the two males hopped about, plucked flowers and laid them carefully around the entrance to their bowers.

They didn't mind being observed as long as people were still. Rachel, Luke and Ava were terrible observers, shifting and fidgeting, wanting to talk. Only Serena understood the need for absolute stillness.

"How many can you see?" Finch asked her. "A flock?"

"Why? Did you get them girlfriends?" She concentrated in the evening light; she could see four she thought. Five.

That night, in the granny flat, Serena checked Facebook. Luke's ex-girlfriend was there, laughing, with bright, parrot-like clothing, long, mirror earrings. She looked free, as if she knew how to fly and was only waiting for the right breeze to come along. She also looked tacky, and much older than Luke. He liked them older. Rachel told her she'd had a lot of money, which had set Luke up. That he'd be nowhere without her. "He's got mother issues. He feels guilty that we weren't sad when Mum died. But she was awful, you know? So mean to us."

She turned out the light and curled up in bed, the moonlight filling the room through cracks in the blinds.

You sick fuck, she was sure she heard. The birds. Another she thought was wailing until it was pleading. *Please, no,* the words drawn out, desperate.

Another, *It's not too late.*

Another, quiet, very quiet, *You're useless, the two of you.*

She pulled on her coat and crept outside. "Did you teach them all these words?" she asked Finch.

He ducked his head, avoiding.

"Some of them came out talking this way."

"They sound like dying words."

He inhaled, shocked or surprised.

"You can understand them?"

It was as if the birds were witnesses to things they shouldn't understand. Their bowers were more beautiful than ever. Serena saw a pair of mirror earrings dangling down, reflecting back more birds, ones without real substance. Piles of acorns, of tiny stones, of berries, were laid out with perfection at the entrances.

"He's got someone home with him," Finch said. It was the first time she'd seen him distracted from the birds. "Come on." He led her around the side to Luke's bedroom. There was a clear view inside through a gap in the blinds.

Inside, a woman of about 35 stood in bright red underwear. She spun around, as if showing herself off. Luke, naked, larger than she'd thought, tanned all over, smooth, hairless, muscly, so strong and in control, stepped up to the woman and kissed her deeply.

Serena turned away.

"You can watch. He doesn't mind."

"Of course he minds. He's not a fucking bower bird."

She didn't want to see it.

"Don't move! Keep still!" Serena felt very visible amongst the dark green leaves, with her bright, layered clothes.

They backed away carefully. The birds called them.

don't luke don't luke don't luke

"I can see five. Or six. I'm not sure. They're all in pain."

"Not them. They're mimicking."

"Mimicking who?"

He didn't answer.

She thought she should do something. Anonymously report him to animal cruelty, although he wasn't guilty of that, and hope it led to an investigation. She thought, *But then they'd be gone,* and she hated that.

"Hey, Serena," she heard. Luke, on the back verandah, sitting in a chair, tipped back, watching them. "Come sit with me. Leave bird boy alone."

She heard a car drive away and wondered how he'd got rid of his lover so easily.

Finch hunched down into his squat to watch his birds. He whispered, "Mummy."

"You shouldn't really encourage him," Luke said. "He'll think you're into him."

She laughed. "He wouldn't! Surely. No woman ever would be and he must know that. He doesn't even make an effort."

"It's all about the effort, isn't it?" He was freshly showered, his hair wet, his skin shiny. He smelt of jojoba or something like that, ginseng. She knew he used some sweet body wash. She'd seen it in his shower.

There was a frenzy in the aviary, birds fluttering about. She stayed focused on Luke, though, not wanting to think about the birds.

How many can you see? Finch had asked her.

"How many birds do you see?" she asked Luke.

"He's only got two. Likes to see them suffer, I reckon. Likes to see them with blue balls, like he's got."

"Cruel!"

"He thinks he's got treasure but all he's got is shit. He thinks the birds are guarding something for him."

"Why don't you ignore him? Why does he bother you so much?"

"Because he's creepy and I don't want him near any of us. Even you." She wondered what he knew. What there was to know. If she was imagining the voices, and that there were no last words.

Finch came up and stood at the edge of the veranda.

"Beer, Finchy? Or something to eat, perhaps? Rache!" he called out. "Rache, bird man wants something to eat."

"They want you to come back," Finch said to Serena. "They want to talk to you."

Luke draped his arm around her. "Serena's just gonna sit with me for a while. Aren't ya?"

She felt her blood racing. This rarely happened; so rarely was she attracted like this, an animal attraction she couldn't control. She liked it, though. She liked the feeling that things were out of her power, that her body knew what it wanted and her brain (he's too old, he's an arsehole, he's just using you, Finch will watch, Finch will be jealous, the birds won't like it, Ava will think it's disgusting, Rachel will think it's disgusting, at least the pill, every morning since 15, daily routine, but still, condoms) could just be quiet.

Finch hunched over and went back to his birds. His shoulders shook and she wondered if he was crying. The male birds pecked and moved their things around, perfecting their bowers. The females in there watched, preened, waited.

Luke gave her a glass of wine, and another. She clutched the glass, claw-like, her fingers cold, and they sat close together. He gave her a delicate scarf that smelled, she thought, of the woman who had just left. Finch lifted his arm and watched from under it, his head twisted.

"He's freaking me out. He's only here a couple more weeks, anyway. Finally convinced Rache he's a health hazard. Bad to have around Ava. What happens when she gets preggers? Won't be forever before that happens. Can you imagine that shit around a pregnant woman? Carrying my grand-niece or nephew? No fucking way. Let's go inside. Rachel's gone for the night, I think. We could watch something. What do you like to watch?"

There were mirrors throughout the house and she caught herself, looking flushed and, she thought, beautiful.

In the glow of the television, with an old sci-fi movie playing, they made love. It was exhilarating. He was an experienced man and he enjoyed her youthful skin, her flexibility. He kept saying, "You're gorgeous, you're gorgeous," which was nice to hear. In the background, the smoke alarm chirped, wanting new batteries, and she thought she heard whispering but it was probably just her blood in her ears.

Afterwards, he gave her more wine, and a rug for her lap.

"I hate the color of these walls," he said. He started shifting furniture, scratching at the wall with his fingernail. "If I prep tonight, I'll hit the paint store first thing. Rach'll be stoked."

She sat for a while, watching music clips. She could hear the birds, though, speaking over the top, and she wondered if the whole neighborhood could hear them.

Wrapping the rug around her shoulders, she padded outside. Luke didn't notice her leaving.

Inside the aviary, Finch lay curled up like a child, his thumb in his mouth, the other arm over his head.

The birds circled in there, showing off their bowers. *Come in, come in,* she heard. *Come in come in come in come in.* These were not words she'd heard them say before; there was nothing weak, nothing of the victim in these words.

Still naked, with the rug wrapped around her, she climbed in.

She realized that the bowers went back far further than they appeared to from the outside. She stepped between them and walked, her hands on the outer walls of each bower, feeling the textures of straw and sticks, leaves and flowers.

It was dark, but her eyes adjusted. How far did they go back? Into the next property?

Here, the walls were threaded with larger bones she knew the birds couldn't have carried, and large clumps of hair, some pieces anchored to what looked like leather.

Underfoot was crunchy and she felt her feet sink deep in debris.

She felt suddenly enclosed and turned to leave, but birds flocked around her, male and female, the gentle breeze of their wings filling her instead with a sense of comfort and a deep restfulness. *I am fashion,* she heard. *I don't do fashion. I am fashion.*

Finally she reached the back wall. The birds plucked at her hair, pecked gently at her skin and the sensation was so comforting she sank down onto her rug and closed her eyes.

She felt bones and seeds press into her back and buttocks. She tried to lift an arm or leg but couldn't. She felt light as a feather but solid as concrete.

The birds got used to her, threaded twigs into her pubic hair. There was a kind of peace about it, a giving up. An end to the relentless striving, decision making.

"There are only two," Finch said. She wasn't surprised to see he'd followed her back there. "The rest are ghosts. Only you and I can see them."

"When you said ghost birds, I thought you meant metaphorically."

"I meant both." The ghost birds flew around him and he ducked gently, as she'd seen him do many times.

He reached in his pocket for sunflower seeds, which he offered to her.

She took a few.

They began to cover her with sticks, stones, jewels. Nesting materials. In her ears, across her eyes. She kept her mouth shut. The birds told her a story to send her to sleep, a long, disjointed story of many voices.

Mate, have you got a spare dollar?
I haven't eaten in two days, help us out.

I been on the street six years.
My mum chucked me out.

As the sun rose, the birds caused a ruckus, singing in their wheezy voices *get up get up*.

She sat up, sweeping off feathers and shit, the twigs from her pubic hair and the stones from her ears.

She opened the cage and moved slowly to the granny flat, feeling as if she was walking over eggshells. The birds had quieted as the sun rose, and there was a warmth in the air that made her take deep, grateful breaths.

Her boxes of sewing things sat open, and she ran her fingers through them, loving the texture, the feel, the tinkly song of them playing against each other.

"You spent the night with the ghost birds," Finch said. He stood at the door, leaning in. Over his shoulders, she thought birds flew, but the sun was bright. "Nothing is the same now."

Ghost birds flocked in to her, plucked at her, picked at her buttons. She felt them in her hair, nudging at her ears, nibbling at her fingers. They bathed in sequins. They flocked around her and she had never felt such a sense of belonging.

Nothing is the same, they said. And *who will you bring for us?*

"Who will you bring?" Finch said, or was it the ghost birds, sending out an invitation, "Who will you bring for us?"

She thought of Luke's determination to move Finch out, move him on. She wondered how they'd get Luke into the cage. Or her sister, whose life was nothing, or any of the idiot customers she served daily. And there was always the homeless, the forgotten. Birds fluttered around her *spare a dollar, mate* and she knew there were plenty of those. All she had to do was entice them.

She decorated herself with makeup, jewelry, clothing, her hair done up and braided with golden ribbons, her legs shaved and smooth. Finch watched as she preened, and Luke was there, and Rachel, all of them watching as she made herself shine.

Memory Lake

Robert Morrish

The story began with the worst drought Karn County had seen in more than a hundred years. Events happened slowly at first, crawling through a seven-year prologue of dry skies and parched earth. But as a thirst for water built, so, too, did a thirst for revenge. And once things started to happen, they happened pretty quickly.

1.

Jack Depp was busy when the phone rang. Not to put too fine a point on it, but he was on top of Randy Mueller's wife, who was one smoking-hot redhead, and Jack didn't appreciate the interruption.

The second ring did the trick. He opened his eyes to a darkened bedroom ceiling and looked over to see his wife lying next to him. Obviously, she wasn't going to answer it. *It's those damned radio commercials*, he thought as he crawled across her to reach the jangling receiver, *the new, racy ones*. Ever since the local station had started running them, he'd found himself acting out his radio role in his dreams. He hoped they'd end soon. The dreams, that is; not the commercials. The ads were doing the trick, so he could most definitely live with them for a while longer.

He answered with a sleepy, tentative, "Hello?"

"Wake up, Jack. It's Frank. I need you."

Jack paused, trying to gather his still-napping wits.

"Who is it, honey?" came a drowsy voice from his wife's side of the bed.

"That's nice," he said into the receiver. "I need you like I need a hole in the head."

"You're not funny when you're awake. Don't waste your time trying to be funny when you're half-asleep."

"Yeah, yeah. Speaking of sleep, what the hell time is it, and why are you calling me?"

"It's about five-fifteen. Shouldn't you be up by now, anyway?" the caller prodded, then continued without waiting for a response. "Listen, I'm serious—I need you to get down here as soon as you can. It's work-related, I can tell you that much."

"Where, exactly, is 'here' and what, exactly, is so all-fired important?" Jack's mouth felt like it was full of half-congealed paste.

"Come down to the south end of Esmeralda, to the Hyde Point boat launch. Murphy or I will meet you there."

"Okay-y-y…" Jack drew the word out to about three times its normal length. "That takes care of the 'where.' Now what about the 'what'?"

"I can't say right now. I'm on a cell phone, so this is an unsecured line…"

"Oh for chrissakes," interrupted Jack. "You're the police chief of a podunk town, not the director of the FBI. You think anybody really gives a shit?"

"Jack," came the measured, patient reply, with just a hint of menace, "you don't have any idea what's going on here, so why don't you give me the benefit of the doubt, quit jerking me around, and get down here."

Something in his brother's tone impelled Jack to comply. "All right, fine. Give me about… half an hour and I'll be there." After a moment, he thought to add: "Is the department gonna pay me for this, by the way, or are you expecting me to haul my ass out of bed on account of brotherly love?"

"Don't worry, you'll get paid. And besides, right now, all I need you to do is take a look at… a situation, and tell me if you can get a 'hoe in there to do some work."

I sort of figured that much, thought Jack, but stopped himself from saying so. A brief urge to ask if he'd get time-and-a-half rates, given the early hour, also died before reaching his lips. Instead, he just said "all right, see you in a bit," and hung up.

"Everything okay, honey?" asked Christie.

"Yeah, fine. Frank has some sort of important job for me. Wouldn't give me any details."

"Be careful," she replied, but he could tell from her tone she was already falling back asleep.

Jack ran a hand roughly across his face, hoping the gesture would somehow wipe away the clinging effects of sleep. It didn't work; he still felt hopelessly groggy and his mouth still tasted as if something had died in there last night. With a groan, he rolled off the bed and to his feet. *I remember when we used to make fun of dad for all the grunting noises he used to make. Now it's me making them. When, exactly, did I get old?*

He flipped on a hallway light, squinting in the sudden brightness, and began a search for clothes and toothbrush, moving carefully so as not to wake Carolyn and Jack Junior.

Fifteen minutes later, Jack "Digger" Depp was on the road, a second cup of coffee in his free hand. The first one he'd thrown back like he was doing a shot, not that he drank all that much liquor any more. Having a wife and two children and owning your own business didn't leave too much time for carousing. Although the first part of that equation—having a family—hadn't done much to slow down some of his friends. *Not me. Couldn't be that irresponsible if I tried. Gotta give thanks to the old man for that, I guess.*

He flipped on the radio and cracked a smile—his first of the morning—in response to a familiar tune. Perfect timing—it was the new commercial. *His* new commercial. What a strange thought that was, although he should be getting used to the notion by now. It'd been over a year since he'd first taken the plunge on a radio ad—his first foray beyond the yellow pages—and nearly a month since the new campaign had started.

Radio advertising didn't seem like the most logical avenue for his line of business. He'd only allowed himself to be talked into it because it was so relatively inexpensive—and because he liked the station so much. The ads only ran on a single station, KFAT, a small outfit with a weak signal, but a big reputation among those with eclectic tastes and a strong *dis*taste for the top 40 crap served up by the big faceless corporate stations.

Because the station wasn't constrained by any corporate standards, it became known for both its DJs' eccentric behavior and its frequent spoof commercials. The irreverent atmosphere resulted in many of the station's "real" commercials being decidedly tongue in cheek.

Digger's first effort at a radio commercial had actually been pretty tame. But when it didn't generate much of a spike in business, he was convinced by the radio's ad department to try a more risqué approach. And so for the second commercial, a new persona was created for Digger Depp, as a studly gigolo whose business consisted of not just excavating the earth but also plumbing the depths of countless panting housewives. Featuring the breathless voices of several such wanton wenches, commenting on his prodigious tool and skillful handiwork, it was really quite racy—or, depending on your viewpoint, extremely juvenile. The new commercial, his second featuring the gigolo version of Digger, was along the same lines as the previous one, but ended with Digger waking up to the sound of an alarm clock and realizing that all the gushing remarks were only part of a dream, and that it was time to get up and go to work for real. Much like this morning's episode: life imitating art.

What really mattered was that the risqué ads seemed to strike a chord with the listeners—at least sufficiently to make them think of Digger's name when they needed a hole dug. Business was up almost 50% since the racy ads started running. And the funny thing—or perhaps not so funny—was that a few housewives had actually come on to him.

Business was up so much, in fact, that Digger had been forced to hire a couple new employees. One of those was an apprentice who reminded him in some ways of himself, some twenty-plus years ago. Jack Depp had been permanently saddled with the "Digger" moniker when, at the age of 19, he took an apprentice job of his own with an excavation company. His last name was actually pronounced "Depp," like the actor Johnny, but once he started the excavating work, his friends had decided it should be pronounced "deep."

Looking back, Jack thought that maybe, just maybe, he'd stuck it out initially with the excavation company only because he enjoyed the novelty of having a nickname. But after a bit, he realized that he actually liked the work. There was actually some variety to the tasks and he enjoyed working with the soil, even if in many cases there was a whole lot of metal between his flesh and that soil.

Fifteen years later, the man who ran Kearsley Excavating had retired, and Digger managed to scrape together enough money to buy the business. He quickly changed the firm's name to Digger Deep Construction, seeking to take advantage of all the novelty his nickname had to offer, and had enjoyed a stable if occasionally slow business ever since—until the radio ads had given him more business than he could handle.

Digger turned onto the road leading to the Hyde Point launch. Headlights were visible at the end of the road, backlit by a gray but rapidly-brightening sky. As Digger drew near, an officer he recognized as Pat Murphy walked out to meet him. Digger rolled down his window, letting in morning air that was still crisp but already held an undercurrent of warmth. It was going to be another hot one.

"Hey, Pat. What's going on?"

"Morning, Digger. I'm just supposed to take you out to Frank. He'll give you the details."

"*Out* to Frank? Where is he?"

"Out there," answered the deputy, turning and pointing across the dry lakebed, "at the old town site."

Fifteen minutes later, Digger was still grumbling as he trudged across the cracked moonscape surface.

"I still don't understand why we couldn't drive out here. The bed's dry enough, and obviously Frank drove out here, unless that car I see is just a mirage."

"I told you—he doesn't want any more cars driving out here right now."

'Yeah, but why?"

"Ask him yourself," answered Murphy, pointing at Frank, who was striding out to meet them. Although Frank was taller—more like 6'3" to Digger's 6'1"—and broader—built more like their father than Digger, who tended more towards wiry muscle—the resemblance between the brothers was clear. Both sported unruly brown curls that passed for hair but refused to be tamed; prominent, borderline-chiseled jaw lines with cleft chins; Roman noses that tapered off just short of being unattractively prominent.

"'Bout time you got here," said Frank, by way of greeting.

"I would've been here a long time ago if you hadn't insisted on this boy scout hike."

"I figured you could use the exercise. Noticed you been starting to get a little bit of a gut on you."

"The only thing getting fat around here is your head. All bullshit aside, Frank, what's going on here?"

"I need you to do some digging for me. I wanted you to come out here first to make sure there's no problem bringing a backhoe out, right up to where the edge of the water is now, where it's still pretty swampy."

"I'd figured that much out, or most of it. Tell me the rest."

Frank looked back in the direction of the water, and Digger followed his gaze, taking in the pathetic remains of a drowned town.

Since its founding in 1858, the town of Placerton had slowly taken hold here, along the banks of the Karn River. Over the years, the population had grown and more and more businesses opened their doors, including the likes of a hotel, a barbershop, a general store, and two bars. But in the springtime, floods would often plague the area as snowmelt swelled the river into an angry torrent that escaped its banks and inundated the surrounding, low-lying areas. When the floods became too frequent, and the losses too great, it was decided that a dam was needed to tame the raging river—and the location chosen for the dam meant that, after more than 100 years of life, the town of Placerton would have to die.

Ignoring a virtual flood of complaints and controversy, the federal government bought out everyone and relocated the town five miles to the east, allowing the U. S. Corps of Engineers to build a massive earthen dam across the span of the Karn River and create the Esmeralda Reservoir. With the dam's completion in 1971, Lake Esmeralda soon became the centerpiece of the Karn River Valley, ultimately growing to include nearly forty miles of shoreline.

But now, after seven years of dry skies that had withered hopes and dried up dreams, the water level of Lake Esmeralda had receded so far that the ghost of the former town had emerged from the murky depths. Here and there, the remnants of stone fireplaces reached pitifully for the sky, and a few warped, sagging walls stood stubbornly like ribs of a skeleton. Crumbling cement foundations dotted the landscape like broken teeth; a concrete bridge stood uselessly, connecting nothing and no one; and the passage of water and time had done little to dull the red radiance of the old schoolhouse steps, a stairway to nowhere.

If he'd been asked to picture a ghost town, Digger never would have come up with a desiccated patch of vacancy such as this. But now that it was right in front of him, he couldn't think of a more apt defining image. He'd only been three years old when the town was submerged, and what few memories he had of it were happy, almost dream-like. Looking at it now, he shuddered, for reasons he couldn't name.

"We got a call last night," said Frank, bringing Digger back to the here and now. "A couple kids were out here on bikes to take a look at the old town, said they found a body. Pat here," he glanced at the other cop, "came out, confirmed it, and called me out." Frank started walking in the direction from which he'd come, and motioned for Digger to follow.

"The thing is, it's not exactly a body—all that's left is a skeleton. At first, we figured somebody must have dumped a body in the lake a long time ago. But then we started nosing around, and we found this." He pointed toward a spot a few feet away, turning on his flashlight to highlight the spot, although the beam was barely noticeable in the dawning light. Sizable shards of splintered wood were visible through the mud.

"Is that…a coffin?"

"Yeah. And we've since found pieces of another one. It appears that we're standing in the middle of the old cemetery."

"But…" Digger paused, confusion playing across his features, "they wouldn't have just left all the bodies here when they flooded the town. Would they?"

"Good question. I made a couple calls, woke up a couple folks—besides you, that is—and the answer, supposedly, is no. All the coffins were supposed to be dug up and moved to the new cemetery."

With his right hand, Digger pushed his hair up off his forehead, exposing his widows-peak hairline, and held it there. It was a common pose for him when his brain was working overtime.

"You think somebody, umm, shirked their duty? Figured that nobody would ever know if some bodies didn't get relocated to their new neighborhood?"

"That's my guess. From what I've gathered, the cemetery owners got paid a pretty good sum to do the moving. Could be they just pocketed some of it as pure profit. I'm gonna ask some more questions, do some digging of my own, and I want you to do a little digging out here—see what else, or who else, you can find."

"Gotcha." Digger toed the ground. It gave a bit, sucking in the bottom of his foot, but not much. "Shouldn't be a problem." He walked towards the water. "Not even over—"

"That's far enough," warned Frank. "Just to be safe, I'm treating this as a crime scene until we've got enough daylight to check things out carefully. That's why I didn't want you to drive out here—if there are other vehicle tracks out here besides ours, I want to keep them distinct. If you come back with a 'hoe around noon, we'll be ready for you."

"Guess I better start walking then—it'll take me damned near that long to get back to my car."

2.

Ellen Rankin's feet were killing her already, and she'd only been on shift for a couple hours. Wearing these new shoes without breaking them in first had been a very bad idea. She pushed the breakfast cart toward the last door on the hallway, thankful that this task was almost done. She pushed open the door and saw Colleen was drowsing, as usual, while Agnes sat staring out the window.

"Beautiful morning, isn't it, Agnes?"

The older woman turned from the window. "Yes, it is, Ellen. A beautiful morning, indeed. A brand new day."

Nurse Rankin stopped dead in her tracks, the breakfast tray in her hands listing precariously. Agnes was the elder equivalent of a poster child—for senile dementia; she hadn't said anything remotely sensible in the five years Ellen had worked here.

"Agnes? Are you…feeling all right?"

"Absolutely. I'm back."

"Back? Back from where?"

"I hid. All these years, I just hid. But you know the worst thing?"

"Wh-what?"

The old woman was staring at her, pupils dilated and distilled with a strange gleam.

"I remember."

Ellen had to fight the urge to take a step back, so intense was the woman's expression.

"I remember all of it."

After so long spent huddled in a dark corner of her mental cell, Agnes Woolrich found it invigorating to step out into the sunlight and come alive again. But she stopped short of being happy about her emergence. For with consciousness came memories, and with memories came shame.

At long last, Agnes remembered… and on this day she was not alone in remembering.

3.

"Well, if you fellas happen to see Leon, you be sure and tell him I want to talk to him, all right?"

"Will do, Chief."

"Sure thing, Frank."

Frank Depp nodded and turned to cross the street. Behind him, the two old-timers continued murmuring as he walked away. He couldn't hear exactly what they were saying, yet he felt sure he knew the gist of it.

"You know, Frank has turned out to be a fine young man."

"Yeah, but he's not his father."

"No. But who could be? He was one of a kind."

Ad nauseam.

It was a sentiment that he'd grown used to. When your father was a local hero, it wasn't easy walking in his shadow, let alone his very footsteps, but you either learned to live with it or let it drive you crazy. Frank had finally done the former, but it hadn't been easy.

Ken Depp had been a three-sport star in high school, a stellar student, a war hero, a devoted family man, active in his community, and the chief of police—what wasn't to love about him? And loved he was, as evidenced by the many friends he counted and the endless adulation he received. The hero worship even went so far that he'd been on the receiving end of years' worth of deep discounts, outright gifts, stock tips, and the like—despite his protests—to the point that the Depp household had never wanted for much, and Julia Depp had wound up a pretty well-to-do widow. Even Ken Depp's death two years ago from a heart attack hadn't served to stem the flow of admiration. Frank was surprised that they hadn't yet erected a statue in his father's honor in the town square.

Of course, something as solid and permanent-seeming as a statue might not fit in all that well in Placerton. The town had an unsettling *newness* to it, a complete lack of history and tradition, owing to the fact that it—or more accurately, the current version of it—had only been in existence for thirty-some years. To Frank, the town somehow seemed incomplete and superficial, all tilt-up walls and prefab structures; sort of like a Stepford village. The town's elders liked to say that the new Placerton had no soul, usually just prior to launching into a nostalgic, almost reverential description of the old town.

One of those old-timers was Leon Urban, the cemetery owner, and Frank's search for him so far this morning had proved fruitless. Urban had begun managing the cemetery in the early '60s, after his dad retired, and had apparently overseen the move to the new cemetery—which, not coincidentally, was also located on land owned by his family. Frank wondered just how *that* transaction had gone down, way back then. That particular suspicion was just one of several that Frank was harboring like a yacht club beset by a squall. He thought, for example, that it was likely not an accident that Urban was nowhere to be found at the moment. Word had no doubt traveled quickly in certain circles following Frank's wake-up calls the previous night to Henry Orthlieb, the town's mayor during most of the '60s and '70s, and Carl Eckersley, the long-time head of the water company. If there was anything shady that needed to be kept covered up, chances were the parties involved were laying low and making sure they had all their ducks in a row. Frank realized he was jumping to all sorts of conclusions, but that was the problem with being a cop—you got so used to people lying to you that you got to the point where you didn't trust anybody anymore.

But he'd decided to abandon, for the moment, his search for Urban. Frank was only a couple of minutes from Orthlieb's house, and thought that paying an unannounced follow-up visit to the ex-Mayor was a grand idea.

After three rings of the doorbell and several knocks, Frank had been about to give up on his brilliant Orthlieb-interrogation idea when the door finally opened. He suspected... but there he went again; he needed to keep those lunging suspicions at bay. A housekeeper had led him through the cavernous house, which sat on a bluff overlooking Placerton, with spectacular views across the lake to the west. Orthlieb was lounging in a backyard Adirondack chair, half in the shade, with a cup of coffee and the day's newspaper.

And, so far, he'd proven just as unreceptive to Frank's queries in person as he had the previous night on the phone.

"It's like I told you—that was a very long time ago. I don't recall much about it, mostly because there's not much *to* recall. There were a great deal of logistics involved, but they were all just tedious details, really. There were no under the table deals, as you seem to be insinuating. If there had been, I'd certainly have known about them, because I was in the middle of everything."

"So the cemetery move was by the book, as far as you know?"

"Yes," sighed Orthlieb, not bothering to hide his exasperation. "As I said, the decision was made to move *all* the graves to the new cemetery. There weren't nearly as many graves back then, so it wasn't an enormous undertaking. So to speak."

"And you don't think that Urban decided to maybe pocket some of the proceeds and leave a few coffins behind?"

"No, I can't see Leon doing that. In fact, I was out there one afternoon when he was ... disinterring caskets. I couldn't forget it if I tried—one of the caskets fell to pieces as they were levering it out of the ground. Not a pretty sight.

"Regardless, I *saw* him removing caskets, just as he was supposed to. I guess it's possible that he could've missed one, or even more than one. Not all the graves were well-marked, especially the ones in the potter's field section."

"Potter's field section?"

"Yes, you know—the drifters, the vagrants, with no money of their own for burial. When such a person dies, the city takes the expense of burying them—or at least we did back then; I expect it's the same now. But there wasn't enough money to buy them headstones. I believe the cemetery manager just kept track of their plots in a chart in his office. It could be that one of those vagrants was accidentally... misplaced. So to speak."

"Seems like a convenient excuse."

"Chief... Mr. Depp... Forgive me, but were you even born then? Your father was in charge of this town in those days. I may have been the mayor, but he was the Chief of Police; he ran this place. You think a man such as your father would've stood for anything like what you're suggesting?"

Frank understood the comparison, and implied insult, for what it was.

"No," he said slowly, refusing to rise to the bait. "No, I don't expect he would have."

"You're chasing ghosts, Chief. Things that happened so long ago that there's not even many of us left now to remember it. And nothing illegal about any of it. My advice is to let it go. Just…"

4.

"'…let it all go.'"

"So, pretty much the same thing that Orthlieb told you, huh?"

"Not pretty much—*exactly* the same thing Orthlieb told me. It's like him and Eckersley got together to get their stories straight, but got them a little *too* straight."

"Sounds pretty fishy," said Digger, raising one eyebrow.

"Yeah, it does to me—" Frank's voice faded, as he realized his brother was kidding him. "Look, just because I'm paranoid…"

"…doesn't mean everybody *isn't* out to get you," finished Digger. It was a time-honored exchange.

Digger cracked his knuckles, stretched his neck a little. He was enjoying the late afternoon sunshine and the break from his work, but knew he should get back to it before the light started to fade and see what else he could find. The day's digging had so far yielded two more bodies.

"You want my two cents?" he asked over his shoulder as he started to walk to his backhoe.

"Why not? You're going to give it to me, anyway."

"The potter's field story seems pretty reasonable to me. I haven't found *that* many bodies, and they all seem to be in the northwest corner."

"I know," sighed Frank. "You're probably right. It's just… I'm not ready to close the book and absolve everybody just yet."

"Of course not. If you gave up that easily, Dad would roll over in his grave."

Digger climbed up into the backhoe's cab, yanked the throttle, and fired up the engine before Frank could offer a reply. He swiveled his seat around, swung the bucket back over the edge of the hole with practiced precision, and lowered it in.

He was taking his third bite out of the soil when he saw from the corner of his eye Murphy go running past, heading for Frank. Something about the deputy's urgency, and the expression on his face, made Digger stop what he was doing and watch. He realized the deputy was trying to shout over the din, and cut the engine.

"Say again?" yelled Frank, as the sound spiraled down.

Murphy was half-covered with mud, and a little out of his breath from his run. "Another skeleton," he exhaled. "Over there."

"Another one?," asked Frank. "This goddamned cemetery is leaking people. They must've floated all over the place."

"This one isn't from the cemetery. And it didn't float anywhere."

"How do you know?"

"Come see for yourself—it's in a basement over here."

Curious, Digger climbed down from his cab and followed the two men as they made their way across a debris field of bricks, rotted lumber, and the occasional stump. When they were about a hundred yards from where he'd been working, the deputy slowed and pointed to a rift in the ground.

"It was partly filled in with mud, so I didn't notice anything at first. But then I noticed the sun was glinting off something, so I climbed down there. That's when I uncovered him."

"Uncovered—" started Frank, but stopped when he got close enough to see over the lip of the hole.

There, looking up forlornly at them with empty eye sockets asking where his rescuers had been decades ago, when he needed them, was another skeleton. But this one was chained to a thick, rusting pipe.

5.

"I have to admit—it's one of the stranger things I've seen."

"It just seems so… spontaneous."

"Well, her recovery may have been prompted by some external factor, or it may have just happened, for reasons that we don't yet understand."

Nurse Rankin looked down the hall and through the open door, where Agnes was again gazing out the window, as if seeing the world for the first time.

Rankin lowered her voice further, and asked, "Is it a permanent recovery, do you think, or could she slip back into dementia?"

The doctor shook his head. "It's temporary. People with her condition can sometimes experience periods of lucidity, but the recovery is never permanent."

"Before you got here, I was looking at her file. I knew her condition had never changed during the time I'd been here, but I wanted to see how far back it went. *Sixteen years* she's been here—and displaying Alzheimer symptoms the entire time! And for who knows how long before she got put here? How common can it be for someone to experience this kind of recovery after that long of a time?"

"*Extremely* uncommon—but not unheard of."

"There's a reason, you know." The corner of Nurse Rankin's mouth curled upwards.

"There usually is."

"I mean, a reason why she's been in this condition for so long—and for years before her family even brought her here, from what they say."

"I know, I've heard the rumor. I've heard just about everything in my day, Ellen. I've been consulting here for more than twenty years, you know." As if to emphasize his point, the doctor ran a hand over his shining bald pate. "I was here when Mrs. Woolrich's family checked her in."

"And…?"

"And what? They didn't walk in and announce 'Please take our mother. She's had Alzheimer's since the old town was submerged,' if that's what you mean. I seem to remember that they did say she'd been exhibiting symptoms for quite a while and that she'd finally become too much to handle, but that may just be my imagination filling in the blanks—whatever they said, it should be somewhere in her records. Her family moved away right after they checked her in. They pay her bills, but as far as I know, they never come to visit her."

As if she'd heard them talking about her, Agnes Woolrich suddenly turned and looked directly at the pair in the hallway, then walked over and closed the door to her room.

❊

Agnes felt better as soon as the door swung shut, cutting off the inquisitive stares and conspiratorial whispers from the hallway. She'd spent so long wandering alone inside the confines of her own head that the presence of others seemed like an intrusion, especially when they were so curious, so intent on peeking into her life.

Relief from prying eyes was easily obtained, but peace from her own thoughts was not something Agnes had managed to achieve. It was likely not something that she would ever manage.

She sagged, her descent stopping only when the backs of her thighs met the edge of the bed. A sluggish breeze crawled in through the open window, rustling her stiff gray curls and bringing with it the smell of lilacs, and the odor of something long dead.

As if brought by the breeze, more memories flowed over her. With them came an overwhelming sense of disbelief at what she'd been a party to.

How had she ever been convinced that the end justified the means? Some meaningless materialistic gains in exchange for the casual manipulation of so many lives…and, ultimately, the loss of one life, a life that had once been so very dear to her. Had she been drunk with power, mad with misplaced love? Or was there truly nothing at which to point a finger, no cause or excuse for her behavior? It was a mental exercise with no benefits, mindless aerobics that would shape no goal.

But while torturing herself with recollections might serve no purpose, Agnes herself did possess a purpose. For just as she'd been a pawn in a larger scheme thirty-eight years ago, so now were her actions being directed. She wasn't sure by who, or what, but she didn't bother to question. She knew what she had to do, and that was enough.

Her gaze was again drawn to the window, where the breeze sent a tattered curtain of leaves fluttering to the ground. Nothing escapes the Earth, she thought. In the bottomless depths of its existence, certain things were neglected for a time, but nothing was ever forgotten. In the end, everything was drawn to its bosom, submerged beneath is smothering soil.

She picked up the phone. It hadn't been hard to get his number; it wasn't even unlisted. He'd always enjoyed the spotlight, and cast himself as a man of the people, even as he was stepping on their heads in order to climb over them. The phone buzzed angrily in her ear.

"Hello?"

"Hello, Henry. This is Agnes."

"My God! I'd heard you had some sort of miraculous recovery, but I didn't believe it."

"Word must travel fast."

"It does when you've got your ear to the ground. I still keep track of everything that goes on in this town."

"I'm sure you do, Henry. And I'm sure you still control a fair share of it, too."

"Now that you mention it, I suppose I do."

"I knew that you would. But you don't control me. Not any more."

"What is that supposed to mean?"

"It means that I remember everything that happened. And that there needs to be an accounting."

"Listen to me, you…" Orthlieb paused. She could hear him struggling to maintain his composure. "If you try to go public with this now, everyone is just going to think that you're exactly what you appear to be—a crazy old woman."

"Don't worry, Henry. I'm not talking about 'going public.' I'm talking about making amends."

A wordless sound of derision came from the other end of the line.

"I want you to meet me, tomorrow, at the old town site. About five o'clock."

"You must still be insane. What makes you think I'd do anything of the sort?"

"You'll do it. You'll do it or else I *will* tell everyone what you did."

There was a long moment of silence.

"And if I do come, what happens then? Just what's your plan?"

It's not my *plan*, she started to say, but knew that would only bring more questions. Instead, she simply said, "You'll have to be there to find out; to keep your secrets secret. Oh, and Henry…? I want you to bring the others with you."

"Bring the others? I can't do that! You have no idea what…"

"Just bring them," she interrupted, and hung up before he could reply. It felt good to turn the tables on him. She sat back, satisfied. Now there was nothing to do but wait for events to play themselves out.

She looked out upon a town she didn't recognize. It was a hollow place, built on lies and deception. The real town lay miles from here, fallow and abandoned. And waiting.

6.

Digger had just cracked his second beer and was walking across his brother's back lawn, deep in thought but idly enjoying the feel of the grass between his toes, when the sprinkler heads suddenly popped up and started spitting in the late afternoon heat. Digger was caught in their midst and swore at the unexpected surprise, even though, he had to admit a moment later, it actually felt pretty good. He looked back toward the house, expecting to see a grinning Frank, hand poised over the sprinkler control, but instead he saw his brother, sister-in-law Mindy, and wife Christie, engaged in conversation around the barbecue grill. The kids had gone next door to a friend's house to hurl themselves into a swimming pool until the food was ready.

Digger walked over to join the gathering around the grill, paralleling the arc of a miniature rainbow over the lawn. But like the skies themselves had proven to be so many times in the last few years, the rainbow was all flash and no substance—as Digger reached the end of the rainbow, it simply faded away, taking its pot of gold with it.

"You ever heard of water conservation, Frank?"

"What?" He looked up from his task of idly poking the meat on the grill. "Oh, the sprinklers…"

"If you're using them at all—which you probably shouldn't be— it should be early in the morning or late at night, so that—"

"I know. Get off your high horse, would you? Our power went out last week, when they were working on the lines. Screwed up the sprinkler timer."

"Those things have battery back-ups, you know."

"I can barely keep fresh batteries in my smoke alarms. You think I'm going to be right on top of my sprinkler system?" He flipped a steak, as if to underscore his point.

"Here they go again," said Christie. "I knew we couldn't have peace for long." There was a jovial tone in her voice, but she exchanged a knowing look with Digger as she said it. He shrugged his shoulders and took another swig of his beer.

"Let's get the rest of the food," said Mindy, nodding to Christie. "Hope you guys are hungry," she called as they walked inside, "I've got corn on the cob and baked potatoes, besides all that meat."

Digger figured it was no coincidence that Mindy had chosen this moment to pipe up about the food—both she and Christie tired quickly of the two brothers' jibes, good-natured though they usually were. Digger didn't always care for his brother's wife—she was a little too manipulative for his tastes—but she'd clearly been good for Frank. Since they'd married, he'd quit carousing and settled down, gotten involved with Lion's Club, won a couple commendations, and wound up receiving the appointment to Chief of Police a little over a year ago. It was too bad that their father hadn't lived to see it, but Frank had turned out to be a real success story; deserving of congratulations.

"Cheers, Frank. Congrats."

His brother's eyes narrowed. "For what?"

"For this," Digger replied, gesturing expansively. "For everything. Just drink a toast with me."

After another moment's hesitation, their bottles clinked and Digger tilted his head back. The beer tasted good, but it was already losing its chill.

"You hear anything from Sharon?"

Frank snorted. "Not since my birthday. That's about all she can muster these days—a couple cards a year on holidays, and a couple phone calls on birthdays. No, when she left, she left for good, that's for sure."

"You shouldn't take it personally. Brad got an offer he couldn't refuse from his company. What were they supposed to do, just ignore that?"

"She was looking for a way out of here before that. You know she was."

"Maybe. But that's her right. It's hard to live with a legacy—you, of all people, should know that. How many times a day does somebody bring up Dad to you? Christ, sometimes I think he should get his own saint named after him. There's a lot of past here for us to want to get away from. I can't say I'm surprised that Sharon left. Can't say that I blame her, either."

Frank's lips were pursed tight enough to become a single white line across his face. He looked like he wanted to spit. "Why are you always so hard on Dad? Sharon's the same way, always talking like he's this huge burden hanging over us. Most people I know would've loved to have had a dad like him. If it's so hard for you to live with his memory, why don't *you* just leave?"

"There you go again, taking it personally. This is my home, and I'm not leaving it. But that doesn't mean I have to be in love with it every single day."

In response, Frank looked away and drained the last of his beer. He turned and threw the empty bottle at a trashcan sitting behind the garage. The bottle sailed in clearly, a perfect toss. It shattered inside, the sound jagged against the quiet suburban afternoon.

Digger reached down and fished a fresh beer from the sweating ice chest. Frank accepted the bottle with a nod, which was usually as close as he came to an apology. But then he surprised Digger by saying, "Sorry. Guess I'm a little tense right now. Lot of stuff going on." He paused. "Guess you heard about the goddamned *gang* fight we had?"

"I heard, but I couldn't believe it. Since when have we had gangs around here?"

"Since now, I guess. The kids we brought in wouldn't say much, but I think they just got together in the last few months. Probably looked cool to them from the movies. And, of course, they have to be *rival* gangs. So much for our peaceful small town."

"I heard a second kid might die."

"It looks like he'll pull through. But besides that gang thing, we've had two bar stabbings in the last week and more fights and domestic disputes than we normally get in a whole summer. It's like this whole damned town's on edge."

Digger started to make a crack about job security, but thought better of it.

"And then there's the 'old town mystery,'" added Frank.

"Any idea yet who that poor guy in the cellar was?"

"No, it'll take weeks to get the forensic results back. And the police files from back then, including the missing persons reports, are in boxes in storage. I sent Grunwald over there to take a look, and he called me up, practically begged me to not make him go through them. They're a mess."

"What'd you tell him?"

"What could I tell him? We've got what looks and smells like a forty-year-old homicide on our hands and we've got to start by figuring out who the deceased is. I told him to roll up his sleeves and dig in."

"Speaking of which, are you sure you really need me back out at the lake tomorrow? I've got a sewer job needs to get done, and I'd rather do that myself. I could send Robinson down to the lake to dig for you while I get started on—"

"No, sorry. I want you at the lake. In case we find anything else, I don't want word all over town that same night."

Digger felt a sudden breeze, cooling the sweat trickling down his neck and back. It felt wonderful. He knew there was likely no escaping another day at the lake, but didn't want to give up just yet. "You really think you're going to find anything else? Your guys have sifted through every inch of mud in that cellar. And you admitted that the Potter's field story seemed to check out after all, in regards to the other bodies."

"No, I don't think we're going to find anything else. I said 'just in case,' didn't I? But we can't quit yet—I have to be as sure as I can be that we're not missing something. Or someone."

Digger felt his hair lifted from his forehead. The breeze had become a wind. He looked up and saw the eastern sky rapidly darkening. He turned back to his brother.

"All right, fine. Lord knows what kind of trouble Robinson'll get into if I let him do the sewer line on his own, but I guess that's how it's gotta be."

"Thanks. I need somebody I can trust, and you're it."

Digger nodded. "So, that's it, then—nothing else new on the old town case…?"

"Not really. We figured out that the cellar used to be under the old Water Department building. I talked to Eckersley, the guy who was running it back then, but he says he doesn't have any idea who the dead guy could be. Why am I not surprised at his answer?"

Thunder suddenly rumbled through, punctuating Frank's remark. As shadows of clouds fell across their faces, he seemed to notice the changing sky for the first time.

"Man, look at those clouds. If I didn't know better, I'd say it was actually going to rain…"

7.

The sky was the Prince of Lies, the boy who cried wolf, and a shameless tease, all rolled into one. If there were any hopes left to wring out of the locals, the current crop of clouds would surely do so. Tufts like off-white cotton candy fled to the east, chased by roiling billows of dark gray and black. To the casual observer, it would seem that a storm must be in the offing. But to valley veterans, it wasn't worth getting one's hopes up.

Agnes was only vaguely aware of the drought that had spent the last seven years slowly squeezing the life out of the surrounding area.

She dimly recalled hearing snatches of conversation about the subject during her stay in the convalescent home, and she understood that the condition must be severe, or else she wouldn't be standing where she was—in the middle of a town that had laid at the bottom of a lake for nearly forty years. But that was the extent of it. To her, the drought was merely a piece of the puzzle, part of a bigger picture she couldn't, and didn't need to, comprehend.

Once the drought was in place, the town could be uncovered. Once the town was uncovered, she could wake from her long sleep. Once she'd awakened, she could bring all the players in this sordid drama back to the scene of their crimes. Once they were all there… well, she didn't know what happened next. It wasn't up to her. She merely had her part to play. Besides, she would find out soon enough.

She could see a vehicle driving toward her across the dry lake-bed, kicking up a trail of dust in its wake. She'd almost started to wonder if they were going to show, but somehow she knew they would. Orthlieb had too much to lose, and he was too eager to reassert control.

It was a late Sunday afternoon, early evening really, and Agnes had been out at the old town for nearly two hours now, making the long, halting walk out after taking a taxi to the former shoreline. She'd taken her time to explore, knees and hips complaining as she hunched beneath the police "crime scene" tape strung haphazardly between hastily-erected stakes, dried mud clinging to her shoes as she wandered about. There were several large mounds of dirt from a series of holes that had been dug. The holes lay patiently, like graves waiting to be filled.

For Agnes, each step brought with it another memory—here, the spot where she'd fallen from her bike as a child, garnering gravel burns that wouldn't fade for years; over there, a lane where she'd strolled with her first boyfriend; a little further on, the bench where she'd collapsed in relief upon hearing that her brother was coming home from the war, safe and sound. There were other, far less pleasant memories as well, but she forced those aside.

When she saw the police tape, she knew they'd found Andrew, but she had to go look, anyway. The old water company cellar was just a mute hole in the ground now, scoured down to its foundation by searchers, the yawning space broken only by a few rusted pipes.

Those pipes...

The events of nearly forty years ago were as clear in her mind as if they'd happened yesterday. She'd turned away then, hoping the past could not yank free its chains from their moorings and come clanking, shambling after her. At least not yet.

Thunder rumbled again, rolling across the cracked lakebed; thunder, and something more, something deeper, a deep-throated growl that seemed to emanate from the earth itself. Agnes felt a first, tentative drop of rain. More followed, caressing soil that had lain untouched for too long.

She watched the vehicle, a Mercedes of some sort, draw close and come to a stop before her. She watched as the door opened, waiting for familiar faces, but only Orthlieb emerged. He gazed back at her with a combination of anger and curiosity.

"Where are the others?" she demanded.

"I tried to tell you, but you wouldn't let me—Gavin moved away a long time ago; Carl refused to come." said Orthlieb, holding up a hand to stop her protests. "And Ken is dead."

Agnes knew she shouldn't be surprised—after all, they were all so old now—and yet she was. She felt her mouth hanging open, but no words came to fill the void.

"I don't know why I agreed to this, Agnes, but here I am. So what now? Do you harangue me for my sins? Lead a prayer for forgiveness? Try to blackmail me? What?"

"Doesn't it bother you?" she asked, ignoring his questions. "Doesn't it keep you awake at night? My God, you killed a man. Chained him up and left him there to drown. You killed..." She found herself fighting tears, even now, after all this time.

"What bothers you the most, Agnes? What I did? Or that it was your own brother who threatened to betray us? Or that you stood by and did nothing when he died? Or that you let it all happen because you stupidly fell in love with a married man who turned his back on you once you were no longer useful?"

"Shut up! God, you're even more of a heartless bastard now."

Orthlieb chuckled. "I could care less what you think of me. The only thing I care about is making sure that you don't start causing trouble after all these years." He was wearing a voluminous short-sleeved shirt, hanging un-tucked over his slacks. He reached beneath the shirt now, and his hand seemed to settle on something tucked in his waistband.

8.

Lightning forked above Frank Depp's house, and the sky's resistance suddenly faded, hesitant sprinkles turning to fat drops. The backyard group started grabbing items and moving inside before it got too wet.

Digger and Frank scurried back out to grab the last of the food but then just stood there, faces upturned to the sky. Digger started laughing, and Frank joined in; Digger danced around in a little circle, and Frank whooped. Finally, when they'd had their fill, they ducked back inside.

"Do you believe it?" asked Frank. "Do you believe it?"

"Un-fucking-believable," grinned Digger.

"Look at you two, acting like a couple of ten-year-olds," laughed Mindy.

"I'm going to get the kids from next door," said Christie. "They probably think it's fun to play in a swimming pool during a lightning storm."

"Do you think it's finally broken?" asked Digger.

"Don't even say that," said Frank. "You'll jinx us."

"Okay, then. Think it's gonna last long?"

"Judging by the sky, I'd say so." Through the window, a cape of gray and black hues surged overhead.

"Weird—there wasn't anything in the forecast about rain."

"Weather forecasters didn't know a damned thing back when it actually used to rain," said Frank. "Why should they know anything now?"

"You've got a point there. Man, just look at it." The rain was pelting down harder now, appearing to rebound well back up into the air after striking the wooden deck outside Frank's back door.

"Shit, I just realized—if this keeps up..." Digger's voice trailed off.

"What?"

"I need to get out to the lake, get my 'hoe out of there. I left it where I was working last, right down by the waterline. It was pretty mucky there already. With this coming down, it's gonna turn into a friggin' bog."

"You and Christie walked over here, didn't you? Do you need a ride?"

"Yeah, if you could run me back to my house to get my car, that'd be great."

"Oh, the hell with that. I'll just take you out to the lake. We can take the Jeep. That way we can drive all the way out with no worries."

By the time they reached the lake's edge, it was raining hard enough that the wipers were having a hard time keeping up.

"Look at this. Man, I hope it rains for a week."

"Let me get my 'hoe out first, then it can rain for a week."

"You should be OK. We're almost there and we're not sinking in at all. I don't—*what the hell?*"

Frank was leaning forward in his seat, eyes narrowed, straining to see through the downpour. Digger followed his gaze, and saw a vehicle parked ahead.

"Kids, you figure?" began Digger, but then he saw the make of the vehicle. Then he saw the figures pressed between sheets of rain.

Digger struggled to form another question, but before he could bring it to his lips, Frank had opened the door and stepped out. "Should've brought an umbrella," Digger said to himself as he followed.

"What the hell are you doing out here?" Frank's voice rose above the wind and wetness. "This is a crime scene. Can't you see—" he stopped, mid-sentence and mid-stride, when he was close enough to see who he was addressing. "Christ, Henry, what are you doing out here? And who are you?" he asked, looking at a diminutive, gray-haired woman.

"Just a little reunion," answered Orthlieb. "A couple of us who remember what the old town was like."

"In the pouring rain? You'll have to do better than that."

Digger stepped closer, straining to hear over the rain's percussion. His feet sank in the growing mire but he didn't notice, absorbed as he was by the unlikely scene before him.

"Are you Ken Depp's son?" This from the woman.

Frank seemed perturbed by the question, although Digger wasn't sure if it was because it was such an out-of-the-blue non-sequitur, or because he couldn't escape his heritage even with a complete stranger.

"Yes," he said finally. "And you are…?"

The woman took a step forward. "My name is Agnes Woolrich. I knew your father very well."

Digger recognized the surname. He knew the Woolrich family had once been major land barons here in Karn County, but he hadn't heard the name in years. The notion that they'd sold out and moved away seemed vaguely familiar.

"We're here," she continued, "to right a wrong that occurred thirty-eight years ago. You see, none of this"—she looked around her, drops of water slewing from her face and hair— "had to happen. There were better places for a dam, more logical places, more economical. But a few influential people, including the two of us, got together and realized we had a way to make even more money than we already had. We bribed a few people, got our way, and made our new fortunes."

"You'll have to excuse her," said Orthlieb. "She's been institutionalized for several years now. I suspect she's here without her doctor's permission, or knowledge."

Agnes Woolrich laughed, but it was a short, unpleasant sound, without a hint of mirth. "Quick thinking, Henry. Well done. But you have much more to worry about than me telling the police you're a murderer."

"All right, I've heard enough," said Frank. "We're all going back to the station and talk about this some more. A lot more."

Night had crept up so that the only real illumination came from the jeep's headlights, and from the lightning strikes, which came every few seconds now, followed closely by thunder strumming low on its backside. But there was enough light for Digger to see that Orthlieb's face was twisted like a wadded-up rag, with a grimace mean enough to kill sitting dead-center.

"I'm afraid not," he said, reaching beneath his shirt. When he pulled his hand back out, he was holding a revolver. "I'm sorry you and your friend have stumbled into this, Frank. You were always a likeable enough buffoon." He moved the gun back and forth between the brothers. "But your timing couldn't be worse."

Digger's heart went from 0 to 60 in a blink. A minute ago, he was about to drive a tractor a short distance and then head back to a warm, dry house. Now…

His ears were prepared to hear the loud crack of a gunshot. Instead, there came a massive, churning rumble, like a gigantic subwoofer, that seemed to spread from his feet up through the top of his head. A moment later, the ground heaved, knocking Digger and the others off their feet.

When Digger looked up, Orthlieb still had the gun, but he was on all fours, both hands thrown out before him, fighting for balance as the ground continued to lurch. As Digger watched, the lakebed suddenly seemed to *liquefy* beneath Orthlieb.

His hands and feet disappeared beneath the surface, the gun going with them. Mud seemed to crawl up his body as he sank.

Alongside him, the Woolrich woman was sinking as well. Digger and Frank seemed to be on solid ground, at least for the moment.

They'd all been stunned into silence by the sudden events, but now senses returned.

"Christ!"

"What the hell?"

"Somebody help me!"

Only Agnes remains quiet. She seems oddly calm as the mud wraps her in its cold embrace.

"Help me, dammit! It's like quicksand!" Panic creeps into Orthlieb's voice, overtaking fear.

The shaking subsides slightly. Frank struggles to his feet and takes a halting step. A few feet behind him, Digger rises unsteadily.

"No!" It's Agnes, finally speaking. "Stay back, or it will take you, too!"

Ignoring her, Frank staggers forward.

Digger watches, not moving, stunned.

Orthlieb is whimpering, swearing, up to his armpits. Sinking faster.

Frank takes another step.

"No!" she cries again. "It will take you in place of your father."

Frank stops suddenly, as if struck. "What?" he shouts. "What do you mean?"

"Just walk away," says Agnes, calmer now that Frank has stopped moving. "Leave us; it's what we deserve." Mud licks beneath her chin.

Frank breaks from his paralysis, leans forward, arm extended. But then the earth lurches again violently, purposefully, throwing him backwards.

Orthlieb is screaming now, thrashing helplessly.

"Your father was a good man," says Agnes, while her mouth is still uncovered. "Remember that."

Digger moves at last. He reaches out, wraps his arms around his brother, holding him back from any last-second heroics.

Agnes's eyes are serene as they slip below the surface.

Orthlieb's screams bubble through the mud, his hands reaching up desperately as he sinks.

Digger holds his brother tightly as Orthlieb's straining fingertips slip hopelessly beneath the mire. Frank's struggles to pull free slowly cease but he continues to shake violently in his brother's arms.

Around them, the lakebed grows darker.

And the rain comes down.

And the earth rolls on.

That Long Black Train

Travis Heermann

"You no ride this one," the nasal voice said, thick with a Vietnamese accent.

The December air was chilly but Sean hadn't noticed it, even in his thin batik shirt, until the sound of that voice. A shape emerged from the shadows along the crumbling train platform. A short, lumpy man with a pencil-thin mustache, wearing the ubiquitous olive-green uniform and red-banded wheel cap with the yellow star above the bill. Vietnam People's Army. The man's uniform had pips on the collar like an officer, and he wore a sidearm.

The train ground to a halt a few feet away, its massive diesel engine growling, rumbling.

Sean scratched his head in a moment of panic. Was this the wrong train? He and Phil glanced at each other.

Phil turned toward the officer and pointed at the train. "Night train to Nha Trang?"

"Yes. You no ride this one."

"We have tickets." Phil pulled out his ticket and showed it to the officer, but the man didn't appear to be interested. His gaze was fixed on Sean.

Sean looked around. Two more shadows lurked near the area from which this man had emerged. A spot of cigarette orange flared against a dark silhouette.

The dim yellow lights of the platform made dull yellow circles on the glossy black cars. The same tone of dull yellow seeped through the closed blinds from inside the cars.

Back toward the ticket office, dozens of other passengers shambled, dispersed along the platform, looking for their assigned car numbers, climbing the steps through the passenger doors. Most of the Vietnamese were going home to the countryside for the Tet holiday, getting out of Ho Chi Minh City to visit their families. But even thirty-five years after the Communists took over, the locals still called it Saigon. In the chilly air, they wore long coats and scarves, compared to Phil's and Sean's short-sleeve shirts and shorts.

The rest of the passengers were foreigners, wearing dreadlocks, beads in their hair, scruffy beards, no bras, lean and carefree as they lugged their massive backpacks. Europeans, Aussies, Israelis, all on a cheap vacation to exotic Southeast Asia. Just like Sean and Phil.

Phil was almost a foot shorter than Sean. He was Filipino by heritage, but he had a generic Asian ethnicity, leading him to be mistaken for Chinese, Vietnamese, Thai, even Japanese. His hair was shaved close to his head. He had the upper body of a heavy-weight boxer and the lower torso of a dedicated beer drinker. By contrast, Sean stood six-foot-three with a stiff brush of red hair and broad, linebacker's shoulders.

The officer looked at Phil. "You no go. He go, OK."

Sean looked at his friend again and felt his insides clench. He did *not* want a run-in with the notoriously corrupt Vietnamese authorities. How many times in the last week had he felt that twinge of nervousness? The feeling of being off the beaten path in a country where anything goes. Until Phil had talked him into this trip, Vietnam had just been a vague painful notion that nevertheless had cast a pall over his entire life. It had made his father into a difficult man, all but ruined him. Vietnam and everything about it was best left at arm's length, just like his dad. That is, until Angie had dumped him, and Phil had called him up and said, "Let's takes a trip to Southeast Asia!" He had been so enthusiastic. "C'mon! I need to get out of this one horse town for a while. We'll meet some girls and tear a swath through every bar that crosses our path! You can forget about that cheatin' ho-bag for a while. Whaddaya say?"

He had to admit, his friend had been very persuasive.

But now, four days into their trip...

Those men in uniform were just the right age to be former NVA or Viet Cong. The same people who had driven the U.S. Army in disarray from their shores. The same nervousness had twinged inside his gut at several points during their trip. At the gleefully propagandistic War Museum, and the graphic photos of "atrocities" committed by "the American aggressors" and the French-made guillotine so proudly displayed, said to have been used only by the "evil South Vietnamese government." And the next day the grim and sullen Cu Chi Tunnel System sixty kilometers west of Saigon, nestled in jungle and rubber plantations that looked as if Agent Orange had never existed. The ingenious subterranean mazes where American G.I. "tunnel rats" had met booby traps and ambush. Now it was a tourist attraction. The prominent displays of booby traps and animatronic Viet Cong freedom fighters. The burned-out shell of an M-48 tank near one of the entrances where it had rotted like a steel corpse for 35 years. And the real U.S. Army issue .50-caliber machine gun that tourists could fire for a mere twenty dollars. The history had pressed down on both of them, made this trip more than just the hedonistic free-for-all that Phil had intended.

Sean stepped forward and pointed at Phil. "My friend. We go together."

The officer gave them one last long look, then shrugged and walked back to the other men standing in the shadows.

They shrugged at each other to try to dispel their mutual discomfort and boarded the train.

The sleeper compartment that matched their ticket number was a dark, four-bed cracker box, two on each side, with frayed, naked mattresses that looked like they were new when the train was built, in about 1974. Sean and Phil took the top bunks.

The small reading light at the head of Sean's bunk helped dispel the gloom. Passengers shambled past the bright doorway, dragging luggage behind them.

It had been a long, challenging evening to make sure they reached the station on time. Neither of them spoke a syllable of Vietnamese, even though Phil made a hilarious imitation. The bar girls had loved it.

They stretched out in their bunks, arranging bags and blankets. Phil pulled out one of the baguette sandwiches they had bought from a street vendor for thirty cents apiece. "So how long was your dad in Nha Trang?"

Sean took out his own baguette and unwrapped it. "His whole tour. A year." The baguette he had eaten yesterday had been fantastic. At least the French had left something worthwhile behind.

"He saw some heavy shit there, eh?"

"It messed him up. Mom said he was kind of gun crazy when he came home. Figured the Russians or the Chinese would invade or something, so we always had a bunch of guns in the house."

"How does he feel about you going to Vietnam?"

"I think he wants to know what it's like now. He really wants pictures of Nha Trang."

"Is that why you came on this trip? Or is it to take your mind off the ex?"

Sean nodded and lied. "For Dad. Maybe we'll have something to talk about now. Angie can go fuck herself." Six years. And for three of it, she had been fucking her yoga instructor.

"That's the spirit!"

He took a big bite of his sandwich, chewed a little, and then the scent of rancid meat smashed him in the nose. He spewed the rotten paste in his mouth onto the wrapping paper. "Fucking hell!"

"Something wrong?"

"It's rotten!" The processed luncheon meat that gave the sandwiches their particular flair stank like a carcass left in the sun for three days, and as he opened the bun, he saw that the meat had a sickly greenish cast. His stomach heaved.

Phil continued munching his. "That sucks, man. Mine's good."

"Are you sure? We were standing right there when the old lady made them both." He grabbed his bottle of water, climbed down, and headed for the bathroom. Passengers clogged the hallway, sifting into their respective berths.

The bathroom was a corrugated stainless steel cell with a six-inch hole in the floor that opened onto the tracks.

He did his best to wash the rancid taste out of his mouth with the bottled water, rinsing and spitting into the tiny steel sink.

Then the whistle blew a long, wavering squeal, and the cell lurched. Through the hole in the floor, he could see the ground beginning to move. Through the small, grimy window, the station platform began to slide.

The whistle squealed again, a strangled, ululating sound, like someone throttling a rabbit. Something rumbled in his belly that was not hunger and was not the lingering taste of putrid meat.

"Toss that sandwich in the garbage, man. It reeks," Phil said.

He was right. The compartment stank of rotten meat, so Sean bundled the sandwich back up into its paper and took it out to toss it into the garbage bin.

As he turned, he found himself belly-to-face with a short Vietnamese woman. Her eyes were milky and half-lidded; her pink, toothless mouth hung slack and open. She stopped one step away from him. Her gray hair was shot with streaks of white, and her skin looked like a desiccated mango. She did not look up at him, just stopped as if she had dimly perceived some sort of obstacle in her path but did not care to examine it. She lifted her nose to sniff the air. He stepped aside, and she moved on without acknowledgement.

By the time he returned to his compartment, the disembodied lights of Saigon were picking up speed outside the window. Haloed globes of halogen white suspended in ink moved across the filmy glass like headlights coming sideways on a dark night.

Phil thumbed through his copy of *Lonely Planet: South East Asia.* "Looks like a couple of good hotels in Nha Trang."

Sean lay back on his bunk wondering what to do about his returning hunger. He felt like something in his chest was vibrating, defibrillating, and it would not let him relax. Finally, he said, "I'm going to go find the dining car, get something to eat."

"Sounds good, man. I'll come with. Maybe we'll meet some of those smoking hot European girls."

After threading their way through three sleeping cars identical to theirs, they came to a different kind of coach, dark and dingy, with quiet people squeezed into ancient cast-iron seats. Furtive eyes flicked their gazes at the pair. They picked their way around boxes, luggage, and haphazardly sprawling legs, down the center aisle between rows of seats. Phil said, "Jesus, man. Who chose the upholstery on this train?"

An old man slept soundly on a seat made of worn vinyl the color of flesh. The vinyl looked deep and soft, like a fat woman's belly.

The clenching unease in Sean's belly returned, stronger. He caught a strange scent on the air, like a tangle of sweat and smoke and…

They found the dining car a couple more coaches forward. As they neared it, the smells of hot steaming noodle broth and warm beer drifted back on waves of rockabilly music. An Elvis song, one of his early ones that Sean had heard many times, but could not name.

"Looks like we're missing the party," he said.

"And me without my condoms." Phil's sarcasm could peel paint at times.

The foreign passengers they had seen earlier looked to be all here. Tables were filled with bottles of Tiger beer, empty noodle bowls, and half-eaten spring rolls. A man and woman were dancing, their bodies grinding at the hips, tank-tops and shorts clinging to their sweaty flesh. His hand was down inside the back of her shorts, cupping one of her buttocks, and her eyes were half-closed and dreamy. The air in here was hot and steamy, like the Mekong delta in high summer. The other partiers watched the couple with hungry, rapt expressions, as if waiting for the man to throw her up on a table and bang her right there.

Behind the counter was a tall cook with a big grin on his face and an array of steaming pots behind him. A half-drunk policeman slouched on a stool, leaning against the wall, clutching his beer and enjoying the spectacle with piss-colored eyes.

The cook's plastic smile did not change as Sean ordered two beers and a bowl of *pho*. The cook ladled out noodles and handed out beers with his lips and teeth in exactly the same position, as if they were glued in place.

Phil squinted, mimicked his expression, and said, "Sank you velly mush."

They sat down near the door, keeping an eye on the other foreigners. The music pulsed from an old, worn boom box on a corner table. Suddenly the music stopped as the cassette player kicked itself off at the end of the tape. The sudden silence roared, and the partiers filled it with a surge of cacophonous conversation. Sean did not speak any of those languages. The two dancers continued their sensuous movements as if listening to hot, juicy, throbbing music only they could hear. Then someone flipped the tape over, and the music resumed with "Surfin' USA."

Sean and Phil looked at each other.

"Wacky Europeans," Phil said.

"Yes, we are quite 'wacky,' aren't we," a man's voice said behind him, with a heavy French accent and an undecipherable tone. "Some of us more than others."

Sean looked over his shoulder at the man behind him. The man's nose was enormous, like a hatchet buried in the front of his narrow, aquiline face. His eyes were a pale slate-gray, and his hair had thinned almost to nonexistence on his dark, weathered skull. He wore a fashionable sport coat and trousers with a light gray T-shirt, Italian leather shoes. His golden watch gleamed in the ruddy light.

He sat down at a table across the aisle, about five feet from the drunken policeman, keeping his gaze fixed on them. "Americans?"

Phil pointed. "He is. I'm Canadian."

"*Parlez-vous français?*" the man said.

"*Je parle français comme une vache espagnole,*" Phil said.

The man's mouth twitched almost into a smile. Sean thought that mouth had not seen a smile in quite some time. His teeth were like an ill-kept picket fence painted tobacco-stain yellow. The man reeled off more French. Phil squinted, listening, as if he was trying to decide if he had heard correctly. The Frenchman's tone wormed under Sean's skin.

The Frenchman put his feet up on a chair, and his gaze flicked back and forth between them as he lit up a slender brown cigarette.

"What did you say to him?" Sean said to Phil.

"I said, 'I speak French like a Spanish cow.'"

A nimbus of blue smoke surrounded the Frenchman's head. Finally Sean tried to be friendly. "You going to Nha Trang?"

The Frenchman nodded slowly, a mere tipping of the head.

"Business or pleasure?"

"My business, heh." His monosyllabic laugh held no mirth. "My business is pleasure. I do have business in Nha Trang, and from there over the border into Cambodia."

"Cambodia, eh? You been to Angkor Wat?" Inside, Sean kicked himself. Could he sound *more* like an ignorant tourist? Well, even though he *was*, he didn't want to *sound* like one.

The mirthless smirk on the man's lips did not change as he nodded. "Of course."

"So," Phil said, "what's the most 'pleasurable' country?"

The Frenchman tapped his cigarette. "Cambodia is a wonderful country. Vietnamese authorities are so uptight, you know? In Vietnam, one can deal only with the police and the military. In Cambodia, there is the police, the military, and the mob. The third option makes my business easier." The Frenchman's dead gray eyes looked past them, toward something within his mind.

Phil and Sean glanced at each other, then at the Vietnamese cop sitting five feet from him.

The Frenchman saw their glances, and that smirk crossed his lips again. "South-east Asia is delightfully corrupt. But the Communists can be... shall we say, touchy." Then his gaze suddenly fixed on Sean, pierced him, and Sean felt like a naked kid at the public swimming pool. "You boys like Asian girls, yes?"

Boys? Both Sean and Phil were thirty.

Phil smiled. "Yeah, Vietnamese girls are hot, man. Curvy, gorgeous."

Sean's mind hearkened back to the night before. Ngao had been like a tall, slim goddess. The first girl he had touched since Angie. So lovely, with such pretty eyes, and an ass that could have sold a million jeans. This morning he had woken up with her scent still thick in his nose; jasmine, coconut, and spices. He imagined American G.I.s going crazy for girls like that. And Phil had had two of them fawning and giggling, one on each knee. A twinge of guilt shot through him that the night had ended so badly.

The Frenchman said, "Did you fuck them?"

"Nah, man," Phil said, "They were hookers. No fuckee fuckee no hookers."

Sean's gaze flicked away.

Another presence loomed behind him, and the hairs on the nape of his neck stood up. Over his shoulder he saw an enormous Caucasian man with a thick, red braid that twined from the back of his head halfway down his chest. His sleeveless shirt revealed barb-wire tattoos encircling his corded biceps. Another tattoo looked like a military insignia. "*Légion étrangère.*" Strange symbols tattooed the callused knuckles on his enormous hands. His face was broad and blunt and looked like it had been smashed flat with a two-by-four. He moved with a precise, purposeful propulsion. The image of an ancient Scots warrior with an axe in his hand flashed in Sean's mind.

The warrior passed them as if they did not exist, then leaned down and whispered in the Frenchman's ear.

The Frenchman got up with a single fluid motion, stubbed out his cigarette. "Excuse me, gentlemen. Business calls. Enjoy your trip." They departed together without another word.

"Jesus Christ," Sean said, "Creepy."

"Scary fucking Europeans, man. You get a load of Braveheart there? French Foreign Legion."

"Yeah." Sean laughed a little too loudly. Was this how sheep felt when they sensed a wolf nearby? He slurped down the rest of his noodles, which had almost grown cold, while Phil turned his attention to the other foreigners across the car.

They all erupted into a rousing chorus of James Brown, "I Feel Good." The two dancers were now seated on a stool, with the woman straddling the man's leg, their hungry lips devouring one another's faces.

Sean looked at one of the girls, caught her eye, and gave her a smile. Her blonde hair was tied into a loose ponytail, wisps of hair grazing her cheeks, with big wide-set eyes and broad cheekbones. She smiled back.

"We're in, dude," Sean said.

"Gosh, you work fast. How ever can I keep up? You got your condoms?"

"Condoms shmondoms."

"Not a good attitude in the Third World, my friend. All those girls last night were triple baggers."

"Not mine. She was as pure as the driven snow."

"Yeah, whatever."

"No, man, I'm serious."

"What happened with her anyway? Where'd you go?"

"Hotel."

Phil's eyes bulged. "I didn't know you fucked her! I thought you were just going to make out or something."

"The wacky European girls are waiting. Come on."

Phil's humor and natural charisma kept everyone entertained, but the girls' eyes were on Sean's tall, athletic build. The girls were Israeli, and spoke perfect English.

The blond girl, Sarah, had moved to sit beside him, edging closer, until he could feel the heat of her breasts on his arm. He should have been interested, but that strange feeling in his belly was getting worse. And somehow he could not get the sickly taste of the sandwich completely out of his mouth. He drank beer, swished it around inside his mouth, but to no avail. That sandwich. Just what he needed was a case of food poisoning in a B.Y.O.T.P. country with squat toilets.

He excused himself and went to the bathroom. The lavatory in the dining car was the victim of numerous drunken attempts at pissing whilst riding in a moving train. The floor was slick and sticky with urine, and the smell hung heavy in the warm, moist air. Scraps of toilet paper clung like diaphanous ghosts to the moist steel floor. He looked down through the hole in the floor, just able to see the tracks moving below in the darkness. He wasn't drunk, but squatting and maneuvering himself above the hole was a challenge in the best of conditions. Suddenly his bowels released a torrent of watery excrement. The train lurched, and warmth splashed his naked ankles.

"*Motherf—!*"

The expletive died on his lips as he looked down between his legs. His ankles, sandals, and the area around the hole were splattered with bright red blood and small chunks of semi-solid, meaty-looking matter.

"Oh. My. God."

Another abdominal spasm expelled another deluge of hot gore. He groaned, and his hands clenched the steel support handle on the wall. God, it hurt. It *hurt*. His eyes misted with tears. The stench of putrefaction roiled around him, filling his nostrils, gagging him.

More agonizing surges, eyes squeezed shut, afraid to look at the awful mess his body was spewing, until the spasms subsided, leaving him gasping and weak, his face against the cold smooth steel of the handle. His legs shuddered. He stood and attempted to clean himself up, but he needed a hose, not a meager roll of flimsy white paper. The floor of the lavatory looked as if someone had just blown his brains out with a shotgun.

He cleaned himself up enough to pull up his pants, swabbed off his legs and feet, and by that time, his supply of toilet paper was gone and his hands were as red and sticky as his feet. The hand towel dispenser was empty.

He couldn't just leave the lavatory like this.

He carefully opened the door, praying for no one to be nearby, trying to be discreet.

Sarah's pretty face looked up at him, right outside, biting her lip. She was squirming and fidgeting. "About time! I'm doing the Pee-Pee Dance."

His face grew hot, and he interposed himself in the doorway. "Um, you don't want to go in there. Not yet. Uh, someone was in there before me, and it's absolutely awful."

"Oh, come on. How bad can it be?" A strange expression emerged. Her eyes narrowed.

"I'm serious. Please, go to a different car."

She sighed. "Okay, okay." As she walked away, she gave him another peculiar expression.

As soon as she was out of sight, he stepped over to the counter. The man with the plastic smile smiled at him. Agonizing moments later, he had convinced Plastic Smile to loan him a towel, and he quickly returned to the rest room to clean up the mess.

He opened up the door. A chill up the back of his neck stopped him dead in the open doorway.

The blood was gone.

For a long time, he stood there, just staring, until he noticed that his hand hurt. His hand clenched the towel ferociously. He switched hands and flexed his fingers. His abdomen spasmed again, and he groaned.

A hand on his shoulder brought him around. "Everything come out okay, man— What the hell? You look like shit!" Phil's eyes bulged.

"I... I... don't know. I do?"

"Yeah, you're fucking pale, eh. Let's go back to our compartment. Maybe you should lie down."

"Yeah, I don't feel so good."

Sean let Phil guide him back toward the sleeping car. His mind was a fog, and he struggled to maintain his balance as the train clattered and lurched.

As they passed through the dim coach full of seated passengers, Sean tried not to meet the glance of any other passengers. The stench of rotting meat, decomposition, putrefaction was so intense here that it brought a wave of nausea over him.

He whispered toward Phil. "Don't you smell that?"

"Smell what?"

He noticed a man's arm moving quickly, rhythmically in a dark corner seat. The man's eyes were squeezed shut, his teeth clenched, his hand clutching his exposed penis, his arm jerking with furious speed. The old woman across from him appeared to be asleep.

Sean snatched his gaze away, shaking his head. "Holy shit."

"What?"

"Never mind. Go. Go."

Back in their berth, they found that the two lower bunks were now occupied by dark, motionless figures. Two pairs of shoes and a worn duffel-bag rested on the floor beside the bunks.

Phil's voice was low. "Do you remember the train stopping for more passengers?"

Sean shook his head. "No." His brain was swimming, and another wave of dizziness washed through him.

Heavy breathing emanated from the figures in the lower bunks. Outside, moonlight glistened on jungle treetops, striking silvery highlights on the dense black forest, sliding inexorably past. A lone pair of dim headlights meandered down a narrow road, blurring together as his vision swam.

Sean clung to the handholds as he climbed into his bunk and flopped down. The ancient mattress ground against his skin. "God, I feel like shit."

"Try to get some sleep, man. We'll be in Nha Trang in the morning."

"Morning… Yeah…" His voice trailed off, leading him into blackness.

He was awake, shambling through the harsh white light of the corridor toward the bathroom. His skin crawled and felt caked with something slimy that had dried against his back. He must have removed his sandals; the stiff carpet rubbed his bare soles like cheap Astroturf. He stepped into the lavatory. The floor was sticky with half-dried urine, and at each step his skin pulled away from the metal with a wet slurp.

He knuckled his burning eyes, then flinched as he glanced at the unfamiliar face in the mirror. His skin was a pasty yellowish-white. The whites of his eyes were blotched with red, with dark purple circles sagging below them.

"God, need a doctor." His voice was a croak.

How much time had passed since he went to sleep? It felt like hours. The darkness still rolled by outside, relentless. The hallways were deserted and quiet. The sleeping compartment doors were closed. It must be getting close to morning, but he could see no sign of imminent dawn.

Then a stab of pain in his belly, stronger than ever, doubled him over, ripping out a visceral cry of agony. A stream of bright red vomit exploded out of his mouth and nose into the small steel sink, tasting and smelling of bile and blood.

His heart thundered, and his body began to shake. A doctor. He stumbled out of the lavatory, down the hallway toward the rear of the train, clutching his belly, the hot vomit cooling on his lips and chin.

"Need a doctor!" His voice sounded so feeble.

Another sleeper car, just like the last, empty hallway and closed doors, desolate and deserted. But at the rear of this one, something different. He saw another car through the window in the door, but the interior was dark.

The door opened at his push into what looked like a baggage coach. There were no seats, no compartments, just a long open space divided by partitions of dark cargo netting, crates and boxes. Most of the windows had been painted over and were covered by bars on the inside. The only light spilled through the door behind him and two dingy windows, casting his shadow long on the steel floor. Pale moonlight congealed in a puddle before him, and he stepped into it, waiting for his eyes to adjust to the gloom.

Something moved in the darkness, breathing, something alive. A few more steps into the darkness. Beyond a stack of crates. Weeping. A heavy, shuddering sigh.

There, bathed in moonlight, were several pale figures. Long black hair hung from their bowed heads, obscuring their faces, cascading around their naked shoulders, their naked backs, their naked buttocks resting on naked feet. Their hands were bound behind their backs. Five of the women knelt on the hard steel floor, and two lay on their sides like limp rags. The stench of rotting flesh made Sean's eyes water.

"Oh, my God." His knees quivered and he grabbed a handful of cargo netting nearby for support.

Until he realized that it did not feel like 'netting' at all. He released the substance with a cry.

An enormous shape lunged out of the darkness. A hand like hardened steel clamped around his throat and drove him back against a stack of crates. Rough wooden angles gouged into his back, and the hand squeezed his throat like a hangman's noose. A quiet deadly voice spoke in a thick French accent. "You shouldn't be here, my friend."

A surge of strength went through Sean's body. His younger days of football and bar-hopping had led him into a few fist fights, but that powerful hand squeezed the strength right back out of him.

The warrior leaned closer, examining him. "You don't look so good, my friend." He sounded vaguely amused. "You sick?"

Sean fought his breath into a gurgle to make the words. "Looking for a doctor."

The warrior leaned his head back and laughed.

Suddenly Sean was flying through the air. His already dizzy head pounded once against the steel floor as he skidded down the central aisle past the cowering women.

As he sprawled like a rag doll, stars dancing in his vision, in that one moment, he saw her. He could never forget that face, peering at him from behind her hair.

"Ngao?"

Her glistening eyes widened.

Then narrowed.

Vehement Vietnamese spewed like acid from her lips. She lunged toward Sean, eyes blazing, but her bonds held her in place. She strained against them, shouting and sobbing.

"My, my, my, isn't this interesting," another voice said. The Frenchman stepped into the pool of light. The orange cherry of his cigarette gleamed in his cold eye. He looked toward the furious girl and spoke in Vietnamese.

She answered with a torrent of invective.

"She says she knows you. Is this true?"

Sean did not have the strength to lie. "Yeah. I met her in a bar last night. Me and my friend, we were just playing pool."

The girl flew into another stream of speech.

"She says you took her to a hotel. She was supposed to have sex with you. It was to be her first time."

"I didn't know she was a hooker!"

"Come now, don't be such a prude. Of course, you did." The Frenchman knelt beside him. "Language is such a curious thing, yes? You call her a 'hooker,' an unabashedly derogatory American term, but the sex industry in this part of the world is so much more… complicated than that, yes? Vietnam, Cambodia, Thailand, girls here often have sex for money, with foreigners, with rich men. They are simply helping their families with money. Some of them even do it for fun."

"She said she wanted to come with me. She was so sweet. And she said she liked me."

Ngao was still talking, her fury subsiding into sobs, trying to get the words out.

"Of course, she did. Humph, she says she really did like you. You're so 'handsome and nice.'" The Frenchman clucked his tongue. "But you wouldn't pay her."

"If I paid her, it wouldn't be real…"

"My young friend, you're looking for *love?*" The Frenchman's laugh was harsh and sharp. "You are in the *wrong* part of the world for such nonsense!"

"She said she liked me! She *wanted* to go with me!"

Ngao's shoulders slumped, and her beautiful breasts with such delicate pink nipples disappeared behind the curtain of dark hair.

"She was waiting for someone she liked to be her first. She was waiting for *you.* And then when you refused to pay her, she left."

Sean's voice grew feeble. "She said—"

"You stupid twit! For women like her, men like you are their ticket out of this godforsaken fucking country."

Ngao's voice had fallen to a whisper.

The Frenchman continued to interpret. "So when she went back to the bar, empty-handed, the madam beat her. A young woman with beauty like this is a valuable commodity, eh? The madam called me, you see. She'd been waiting for months for this girl to start bringing in money. So when the girl finally tried, and then failed, the madam sold her to me. Everything must have its due, you know, eh? Everything must have its due."

A wash of fresh bile bubbled into Sean's throat with his guilt. He turned toward her. "Ngao! Ngao, I'm so sorry."

The Frenchman leaned forward. "So how much was this girl's life worth, eh? How much did she ask for? Thirty American dollars? I can tell you she'll bring me far more than that."

She glanced at Sean, sniffling, then looked away. A single tear dropped from her chin like a falling diamond, glistening in the moonlight.

The Frenchman said, "If you had only paid her, she would not be here like this. You would, but she wouldn't."

Sean sat up. "What are you talking about?"

"Nothing. Go back to your bed. Forget about this."

"What are you going to do with them?"

"That is none of your business."

"There's nothing I can do to stop you."

"I suppose you're right about that, eh." His cigarette flared as he took a drag. "Some of them are coming with me to Phnom Penh. I'll look for buyers there. Some of them... will not."

Sean looked closer at the two women lying motionless in the darkness. "What happened to them?" He staggered to his feet.

"Easy, my young friend. You are not well."

"I'm not your friend. What happened to them?" Sean took a step closer. Then he saw the dark glistening pools surrounding their bodies, the dark, congealing stains, on their lips, on their legs, around their eyes, around every orifice, strands of their dark hair mired in sticky, congealing pools, their deathly pale flesh like alabaster in the moonlight. "What did you do?" A surge of anger rose in his throat, and his hands clenched into fists.

The warrior loomed closer.

"I did nothing to them. Go back to your bed."

Somewhere far ahead of them, the train's whistle cried its long, lonesome wail.

The Frenchman said, "You should go now. Go back to your friend. Enjoy what time you have left."

"What the fuck does that mean!" Sean's voice cracked.

An iron hand clamped over his shoulder and threw him down the aisle toward the door.

"Do not come back here."

Sean scrambled toward the door, toward the light. He tumbled across the space between the cars, falling to his hands and knees in the flickering white glow of the hallway.

His arms could barely support his weight, but he fought to his feet and flung himself down the hallway.

In their compartment, he reached up and shook his friend. "Phil, get up!"

Phil rolled over and squinted at him. "What the fuck, man!"

"Trust me, you need to get up. We need to get the hell off this train."

"What are you talking about?"

"Something's wrong with me. I'm going to die if I don't get off this train *now!*"

"Man, you're not going to die, it's just some food poisoning—"

"No, it's worse than that. I don't care if we have to ride a water buffalo back to Saigon." He pulled his pack down, grabbed his sandals and began to strap them on. "Just trust me! Let's go!"

"All right, fine. Whatever." Phil sat up, rubbed his eyes, and began to gather his things.

"Don't you smell that?"

"Yeah, man, I thought it was your sandwich."

Just then, Sean noticed that their heated exchange had not disturbed the two inhabitants of the lower bunks. Ragged breathing gurgled from the dark enclosure under his bunk. The other bed was deathly silent. The light from the door fell across a whitish-yellow foot and a thick dark stain soaking the mattress. "No, it's coming from them! And *me!*"

Phil stared at the dying Vietnamese man.

"Believe me now?"

Moments later, they were in the hallway. Phil shouldered his duffel bag. "What are we going to do, jump?"

Ngao's face flashed in Sean's mind, and he stopped. He couldn't just leave her with the Frenchman. But the warrior could kill him and Phil both, effortlessly, and not give it a second thought. She was tied up, naked, and under guard. And Sean was not James Bond or Arnold Schwarzenegger.

"What is it?" Phil asked.

"You remember the girl from the bar, Ngao?"

"You remember her name?" Phil's eyes widened. "Yeah, I remember her."

"She's on the train. The Frenchman has her tied up naked in the baggage car."

"Jesus Christ, man. What the fuck are we into?"

"I think it's even worse than that, but I don't know how yet."

"If those guys have a girl chained up naked on this train, they *will* kill us if we fuck with them. If they can get a naked girl—"

"Seven naked girls."

Phil rolled his eyes. "Ok, seven naked girls—onto a train, they're probably carrying guns."

"But we can't just leave them."

"We get off this train, we can contact the police. This guy is probably wanted. They can stop him before he gets over the border."

Sean sighed. A sledgehammer was pounding on the back of his skull, and his bag felt like it weighed more than him. "OK."

They hurried down the hallway to the end of the car, and stopped. Phil said, "Where's the exit door?"

A cold silent hand clamped around Sean's heart, and his vision swam.

Phil threw his bag against the blank steel wall. "Where's the fucking door!"

The exit door was gone, as if it had never been.

Sean grabbed Phil by the shoulder and pulled him toward the door into the next car. "Come on."

In the next sleeper car, they found the same absence of exits. The places that had once been passenger doors were now blank empty walls. The sleeping compartment doors were all tightly closed. As they passed one, Sean spotted a spreading pool of dark blood oozing from underneath, staining the carpet.

Through three, four, five, six more sleeper cars (Had the train always been this long?) all similar, until they reached the car with the seated passengers. They stood on the threshold of a charnel house.

Decomposing corpses filled the seats with rotting flesh and spreading pools of liquefaction. Clothing and skin sloughed away in great oozing swaths, mouths hanging, tongues lolling.

Except for one man.

His face was still raised to the ceiling, teeth clenched, eyes squeezed shut, one hand pounding his cock like a jackhammer. But now his flesh was splotched and pale. Tears streamed down his face, and his hand and member were drenched in blood. The ferocity of his effort spattered droplets of blood in all directions. His head leaned against the dark window that reflected his pale tortured face back against him.

Sean leaned closer. The dark window. Outside, absolutely black. The tracks rumbled under the train's steel wheels, but there was no countryside moving past now, no sky, no jungle. Only empty, inky blackness.

Phil grabbed him by the shirt and dragged him away.

As they opened the door to the dining car, that same rockabilly Elvis song echoed from the darkness.

"Train I ride, sixteen coaches long
Well that long black train got my baby and gone…"

The lights in the dining car were out, except for a single spare bulb gleaming behind the counter, casting solid black shadows high on the steel walls.

The drunken policeman still sat on his stool against the wall, and he would never move again. Nor would any of the former partiers. They all now lay in haphazard heaps of decaying flesh and bone, sprawling across tables and chairs and each other. The two lovers lay together against the far door, their bodily fluids melding in ways they would never have imagined.

To reach the far door, they would have to wade through the bodies, and then clear them away from the door.

The train whistle shrilled again, and the vibration of the rumble increased, as if it was picking up speed.

Sean grabbed Phil. "Back this way."

They went back through three more cars with passenger seating before they once again came upon the masturbating man. The cords stood out of the side of his neck, the veins on his forehead, as he strained, yearned, frenzied for release that would never come.

Back through the cars, nine, ten, eleven, twelve coaches. Until they reached the closed black door that led into the baggage car.

Sean stopped before the door, his breathing wet and ragged, warm rivulets of blood dripping from his ears and nose. A single wracking cough sprayed blood from his lips to splatter against the center door.

He pulled open the door, stepped into the space between coaches, and the train lurched, staggering him for a moment. He glanced around at the diaphragm enclosing the empty space, keeping the outer darkness at bay. Sean could feel that darkness outside, rubbing against the train's glossy black carapace. The dark, membranous diaphragm flexed and shifted like bat's wings. Black veins trailed across the lighter inner surface, pulsing with… What?

He threw open the second door and stumbled inside. There was no moonlight now to light the way, only utter darkness. No sound but the CLACK CLACK CLACK of the train. He struggled to keep his massively heavy bag from dragging on the floor as he crept toward where he thought the women had been tied. He tried to visualize the layout of the car, armed only with his fuzzy memory.

He heard breathing, the slither of hair, the catch of breath. His hand searched the black until it brushed against soft, velvety strands. She flinched away. He leaned forward and buried his nose in her hair. How could he ever forget that scent?

"Ngao," he whispered, "Shhh." She didn't speak a word of English. He just prayed that she didn't make any noise. He knelt beside her and felt his way behind her, looking for her bonds. His touch stopped at the strands around her wrists. They felt like exactly the same material as the cargo netting. Warm and pulsing, growing out of the steel floor like ropy tentacles. He tried his strength against them but there was no way.

A metallic snick.

"Here," said the Frenchman, "Try this."

Something clattered across the floor and slid against Sean's leg. A switchblade knife. He snatched up the knife and began to saw at the girl's bonds. The blade was sharp and sliced deep through the strange sinew. In seconds, he had freed her hands; he went to work on her ankles.

"Just what do you hope to accomplish, my young friend?" the Frenchman said. A match flared, splashing orange across the Frenchman's craggy face.

"Getting out of here," Sean mumbled, sawing.

"You will not survive long enough to get out of here. You have already been claimed. You can hardly stand."

"Why aren't you sick?" Sean spat at him.

"I ride in the belly of this beast. We have a deal, you see. I help feed it, and it gives me safe passage, away from the eyes of the authorities."

Sean stopped sawing, his mind reeling. "How...?"

"Once upon a time, after the Americans left, this rail line shipped countless South Vietnamese north for 're-education.' I've lived in this part of the world for thirty years, and I can tell you that Vietnamese are some of the most cruel and ingenious little fucks to ever walk this planet. For years the Communists consolidated their control. That kind of suffering, that much pain, it has power, you see. It festers. It *does* things. It begets *more*. This train has... brothers, I suspect. In Germany, Russia, China."

"Don't they know about it? The Vietnamese government?"

Sean heard the Frenchman's smile. "Of course they do. They fed you to it, just like all the other 'undesirables.' Last night, you picked up a local girl in a bar and humiliated her, caused trouble for her family. And you're an American. This train is, shall we say, like a bastard step-child they don't know how to rid themselves of. It just keeps coming round. So they use it to throw away their trash. The old, the diseased, the foreign trouble-makers. Power takes its due. And there is *always* a higher power. Every time I ride this train, I must give up some of my cargo, a tribute, shall we say. But it is a fair trade, no?"

"Where's this train going? How do you get off?"

"Ah, my young friend, that is part of the deal. My friends and I are getting off at Nha Trang. But this train doesn't stop, you see. It, too, must give up its due at the last stop."

"To what? Where?"

"To even darker powers, of course."

"Just let us go! Just me and Phil and her. Please."

"Why on earth would I do that?"

"Because you're a human being, right? This train is full of dead people now. Isn't it... full?"

"It doesn't work that way, you see. Your fate was sealed from the moment you set foot on board. I don't make the rules." Sean sensed his crocodile smile. "I just take advantage of them."

"Just me and Phil and her. We don't matter to your plans. We can't stop you."

"My young friend, you're dead already! And I don't think getting off is an option for your friend any longer."

A flashlight beam shattered the darkness, and Sean blinked away tears. The Frenchman shined his pen light toward the towering warrior a few steps behind Sean. The machete in the warrior's tattooed fist dripped dark crimson.

Sean lunged toward the Frenchman. The flashlight tumbled to the floor, and in the dancing beam he caught a glimpse of a surprised expression wiping away the smirk on the Frenchman's dry lips. Sean was surprised at how easily the point of switchblade went into the soft, perfumed throat. A choked gurgle, and Sean shoved in the point until it jammed against skull and spine, then he ripped backward and tore out the Frenchman's throat like he was cutting a bundle of cords.

The women shrieked and dragged themselves away as the warmth spattered over them.

He felt the weight of the warrior bearing toward him, imagined the machete upraised to take his head.

As the Frenchman's body fell like a sack of fresh meat, lungs spewing blood from the front of his throat, Sean felt the hard bulge of a pistol in a shoulder holster under the jacket. Sean followed it down, snatching at the butt of the pistol.

The pen light spun in place on the floor. He seized it and shined the dazzling white beam full in the face of the looming brute. The warrior flinched and blinked for a moment, shielding his eyes. Then Sean switched off the light, jerked the pistol free of its holster and slid away into the darkness away from the Frenchman's body. Spots danced in his vision. The butt of the pistol was warm and hard in his hand. He traced the steel lines with his fingers. An automatic, 9mm or .45. Thanks, Dad. His thumb found the safety, and he eased the bolt back to chamber a round.

The machete blade whistled through empty air four paces away as the warrior flailed for Sean's head.

Sean raised the pistol, popped the flashlight beam on, bathing the warrior like a deer in the headlights. He squeezed the trigger, and the pistol bucked with white thunder. The warrior staggered once, then lunged toward the light. The pistol exploded into a white-hot hail of bullets, and the warrior's head exploded into wet gobbets strobing in the muzzle flash.

Sean didn't know how long he stood there, gasping for breath, trying to ignore the overpowering coppery taste of his own blood.

Until the train whistled, a long, screeching howl.

"Let us go!" Sean screamed at darkness. "You have your due! Let us go!" He broke into a fit of wet coughing.

A rhythmic shiver ghosted up his spine, like cold fingers playing a tune on a dead keyboard, a cacophonic vibration like a thousand violins grating in unison. And suddenly he knew it all, *felt* it all. The train, the scores of dead souls, being digested on their way to their final destination.

He walked over to where Phil lay dead on the floor, his throat slashed to the spine, his head surrounded by a pool of blood. "I'm sorry, buddy." Somehow the pool of blood was shrinking, not spreading. He spotted movement at the edges of the body and looked closer. Hundreds of bluish-purple tendrils like slimy worms as thick as fingers writhed raw from the steel floor and burrowed into the body, pulsing, sucking, throbbing. Sean stepped away.

Yes, the train would let him go, would let Ngao go and all the other girls, just as it had agreed with the Frenchman. And Sean could live as well. There was only a small price.

Morning light suddenly shone through one of the unpainted windows. The girls staggered to their feet, whispering among themselves, glancing at Sean, rubbing circulation back into their wrists and trying to cover their nakedness.

They looked at him in the feeble, grayish-golden glow, and the train began to slow.

He went through his bag, dug out handfuls of clothes, and threw them to the girls. He did not know what the Frenchman had done with their clothes, and probably neither did they. "Put these on."

By the time they were dressed, the train was nearly stopped. Ngao looked striking in his yellow Hawaiian shirt, and her eyes were big and confused. The train ground to a halt, and the door to the baggage car slid open, revealing a small, lonesome train platform, little more than a deserted slab of concrete beside the tracks in the middle of the jungle. But the lone, rusting tin sign was written in Vietnamese, not Khmer.

"Go," he told them, "Get out."

They did, shuffling, sniffling, limping away as he stood in the open door. Ngao only looked over her shoulder once.

Then the baggage car door slid closed.

He was starting to feel better. Perhaps if he could enjoy himself in Phnom Penh for a few days, he might be able to forget the things he had agreed to do.

Beholder

Graham Masterton

"Once upon a time in a faraway land a princess was born who was so beautiful that nobody was allowed to look at her for fear that they would be so jealous that they would try to harm her.

"She was so beautiful, in fact, that nobody could paint her portrait because the paints would burst into flames as soon as they were applied to the canvas, and no mirrors could be hung in the palace because they would shatter into a thousand thousand pieces if she were to look into them.

"The beautiful princess had many servants, but they were all blinded before they were allowed into her presence by having their eyes spooned out of their sockets."

Mummy had read Fiona that story so many times that Fiona knew every word of it by heart, and her lips used to move in silent accompaniment whenever Mummy read it. She loved it, because it made sense of her life. She would sit cross-legged on the end of her bed with the windows open, her eyes closed, feeling the sun on her face and listening to the chirruping of sparrows in the garden below. The garden into which she was never allowed to go further than the patio, in case one of the neighbors saw her, and were so envious of her beauty that they climbed over the fence and tried to disfigure her, or even kill her.

Mummy closed the book. It wasn't a proper printed book, but an exercise book with a purple marbled cover and the story of the beautiful princess had been written by hand. Fiona thought that Mummy was beautiful, although she knew that she herself was even more beautiful. At least Mummy could go out and meet other people, without them shouting at her or chasing her down the street or throwing acid in her face, which Fiona knew would happen to her, if *she* ventured beyond the front door.

It was a warm morning in the middle of May, and Mummy came into Fiona's room and said, "Why don't you take Rapunzel into the garden, Fee-fee? I have to go to the shops and it's such a nice day."

Rapunzel was Fiona's doll, which Mummy had made for her. Rapunzel had a completely blank face, with no eyes or nose or mouth, but she had very long fair hair, like Rapunzel in the fairy-story, who had been locked up in a tower by an evil enchantress. When she had first given Rapunzel to her, Fiona had asked why she didn't have a face, and Mummy had said, "You don't need a beautiful face to be beautiful. Beauty is in the eye of the beholder."

"Who's The Beholder?" Fiona asked her.

"Anyone who looks at you. Anyone at all. They're all beholders."

Mummy called out, "'Bye, darling, won't be long!" and Fiona heard her close the front door behind her.

Fiona picked up Rapunzel from her pillow, where she had been lying between Paddington Bear and Barbie. She went downstairs and out through the kitchen door, onto the York stone patio. The sun had moved around behind the horse-chestnut trees at the end of the garden, so the patio was in shadow now, but the stone was still warm. There was a low wall around it, with steps in the middle that led down to the lawn, and on either side of the steps stood two square pillars, with geraniums growing in them. Fiona thought that they looked like the towers of a fairy-tale castle, so she always knelt down and perched Rapunzel on top of one of them, amongst the geranium stems.

A breeze was rustling through the trees, as if they were whispering to each other, and she could hear the children next door laughing as they ran around their garden. Fiona sometimes wondered what it would be like if she hadn't been born so beautiful, and could play with them. She knew that the boy was called Robin and the girl was called Caroline, because she had heard them calling out to each other, but that was all. She had never seen them, even from her bedroom window, but she imagined that they were probably quite plain. Ugly, even.

"Rapunzel! Rapunzel! Let down your hair!" she repeated, in a creaky voice that was supposed to sound like the evil enchantress. In the story, there had been no door in the tower where Rapunzel was imprisoned, and no steps that led up to her room, so the only way in which the evil enchantress had been able to visit her was by climbing up Rapunzel's twenty-foot tresses.

Fiona took the hair-grips out of Rapunzel's silky blonde braid and hung it down the side of the pillar. Then she started to make her fingers crawl up it, spider-like, to represent the evil enchantress. But her fingers were less than halfway up to the top when a yellow tennis-ball came flying over the fence from the next-door garden, and bounced in the middle of the lawn.

She heard Caroline saying, "*Now* look what you've done, stupid! You'll have to go round and get it back!"

But then Robin said, "There's somebody there…that girl we never see. I heard her."

Fiona stopped her fingers from climbing Rapunzel's hair. She knelt up very straight, listening. She could hear Robin approaching the fence, and then he called out, "Hey! Can you throw our ball back, please?"

Fiona stayed where she was, hardly daring to breathe. She knew that she couldn't go down the steps and onto the lawn to pick up the tennis-ball because then Robin and Caroline would be able to see her, and realize how beautiful she was. Before she knew it they would be clambering over the fence with kitchen knives or broken bottles or bleach or who could only guess what, to ruin her face.

Very, very carefully she stood up, lifting Rapunzel out of her flowery tower. Then she tip-toed backward toward the open kitchen door.

"Hey! Can you hear me?" Robin shouted. "Can we have our *ball* back, please?"

"There's nobody *there*," said Caroline, impatiently.

"Yes, there is, I heard her. All she has to do is throw it back."

"She's probably gone inside. You'll have to go round and knock on the door."

Just as Fiona was stepping back into the kitchen and closing the door behind her, she heard Robin shouting out one more time, "Excuse me! Deaf ears! Can you throw our ball back?"

Fiona locked the kitchen door and went through to the hallway. Over the front door there was a semi-circular stained-glass window, so that the hallway was lit up with green and red and yellow light, like a small chapel.

"Mummy!" she cried out. "Mummy, are you back yet?"

Silence. Fiona held Rapunzel tighter. "Mummy?"

At that moment, the doorbell rang, one of those jangly rings that left a salty taste in Fiona's mouth. It must be the boy from next door, Robin, wanting his tennis-ball back. What if she opened the door and he saw how beautiful she was and attacked her? She stood in the hallway for a moment, clutching Rapunzel, not knowing what she should do, but then he rang the doorbell again and she ran quickly and quietly upstairs.

"Mummy!"

She stood on the landing outside Mummy's bedroom. The doorbell rang again and she was so frightened that she wet herself, a little bit.

"*Mummy!*"

"I can *hear* you!" said Robin. "I know you're in there! We only want our ball back!"

Mummy always locked her bedroom door, when she went out, but all the same Fiona pulled down the handle, and to her relief, it opened. Mummy must have come home and perhaps she'd gone to the toilet and hadn't heard her.

"Mummy?" she said, stepping cautiously into her bedroom. There was still no reply. Mummy wasn't here, in the bedroom, and the door of her en-suite bathroom was open. She wasn't in there, either.

Fiona made her way around the bed, with its pink satin quilt and its array of lacy cushions. On the left-hand nightstand stood a gilt-framed photograph of Daddy, with his hair receding, but smiling all the same. Daddy had died when Fiona was only nine months old, although Mummy never said why he had passed away so young.

There was a smell of talcum powder in the room, mingled with that distinctive dustiness of people who live on their own.

The doorbell rang yet again, but in Mummy's bedroom Fiona didn't feel afraid any more. She touched the quilt, which felt so cool and silky, and she went to the window and looked out, and saw the street outside, with its neat front gardens and cars parked in everybody's driveway. She felt like Rapunzel in her tower—not imprisoned by an evil enchantress, but by the beauty with which she had been blessed as an accident of birth. She was sure that one day a handsome prince would come to rescue her, just like the prince in Rapunzel.

In the story, the prince had tumbled from the top of the tower into the thicket of thorn-bushes that surrounded it, and both of his eyeballs had been pierced, so that he had been blinded. Perhaps Rapunzel had been too beautiful for anybody to look at, too.

She went over to Mummy's built-in closet. Even with the doors closed, it smelled of Mummy's perfume and Mummy's clothes. Mummy had never let her look in her closet before, at all of her lovely clothes. She was sure, however, that Mummy wouldn't be cross if she had a quick peek. She needn't even tell her.

She turned the little key and opened the right-hand closet door. Hanging neatly inside were Mummy's dresses, in order of color, and Mummy's skirts, and on the shelves were all of Mummy's jumpers and cardigans, neatly folded. On the floor of the closet were Mummy's shoes, her sandals and her court shoes and the high heels she never seemed to wear these days.

Then Fiona opened the left-hand door. Immediately she gasped in shock, and jumped back, almost stumbling over. Standing in front of her was a girl, wearing exactly the same pink gingham dress as Fiona, and with her blonde hair tied up with two pink ribbons, exactly the same as Fiona's hair.

This girl, however, had a hideously distorted face, with a bulging forehead and eyes as wide apart as a flatfish. Her nose was not much more than a small knot of flesh with two holes in it, and her mouth was dragged down as if she were moaning.

Fiona was about to demand what this monstrous girl was doing, hiding in Mummy's closet. But when the girl raised her hand in exactly the same way that Fiona was raising her hand, Fiona began to realize, with a growing sense of horror, who she actually was. On the back of the left-hand door there was a mirror, and the girl with the hideously distorted face was *her*.

She touched the surface of the mirror, and the girl with the hideously distorted face did the same, so that their fingertips met.

"But I'm beautiful," she whispered, and the girl with the hideously distorted face whispered it, too. "I'm so beautiful that nobody can look at me, because they'll be too jealous.

"I'm *beautiful*."

It was then, however, that everything started to make sense. The reason why she could never go out, and meet other people. The things Mummy said to her. *Beauty is in the eye of the beholder.* She hadn't really understood what that meant, but now she did. She *was* beautiful. She was very, very beautiful. But too many beholders had looked at her, and every one of them had stolen a little bit of her beauty away.

Her beauty was still there, but now it was inside their eyes. Somehow she had to find a way of getting it back.

She took one more long look at herself and then she closed the closet doors and locked them. Her heart was beating very fast and she was breathing quickly, too, as if she had waded chest-high into an icy-cold swimming pool.

What could she do to get her beauty back? Mummy always kept her protected, inside the house, in case any more beholders saw her, and made her look even more hideously distorted than she was already. But had Mummy ever tried to confront those beholders, and demand that they return her daughter's looks? Perhaps she didn't know who the beholders were, or if she did, perhaps she was afraid to ask them. Anybody who would deliberately steal a young girl's beauty would probably be very selfish and vicious.

Fiona went downstairs, and as she did so the front door opened and Mummy came in, carrying a bag of shopping.

"Why aren't you out in the garden?" Mummy asked her. "It's so lovely out there."

"The boy from next door threw his ball over the fence and he came to the door to ask for it back."

Mummy put down her shopping-bag. "You didn't open it, did you?"

Fiona shook her head, and now she was conscious of how loose and wobbly her lips were. "I went upstairs to see if you were there, but you weren't."

"Well, I'm here now. I'll throw his ball back over for him. Would you like some lunch? I can make you some sandwiches, and you can eat them outside, like a picnic."

"Mummy—" Fiona began. She wanted to ask her about the beholders, and how Mummy had allowed them to take her beauty away, but then she thought better of it. Mummy always took such good care of her. She had probably done everything she could to keep the beholders away, and Fiona didn't want to upset her or make he feel guilty about something that she had been powerless to prevent.

There were many times when Fiona had heard Mummy sobbing in the middle of the night, or she had come downstairs late in the evening for a glass of water and Mummy had quickly torn off a sheet of kitchen towel to wipe her eyes.

They went outside. Mummy picked up the tennis-ball in the middle of the lawn and threw it back over the fence. There was no reply from next door. Robin and Caroline must be inside, having their lunch, too. Fiona knelt down on the patio and put Rapunzel back on top of her tower.

"Rapunzel! Rapunzel! Let down your hair!"

As she said that, she saw a large brown snail creeping across the patio, leaving a silvery trail behind it. It had only one pair of tentacles sticking out from the top of its head, and she knew from her children's encyclopedia that the shorter tentacle was for feeling its way around, while only the longer tentacle had an eye on the end of it. All the same, that single eye was definitely looking at *her*.

She hesitated for a moment, and then she stood up and went back into the kitchen.

"Won't be long, darling," said Mummy, spreading butter on four slices of bread. "Would you like tomato in your cheese sandwich, or brown pickle?"

"Brown pickle, please."

Mummy was standing with her back to her, so Fiona was able to slide open the drawer next to the cooker and quietly lift out the black-handled scissors which Mummy used to cut the tips off chicken wings. She dropped them into the pocket in the front of her dress and went back outside.

The snail was still only a third of the way across the patio. Fiona knelt down close to it, and peered at it intently. Its eye was unquestionably swiveling in her direction, so in its tiny way it, too, must be a beholder. Even if it had taken only the minutest part of her beauty—a pretty little dimple from her chin, perhaps—she wanted it back.

"What do you want to drink?" called Mummy. "Orange squash or lemon barley water?"

She would be coming outside in a minute, so Fiona couldn't hesitate. She took the scissors from out of her pocket and snipped the snail's eye from the end of its tentacle. Instantly, the snail rolled both of its tentacles back into its head, but it was too late. Fiona had its eye now, and everything that its eye contained.

As Mummy stepped out of the kitchen, carrying a small tray, Fiona popped the snail's eye into her mouth and kept it on her tongue. It felt very small and bobbly, and it tasted *beige*, if there was such a taste.

"Here you are, Fee-fee," said Mummy, and set the tray down on the top of the steps that led down to the lawn. "Cheese-and-pickle sandwiches, and a strawberry yogurt."

Fiona nodded and tried to smile. Mummy affectionately scribbled her fingers in Fiona's hair. "You are a funny girl, aren't you?" she said, and then she went back inside.

With the tip of her tongue, Fiona pressed the snail's eye as hard as she could against her palate, but it refused to pop. In the end, she maneuvered it between her front teeth, and bit it in half, and swallowed it. It was far too miniscule for her to taste any optical fluid, but she knew that she had taken back at least a tiny part of her beauty, and that was a good start.

The snail stayed where it was, not moving, as if it had been paralyzed by the shock of losing its eye. Fiona watched it for a while, as she ate her first sandwich. After five minutes, when it still hadn't moved, she stood up and stamped on it, with a crunch. *Serve you right*, she thought. She touched her chin to see if she had regained a pretty dimple, and she was sure that she could feel some indentation. This seemed to work, taking the eyes from her beholders. She wondered how many more snails were carrying images of her beauty around in their eyes; or how many birds, for that matter.

As if in answer to her question, she heard a tinkle, and a gray tortoiseshell cat jumped up onto the fence, with a little silver bell around his neck. He belonged to old Mrs. Pickens, who lived on the other side of Fiona and her Mummy. Fiona knew that the cat's name was Zebedee, because she had heard Mrs. Pickens calling him in at night. Zebedee was always sitting on top of the fence, staring at her unblinking with his yellow eyes, so he must be a beholder, too.

"Here, puss!" Fiona called him. "Come on, Zebedee! Come here, puss!"

Zebedee remained aloof on top of the fence. Fiona stood up and walked across the patio until she was standing directly beneath him.

"Come on, puss! Come down and play!"

Zebedee stared at her for a long time but still stayed where he was. Fiona took the top slice of bread off her half-eaten sandwich and threw it out into the garden, so that it landed on the lawn. Zebedee yawned and looked the other way.

Less than minute later, however, two fat pigeons landed on the lawn, and strutted toward Fiona's sandwich as if they had ordered it specially. They started to peck at it, and that was when Zebedee crouched himself down and arched his back and scratched at the fence with his claws as he re-positioned himself, ready to strike.

"Go on, puss!" Fiona urged him. He ignored her at first, as he tried to balance himself in the best position for leaping off onto the lawn. But then—as the pigeons started to squabble with each over the last remaining fragment of crust—he sprang off the fence and landed less than two feet away from them, making a southpaw lunge for the nearer pigeon and catching some of its tail-feathers.

The two pigeons immediately flapped up into the air, and were gone. Zebedee circled around the lawn, looking up at the sky as if he had intended only to chase the pigeons away, and was just making sure that they didn't have the temerity to try to come back.

Fiona was sitting on the top step now, watching him. He came toward her, climbed the steps and started to sniff at her sandwiches.

"Cats don't like cheese-and-pickle," said Fiona. Zebedee stared at her and licked his lips, as if he expected her to offer him something else, like sardines. Or maybe he only wanted to show her how much he relished the beauty that he had taken from her.

"You're a beholder, too, aren't you, Zebedee?" Fiona asked him. "I can tell, because you're so beautiful. 'What a beautiful pussy you are, you are.'"

Zebedee came up closer to her and sniffed at her. She reached out and stroked his head, so that he half-closed his eyes and flattened his ears back.

It was then that Fiona suddenly snatched his green leather collar and twisted it around tight, so that it was almost strangling him. He yowled and struggled and scratched, jerking his body wildly from side to side, but Fiona held onto him, and pressed her thumb into his furry throat until he was whining for breath.

Gradually, his convulsive kicking became weaker and more spasmodic, and at last he stopped struggling altogether. Fiona laid him on his back across her knees, and tried to feel if he still had a pulse, but she couldn't find one. His eyes were closed and his upper lip was raised in a silent snarl.

"*Now* let's see who's beautiful," she said. She picked up the small stainless-steel spoon that Mummy had given her for eating her strawberry yogurt. Then, with her thumb, she raised Zebedee's sticky left eyelid, so that his eye was exposed, with its sunflower-yellow iris. He didn't try to blink, so she assumed that he must be dead. She felt that it was a pity, in a way, that he was dead, because she would have liked him to be aware that she was taking back her beauty. He had stared at her. A cat may look at a queen, she thought, but that doesn't mean that the queen won't be angry for being looked at.

Very carefully, with the tip of her tongue clenched between her teeth, Fiona dug the tip of the yogurt spoon underneath Zebedee's eyeball. The eyeball made a slight sucking sound as she lifted it free from its socket, but it wasn't difficult to lever it out. Soon it was hanging on Zebedee's cheek, staring sightlessly at his whiskers. Fiona picked up the scissors and cut the optic nerve, and then she carefully placed the eyeball on the tray next to her plate of sandwiches.

She took out the other eye the same way, and then she had both eyeballs side by side. She couldn't help smiling because they were squinting, like cartoon eyes.

"Fee-fee!" called Mummy, from the kitchen. "Have you finished your lunch yet?"

"Nearly!" Fiona called back. She lifted Zebedee off her lap and stood up. Then she carried his lifeless body over to the side of the house, where the dustbins stood. He was surprisingly heavy, and his legs swung from side to side like a pendulum. She opened the lid of the dustbin and dropped Zebedee into it, on top of a black plastic bag.

She had half-closed the lid when there was a frantic rustling of plastic, and a scrabbling sound, and then, with a screech, Zebedee came jumping up the inside of the dustbin, blindly scratching at the sides in an attempt to climb out. He managed to get his front legs and his head over the rim of the dustbin, but the plastic was too slippery for him to get any purchase with his back legs.

Fiona slammed the dustbin lid down on his neck, and pressed down as hard as she could. Zebedee spat and hissed at her, his eyeless face contorted with fury and pain. She pressed down harder still, and at last she heard a snap as the vertebrae in his neck were dislocated. He stopped hissing, and when she lifted the lid up a little he dropped back heavily onto the plastic bag full of rubbish.

Serves you right, too, thought Fiona.

She returned to the steps and sat down. She picked up one of Zebedee's eyes and held it up, so that she could stare into it. It stared back at her, sightlessly, with a shred of optic nerve hanging from the back of it. *In there, that's where my beautiful face has been hiding.* She hesitated for a moment, not because the eye disgusted her, but because she was so pleased that she had discovered how to get her beauty back, and it was a moment to savor.

She placed the eye on her tongue, and then she slowly closed her mouth. The eye felt like a grape, although it had a strange taste to it, oily and slightly musky. She waited a few seconds longer, and then she bit into it, so that it popped, and this time she could actually feel the small blob of optic fluid sliding down her throat.

She picked up the other eye, and bit into that, too. This eye had a longer string of connective tissue still attached to it, which stuck to the back of her throat and made her gag. For a few seconds she thought she was going to be sick, and lose all of the beauty that she had retrieved from Zebedee's eyes, but then she took a mouthful of lemon barley water and managed to swallow it.

She finished the second half of her cheese-and-pickle sandwich, and then she ate her strawberry yogurt. The sun flickered through the leaves of the horse-chestnut trees at the end of the garden and made Fiona feel as if she were an actress in a film. She kept touching her face and she was sure that she could actually feel her beauty coming back to her, little by little.

She sang, in a high, reedy voice, "I feel pretty…oh so pretty! I feel pretty and witty and gay!"

From next door, she heard old Mrs. Pickens calling out, "Zebedee! Zebedee! Where are you, you naughty cat?"

Later that afternoon, when Mummy was busy in the kitchen, Fiona crept upstairs again and went into Mummy's bedroom. As quietly as she could, she turned the little key in the lock and opened the closet doors.

There she stood, in the mirror, the girl with the hideously distorted face. Fiona peered closely at her, so that their lumpy little noses almost touched, and she was sure that she wasn't quite as ugly as she had looked before. So it *did* work, finding beholders and swallowing their eyeballs. But it wasn't working as dramatically as she had hoped. She needed more—many more—and the bigger the eyeballs, the better.

A *person*, that's what she needed. A person who had seen her.

But who had seen her? Daddy was dead and presumably buried, or cremated, and Mummy had never taken her out of the house. She had never been to school, because Mummy taught her everything. She had never been to a shop, although she knew what they were because Mummy had shown her pictures of them.

She thought she could remember a man and a woman looking at her. They had both been wearing white coats and said things which she hadn't been able to understand. But that had been a very long time ago, and she had no idea who they were or where she could find them.

She carefully closed the closet doors and went back downstairs. Mummy was Hoovering in the sitting-room so she was able to go through the kitchen and out onto the patio without Mummy seeing her.

She sat on the steps with Rapunzel and started to braid Rapunzel's hair, in the same way that Mummy braided *her* hair. The sunlight was still flickering through the trees, but it was much lower now, and the shadows across the lawn were much longer. After she had pinned up Rapunzel's braids, Fiona turned her around and looked at her blank, featureless face.

Beauty is in the eye of the beholder. That's what Mummy had said. And it was then that it occurred to her. *Mummy.* Apart from those two people in the white coats, Mummy was the only person who had seen her, all these years. There had been no other beholders, apart from the insects and the animals and the birds in the garden. Mummy was the only one.

Mummy came outside and sat beside her on the steps.

"Phew!" she said, with a smile, wiping her forehead with the back of her hand. "That's all *that* done!"

Fiona stared at Mummy's eyes. Her irises were pale blue, like hers, but in the late afternoon sunlight her pupils were only pin-pricks. But now Fiona knew. Inside the blackness of Mummy's eyes, that was where her beauty was hidden. It must be. Nothing else made sense.

"What shall we do this evening?" asked Mummy. "What about a film? We could watch *The Cat in the Hat* again, if you like."

Fiona thought of that stringy shred of tissue sticking to her throat and shook her head. "I've gone off cats."

Once she was in bed, she was allowed to read for half an hour, but this evening her storybook remained unopened, because she was too busy thinking.

Mummy had always done everything she could to protect her and take care of her, ever since she was little, so she was sure that Mummy would understand why she needed to take out her eyes. Mummy would be blinded, yes, but blind people could still go shopping, couldn't they? and Fiona could help her around the house, cleaning and cooking. Fiona could roll out pastry and she knew how to make baked potatoes with grated cheese in them.

Perhaps they could get a guide dog, so long as the guide dog didn't look at her, and become another beholder. A guide dog with no eyes wouldn't be much good. The blind leading the blind!

The main problem would be keeping Mummy still, while she did it. And quiet, too. Zebedee had fought like a demon, even though he must have known that what was in his eyes belonged to her, and not to him.

At eight-thirty, Mummy came into her bedroom to tuck her in and give her a goodnight kiss.

"Sleep well, darling. Pleasant dreams."

"Mummy?" said Fiona, as Mummy switched off the light.

"What is it, Fee-fee?" she asked, standing in silhouette in the doorway.

"If I did something terrible, but I did it because it made me happy, would you forgive me?"

"What do you mean by 'something terrible'?"

"If I hurt somebody, really badly."

"I don't know what you mean, darling. You don't *know* anybody, do you, apart from me?"

Fiona was tempted to tell Mummy what she wanted to do. Perhaps Mummy would agree to gouge out her eyes voluntarily, so that

Fiona could be beautiful again. She had already given up her whole life for her, what difference would it make if she gave up her sight?

But then Fiona thought: what if she says no? What if she finds the idea really horrifying, and refuses to do it? After that, she will always be on her guard, and I won't be able to sneak into her bedroom in the middle of the night and take out her eyes, even though she doesn't want me to.

"I know, Mummy. I was just being silly."

Mummy blew her a kiss. "You are a funny girl sometimes. You know that I'd forgive you anything, don't you? Since Daddy left, you're all I have."

"Daddy *left*? I thought Daddy died."

"That's what I meant, darling. Since Daddy left us, and went to Heaven."

"Oh."

Mummy closed the door, leaving Fiona lying in darkness, except for the illuminated green numbers on the digital clock beside her bed. For some reason, she thought that Mummy had sounded strangely unconvincing when she had said that Daddy had gone to Heaven. Perhaps he hadn't gone to Heaven at all. Perhaps he had gone to Hell.

She waited for over an hour, trying hard to keep her eyes open. She could hear the television in the sitting-room below her, as Mummy watched the news and then some comedy program with occasional bursts of studio laughter.

This is the last time she'll ever be able to watch TV, thought Fiona. But she can listen to it, can't she? And she'll still have the radio in the kitchen.

At last she heard Mummy switch off the television and come upstairs. Mummy closed her bedroom door behind her and a few minutes later Fiona heard the bathwater running. The water tank in the attic always made a rumbling sound like distant thunder, followed by a high-pitched whistle.

Fiona waited for another half-hour, and then she sat up. She went across to her door and opened it. Mummy had switched off her bedside lamp, and the landing was in darkness. She knew that Mummy almost always took a Nytol tablet before she went to bed, so it was likely that she was asleep already. Mummy said she took Nytol because she found it difficult to get to sleep, and even when she did she had nightmares about monsters.

Fiona closed her door and turned on her light. She went over to the window and unhooked the pink braided cords that held her curtains back during the day. Then she took a small blue plastic-bound dictionary off her bookshelf, and a brightly colored cotton scarf from the top drawer of her chest-of-drawers.

Last of all, she picked up a dessert-spoon which she had taken from the cutlery drawer in the kitchen, as well as the poultry scissors.

She switched off her light and opened her door again. She stood there for a few seconds so that her eyes could become accustomed to the darkness. She didn't want to trip over something and wake Mummy up too soon.

In her head, over and over, she could hear Julie Andrews singing *"I feel pretty...oh so pretty! I feel pretty and witty and gay! And I pity... any girl who isn't me tonight!"* and she softly panted the words under her breath.

Very gently, she pulled down the handle of Mummy's bedroom door, and then opened it. When it was only a few inches ajar, she stopped, and listened.

At first she couldn't hear anything at all. But then Mummy turned over in bed, with a slippery rustle of her satin quilt, and muttered something that sounded like *"never!"* After that, Fiona could hear her breathing quite steadily, with a slight sticking noise in one of her nostrils.

Fiona crept across to Mummy's bedside. By the light of her luminous clock, she could see that Mummy was lying on her back, with one arm raised on the pillow beside her, and that she was deeply asleep.

With great care, she lifted Mummy's upraised arm a little further up the pillow, until Mummy's hand was poking through the brass rails of her headboard. She took one of the curtain cords and tied Mummy's wrist to the nearest rail, using the double knots that Mummy had taught her when she was showing her how to sew.

Next she walked around the bed and climbed up onto it so that she could gently tug Mummy's other arm out from under the bed-covers, and tie that to the headboard, too.

Now she lifted Mummy's head up from the pillow and slid the cotton scarf underneath it. Mummy stirred and said "*what?*" and then "*never!*" but still she didn't open her eyes. However, Fiona knew that what she did next was certain to wake her up. She took three deep breaths to steady herself and made sure that she had the little dictionary ready in her left hand and the spoon and scissors waiting on the bedside table.

I feel pretty, she breathed. *Oh so pretty.*

She parted Mummy's lips and then she pried her teeth apart. Mummy almost immediately opened her eyes and jerked at the cords that were keeping her wrists tied to the headboard. Without hesitation, Fiona jammed the dictionary between her teeth, as far as it would go, and then she took hold of the two ends of the scarf and tied them quickly in a tight knot over Mummy's mouth, so that she couldn't push the dictionary out with her tongue.

Mummy's eyes rolled in panic and bewilderment. She pulled at the cords around her wrists until the headboard rattled, and when she couldn't free she began to twist and kick and bounce herself up and down on the bed—all the while grunting and mewling at Fiona to untie her.

Fiona leaned over her, almost as if she were about to kiss her. Mummy stared up at her and stopped thrashing and kicking for a moment.

"Mmmm-mmmmfff-mmmmff," she said, through the diction-ary. Saliva was beginning to run down on either side of her mouth.

"It's all right, Mummy," said Fiona. "I'll try not to hurt you, I promise."

"*Mmmmmfff!*" Mummy retorted, and this time she sounded an-gry.

Fiona pinched Mummy's left eyelid between finger and thumb, and pulled it upward as far as she could stretch it. Mummy started kicking again, and trying to shake her head from side to side, but

Fiona was holding her eyelid too tightly. She reached across to the bedside table for the spoon, turned it upside-down, and pushed the tip of it into the top of Mummy's eye-socket. Mummy let out a harsh grating scream, and bounced up and down on the bed as if she were suffering an epileptic fit. But Fiona dug the spoon in deeper, until it curved around the back of the eyeball, and she could easily gouge it out onto Mummy's cheek. Blood welled out of her hollow eye-socket and slid down onto the pillow.

Mummy started shaking uncontrollably. The mattress made a furious jostling noise and the bedhead banged repeatedly against the wall behind it.

"Mummy! Mummy! It's all right, Mummy!" Fiona pleaded with her. "I promise I'll be quick!"

She hadn't realized how violent Mummy's reaction would be, and she started to sob. But it was too late now. She couldn't push Mummy's left eye back in and pretend that nothing had happened, and she so badly needed her beauty back. She reached across for the scissors but Mummy jolted her and she dropped them onto the floor.

Weeping, she climbed off the bed, but she couldn't see the scissors anywhere. She felt underneath the bedside table, but they weren't there. She felt underneath the bed, too, but there was a gap of only about an inch off the carpet and she couldn't feel them there, either.

Mummy was quaking and snorting now, with her gouged-out eye staring at Fiona accusingly from her cheek. There was only one thing that Fiona could do. She climbed back up onto the bed, and grasped Mummy's hair with her right hand to keep her head still. Then she took the eye between the thumb and middle finger of her left hand, leaned forward and bit it in half. She sucked the clear optic fluid out of it, and swallowed. Her eyes were still filled with tears, but she could almost feel her lost beauty slipping down her throat.

Mummy was still trembling, and she felt very cold, but she had stopped kicking and struggling. Fiona lifted her right eyelid, picked up the spoon, and gouged out her right eye, too. Again, she bit it in half and swallowed the fluid inside.

She knelt on the bed for a while, feeling slightly sick. Then she climbed off it again, untied the scarf that covered Mummy's mouth and gently wiggled the dictionary until it came out from between her teeth. Mummy had bitten almost halfway through it.

Next she untied her wrists and dragged up the bedcovers to try and get Mummy warm again. She didn't know what to do with the empty shreds of half-bitten eyes that were hanging out of each socket, so she carefully poked them back in again, and closed Mummy's eyelids, and then she tied the scarf around Mummy's head like a blindfold.

It didn't occur to her to call for an ambulance. She had seen ambulances on television, but they were only in stories. She had never seen a real one, and she didn't know that you could call one yourself, and it would actually come to your door.

Besides, the most important thing was that she had regained her beauty, and in spite of being so beautiful, she would risk going out into the world, no matter how jealous other people might be. Mummy might be blind now, but she was so beautiful that she would be able to become a famous actress, and become rich, and support them both.

It was only now that Fiona realized what a sacrifice Mummy had made for her—keeping her beauty in her own eyes for all of this time, in order to keep her safe. She must have known that one day the time would come when she would have to give it back to her.

She crossed over to Mummy's closet and unlocked the doors. There she was, in her pink pajamas, which were spattered with a fine spray of blood. But something was badly wrong. She wasn't beautiful at all. She looked the same as she had before, with that bulging forehead and those wide-apart flatfish eyes and that dragged-down mouth.

Perhaps it took time for the beauty to make its way into your body, she thought. After all, if you ate a bar of chocolate, you had to digest it first, in your stomach, before the sugar went into your bloodstream.

She sat down cross-legged on the bedroom carpet in front of the mirror, and waited for Mummy's optic fluid to work on her face. It *had* to work. Mummy had said that beauty is in the eye of the beholder, and she had swallowed the beholders' eyes. What more could she have done?

❋

She woke up and the bedroom was filled with sunlight. She glanced over at Mummy's bedside clock and saw that it was 7:17 am. It looked as if Mummy was still asleep, with her blindfold over her eyes. It was the blindfold that reminded her what had happened last night, and what she was doing here in Mummy's bedroom.

She looked in the mirror. She hadn't changed at all. She was still just as hideously distorted as she had been before. She couldn't understand it. She had swallowed those eyes for nothing.

She slowly stood up.

"Mummy?" she said. "Mummy, are you awake?"

She went over to Mummy's bedside. Mummy was very pale and she didn't appear to be breathing. Fiona shook her shoulder but all she did was joggle unresponsively from side to side.

"Mummy?"

She realized then that she must have misunderstood what Mummy had said to her. The snail hadn't been a beholder, and neither had Zebedee, or Mummy. She—Fiona—she was the beholder. It was she who had seen her own face in the mirror and thought that it was ugly. That was why Mummy had kept her away from mirrors, and stopped her from going out to meet other people. So long as she didn't know what she really looked like, she had remained incandescently beautiful.

She went back and stood in front of the mirror. Her hideously distorted face stared back at her. It always would, for the rest of her life, every time she saw her own reflection.

There was only one remedy. She went over to Mummy's chest-of-drawers. In the second drawer down, there was a purple biscuit tin with a picture of Prince Charles and Lady Diana on it, to celebrate their wedding. Mummy kept her sewing things in it—her spare buttons and her button thread and her needles.

Fiona picked out a large shiny darning needle and went back to face the mirror. With her fingers, she held her left eye open wide.

I feel pretty, she whispered, and stuck the needle into her pupil.

She felt nothing more than a sharp prick, but her eye instantly went blind. She held her right eye open in the same way, and stuck the needle into that eye, too.

She stood there, in total darkness. She couldn't see herself now. She couldn't see anything at all. But she could imagine how beautiful she was—so beautiful that if anyone tried to paint her portrait, their paints would burst into flames, and mirrors would shatter into a thousand thousand pieces if she ever looked in them.

She started to circle around and around, and as she circled she sang *I Feel Pretty*, over and over, until she was so giddy that she dropped to her knees. Outside, in the street, she could hear traffic, and people talking, and her blind eyes filled with tears again, although she no longer knew why she was crying.

Feel the Noise

Lisa Morton

I was on the club floor waiting for the show to start, feeling the anticipation in a wave of smells like a girlfriend's body after a shower, the stage lights overhead making me taste whiskey, when a young man walked up to me. His approach brought the wary tang of mustard, and he sounded like an itch when he asked, "Private Jackson Howard?"

I'd been out of rehab at the V.A. hospital for two years, but it still took me a few extra seconds to turn his gush of sensations into words. Then I answered, "I haven't been a private for a while."

The kid—ironic, since he was probably my age, but I thought of myself as old—smiled, and asked if we could go outside to talk.

'To talk'…sure. It was still easy for him.

His name was Kevin. He worked as a blogger for a news outlet.

Here's what I told him, when he asked what being scrambled was like:

You wake up, and you're not sure where you are or what happened to you. Some part of you recognizes a hospital, but the man standing over you tastes like aspirin, and the antiseptic smells sound like a low buzz, and the feeling of the meds in your system reminds you of the scent of your grandmother's mothballs, back when you were a normal little kid playing in the attic in her big old house down in your home town. And you start to panic, you think back to your last memory—in the desert, and some bad shit had just gone down, and the sergeant was screaming and no one was paying attention as we made our way back to the Hummer, and—

Scrambler.

Suddenly you know. You were hit by a scrambler. You've got a condition now called "systemic synesthesia", and it's every soldier's second worst nightmare; you'd rather lose an arm or a leg or an eye than have your brain rewired so no two senses match up right. In fact, a lot of scrambleheads say they wish they'd just died, so maybe it's Nightmare #1. You frantically try to think back to that day in basic training when you sat in a classroom and they told you about this new weapon the other side had called scramblers, and how they're electronic bombs that were really designed to mess up communications equipment, but they messed up soldiers instead, and you curse yourself—fucking idiot—for getting bored then, for sitting there thinking, That'll never happen to me, and when do we finish with this pussy training and get over there to mix it up?

Mix it up. That's rich.

They kick you out of the main hospital after a week and send you to the special clinic, and over the next year you hang out with a lot of other scrambleheads like yourself while they try to teach you how to alter your thinking and reprogram your brain, and you spend that year screaming a lot, but what comes out feels like a slap and looks jagged and smells like death. And after a while you start to figure it out: That seeing red means you just ate some meat, and hearing a screeching noise means you just smelled something bad. You learn to read again by examining the tastes the letters make, and you know who's touched you by how nice the smell is. You scream a little less every day.

And then you find the one thing makes you feel something strong: Music. And if you want to feel like you're with the world's sexiest woman, and she's rubbing all over you and you think you could take on everything, then you need it fast, loud, and hard.

And that's why all the scrambleheads who used to spend their furloughs chasing pussy are chasing music now instead.

It took me another year to be able to figure out how to talk again.

And during that year, I went a little crazy (crazier?) locked up in my head, because I had to tell someone what happened. What I saw every night when I closed my eyes. What fucking Sergeant Dean Craig had done.

He'd popped off and shot a kid. The parents, too.

We'd been doing a routine patrol on the outskirts of a desert town. Searching abandoned houses, making sure the bad guys weren't still hiding out, or hadn't left some presents behind.

In one of the houses we found this family, this poor family. Mother, father, young son, couldn't have been more than five years old. Sergeant Craig started screaming at 'em to put their hands on their heads and get on their knees, but they didn't speak English and they just kind of flapped their hands a lot and argued.

The kid had started to reach for something inside his shirt.

Craig shot him.

Just like that. A five-year-old with a bloody hole in his chest. No one should ever have to see that.

The parents screamed and charged, and so Craig shot them, too. Three people dead. Three people who'd wanted nothing but an abandoned house to squat in, to be left alone to scrounge whatever kind of living they could. Now they were dead, because Sergeant Dean Craig was a fucking terrible soldier who should have been back home yelling at his junior salesmen, not deep in the shit with an assault rifle.

There were three of us who saw it. Craig turned on us next, and if he didn't exactly point that rifle at us, he didn't completely lower it, either. He told us the kid had drawn a gun, right? That's what we'd all seen, RIGHT? And Private Quint, he was this o.g. from Detroit, he just walked out. And Craig followed him, shouting, and neither of them noticed the sensors in the sand, I guess, because the next thing I knew, I was in that hospital bed that felt like the stink of naphthalene, and I was screaming.

There, outside the house, with a five-year-old's blood splattered on me, just as a scrambler hit, was the last time I saw Craig.

Of course I told them what had happened, once I could communicate again. I saw an army shrink who said he'd ask around, find out what'd happened. He couldn't turn up anything on either the incident or Craig. Sergeant Craig had ceased to exist, as far as the feds were concerned. It was a convenient way to deal with an inconvenient problem. The war was already unpopular, and the government didn't need to have the public hearing about soldiers gunning down five-year-olds.

And then my benefits ran out, and they threw me out into the world and told me to deal with it.

So I did. I got the simplest job I could find—washing dishes in a restaurant—and a one-room apartment that was the only thing I could afford. I slept a lot, got free meals at work, washed dishes, stayed to myself.

Dreamed a lot about five-year-olds wearing bullet holes, who followed me down dark alleys and looked at me with bloodshot, sad eyes, until I woke up gasping, maybe crying.

Only the music kept me going.

When you're scrambled, you find out pretty quickly that music can still get you off, but it has to be live; recorded music is like watching porn—close but not the real thing. So you go to a lot of clubs and concerts, and you soon realize that some bands are better at it than others. But only one band really gets it and plays to scramble-heads: The Violence. They play medium-sized clubs, so all of us can stand right in front of those fucking amps and feel every guitar lick and wailed lyric right in our groins. There are always a few civvies at the sidelines, and they must be wondering what the fuck's going on—they see a bunch of guys in old army fatigues jerking around near the stage with these ecstatic looks on their faces, because they can all feel the noise. We'll be there all night, and we'll come back every night.

The music was the only thing that kept my mind off the horror of what I'd seen. My job sure didn't; there's nothing more tedious than doing the same task over and over, and your thoughts start to wander. In my case, it always wandered right back to a desert on the other side of the world and a trigger-happy asshole who'd killed a kid. My elbows immersed in warm, sudsy water meant seeing a five-year-old take a bullet in the chest yet again. And again. And again. Of course everything meant that; I saw it while I worked, while I ate, while I rode the train from home to work, and in my dreams while I slept. I saw it while I tried to parse what the boss said, while I tried to buy the right breakfast cereal, while I tried to read or watch things on television that I couldn't completely understand.

Sometimes I thought about really trying to find Craig; find him and somehow bring him to justice. If I could locate Quint, and the other two guys who'd been there, we could all testify. But then I'd remember that the dishes I washed felt like the smell of spoiled food, and I knew I'd never find Craig or any of them on my own. I was fucked, and Craig was free.

And then Kevin arrived.

When we walked outside, what it was like getting scrambled wasn't the first thing we talked about; that actually came later. No, the first thing was what Kevin showed me. He held up his smart phone, hit a button, and let me watch a video.

I didn't do well with movies—they unreeled in my head with a stream of tastes and the feeling of being prodded all over. I couldn't figure this one any better than the latest 3D Hollywood blockbuster, and I asked Kevin what it was.

"It's video from a helmet-cam. *Your* helmet-cam, specifically."

My heart did an arpeggio in my chest. "Is it Craig? Is it…?"

Kevin nodded. "Shooting a little boy. And two other people. Do you remember this?"

I thought I might cry. My face grew hot, which in turn made me smell smoke. "Remember it? Man, I've been trying to forget it for three years."

"We acquired this from a source. The government thought they'd squelched it, but they just don't pay some of their workers enough."

"I tried," I told him, and I didn't care if he saw me wipe at my eyes, "God damn it, I tried to get them to listen to me, but they wouldn't, they told me it never happened, and – you're going public with it, right?"

The heady scent of a meadow on a warm summer day nearly overpowered me just then, and I knew that meant Kevin had put a comforting hand on my shoulder. "It's okay. Yeah, soon the whole world's going to see what Craig did, and know what happened to you. We just want to know that you'll back it up."

"I will. Fuckin' A, I will."

"Good. We'll take him down, then."

"If you can find him."

I tasted something odd – Kevin was looking at me strangely. "Uh, Jackson…"

"Call me Jack."

"Jack…" He stepped back, and I think he was looking deep into my eyes, like he was trying to see if my pupils were dilated, if I was high. I get that a lot. "He won't be hard to find."

"He won't?"

Kevin made a sound like a muscle jerk. "You can't recognize him, can you?"

My stomach started to knot. "Why?"

"Because he's right inside. In the club."

I went cold, and smelled nothing at all. "He's…" I couldn't get out anymore. It couldn't be true. "Show me," I said, a croak.

Kevin motioned, and I followed his blur of shifting flavors back into the club.

Just as we stepped inside, the band took the stage. The opening guitar chord struck me with a shiver, and I knew it'd hit the rest of the scrambleheads the same way. There must've been fifty of them there – every fucked-up vet on the eastern seaboard had come to get laid by the music, and as the guitar player lashed into the first song, they trembled with the foreplay stroke of fingers against skin.

I had to struggle to stay focused on Kevin, as he pushed through them. The rhythm had kicked in now, and the ex-soldiers before the stage had become a seething, gyrating mass. A lot of them must have been wearing their old fatigues, because I tasted sand-blasted metal and sweat. Kevin paused just long enough to examine each face before pushing through again, pulling me after him. They ignored him; he was just a whiff of smell intruding on the beautiful noise they were feeling.

Finally Kevin stopped, and I tried to look where he was looking. He'd paused before a man who tasted the same as all the rest, whose gasps provoked the same sandpaper-y sensations that the others did.

I must have looked perplexed, because Kevin leaned over, put his mouth up against my ear, and I felt, "Craig."

I tried to look, God *damn* it, I tried, but the confused synapses in my brain sent the same wrong message. I had to take Kevin's word for it, that this was Sergeant Dean Craig, that this flood of sour tastes that made me gag was the murderer who had haunted me for three fucking years.

And then I knew: It was Craig. It had *always* been Craig. Of course – he'd been here right next to me, every time the band had played, show after show, night after night, for at least a year, and I'd been too fucked up to know it. He'd stood by me, shouting and gasping and ejaculating into his stained army pants just like I had, and every night I'd let him walk away from the show. Every night I'd let this fucking killer go home; it was practically like I'd helped the army bury Craig's crimes. Except they'd done it skillfully; I'd done nothing, just sat back like a useless lump of flesh and let them all go on.

No more. Not tonight.

"Can I have your phone?" I asked Kevin. My new best friend Kevin, a man my age who would never really understand what it was like to wake up screaming and feel the sound, although later I'd try to explain it to him, and he would nod and I'd taste his nod rather than see it, but he wouldn't get it. And then he'd put Craig away while I struggled against my own senses just to wash other people's food-stained plates.

Kevin gave me his phone. It was still set up to the helmet video, the one that would show the whole world what Craig had done, and his supporters had covered up. I fingered the "play" arrow. The video started. I hoped it was at the right place; I only knew I tasted something like the bottom of a garbage pail.

Craig was bouncing around with the rest, but he slowed and then stopped when I held the video up before his face. He was being assaulted with tastes that he couldn't put together, even though he tried. He knew it was bad. Really fucking bad.

I leaned over to him, screaming to be heard over the music, hoping he was at least as good as I was at unscrambling our scrambled signals.

"Craig," I shouted, my lips an inch from his ear, "you're fucked."

He felt that, all right, because he turned and stared at me. "Who the goddamn hell are you?" he asked, his body still trying to jitter to the music.

"Private Jackson Howard, SIR." I saluted him – and then, while my hand was still on my forehead, I uncurled only my middle finger.

That got through, because Craig panicked and bolted.

He didn't even make it off the dance floor before I caught up to him. I grabbed a fistful of his shirt and yanked him around, and for a split second my senses unscrambled, and I saw his face, his real face, at the same time as I saw his memory face, three years ago, as he stood over a dead family.

When my fist connected with Craig's face, I smelled ozone and rank fear sweat, and he dropped to the floor as I tasted bile…but the image in my head of a shot-up kid wasn't tainted with any sensation but horror, it was clear as yesterday, and it drove me to squat and hit him again. The music was still going, and they were playing my favorite song, but the release I was feeling was anything but sexual. It was knowing that the nightmares might end now, and that I might be able to get through a day without feeling/smelling my gut drop out whenever I thought about the war. It was knowing that the dark alleys in my dreams might be empty at last.

Then somebody – Kevin – was pulling me back, and I stumbled to my feet, and he shouted, "You got him, Jack. It's done."

I was panting and I knew there was blood on my knuckles, but I didn't care. The music took me, then, and it was a victory dance and an orgasm and a giant jitter of joy and relief all together.

The noise had never felt so good.

Plant Life

Greg F. Gifune

"Mary, Mary, quite contrary, how does your garden grow?"
—Mary, Mary, Quite Contrary

1.

Unseen things began to move, slithering, growing and coming alive in ways he did not understand. Wrapping around him, they coiled like dozens of tiny snakes slowly tightening around his head and throat, over his eyes, across his nose and mouth, a jungle of them enveloping his face and body until they had come together to form a hideous cocoon. Though he attempted a scream and struggled to free himself, he knew it was all in vain. There was nothing he could do to shed this new skin, even as it blinded and choked him, and his body bucked with violent resistance. And as his final breath rasped free, barely audible beneath the networks of vines, he wished for death. But he understood even then, as these things pierced his flesh and moved deeper inside him, that he was changing instead. He was becoming something else, something horrible and hideous, but something still profanely *alive*.

Ed awakened gasping for air, his hands fumbling at his throat. As he lay atop the sheets, the ceiling fan overhead spun furiously but did little to decrease the humidity in the bedroom. As he escaped sleep, his vision focusing and his head clearing, he listened a moment, but all he could hear was the steady hum of the ceiling fan. He was alone—his wife Hannah had evidently gotten up ahead of him, which was her custom—but the house seemed unnaturally still. Theirs was the last house on a rural road, so they got little traffic, and their neighbors were mostly elderly. Generally, the area was quiet. But this was different, as on this day, the normally peaceful silence of their neighborhood left Ed instinctually uneasy. Still bleary-eyed, he rolled from bed and headed downstairs to see where everyone was.

That summer was their dog Corky's second, and although he was nearly two, he was a lab, and labs have notoriously long puppy-hoods. Perhaps because he'd been raised in a household with cats (they outnumbered him three-to-one), Corky had become much like his feline brother and sisters, a creature of habit, and so, he'd get up every morning a bit earlier than Ed, and accompany Hannah downstairs. She'd let him out to do his business while she put the coffee on. Once Corky was back inside, he'd sit in the kitchen with Hannah until she became sufficiently distracted then he'd sneak away and creep back upstairs. While Ed slept (or sometimes only pretended to still be asleep), Corky would select one of his toys from the myriad littering their bedroom floor, and then furiously wagging not only his tail but his entire back end (a maneuver Ed had dubbed Corky's "happy dance"), Corky would launch all eighty-five pounds of himself onto the bed and come crashing down on top of him. This had become the norm for Ed, to awaken to Corky wiggling about on top of him doing his happy dance. When he'd been a small puppy it was adorable, but the larger he got, the harder it became to survive unscathed. Ed didn't mind though, as once he was fully awake, Corky would drop the toy, shower him with kisses then flop down next to him and stare at him with those big, dark, adoring eyes. It simply wasn't possible to be upset or to wake up anything but happy when one's day began with that level of unconditional love.

But there was no sign of Corky either.

Still suffering the ravages of vague but terrifying nightmares, as Ed stumbled down the stairs, he couldn't shake the feeling that there was something horribly wrong.

The den was empty, as was the kitchen. The coffee pot beckoned from his peripheral vision, but he ignored it and shuffled over to the sliders overlooking the backyard instead. They'd had a fence installed around the entire yard when they got Corky, so they could let him out and he could run and play out back safely. Ed looked to the gate. It was closed, so he turned his attention beyond the deck to a modest raised-bed garden Hannah had planted earlier that year. She'd been laid off from her job several months before, and though she'd always been interested in gardening, until recently, she'd never had time to pursue it. In many ways her garden had become a saving grace, as it gave her something enjoyable to focus her time and energy on when she wasn't searching the online job sites or going on interviews, neither of which had yet amounted to much.

When Ed stepped out onto the deck, the first thing he saw was Corky sitting a few feet from the garden. The dog seemed oddly docile, just sitting there and staring straight ahead. Nearby, Hannah stood gazing at the garden as well. Although he felt better the moment he saw them, Ed moved to the edge of the deck, and without saying anything, watched his wife and dog awhile, his eyes darting between them and the garden. What were they both staring at so intently?

"Honey?" he said.

"Morning," Hannah said softly, without turning around.

Ed slowed his stride long enough to give Corky a quick pat on the head before sidling up next to Hannah. He slid an arm around her waist, leaned in and kissed her on the cheek. "Why are you guys staring at the garden?"

The word *garden* seemed to snap her out of her trance. Hannah blinked a few times, wiped away some perspiration from her forehead with the back of her hand then returned the kiss. "Trying to figure out what happened," she finally said.

Ed knew nothing about gardening, and did his best to just stay out of Hannah's way when it came to such things, but when she pointed to a specific area of her garden he saw that one section of large-leaf squash plants had all been yanked free and left flattened in the soil. They looked as if someone had pulled them up then stomped them down.

"With the fence, some small critters can get through underneath—maybe a bunny or even a raccoon—but whatever did this had to have some weight behind it," she explained. "It'd have to be something…*big.*"

"Was the gate locked when you got up?"

Hannah nodded, the perplexed look on her otherwise pretty face growing worse. "Yeah, so I can't figure out how anything that size could've gotten into the yard."

"I suppose some kids could've scaled the fence, maybe, but—"

"What kids? And why would kids take the time to climb a six-foot fence in the middle of the night just to pull up and stomp some squash plants? Besides, Corky would've heard them. He hears everything, especially at night."

Not this time, Ed thought. "Are there any footprints?"

"Nope, and that's bizarre too."

"What do you think, pal?" Ed slapped his leg, which usually resulted in the dog bounding over to him joyfully. This time Corky slowly strode toward him and sat at Ed's feet, but the dog's eyes remained trained on the garden. "It wasn't you was it, buddy?"

"No," Hannah answered. "When I let him out before we went to bed last night I was out here with him and I checked on the garden. It was fine and Corky never went anywhere near it."

Ed squatted down and petted the dog. "You feeling all right, puppy?"

"I think he's a little spooked." Hannah pushed her bottom lip out and blew a renegade strand of her short brown hair away from her eyes. "I am too."

"I really don't think it's anything to be frightened of."

"Someone came into our yard in the middle of the night and did this while we were sleeping, Ed."

"Honey, listen, nobody came into the yard. It could've been raccoons, maybe a whole family or something. A bunch of good-sized ones could've tried to eat them by pulling them loose like that and trampled them in the process."

She thought about it a moment. "It's possible, but where are *their* prints then?"

"Who knows? Faded overnight, maybe, or—I don't know—but doesn't that seem more likely? Besides, why would anyone want to hurt your garden?"

"I don't know." Hannah shrugged her narrow shoulders. "I'm just pissed."

But there was more to it than that. Ed could tell she felt some-thing deeper because he felt it too, something he couldn't quite put his finger on, an instinctual sensation that crawled up the back of his neck and whispered in his ear that despite what common sense dictated, there was more to this than raccoons or other critters. He'd felt it even before he knew about the vegetable garden. Memories of his nightmare flickered through his mind in blinking segments. Still, Ed forced a smile and did his best to mask his own feelings, to calm Hannah and to defuse the situation as best he could. "Let's go in and have some breakfast," he said.

Together, they strolled back toward the house.

Corky remained where he was, watching the garden. After a mo-ment, there emanated from deep within him a barely audible sound somewhere between a growl and a whimper.

2.

That afternoon, Hannah pulled the ruined plants from the gar-den and planted some new ones. She figured it was early enough in the season where if she got them into the ground now they'd still be ripe and ready to be picked at some point late in the summer. But as she worked beneath a brilliant sun, down in the dirt of her garden on her hands and knees, she couldn't seem to stop running various scenarios in her head. *What could've done this?* She wondered. The work done, she sat back on her heels, wiped some sweat from her brow then looked around. Behind the garden was fence. To the right was open yard, to the left a series of wild plants growing along the fence. Mostly weeds and a few leafy plants, but they were all fine. Beyond them were several birdfeeders and a cement birdbath. Han-nah stood and inspected the area to see if any additional damage had been done. Though the birdbath needed to be filled, otherwise, far as she could tell, nothing else had been disturbed or looked in any way out of the ordinary. She plucked a bottle of water from the pocket of her shorts and took a long drink. As she screwed the plastic cap back on the bottle she suddenly felt lightheaded. The world swayed a bit, tilting one way then the next, until she nearly fell.

Corky must've sensed something was wrong, because he vaulted from his step on the deck and ran to her immediately, placing himself between Hannah and the garden and nuzzling her thigh with his nose in an attempt to push her back toward the deck and away from…*Away from what,* she wondered, *the garden?*

"It's OK, boy," she said, suddenly breathless. Nausea had joined the wooziness. She carefully lowered herself down onto the grass and sat there a moment. After a few deep breaths the feeling left her, but the dog continued to gently push his nose into the side of her shoulder. "Corky, stop, baby, I'm fine," Hannah told him. "I think I just got overheated. I should really wear a hat if I'm going to be out here in direct sunlight so long. Mommy should know better."

Corky moved directly in front of her, blocking her view of the garden. Though his tail wagged, his face continued to register not only concern, but anxiety.

Hannah looked to the garden. Was she missing something?

A dark blur slipped quickly along the very edge of her peripheral vision.

She snapped her head in that direction, but the black form she would've sworn had just glided right by her was nowhere in sight. "Christ," she said softly, running a hand over her forehead and across her hair. "What the hell?"

Again, Corky's nose pressed into her shoulder, this time harder than before.

"You don't want me anywhere near that garden, do you, Cork?"

He gave a single high-pitched bark, as if to say, "Duh!" then ran toward the deck and looked back like he'd expected her to follow.

Strange, she thought. *Even the dog senses something's not right.*

Hannah struggled to her feet. Her tank top was stuck to her like a second skin, matted down against her body with sweat. As she and Corky went inside, she tried to convince herself that it was simply the sun that had gotten to her just then.

She failed.

3.

That night, heavy summer winds blew in off the nearby Atlantic, bringing with them torrential rains that soaked everything down and lashed the house with a steady drumming sound. Ed lay awake in bed, watching the ceiling fan spin through the darkness overhead. He wanted to sleep, had every intention of it when he and Hannah had gone to bed earlier, but so far it had eluded him. Instead, he lay there wondering about the garden, about the strange way he'd felt since that morning, and how oddly Hannah and Corky had behaved since. Something was wrong. He knew this—knew it on an instinctual level—but he had no idea what. Earlier, while Hannah had taken a quick shower, he and Corky had gone outside. Ed had walked the garden, inspecting it and searching for…for what? He still wasn't sure. The dog had kept his distance, refusing to accompany Ed beyond a certain point. That had never happened before. None of this made any goddamn sense. Hannah had removed the damaged plants and planted new ones. Nothing else in the garden had changed or seemed out of the ordinary. He even went so far as to check the wild lilac bushes along the fence nearby and behind the garden. All were in place and undisturbed. But not long after he'd started back for the house he'd found himself lightheaded and nauseous to the point that he had to sit down for a spell.

Now, hours later, those symptoms had left him, but he still felt…*strange*…unsure of himself and his surroundings. He reached over for Hannah, his hand coming to rest against her bare thigh. She was sound asleep, partially wrapped in a sheet.

Ed swung his feet around to the floor. The window next to their bed was open, the screen soaked with rain. Beyond, nothing but a stormy night…why then did he have the sudden overwhelming feeling that he and his wife were not alone?

A quick glance to the foot of the bed revealed Corky, asleep and snoring quietly. Odd, he always came awake whenever Ed or Hannah did. In fact, Ed could not recall a time when he'd gotten up and Corky hadn't woken up as well.

He rose from the bed, padded quietly in his bare feet across the carpeted floor and to the stairs. Hesitating, he looked back at the bed. Neither Hannah nor Corky had moved. *Something's wrong,* a voice in his head whispered. *There's someone or something here. Not in the house but...close...nearby...*

Ed started down the stairs, thunder growling in the distance, barely audible above the relentless rain. "The garden," he whispered to himself. "There's something in the garden."

Even as he moved through the house, stumbling a few times in the darkness and shaking with nervous energy, Ed felt ridiculous. But he was also gripped with fear the level of which he had never before experienced.

As he reached the sliders, he flipped the outside light on and leaned close to the glass. The light illuminated most of the deck while rain and darkness conspired to make visibility beyond it essentially nonexistent. Still, Ed strained his eyes and continued staring into the night, the sounds of the storm clamoring all around him, so close and violent on the other side of those doors. *Such a thin separation,* he thought, *such a flimsy barrier.* If someone or something wanted in, would it be so hard to smash through these doors or perhaps a window? Since many of the windows were open, a screen could simply be torn free and that which separated *out there* from *in here* would be no more.

And then he saw it.

Something separated from the darkness. It was too dark to make out, but Ed could've sworn he'd seen movement *within* the rain, a dark form slinking through the storm in the direction of the garden.

"What are you doing?"

"Jesus Christ!" he gasped. Hannah stood a few feet away. Behind her, halfway down the stairs, Corky watched through the balusters. "You scared the shit out of me."

"Is something out there?" she asked, taking up position at the sliders.

"I don't know." Ed tried to calm down but couldn't stop trembling. Was this a dream? Why did everything feel so *wrong?* "Am I asleep?"

"You're awake," she told him.

"Are you sure?"

She hugged herself against the gooseflesh rising along her skin. "Yes, I—of course—we're both standing here talking. It's storming outside and you—tell me what you saw out there, Ed."

"I'm not sure. I thought I saw something move across the yard but—"

"I'm calling the police." Hannah spun and headed for the phone. Why was she moving with such a strange gait, as if drunk?

"Wait, I can't be sure. I just…"

"You just *what?*" she snapped. "Ed, it's the middle of the night. If there's someone walking around in our yard we need to call the police."

"I can't be sure I saw anyone."

"Are you sure you *didn't?*"

"No, but—"

"Then I'm calling the cops."

"It was probably the storm playing tricks on me. I looked out through the sliders and I thought I saw something but…" He swallowed, cleared his throat. "I just don't…Hannah, do you feel all right?"

"Do *you?*"

"No, I don't feel like myself."

"Were you sleepwalking?"

"I've never sleepwalked in my life." A chill gripped him. "Why?"

"Because you just asked me if you were asleep." The troubled look on her face grew deeper with concern. "And you don't remember going outside, do you?"

"I didn't go outside. I just looked out the sliders."

"Ed," she said softly, "you're drenched."

"What are you talking about? I just got out of bed and…"

The rest of the sentence died in his throat as he looked down and saw a small puddle on the floor slowly forming a halo around his bare, mud-caked feet.

4.

Though it took a while, Hannah eventually convinced Ed he'd simply had a bad dream and sleepwalked. Once he changed into dry clothes, she got him to bed, but it was nearly four in the morning when he finally fell back to sleep. Hannah, on the other hand, was up for the night. She returned downstairs with Corky, made sure the back light was on then went and got their video camera from the front hall closet. They'd purchased it a couple years before but rarely used it. The battery would give six hours of continued use, so if she set it up just before they went to bed the following evening, it would record throughout the majority of the night.

As the sun came up, Hannah ventured out onto the deck. Corky ran off into the yard to do his business while she checked on the garden. The rain had stopped an hour or so before, but the ground was still soft and wet. A series of footprints led from just beyond the deck to the garden then back again. Further proof that Ed had sleep-walked out there in the storm, and yet…

More plants had been pulled up out of the ground and left trampled in the garden again. Even sleepwalking, why would Ed damage the garden? It made no sense.

Hannah crouched down. Ed's footprints appeared to stop about four feet from the garden. Had he jumped the rest of the way and come crashing down? It would certainly explain how two tomato plants had been ruined. A closer look around the smashed plants revealed no footprints—same as before—but the soil was so disrupted by the rain and mud and damage, it was impossible to know for sure if the storm had simply masked them.

Though the mystery had likely been solved, Hannah still wasn't buying it, not completely anyway. She still felt there was something more to this than a sudden case of destructive sleepwalking. Besides, why was her husband suddenly sleepwalking in the first place? He'd never exhibited such behavior. And why was he ruining the garden? Had he developed a subconscious dislike for vegetables? The entire thing was so ridiculous it might've been humorous, had it not been so oddly terrifying.

With the video camera slung around her neck, Hannah began to pull the ruined plants from the garden. By the time she returned to the house, she'd again begun to feel frightened and uneasy, certain someone or something was watching her.

Later, she'd set the camera up to record from the edge of the deck, and she'd leave the back light on all night.

Then, she thought, *we'll know for sure what's happening out here after dark.*

5.

"I think I should make an appointment with the doctor while I'm still on vacation," Ed said. "If I'm sleepwalking there must be treatment for it."

Hannah nodded, but she wasn't really listening, she was too pre-occupied with the camera, positioning it just right on the edge of the deck so it would be sure to record the garden once night had fallen. "What I don't understand is how something could trample the plants like that and not leave a footprint. The rain left the ground soft, there should've been footprints—I mean—there'd almost *have* to be, right?"

"Did you hear what I said? Why are you preoccupied with filming the garden tonight? Obviously I'm the culprit and didn't even realize it."

"You would've left footprints," she said, continuing to fiddle with the camcorder.

"Hannah, this is serious. I'm concerned about my health, not the garden."

"In fact, you did leave footprints all around the garden and leading up to the garden, but not in the garden itself, where the plants were destroyed. It's as if something dropped down from *above* the plants and did it without touching the ground."

Ed sighed. "Do you hear yourself?"

"But that's not possible, because there's nothing there for something to hang from. No trees, nothing. Even if they could, it doesn't explain the plants being trampled. Unless…could we be misinterpreting what we've seen somehow?" Apparently satisfied with her positioning of the camera, she stood up and put her hands on her hips. "Tonight we'll know for sure what's going on. The camera won't lie."

"It's going to show me sleepwalking and trampling your garden."

"Fine, if it does, we'll get you to a doctor pronto. But I think there's more to it. I can *feel* it. Can't you?"

He could but didn't want to admit it. "I don't feel like myself. I haven't since this began."

"Same here," she said. "Even Corky hasn't been himself these last few days."

Let her do her experiment, he thought. The night would reveal the truth.

Ed gazed out across the yard. The heat was rising, blurring the landscape. Even their uneventful little neighborhood seemed ominous now, as if just behind the curtain they'd mistaken for reality, a predator was slowly crawling free, slinking closer…and closer still.

6.

Beneath dark and starless skies, Ed slept. Though he somehow knew he was asleep and dreaming, the fear exploding through him was real. He struggled to move, but unseen things held him tight, coiling, tightening around his limbs and torso, his throat, across his face and mouth and forehead, pulling, dragging and choking him with impossible strength. He tasted dirt and grit. It gagged him, but even as he attempted to thrash about, he knew these things were also entering him, piercing his flesh and slithering deep inside his body. He could feel them scurrying through him, beneath his skin. His eyes were wide with terror, but he could just barely see, and his attempted screams were little more than gurgling groans trapped in the base of his throat. And yet he knew he wasn't dying. He was still alive. Alive…but not the same…

He'd become something new.

7.

In the morning, Ed found Hannah at the kitchen table sipping a cup of coffee, the recorder before her. For the first time in recent memory, she was smiling broadly and looked completely at ease. Corky lay at her feet sleeping. "Have a seat," she said, patting the chair next to her. "You need to see this."

He shuffled over to the table and plopped down next to her as she turned the viewer toward them and hit PLAY. "Watch," she said, "and you'll see we've solved the mystery of the garden."

The light from the deck behind the camera gave off enough illumination to clearly see the garden and fence behind it. Ed watched awhile but saw nothing unusual.

"There," Hannah said, pointing to a section of fence directly behind the garden.

After a few seconds, something moved. Atop a red stem growing along the fence, a white-petal flower with a purple center and outer edges slowly came into full bloom. "Is that the wild lilac bush?"

"We *thought* that's what was growing along the fence." She hit PAUSE. "But it's not. I've been on the Internet checking it out. You're not going to believe this, but it's a nocturnal strain of a plant known as the *Devil's Trumpet*. It's a highly toxic plant. Every part of it is poisonous. Even smelling it can affect you. It's a goddamn hallucinogen. Even indirect interaction with it can cause disorientation, blurred vision, dry mouth, severe hallucinations and paranoia. It has affects similar to LSD. That's why we kept seeing strange things and having all those odd feelings. It's why you were wandering around out in the storm the other night without any memory of having done so."

Ed rubbed his eyes and tried to absorb everything she'd told him. "What's something so toxic doing in our yard?"

"That's what I wanted to know. A little more research revealed that its seeds are sometimes found in wild birdseed—like the kind we buy for the feeders—only it takes a long time to germinate, and oftentimes it never even blooms."

He stared at the flower on the screen, so white and solitary in the surrounding darkness. It seemed hard to believe something so beautiful could've caused such havoc. "So all this time we've just been *drugged?*"

"Higher than kites," she giggled. "It's all been a bad drug trip. We're not crazy, we're not sick, and there's nothing coming into the yard at night pulling up our garden."

"Are there any lasting effects? Should we still see a doctor?"

"Nope, the reactions wear off in a matter of hours. Problem was we kept poisoning ourselves every time we went anywhere near the damn thing so we never had a chance to recover unless we were asleep."

That would explain the nightmares, he thought. "We have to get rid of it."

"Already took care of it. Put on a pair of gloves, covered my nose and mouth with a bandana, and cut the thing down. I walked it out into the woods and buried it."

Ed glanced down at Corky. He'd come awake. His tail thumped the floor as if in joyful agreement. "So that's it, huh, Cork?" he said before leaning over and planting a kiss on Hannah's lips. "Good job, babe."

As they hugged, Ed couldn't help but look beyond her to the sliders and the deck and garden beyond. He shuddered.

"What's wrong?" Hannah asked.

"The whole thing's just so damn creepy."

"But it's over now," she said through a wide smile. "It's all over."

8.

Ed sat on the deck, watching the birds fly about from feeder to feeder, while others hopped in the birdbath, or searched the ground for fallen seed. The sun was high in the sky and beating down on him mercilessly, but he remained where he was, sipping ice tea and listening to the birds sing. It wouldn't be long before vacation was over and he'd return to work, so despite the heat, Ed intended to enjoy the weather as best he could. But his mind kept returning to the *Devil's Trumpet.* He pulled his sunglasses down onto the bridge of his nose and looked out across the yard to the garden. *Damndest thing I've ever heard,* he thought, and although he now knew the reasons for their strange behavior, thoughts and nightmares, and the previous symptoms he'd suffered were no longer evident, there was still something about that garden that gave him the creeps. He rose from his chair and stepped down onto the lawn. Hannah and Corky were inside, and a part of him wished they were out there with him, as just then, he didn't feel entirely comfortable being alone. Even though Hannah had said the effects didn't last, maybe some were still lingering within him.

He felt it necessary to approach the garden, almost as if it were beckoning him, drawing him closer to something he could not quite comprehend. His chest tightened as pieces of the nightmare flashed in his head—*living things coursing through him, vines tangling and sliding around and within him, dragging him down beneath the dirt—* so he drew a deep breath and let it out slowly. *No,* he thought, *I will not let this get the better of me. The mystery is solved. What the hell are you afraid of?*

He returned his gaze to the garden. *What was I really doing out there at night?*

Ed moved across the yard, stopping just prior to the raised bed. He crouched down and inspected the garden. No more damaged plants, everything looked fine. He looked over at the bird feeders and bath. Strange, the birds were suddenly gone and the area had grown deathly quiet, much the way it did when a hawk or other predator was nearby. Shielding his eyes from the sun with a hand, he looked to the sky, expecting to see a large bird of prey circling overhead.

The sky was clear.

His eyes panned back to the garden, slowly considering each plant. Had he really pulled them up without realizing it? Had Hannah? It seemed they had, yet despite the evidence, deep down he wasn't sure he bought it, and he had no idea why.

Hannah's words echoed in his mind.

What I don't understand is how someone or something could trample the plants like that and not leave a footprint.

Sliding forward onto his knees, he dropped a hand to the loose soil and pushed it around a bit.

It's almost as if someone dropped down from above.

Ed's finger brushed something foreign.

But that's not possible, because there's nothing there for someone or something to hang from. No trees or anything.

Using both hands now, Ed pushed more dirt aside, digging a bit deeper into the garden with his fingers.

Unless…could we be misinterpreting what we've seen somehow?

His fingers touched something soft but also hard. What the hell—

And then it hit him. What if the plants hadn't been trampled at all? What if it only *appeared* that way? Not because someone above had pulled them up, but because something *below* had pushed them *out*.

Frantically clearing the dirt, Ed stopped as quickly as he'd begun, paralyzed with horror so terrifying he could feel his entire body shutting down. What appeared to be a human face was buried in the garden. *His* face—dirty and tangled in weeds and vines, eyes wild, mouth open like a hungry baby bird—and something resembling human hands not quite finished, rising up through the dirt, through the garden floor to clamp onto his wrists.

As his mind shattered, he tried to scream, but even as he slammed forward into the dirt and felt whatever had a hold of him squeezing and pulling him down, he knew it would do no good.

9.

Corky sat in front of the sliders growling.

"What's the matter?" Hannah asked from somewhere behind him.

The dog cocked his head, confused and trying to understand not only what he'd just witnessed, but what he was now seeing.

"What's Daddy doing? Do you see Daddy?"

No. Not Daddy. Something *like* Daddy. But not Daddy. Not anymore. Something…finishing…growing…*becoming*. But not Daddy.

As Hannah reached for the sliders, Corky barked, jumped up and tried to block her from going outside.

"Down boy!" she scolded, grabbing his collar.

Reluctantly, and with a whimper, the dog sat down.

"Stay. Be a good boy and stop it now, it's just Daddy."

No...not Daddy...

Hannah opened the sliders and moved out onto the deck to find Ed coming up the steps. He was filthy and disheveled. "What the hell have you been doing, rolling around on the ground? You're scaring the dog."

"Come with me." Coughing, he wiped dirt from his lips and took her hand. "I want to show you something."

His hand felt odd. "Why," she asked, "what's up?"

"There's something you need to see," he said, "something in the garden."

As he led her across the yard, Corky hurled himself against the sliders, growling and barking with furious violence.

Not Daddy!

And there, just beneath the dirt...slowly emerging...growing impossibly from the garden soil...

Not Mommy.

I Am Become Poe

Kevin Quigley

You may think me mad, I suspect, but I assure you, I am quite sane. My name is Bill Wilson—some know me as William Wilson—and it is the name attached to me at birth. Perhaps that gives some indication as to why my life has run the course it has, and why I felt compelled to follow in that path, though I knew certain destruction lay at the end.

My parents were both Poe aficionados, going so far as to name both their children after characters in Poe's canon. My sister, Lenore, died early, at the age of six, having fallen down a well and broken her neck. I, William, was but a child at the time, but I do recall the sight of her limp, horrifically twisted body as the paramedics dragged it to the above world. I stared at her—unable to stop myself. I stared at Lenore as she lay on a blanket my parents laid out on the lawn, as she lay mangled and distorted and not my sister but a dead thing which somehow took her form. I gazed, and a phrase, called forth from the depths of my five year old mind,

Nameless here *forevermore.*

The line, the words, recited often by my parents since I was born, and perhaps that was where the descent really began. I forced myself to learn to read, forced myself at that age to read and forget the death of my sister. By the age of seven, I had read all the works of Edgar Allen Poe, and could recite "The Raven" by heart. Let that be a point of fact to those who would call me mad. Since my earliest days, I have been a fastidious one, an exact one, and some may perceive that precision as madness. So be it. Perchance my tale will change such a one's mind.

I decided early on that the primary source of pleasure in my life would be derived from the words and works of Poe. This was not a conscious decision; all vital acts, I believe, emerge from the subconscious. In my school years, I became a student of Poe, often knowing more of the man than my professors did. I sought out collections of his work, delighting in the rarest manuscripts. A mere dozen copies of Poe's first collection, *Tamerlane and Other Poems*, still exist, and I have held one. In school, my essay titled "Edgar Allan Poe and the Dark Art of Madness," won me the position of head editor on the school literary magazine, and a partial scholarship to the university of my choice. I, of course, chose the University of Virginia, where Poe studied, later neglecting my work and dropping out, just as he did.

I actually did spend a brief time in the Army, but opted out after only a few short months. It was then my true life began, as a newspaper editor and part-time carpenter in a small town named Buxley, Massachusetts. I chose the town for two reasons—firstly, because it was within driving distance of Boston—Poe's hometown—and secondly, because it was the only place in the country where I was able to locate a street actually called Tamer Lane. I purchased a small house there, and took a wife by the name of Virginia. As I have said, I had done none of these things consciously, nor with any ebb of sanity. From my youngest days, I have felt that my life has been mapped out in the course that Poe navigated. I believe I was born unto this world to resume the shape and form that Poe originally designed—to become Poe, to live again as Poe once lived. And I was almost successful, almost, almost.

It was the frequent appearance of the bird, I believe, that caused my downfall. The bird ever so gently tapping at my window in the dead of night. I awoke late one evening, plagued by headaches that remained as remnants from the opium-laced drink in which I'd earlier indulged. Virginia slept in the other chamber, and perhaps it was for the best that she could not hear the tapping. O, it was maddening! I came to with a start, my head pounding, and I looked toward the window, at the ebony bird beguiling, tapping its beak against the pane of glass. Tapping, tapping. I stood slowly, rising to stand, staring at this bird. This black bird. I knew, in my heart, that this, as with the rest of my life, had been scripted. I delighted in knowing which words to say, and which actions to take.

I threw the window open, and the bird, of course a raven, fluttered in and did indeed perch above the bust of Pallas just above my chamber door. I'd had the bust made to my own specification, no expense spared. To become Poe, one must live as Poe—and as the people he wrote about.

I turned toward the bird, my bedclothes clinging to me with the slick perspiration sliming my skin. "Though thy crest be shorn and shaven thou," I said, "Art sure no craven, ghastly grim and ancient Raven wandering from the nightly shore. Tell me what thy lordly name is, from the night's Plutonian shore!"

Yes, yes he did. Quoth the Raven, "Nevermore."

I stood, terrified and exalted, my mind reeling. *This* is what I had been waiting for! *This* was my entire life's journey, coming to summation here in my chamber! But, as I was to learn, it was simply the beginning. The quiet dedication to my master was finally being rewarded—I was to for once and forever become Poe!

Presently I gathered my wits about me. My heart was racing—the time had come to put Poe's words into action. I slowly opened my chamber door and allowed myself into the hallway that connected my room and Virginia's. I would have to be careful—this would have to be precise. I was nervous—very, very dreadfully nervous, but I was calm, and my senses were sharp. I knew what to do.

Slowly, I crept past Virginia's door and to the stairs, moving slowly so as not to wake her. I had almost reached the bottom when our cat, Plutonian, raced past me in the dark. It was all so perfect, so right. I reached out blindly and caught the cat by its tail, hoisting it up to me. It jerked about, its claws flying in the air. It could scratch me all it wanted—I was no longer myself. I held the beast at arm's length and carried it out to the backyard, moving slowly, slowly. It scrambled to and fro and I believe even then, it may have known what was to happen to it. I felt an odd sort of pity for the cat, but it was no longer my will which brought the animal to its destiny. It was Poe's will, Poe's story, just as it had always been.

Still grasping the creature by its tail, I entered the tool shed I had built in the backyard several years ago. From within I retrieved the two items I would need. The first was a length of rope. I exited the shed and proceeded to the large elm tree looming above. Securing the mewling, scratching creature under one arm, I tossed one end of the rope around a thick high branch. Swiftly, I made a layman's noose—a sloppy job, but one that would suit my purpose. I dug my hands into the bristly fur on the creature's back and thrust its head through the noose, yanking the rope tight and killing Plutonian instantly. It jerked twice and hung there, suspended in the moonlight, its tongue lolling out and spittle drying on its whiskers. I looked at it a moment longer, and saw with no surprise that the white patch splayed across the creature's back was no longer shapeless—it *had* formed into the shape of a Gallows, that mournful and terrible engine of horror and of crime! It was then I knew I was following Poe's prophecy to the letter—I could feel myself fill with the entity and being that was the man. My actions had shocked me, and I was terrified. Yet that terror was not fright, but a tremendous delight, and I felt the same exaltation I had felt in my chamber, the feeling that my entire life had been lived to be paid off in this moment.

I took the axe, the other item I had removed from the shed, and slowly made my way back to the house.

I stood outside Virginia's door, my hand on the doorknob. I needed to be slow, slow—as slow as possible. I turned the knob with exquisite care, opening the door just a crack. Little by little, the door opened, and I prided myself on my patience. An hour or more sped by as I continued to open the door, and finally it was open enough for me to look inside. Virginia lay sleeping, curled up in a ball near the head of the bed. For a moment, some of my original consciousness overtook me—I saw her beauty, and her innocence, and no part of me wanted to do what I was about to do. Yet just then, her eyes flew open, and she saw me and screamed, and the mind and will of Poe rushed back in me and I fled forward, axe high. Bringing it down, I screamed, as if gripped in a mania, "I am chilling and killing my Annabel Lee! I am chilling and killing my Annabel Lee!" I couldn't help it—the axe sliced down into her pretty face, into her bosom, erasing the young Virginia in a dark spray of blood. My young Virginia, my Annabel Lee.

❋

After I had buried her parts beneath the floorboards on the first floor, I glanced out the window to see the sun was coming up. I showered briefly, and then set about to telephone my good friend Charles Forten. Here, I would need to stray a bit from the path set before me, but what was important was the end, not the means.

"Hello?" he asked, and I found myself pleased that he was groggy, and that he would be more susceptible.

"Charlie," I said, keeping my voice regular, "Could you come over, please? I have some matters to discuss with you."

"Come to the House of Usher at seven in the morning? Why?" I smiled a bit at that. Charlie had always indulged me in my obsession.

"To tell you the truth, Virginia left me," I said. "We had a fight and she went all to pieces."

"Oh," Charles said sympathetically, "Oh, I'm sorry. Sure, I'll be right over."

As I waited for him, I prepared his drink—a glass of wine laced with opium. For once, I didn't take any opium for myself—I would need to be clear-headed for the work I was to perform.

Charles arrived soon after, and I immediately made it clear that I most wanted to be drunk at this time. We could discuss Virginia's leave at another time, but now was the time to drown my misery in wine. It being a Saturday, and Charles being a man who never passed up a drink—even early in the morning (in this, we were remarkably similar), he agreed. Before we set down in the sitting-room, he noticed the bottle from which I had drawn the wine.

"Amontillado, is it?" he asked.

"But of course, " I said, smiling. Once more, I felt a vague unease begin to creep into my senses. Perhaps this was not the way. Perhaps...

But then Charles put the glass of opium-wine to his lips, and I thought, *Nemo me impune lacessit.* No one challenges me with impunity. True, Charles hadn't challenged me with anything, but they were the right words at this point in the path, and again, I felt the presence of Poe grow strong within me.

❋

By his fourth glass of Amontillado, Charles began to halluci-
nate—imagining he saw rats traipsing about the floor, and blood
pouring out of the walls. I tell you, his imaginations of blood un-
nerved me, in light of Virginia's leave of this world. I knew the time
had come to rid myself of Charles Forten, and that in doing so, my
transformation would be complete. No longer just William Wilson,
a character, but Poe himself. I would become Poe.

Charles nodded, nearly napping, and I dragged him by the armpits to my cellar door, kicking it open. His boots thumped softly on
the cellar stairs, and he grunted once or twice from the depths of his
stupor. I had used this place mainly as a wine cellar and a workroom,
but I had also constructed something in the under dwelling my wife
had never discovered: a sub-cellar. As with all things, I had built it
primarily without knowing why, but I had persevered in the project,
and eventually had a small warren of rooms nearly the size of the
actual cellar itself. One could get there through means of a trapdoor,
if one knew the exact place it was set into the basement floor (I had
cleverly hidden the whole floor with a carpet several years before.) It
was here I bought Charles.

The ladder leading into the sub-cellar was steep, and I had to
hoist Charles down bodily. I would have to hurry—the movements
were quickening Charles' revival, and I wanted him to be in place
before that happened. I dragged him to the smallest room in the cellar—not more than an alcove, really, with twin iron supports standing parallel from the floor to the ceiling. I dumped Charles into the
room and quickly went to retrieve a box I had kept down here for
years without knowing why. Now, I understood.

Inside were four pairs of handcuffs, a bag of cement mixture,
and a straight razor. Another room in the catacomb was filled with
solid red bricks. I smiled as I realized my plan and set to work securing Charles' feet and legs to the iron supports. He finally began to
come around when I got the last appendage—his left foot—clinched
tightly.

"What are you doing?" Charles asked, his mouth moving slowly
and deliberately as if stuffed with cotton.

"I am exacting the thousand injuries of Charles Forten," I said, smiling. "You have done nothing out of sorts to me, so I must prepare the injuries myself. Stand still, Charles." It was then I brought the straight razor up and proceeded to cut my friend, over and over. Murder was not my intention, oh no, and the cuts I made were shallow. I counted—I was ever so precise—one thousand times I cut him, one thousand injuries. As it was written.

Charles stood alert, bleeding and whimpering, as I began to brick up the entryway to the alcove. He had weakened, and he called my name over and over. He begged of me. Once, he tried to laugh and pretend as if it were a joke. It appeared as if he remembered the story, and thought that by playing along he would appease me. I needed no appeasement, however. The horror and dread which had gripped my heart during the previous encounters had departed—and I felt free.

Before I fastened the last brick into place, I looked in at Charles. He had grown quiet, and now, I saw, his eyes had closed. "Charles," I called in a singsong manner.

His eyes opened slowly, and he turned his face to me. It was a bloody ruin. He began to grunt at me, trying to fight weakly against his bondage.

"Now you dwell alone, in a world of moan," I said, laughing, and put the last brick in. Satisfied with my work, I retreated to house above, where I partook in a bit of opium myself.

The police arrived some time later, answering calls regarding strange noises from my house. I appeared to them puzzled, then knowingly I revealed that my wife and I had had an argument the night before. They nodded, smiling, and I was about to send them on their way when I was taken by an overpowering need to extend hospitality to them. I invited them to stay for cookies and ale, and they stayed awhile with me, joking and talking. I began to show them around the house, noting all the additions and improvements I made. Eventually, God help me, I led them to the cellar, feeling an overwhelming and compelling need to show them the sub-cellar. I was so taken with pride over its construction, and no one had seen it but Charles, who was well on his way to dying in it.

"And here," I began, after showing them the workstation, and the wine racks "Is something I'm especially proud of. A sub-cellar I built entirely alone..." My voice trailed off. I had begun to hear it. It had been inevitable, of course.

The low, steady thump-thump of my wife's tell-tale heart coming from the floorboards above. My voice cracked, my head swooning. This was where it ended, I thought. This must be the ending to the story.

But it wasn't, for then a high-pitched scream of agony erupted from the trapdoor I had opened for the police. It was Charles, still alive and shrieking. My mind fluttered. Oh, God, my torments have arisen!

A shatter of glass came from behind us—I knew at once a force had broken the cellar window inward. I spun crazily to see the cat—*the very cat I had murdered the night before*—leaping through the window, snarling at me. Immediately following the wretched beast were birds—scores and scores of ravens, fluttering and flittering through the burst glass. They flocked upon me, pecking at me, each and every one screaming *Nevermore! Nevermore!, Nevermore!*

"Get thee back!" I howled! "Get thee back into the tempest!" They paid no mind, beating me to the floor of the cellar, and I lay screaming "I did it!" Shrieking, spewing forth my guilt and admittance, anything to stop the scourge of ravens!

The police lunged at me and dragged me up, rescuing me from the rats that had begun streaming up from the sub-cellar. The rats with their sharp, rodent teeth—hurrying at me in troops, wanting to gnaw and bite. The rats and the ravens and the cat, oh dear God!

It was then I fainted, and awoke in this place, sitting in a corner, wrapped in a tight vest that allows me no movement.

And still I am here, still am sitting, *still* am sitting, listening to the clanging of bells somewhere outside of my room. Surely you must not think me mad, but the people here do. They have begun to move the walls in on me, and I know that soon they will send me hurtling into the pit I cannot yet see. But they may have their torments, for I am become Poe, and I will just sit, just sit, and listen to the bells outside the walls of my room. They toll for my death, you see.

Bells, bells, bells.
Bells, bells, bells.

Arbeit Macht Frei

Del James

When David Bradshaw's parents told him about the month long vacation they were giving him as a graduation present, the seventeen year old almost felt like an adult. All of the hard work he'd done to bring his grades up so that colleges would consider his application, working two part-time jobs to make his car payments, and enduring all the drama that came with his final year of high school seemed worth the effort. His first trip overseas included London, Paris, Berlin, Rome, Barcelona, and a few other spectacular destinations.

The catch— his parents planned on chaperoning.

David couldn't believe they were tagging along. Talk about losing one's erection. Going to Europe with his folks seemed like the equivalent of being given a motorcycle with training wheels. So much for the coming of age adventure-- the road trip that includes meeting exotic young women in exotic places before travelling to the next city or country. Now, with his cock-blocking mom and dad along he wouldn't even need to program a 'European Hookups' play-list for his iPod.

If David had his iPod handy, "Teenage Lament" by Alice Cooper might be the most appropriate song for his feelings toward the month of July. Seriously, why call it a present if it had stipulations attached? This trip wasn't a gift to him. It was a family vacation for them. If they thought he couldn't see the reality of the situation they were wrong.

Nothing was ever quite as it seemed and behind their upwardly middle-class appearance, the Bradshaw family was mired in fiscal turmoil. Mom and dad declared strong annual incomes but they were heavily taxed and lived way above their means. When they weren't fighting over bills they squabbled about who spent more. To David it seemed as if they enjoyed arguing over money more than anything else they did together. Certainly more than whatever they were supposed to be doing behind closed bedroom doors.

For the duration of this so-called vacation where the Bradshaws would get cozy in one room, David would have to try his damndest to smile his way through boring sight-seeing tours and tune out his parent's constant bickering. Hence, the iPod must always be charged.

Big Ben is a big clock.
The Eiffel Tower is tall.
The Berlin wall isn't much of a wall anymore.
The Mona Lisa is ugly.
The Salvador Dali museum is bugged out.
English food is bland.
French food is not bland and not good.
Germans make great schnitzel.
Italian food is fantastic.
Spanish food is better than Italian food.
Wi-Fi rarely works well in Europe.
The subway system is manageable.
Tits on topless beaches are rarely tits that a young man wants to see.
No matter what language it was broadcast in, European television sucks ass.

Toward the end of the Bradshaw family vacation, mom and dad decided that instead of visiting Athens they would check out Krakow instead. Greece teetered on the verge of economic collapse and David's great grandfather was Polish so Mom felt a connection. Dad became sold on the idea when he learned how inexpensive Poland was.

Much to David's surprise, Poland was one of the most beautiful countries they visited. Other than its role as a punching bag in World War II and as a punch line for tasteless jokes, the teen knew very little about Poland. He learned that that Krakus founded a stone-age settlement on Wawel Hill. The settlement stood above a cave occupied by a dragon and would eventually become Poland's second largest and second most important city, Krakow. Many works of Polish Renaissance arts and architecture were created in Krakow during the 15ᵗʰ and 16ᵗʰ Century- Poland's Golden Age. Wawel Castle is the city's centerpiece and a must-see but most visitors are drawn to the Old Town. With its soaring Gothic churches and gargantuan Rynek Glowny, it is the largest market square in the nation.

Blue eyes trying to absorb it all, there was always something captivating to see in Krakow, especially the babes.

Polish girls are stunning. Drop dead gorgeous; even the average ones could pass for models—pale with high cheekbones, seductive eyes, long legs, and bouncy breasts. Judging from the looks of things Polish girls liked to drink beer and meet foreigners but other than observing, David never had the opportunity to find out. His parents never let him out of their sight. He even offered to give them some "alone time" back at the hotel but neither took the hint.

The day before flying back to God Bless America his parents booked a daytrip to Auschwitz. To David it seemed really strange that a place with such a vile history could somehow be a tourist destination but every year over a million people visited the concentration camp. For thirty euros per person, a company called Visit Auschwitz picked them up at their hotel and took them in an air-conditioned minibus to Auschwitz. Headsets and an English-speaking tour guide were included as part of the fee. Besides visiting the main camp at Auschwitz, the three-hour visit also featured a trip to the Birkenau death camp.

As they travelled along the quaint Polish countryside, a strange sensation began to slowly seep in. These roads were the same roads that the Nazis conquered. This was the exact same route that many soon-to-be exterminated Jews travelled. Dark history had been written here. Dark history inspired dark lyrics. Dark lyrics made for a fitting soundtrack. Fortunately David brought his iPod for the forty-five mile journey. Besides blocking out his parents and the other tourists, mandatory listening for the ride called for "Angel of Death" by Slayer.

When they arrived, the sky shone bright blue with plenty of billowy white clouds. Healthy trees stood in full bloom and the grass a vibrant green. Instead of some malevolent shadow hanging over the grounds, Auschwitz appeared surprisingly serene. If not for the diabolical history, this picturesque location could be where picnickers spent a relaxing afternoon.

The minibus parked in a lot with other vehicles from other tour groups like Escape2Poland and Never Forget Tours. Guides led hundreds of people from every ethnicity into the camp. The irony of being herded into a concentration camp was not lost upon David. It wasn't too difficult to mentally substitute the tour guide's casual attire for an SS uniform or add cloth stars to the summer clothing of the tourists. Maybe throw in a few snarling German Shepherds to keep everyone in line.

Everywhere he looked he saw men, women, and children lining up. Jews, Catholics, Slovaks, Germans, Latinos, and Asians... everyone had a different reason for visiting. Some people seemed quite affected by their surroundings. Others were posing for Facebook photos.

A dirt road cratered with rocks. A black and white gate, like a tollbooth, was raised. Steel and barbwire fences surrounded certain locations. Watchtowers with loud speakers, wooden signs with a skull and cross bones warned HALT! STOJ!

The tourists each wore transmitter radios around their necks and headphones to be able to listen to their tour guide. As David and the others entered the grounds, a Polish-accented voice in his headphones declared; "Konzentrationslager Auschwitz was a network of extermination camps built and operated by the Third Reich after the invasion of Poland during World War II. These were the largest of the German concentration camps, consisting of Auschwitz I, the Stammlager or base camp; Auschwitz II–Birkenau, the Vernichtungslager or Extermination camp, and forty-five satellite camps. In the years 1940 through 1945, the Nazis deported at least 1,300,000 people to Auschwitz. 1,100,000 were Jews. Most of them were murdered in the gas chambers as part of Hitler's Final Solution. Those not killed in the gas chambers died of starvation, forced labor, infectious disease, individual executions, and medical experiments. Everybody follow me and stay together please."

The group did as instructed and walked toward the infamous sign that greeted all arrivals to Auschwitz.

"Arbeit Macht Frei is a German phrase, 'labor makes you free' meaning work sets you free," the tour guide explained. "The expression comes from the 1873 title of a novel by Lorenz Diefenbach in which gamblers and fraudsters find the path to virtue through labor. The slogan was placed over the entrances to a number of Nazi concentration camps including Dachau, Gross-Rosen concentration camp, and Auschwitz I. Prisoners with metalwork skills made the sign above your heads and it was erected in June 1940. The phrase Arbeit Macht Frei seems not to have been intended as a mockery, nor as a false promise that those who worked to exhaustion would eventually be released, but rather as a kind of mystical declaration that self-sacrifice in the form of endless labor does in itself bring a kind of spiritual freedom."

Even wearing sunglasses, the bright sun forced David to squint. Clouds rolling by overhead, he stood utterly captivated by wrought iron and the power of the slogan. It was the first time he'd ever stood on a threshold.

Staring up at the sixteen-foot long sign while other visitors took photographs, he could relate to why five men tried to steal it a few years ago. According to the News, the ninety-pound sign had been half-unscrewed and half-torn off from above the death camp's gate. The thieves carried the sign to an opening in a concrete wall. Four metal bars that blocked the opening had been cut and the sign was loaded onto a vehicle and driven to a safe house. Before the thieves could sell the infamous sign, a countrywide search led to its recovery. The sign had been cut into three pieces but soon Arbeit Macht Frei was repaired and put back where it belonged.

Dressed in a black t-shirt with the Monster Energy Drink neon green logo, baggy camouflage pants, and hi-top sneakers, David walked under the sign and entered the death camp with a mission.

He wanted to steal a piece of history.

Obviously the sign was out of the question but there had to be something else he could swipe. A keepsake… a memento of some sort. Everything about Auschwitz held some sort of sinister history. Fuck bringing home a piece of the Berlin wall! Imagine what his friends would think if he brought home a tile or a piece of wood from Hell on Earth?

Tour groups shuffled in and out of various creepy red brick buildings. Square wooden signs, black with white numbers, denoted different blocks- BLOCK 5 or BLOCK 11, etc. David's tour group learned that prisoners who committed minor behavior infractions were sent to "The Dark Cell", a series of small jail cells in the basement of block 11, nicknamed "The Death Block." These small cells were entirely deprived of light and poorly ventilated. Prisoners served out the hours or days of their sentence in utter blackness, and often suffocated from lack of air. Although a trip to The Dark Cell did not mean certain death, it meant misery and possible death in the loneliest, most terrifying environment possible.

For major infractions of camp rules, the worst type of specialty cell in the basement of Block 11 was utilized. "The Starvation Cell" was very simple - prisoners were thrown into an empty cell, the door was locked, and they were left inside until they starved to death. Depending on the condition of the prisoner, this could take a day or a week; all while the captives of nearby cells heard their screams and pleas for food. Following the escape of one prisoner from Auschwitz in 1943, ten prisoners were put into starvation cells to die, as an example to others.

As if on cue, either mom's or dad's stomach made a gurgling sound.

Inside different buildings were different exhibits. Large signs explained what atrocities had occurred and included staggering historical facts. Encased behind glass were ceramic models of prisoners packed in trains and inside the gas chambers. David also examined train ticket stubs, record books, photographs, and a large mound of empty Zyklon B canisters.

"Judged by their physical appearance, people were selected as they exited the trains. Those to be gassed were assured that they were going to take a bath. Dummy showers were fixed to the wall. Menaced by attack dogs and beaten into formation, two thousand victims were crammed into the 210 square meter chamber. The chamber door was locked and the Zyklon B was poured. After fifteen minutes, the chamber was opened. Corpses were stripped of gold teeth, hair, earrings, rings, and anything else of value. Each day 10 kilos of gold were removed from the mouths of the dead. The victims' personal documents were destroyed."

As they moved further through the building, David couldn't believe the mountain of human hair on display. It stood forty feet in length and taller than he. *Then he observed a mountain of eyeglasses.... A mountain of prosthetic limbs and crutches.... A mountain of leather suitcases bearing the names of their previous owners... A mountain of toy dolls.... A mountain of shoes.*

An entire hallway displayed framed photographs of prisoners in their striped prisoner outfits. Like mug shots, these photographs contained the prisoners' name and their identification number. The tour guide explained that Auschwitz was the only camp to tattoo numbers on prisoners. A bottle of ink that had been used to tattoo thousands of prisoners was also on display.

Several bronze statues showed emaciated Jews in various poses. Unlike the statues David had seen all over Europe that tried to immortalize beauty, these somber statues were riddled with strife. Bony limbs and sallow eyes seemed to plead for mercy while tourists snapped photos on their smart phones.

Instead of taking a picture, David stroked the statue trying to feel whatever energy it contained.

The long face with sunken eyes stared back at him.

Next the tour group was taken outside of BLOCK 21. A bullet riddled wall known as "The Death Wall" served as a somber reminder that most of the executions took place at this spot.

"For serious infractions like insubordination or refusing to work, the Nazis would shoot a bullet into the back of the head of a kneeling victim," the tour guide said in a neutral tone. "These executions were carried out in full view of other prisoners, to set a horrifying example, but at least it was one of the quicker ways to die at Auschwitz. Okay people follow me."

The tour group was led to the wooden frame of a hangman's gallows. There was no rope, no noose but it wasn't very difficult to imagine where one would go.

"After the war, the First commandant of Auschwitz, SS Obersturmbannführer Rudolf Höss, was tried by the Polish Supreme National Tribune. Höss is credited for improving upon the methods used at other death camps by building his gas chambers ten times larger so that they could kill 2,000 people at once rather than 200. Found guilty of war crimes, Höss was hanged at this exact spot on April 16th, 1947."

A slight creaking sound, like a rope swinging, quickly came and went.

A faint breeze neither confirmed nor denied anything.

After finishing the Auschwitz I tour, the tour group was given a half an hour to visit the gift shops or grab a snack. Curious, David scoped out the gift shops while mom and dad sought out sandwiches and cold beverages. Items for sale at the gift shops included books like *Auschwitz- The Residence of Death, Auschwitz as seen by the SS, Josef Mengele: The Angel of Death,* and *Auschwitz- A History in Photographs.* Plenty of tourists purchased the picture books.

Also available were post cards.

Auschwitz is a gas. Wish you were here.

And nothing livens up a room like a concentration camp poster.

When the break was over, the tour group hopped on the mini bus and drove over to the largest and most lethal of the Auschwitz camps; Birkenau. The Polish government has maintained the Birkenau death camp as a memorial for all those who perished there during World War II. Unlike the main camp at Auschwitz I, Birkenau is not a museum or research archive. It is preserved more or less in the condition it was found at liberation in January 1945. Some the wooden barracks were being restored. Brick barracks and other structures still stand including the women's camp where Anne Frank was imprisoned.

The Visit Auschwitz bus parked next to a fleet of other tour buses. Tourists got off and walked toward the main gate rail entrance. A familiar voice inside their headsets explained:

"By July 1942 the SS were conducting the infamous selections where incoming Jews were divided. Those deemed able to work were sent to the right and admitted into the camp. Those sent to the left were immediately gassed. Prisoners were transported from all over German-occupied Europe by rail, arriving in daily convoys. The SS forced an orchestra to play as new inmates walked towards their selection and possible extermination; the musicians had the highest suicide rate of anyone in the camps… Follow me and stay together."

Tourists ambled along a train track that led them inside the death camp. A withered red train stood as a monument to the past. Jewish visitors placed rocks on the motionless train. Like sentinels watching over the entrants, wooden guard towers stood close by. Many of the corroded planks appeared to be rotting.

The group walked toward a massive mound of rubble. These piles looked like burned-out apartment buildings.

"When four new crematoriums went into operation in the spring of 1943, the SS in Auschwitz had virtual death factories at their disposal. For the first time in history, human beings were murdered and their corpses burned in assembly-line manner. These practices made it mathematically possible to burn as many as 2,500 corpses each in Crematoria II and III and as many as 1,500 each in Crematoria IV and V per day. In the summer of 1944, during which more than 9,000 persons were murdered daily, the incineration capacity of the ovens no longer sufficed. The SS had corpses burned in ditches as well."

David noticed something about this area of the camp that was not noticeable at Auschwitz I.

A faint smoky scent lingered in the air.

"Before the Nazis fled from Birkenau in January 1945 they tried to destroy the evidence of their atrocious war crimes by blowing up the crematoriums. The last extermination selection took place on October 30, 1944. In November, SS Reichsführer Heinrich Himmler ordered the crematoriums be destroyed before the Soviet Army reached the camp. Using dynamite, the gas chambers of Birkenau were blown up. The SS command sent orders on January 17, 1945 calling for the execution of all the remaining prisoners in the camp but in the chaos of the Nazi retreat the order was never carried out. On January 17, 1945, Nazi personnel started to evacuate the facility and it is estimated that only ten percent of the SS soldiers who worked at Auschwitz ever stood trial for their heinous war crimes."

Sun beating down upon them, the group lumbered over to examine the burnt-out ruins. In certain spots some of the support structure still held so it was possible to formulate architectural angles amidst the destruction. Rocks with the names of victims written on them were left in tribute. Broken bricks, twisted steel, soot, and rubble all combined to form another strange monument.

While the rest of the group started away, David lingered behind. Something had caught his eye—a charred brick. Actually it was half a brick that could fit in his palm. If he could place his hand over the broken brick without anyone noticing, he felt certain he could make it fit into his pants pocket. Then for the rest of the trip, he would just have to keep his hand in his pocket so that the weight of the brick did not make his camouflage pants fall down.

The perfect size brick seemed to be conspiring with him.

After making sure no snoops were watching, David kneeled down as if to tie his shoelaces. Then in the blink of an eye, the half brick that felt cool to the touch was pocketed.

After four weeks of travelling through Europe and a ten-hour flight, the Bradshaw family made it back exhausted. It had been a long time since they truly appreciated their house in the quiet suburbs and the privacy of their own bedrooms.

One of the first things David did was unpack the Birkenau brick. He placed it on a shelf next to his bed. The coarse texture, the reddish and blackened tints, and all of the history imprinted upon it made it display worthy. Tomorrow he would show off his über-creepy souvenir.

Was the Holocaust a terrible event in human history? Absolutely. *Did he or any of his ancestors have anything to do with it?* Not as far as he knew. To David it seemed like every great empire, from the Romans to the Mongols to the Russians, enslaved and sadistically eradicated their enemies by the millions. The Nazis were arguably the most blatantly racist but they were not the first to impose such hateful, malevolent practices nor would they be the last. Hell, it happened in America at the Japanese-American internment camps authorized by President Franklin D. Roosevelt.

History… you can't make this stuff up.

Wiped out, David slipped under the covers, closed his eyes, and gently gripped his circumcised cock. The head always reminded him of a Nazi helmet but before getting too involved with any sort of self-exploration, the teenager drifted off.

David awoke to a horrendous cacophony inside his head. He could not block out timbre of choking panic inside the gas chambers or the unbearable sizzling of fire consuming flesh. Shrieks twisted into dreadful groans. Yelps mutated into ghastly screeches. Squeals became mournful cries. The reverberating misery pounded and pulsated relentlessly, unsuccessfully trying to escape the confines of his throbbing skull. Like a CD skipping, sickening screams repeated over and over and over from each of Auschwitz's 1,300,000 victims.

He heard the shrill shrieks of children being bayonetted by German soldiers.

He heard the terrified yelps of a person getting mauled by a German Shepherd.

He heard the helpless screeches of a prisoner entangled in barb-wire.

He heard the delirious squeals of twins being "experimented" upon by sadists.

He heard the gut-wrenching cries of mothers watching their children die.

These non-stop shrieks echoed inside his thumping head, reminding him that *"the one who does not remember history is bound to live through it again."*

The brick. David had to get the brick.

If he managed to get the brick, the screaming might stop.

Inside a darkened bedroom, husband and wife lay side by side, fatigued yet satisfied from their European vacation. Even though the trip had been quite a drain on their savings account, experiencing Europe with their college-bound son was well worth every penny.

Space divided equally on each side of the bed, they heard an odd sound.

Maybe David was making an omelette?

But if he was making an omelette shouldn't he be downstairs in the kitchen?

And how many eggs was he going to crack?

❄

When Mr. and Mrs. Bradshaw opened David's bedroom door, they barely recognized the battered young man whose bloody forehead was caving in under the force of self-inflicted blows. David's bloodshot left eye bulged out unnaturally and threated to pop out of the socket.

"Work will set you free."

THWAPP!

"DAVID!! STOP IT!!"

But David couldn't stop. He had more work to do.

His grip on the half brick tightened.

"Work will set you free," David declared in a slurry tone, determined to bash himself even harder and hopefully silence the screams.

Bovine

Joel Arnold

See, the ice shapes this land, and the land shapes us. Simple as that. You got that?

"Yes, sir."

And you know what we shape?

"What, sir?"

We shape everything else. The buildings, the livestock, our women. You got that?

"Yes, sir."

See, the livestock ain't nothing but dumb beasts. Women ain't much different. You got to make sure they know that, make sure they know where they stand and what they mean to you, 'cause otherwise...

"Sir?"

Otherwise they'll kill you. You got that, boy?

"Yes."

Yes?

"Yes, sir."

Herb Collins saw her from the window, saw her collapse in the cow pen in a heap. He stared for a moment, sucking in breaths of brandy scented air, then realized he ought to move.

He walked out of the farmhouse slamming the door and muttering, "What the hell you doing there, Cam? Get up off the ground." He opened the gate to the pen. Her eyes were open, but they seemed fixed. Unblinking.

He stepped closer. One of the twenty-six head of cows, heifers and yearlings ambled in front of him. He swatted its flank. "Get out of the way."

It stepped aside, but another one, a thick, leggy heifer, wandered in front of him, its square head staring at him with dumb, rheumy eyes, its bristly ears twitching.

"Goddamn it, move!"

It stood its ground, chewing a mouthful of cud and blinking sleepily.

Herb walked around to its rear, but more cows came, four of them, stepping mutely between him and Camille. More shuffled in, slow and steady, forming a lazy circle around the prone body of his wife.

Herb grinned hotly. *So this is how it's gonna be. Gonna protect the missus.*

"Camille!" he shouted. "Get up." He circled the cows, looking for gaps between their huge lumbering bodies. "Camille? C'mon. Tell your cows to get the hell out of my way. Camille? Come on, now. Camille?" The words began to crack in his throat like brittle sticks.

He was an old man now, but he still did all the farm work.

Most of the work, anyway. Camille had taken over the cows after his second heart attack. (His son, Jack, did the work a short while after the first.) Once Herb got up and around after his attack, he went out to feed them, same as he used to, as if the heart attack had been a rude daydream. But Camille stood there with a bucket of corn straight from the hammermill. She pulled away when he tried to take the feed from her, and said, "Cows are mine from now on. You never treated them right."

He stared at her. "Never treated 'em right? The hell you mean?"

Camille swallowed, her voice scratchy with defiance. "You never treated them with respect. You never treat anything with respect."

Herb laughed. He hocked up a mouthful of phlegm and spit it at Camille. "You want to treat 'em with respect, you go right on ahead. You're more cow than woman anyhow."

He figured she'd tire of it soon enough, or kill them off with stupidity, but the big dumb beasts were still alive.

But Camille...

He punched the brown and white flank of a doe-eyed cow, then shoved hard at its rear. It didn't budge.

"Cammy?" he called.

More cows came, gently but forcibly nudging him aside.

"Move!" The frustration was like wires coiling around his lungs, tightening. He sucked in a breath. His mouth watered for a cigarette. A drink. *Goddamn it, Cam, what did you get yourself into?*

He reached into his coveralls, undid his belt buckle and slid the belt from his pants. He snapped it over his head and brought the teeth of the buckle down hard against the rangy neck of a heifer.

It turned its head. Mooed like a loosely strung cello. Herb swung the belt again, and again. The cow merely turned and kept its position within the tightening perimeter.

"Goddamn it..." Herb's arm tired. He dropped the belt to his side, catching his breath, rubbing a hand absently back and forth across his chest. He looked at his dirt-caked boots. "Fuck it," he muttered. *She's dead.* He trudged out of the pen and secured the fence behind him. He walked back to the house and shut the door without looking back at the lowing cattle that surrounded his dead wife.

She'll keep, he thought.

He had chores to do.

He dialed his son's number. The rotary phone had been there since Jack's birth.

"Herb." Jack stopped calling him "sir" a long time ago.

"How'd you know it was me?"

"Caller ID. What do you want?"

What did he want? Why the hell did he—

He remembered. "Your—" He cleared his throat. Almost said *Your mother,* but then why should he say anything to Jack? What kind of a son was he, anyway? No kind of son. A good-for-nothing kind of—

"Is it Mom? Something happened to her?"

"No," Herb said quietly.

"You sure?"

"Course I'm sure. Everything's fine. Got that? Everything's fine." Herb slammed the phone into its cradle and dropped to the white linoleum of the kitchen floor. He put his face in his hands and tried hard to swallow it all down, swallow *everything* down, but he couldn't hold back, and it came out in violent hiccups. Tears and snot ran down his hard, raw hands. He felt a hard lump like a shotgun cartridge lodge deep in the back of his throat. He grabbed the door of the fridge and slowly pulled himself up, his legs boneless. He opened the fridge, moved aside a bottle of fresh milk, and pulled out a bottle of apricot brandy. He unscrewed the cap. Didn't bother with a glass. Sat down at the kitchen table and took a good long drink, trying to dislodge the growing lump he felt deep in the back of his throat.

Once he made her castrate pigs with him. Thought he'd give her a taste of what a man had to do to keep her in food and clothes and the roof over her head. Jack used to help, but he stopped coming a few years ago; Herb couldn't remember exactly when. He didn't want to ask Walt or Berry to help, so why not show Camille what it was like, the rough business of being a man, a farmer. Maybe she'd appreciate him then, get it through her thick skull that he didn't just wave a magic stick to get shit done. So he grabbed the castrating knife and grabbed hold of her hand and pulled her to the pigpen and told her what to do.

Herb grabbed a week-old pig and hugged it tight against his chest. He dropped to his butt, legs splayed out, the critter squirming in his lap.

"Don't stand there with your mouth hanging open," Herb said. "I can't hold on forever."

Camille's hand flexed on the knife's handle, and as Herb struggled to hold the pig still, he saw something in her eyes, something he didn't like, and for a moment he felt helpless as she stood there, hand tight on the knife, that *look* in her eyes. A thoughtful look. A "what if" look.

"Come on," he grunted. "Do it."

She hesitated, then tightened her grip and performed the castration through squinted, disgusted eyes. Her hands moved quickly.

The piglet screeched hellfire. Herb almost lost hold. Camille dropped the knife and scooped up a double handful of diesel fuel and splashed it on the animal's fresh wound to sterilize it.

A drop of fuel hit the corner of Herb's eye. He dropped the pig as if it bit him, and it raced away screaming.

"You trying to blind me?"

He got to his feet, tears dripping from his eye.

Camille said, "I didn't—"

He grabbed her hands, both of them in one of his, then slapped her across the face.

"I'm sorry," she said. "I didn't mean—"

"Shut up." He let go of her and wiped again at his eye, the surrounding skin an angry red.

Herb coughed hard. Damn! He pounded on his chest. Something shifted inside of him and came up from the back of his throat. He spit it out. It landed at his feet on the kitchen floor. He looked at it, wondering if it was a piece of lung.

"Geez-um," he said. It looked fleshy. Big as a quarter. Can't be a good thing, he thought. He wondered if he should put it in a plastic sandwich bag and take it to the doctor. But what could they do about it? He scooped it off the linoleum with a spoon and flung it into the garbage disposal. He looked out the window as the disposal gargled and spat.

The herd stood in a silent circle around his wife's prone body.

That's all right. Let 'em starve for a few days.

Then he'd fill the troughs and watch them come running.

Once upon a time, Herb had slapped Camille hard across the back of her neck. The reason was—well, he couldn't recall the reason, but what he *did* remember was ten-year-old Jack pleading to Camille, "Why don't we leave, Mom? We don't need this son of a bitch."

And Herb slapped Jack for calling him a son of a bitch. But then he asked, "Why *don't* you leave, Camille? You think I'm gonna stop you?"

She held Jack against her red and white checked apron splattered with bacon grease and flour. She ran her fingers through his red crew-cut hair.

Herb's rage turned to bemusement. "Why the hell don't you just up and leave? Get the fuck out of here?"

Camille said quietly, "There's not enough left of me any more. You took it all, like I was a Sunday dinner. You ate all the good parts of me and all I got left are the gnawed-on bones."

Herb furrowed his brow, then chortled. "You're dumber than I thought. Go ahead and stay, then."

Jack started to protest, tugging at his mother's apron, but she shushed him and said, "We ain't going nowhere, son."

"Cam? I'm hungry. Where you at?"

He waited for an answer, waited for her reedy voice to shout, "Coming!" Waited for her footsteps over the hardwood floor of the living room, or the flush of the toilet. But there was nothing. Not a peep.

"Damn it, where are you?" He looked out the window. Saw the circle of cows.

Oh geez-um. He remembered. *There you are.*

The next day, he shoveled field corn into the hammermill, where it exploded against the swirling hammers and shot out of the mill's strainer-like holes. He filled two buckets and lugged them over to the cow pen. He emptied the buckets into the feed troughs, grinning and watching the tightly grouped beasts.

"Hungry?" He set down the buckets and lit a cigarette. He put a foot up on the trough and leaned forward, elbow on knee, smoked and waited.

The cows turned to face him. They mooed and bellowed and shuffled on the frozen ground.

"Come on," Herb said, blowing out smoke in a ragged halo. "What are you waiting for?"

The cows turned their backs to him, their breath billowing out in wavering sheets.

Herb flicked his cigarette at the small herd, and it bounced off a yearling's muzzle in a small shower of sparks. "Goddamn bunch of scrubs. You don't think I know patience?"

The cows merely lowed and farted.

"Pieces of shit." Herb headed back to the house. Halfway there, he turned to look. The herd had turned to stare at him. Matter leaked from their eyes, leaving dark trails on their cheeks. A thin frost circled their nostrils. Herb shook his head. He saw one of Camille's legs through a small crack in the bovine wall. Her shoe had come off her heel but held on to her toe, forming a tent of foot and shoe.

Tiny cold flakes of snow began to fall. "She ain't worth it," Herb muttered. He shouted at the cows, "She ain't goddamn worth it!"

Eventually they'd move. They couldn't stand there forever.

Herb went inside.

There were chores to do. Tractor's fan-belt busted as he was harvesting the last of the corn over a month ago, so Herb figured it was as good a day as any to get around to fixing it. He pretended to ignore the cows, watching them out the corners of his eyes. Their udders leaked on the ground beneath them. Their backs were dusted with snow.

He fell asleep that night to a stillness that comes only with fresh snow; a kind of stillness where the slightest sound seems big and clear and lonely. He listened to the stillness, the loneliness, and fell asleep.

He woke up an hour later and couldn't breathe.

Something was caught in his throat. Something big. Like he'd forgotten to swallow a piece of steak before settling in. He fell out of bed, trying to cough the object out, but he couldn't get any air around it.

He got up off the floor and stumbled to the mirror. Tried to breathe.

A bit of air whistled into his lungs. His face grew the color of beets. He sucked in, then coughed and pounded hard on his chest. The object in his throat moved. He breathed in some more air through his nose. Opened his mouth wide and looked frantically in the mirror at the inside of his mouth. Couldn't see anything, so he coughed once more. His lungs burned, and his heart galloped. The object moved forward. He reached into his mouth with a rough old finger and grabbed hold of the thing. He yanked it out and flicked it into the sink.

He sank to his knees, sucking in air, filling his lungs, fighting back the grayness that threatened to wash over him. He pounded the counter around the sink, then slowly pulled himself up. He steadied himself. Looked down at what he'd coughed up. Something pink and shiny. As he watched, it unfolded and flattened out. His hand shook as he reached down to touch it.

"Oh, God."

It was an ear. A human ear.

"Oh, geez-um."

A thin, jagged white line ran from the center of its lobe to the lobe's outside edge. A scar.

He recognized the scar.

He'd given Camille the scar. Grabbed hold of an earring she wore one night and ripped it right off.

"Oh God, oh God." He grabbed hold of the ear, pinched it between thumb and forefinger, walked it over to the bedroom window and tossed it out into the darkness.

In the morning. He'd bury it in the morning. Maybe throw it in the hammermill. Destroy the goddamn thing.

How did it get in my throat?

He'd wait until morning. Deal with it then.

Of course, morning came early. Good thing, 'cause after he'd coughed up Camille's ear, he couldn't get back to sleep. Each time he drifted off, he felt like he couldn't breathe, like something new had lodged in his throat, but each time he sat up in bed and took a breath, there was nothing there.

He got up as the first hint of light threatened a new day. He scraped a thin layer of frost off the inside of his bedroom window, and saw that the cows lay down around Camille, asleep or resting, huddled together for warmth.

Herb cursed himself. He'd left the feed out. A trail of teardrop hoof-prints had been pounded out of the snow to the trough.

He found Camille's binoculars, the ones she used for bird watching, and looked out the window at his wife.

She'd been there almost three days now, and a skin of snow covered her. He focused on her head. Tried to look at where her ear should be, but her gardening hat, a straw, wide-brimmed contraption with daisies circling the hat above the brim had been knocked askew just enough to block his view of her ears.

Cam, you idiot, why'd you wear your gardening hat in the middle of winter? *And her gardening gloves.* What the hell?

A stroke, Herb thought. Got disoriented. Thought it was spring, time to plant her garden. She went outside and wound up in the cow pen. Passed out. Froze to death.

Stupid. She never had no sense.

Not gonna feed 'em. No more. As long as they won't let me at her, they're gonna starve.

He put on a shirt, jeans, coveralls, socks and boots. Sat down at the kitchen table to a breakfast of steak and eggs. Burnt steak and eggs. *I'll get the hang of it.* Camille had the cooking down, he'd give her that. Cooked everything just right. And when she didn't, he let her know. Sure did. He chuckled over a forkful of solid egg yolk.

Dropped the fork and grabbed his throat.

Shoved himself away from the table gagging, staggering across the kitchen floor.

God no. Not again.

He doubled over. Tripped on the garbage can and fell forward onto his stomach. The force from the fall dislodged the object in his throat. He spit it out. Pushed himself up. Felt something else in his mouth. Something hard and round. He hooked it out with his thumb. Dropped it as if it bit him, and scooted back across the floor.

The thing he'd spit out was a finger. The hard round thing—Camille's wedding ring. It glistened with Herb's spit.

He coughed up two more fingers before he made it to the living room. These came up easier, and one of the fingertips was misshapen, flattened from the time she'd dropped a match she'd used to light Herb's cigarette. When she squatted and reached out to pick it up, he stomped her finger with the heel of his boot. Just one of those things you do when you can't even stand to look at your wife.

He grabbed a rifle off the gun rack, chambered a round and tossed the gun over his shoulder. He tramped out of the house onto the front porch.

The cows were up, standing mute and sentinel around Camille's frozen body.

Herb flicked off the safety, shouldered the gun and aimed.

A waste of a good marksman to shoot a standing cow.

He hit the first one between the eyes. It fell in a heap.

He chambered another round. Another clean, perfect shot and the cow fell where it stood.

The rest of the cows mooed and shuffled, but stood their ground. "Stupid scrubs!"

Herb took aim and dropped another. Blood turned the snow into pink slush.

His breath faltered. He gagged. Coughed out a hunk of flesh the size of a pocket-watch. It steamed in the cold air.

He fired again at the herd. Another animal went down. He counted a dozen still standing.

He shouldered the rifle, but coughed again, throwing off his aim, sending a bullet into a cow's withers. It bawled in pain. Herb spat out an eyeball. He gagged again, doubling over, leaning on the butt of his rifle. His heart thundered in his ears. He coughed up a chunk of flesh and it splattered on the porch. Again, he recognized it. It was the bruised areola and nipple of Camille's right breast. He'd bruised it a week ago when he bit down too hard on it. She wasn't even a good fuck any more. Just lay there like a bale of hay. Sheep fucked better than her.

He stood. Aimed. Fired.

Aimed. Fired.

Soon, only four were left standing. He decided to go into the pen. No need to waste any more bullets. And who should he call to pick up the beef that lay steaming in the snow? He'd have to think of something.

He set the rifle down on the porch and walked out to the pen. The live ones eyed him, their big flat heads bobbing back and forth like boxers gauging an opponent. *Why didn't I shoot the fuckers days ago?* he wondered.

His throat clogged and he spit out a toe. Spots of red polish glistened on the cracked nail.

He stepped up to the circle of cows. The remaining four shuffled in front of him.

"Don't learn a goddamn thing, do you?"

Fuck it. Not putting up with 'em any more. Too old to dick around.

He backed up to the fence where a rusting awl rested against a post. He carried it to the cows, lifted it to the air and brought it down hard on top of a wobbling head.

Fell like a rock.

He did it three more times until all the cows lay dead and steaming. He swung a few more times on the prone, bulky flesh because it made him feel alive, made him feel like a man. And wouldn't his father be proud? This is what being a man is all about.

He dropped the awl and stepped onto a bloated belly, steadied himself and hopped into the center of the circle where Camille lay.

He reached down to pick up his wife of fifty-three years. His hands broke through the icy crust that had formed around her body.

There was nothing there.

Nothing left of her.

Not even a pile of old, wet bones.

Again, he felt a pressure on his lungs. Something crept up his throat. He sat down in the middle of the cows.

"Geez-um," he mumbled.

He wondered how long this was going to take.

He began to cough.

Depth

Rio Youers

Donations were to be made to the Bluebell Hope Foundation, a charity established in support of children with acute lymphoblastic leukemia, and one that James Cloak held close to his heart. His son, Stuart, had been diagnosed at the age of four, and had battled courageously for over two years. Twenty-six and a half months, in fact. Eight hundred and six days. James had counted every one of them. At the end, he saw a place where peace and pain were intertwined. The shape they made was crystalline: almost too bright to look at, formed of many moments, and with edges that could cut to the bone.

James spent five hundred pounds on a ticket to the fundraiser dinner, and another two hundred on the raffle, winning a makeover at Maison d'Allure and a signed copy of some bawdy pop star's book—prizes he had no use for, and which he passed on to the silent auction. His interest—and a contributory reason for attending the event—was in the artwork displayed around the hall, donated by local artists, primarily to raise money for the cause, but also to bring attention to their work. Much of it was not to James's taste. Landscapes and still lifes, for the most part, suggesting talent but little depth. He wanted to be spoken to, carried away. If he could view an entire painting within thirty seconds, every brushstroke and intention, it would never inspire him. James demanded layers, in art and in life. He was moved by character…by story.

Angelique Mayer was the curator of the Simpatico Gallery in Upper Marton, and had procured, through wile and influence, the paintings for tonight's event. She was a tall woman with a savage buzz cut and a ring through her septum. Electric blue fingernails and a barcode tattooed on the back of her neck. She had a pierced tongue, too, which James heard rattling against the backs of her teeth when she spoke.

"*A Measure of Sin.*"

"I'm sorry?"

"The title of this piece." She tilted her chin toward the painting that James was looking at. "The artist is Belarusian, but lives in Bickford now. She does her initial sketch work in the dark, to better 'channel her essence.' Obviously, the work is completed with the lights on."

James nodded. "An apple," he said. "Alone, in a bowl."

"It symbolizes greed, consumerism, and materialism. She was going to call it *iWant.*"

"Well," James said, moving on. "I *don't* want. I'd be far more interested if the apple were outside the bowl. It would make me wonder what was happening beyond the canvas. It would ask more questions."

"Do you feel it's the artist's responsibility to ask questions?" Angelique asked. A smile tweaked the corners of her mouth. "Or to provide answers…to recreate what *is?*"

"Both, I'm sure," James responded after a little thought. "I can only tell you what moves me, as an enthusiast. It's that…*unseen* thing, that invisible wash of genius that turns a painting of an apple into a masterpiece. It's the same with literature. All writers use the same twenty-six letters of the alphabet. They have the same words available to them. But with great writing, there's a power that breathes between the lines. It's about placement and weight; the shaping of a thing that has no name, and no face. Anything less is akin to joining the dots."

"Indeed," Angelique said. "But all things—not only beauty—are in the eye of the beholder."

"And so the world turns," James said, and with a grin stepped to the next piece. He held out both hands. "Here, this is better. See how the man's shadow, and the building's shadow, fall in opposite directions. And look…an old gramophone in the grass."

"It's called, *Fracture of Time.*"

"It's not great," James said. "But it's better. It has depth, at least. Ambition. I think I'll bid on it, because I'm here to support the foundation…although I don't want to outbid someone who actually wants it."

He took a pen from his jacket pocket and looked at the bidding slip accompanying the piece. So far the highest bid was three hundred and fifty pounds. He'd go four hundred, he decided, keeping it within reach for anybody with a genuine interest, and earning a few more coffers for the foundation in the bargain.

He was about to set pen to paper when he felt Angelique's hand on his upper arm.

"There *is* another painting," she said. Her bright eyes shone and the corners of her mouth tweaked again. "It's in the back; I deemed it too inappropriate to display."

"Really?" James popped the cap on his pen and slipped it back into his pocket. "Now you have piqued my interest."

She nodded, curled her finger in a come-hither gesture. "You want depth?" Her blue fingernail flashed and her tongue bar tapped against her teeth. "Follow me."

"You know what you want, at least," she said as they walked. "I can appreciate that."

"I've been an art lover for many years," James said. "It's only now—well, since my divorce—that I've been able to begin collecting."

"Your wife didn't approve?"

"We had a difficult marriage," he replied. There was no need to elaborate; unburdening on a stranger rarely made the best first impression. He adjusted the conversation instead. "I'm something of an aspiring artist myself."

"Interesting."

They progressed down a short corridor to a door marked STORAGE. Angelique took a cluster of keys from her handbag and jangled through them until she found the correct one. She unlocked and opened the door.

"And do you possess," she began with a smile, "that invisible wash of genius?"

"Hardly," James admitted. "I've yet to paint anything, in fact."

"Oh?"

"I'm waiting until I have something to say."

They stepped into a room cluttered with folding chairs and tables, and boxes stacked in a manner that defied the laws of physics. There was a desk beneath the window, its broad surface the only free space in the room. A mounted canvas, covered by a drop cloth, leaned against the nearest wall. Angelique snaked toward it, removed the cloth, and placed it on the desk.

"I apologize...the light isn't great in here."

"It's fine," James said, leaning forward—almost pulled toward the piece. "Abstract expressionism. Drip painting. Reminiscent of Pollock's *Number 23*...though less busy, of course. And in red."

"Red," Angelique said. Her smile wasn't particularly warm.

It was a portrait canvas, measuring, by his eye, three feet by five. The background was white, slightly yellowed by age. The paint—dripped haphazardly across the canvas—was a deep red. Almost maroon.

"Is that acrylic?"

"No."

Upon closer examination, James saw varying tones to the color, some drips a brighter red, some almost pink, relative to how they'd been applied. This gave the piece a linear perspective—depth to the eye, as well as the mind. There was also something familiar about the placement of the drips. Not so haphazard, after all. Or maybe, James thought, he was inventing something that wasn't there: a reason to want it. He'd done the same thing in the last bitter months of his marriage.

"These drippings," he began, twirling his finger. "There's something about them. A familiarity. I can't quite place it."

"A distinct pattern?" Angelique asked.

"I'm not sure," James replied. "And next time I look at it, I may see something completely different."

"Enough depth for you?"

"It's certainly striking," James admitted.

"In that case," Angelique said, "I believe full disclosure is in order. I have endeavored to find out as much about this painting, and its artist, as possible. But it hasn't been easy. So I'll tell you what I know, and you can make a decision from there."

James frowned. "Should I be alarmed?"

"Well, I found it just unsettling enough that I wouldn't exhibit it tonight." Angelique stepped back and looked at the painting. Her eyes glimmered in the off-yellow light. "But not so much that I didn't bring it with me, or that I wouldn't sell it to an informed and willing patron."

"Go on."

"The artist is Edward Stickling. Have you heard of him?"

James shook his head.

"His most famous piece is *Rise of Tides,* once owned by a young Adolf Hitler, which is extraordinary when you consider the Nazis' distaste for *entartete Kunst*—degenerate art. It is now displayed at the Pinakothek der Moderne in Munich. Stickling himself went insane and committed suicide in 1953."

"Not the first artist to lose his marbles."

"Quite," Angelique agreed. "This piece—it's called *Typing the Canvas*—was completed in 1942. Five years before Pollock's drip period, incidentally."

"I'm already sold," James said.

"Allow me to finish." Angelique narrowed her eyes. "There's very little about it in biographies. Perhaps because it was hidden for so many years…"

"Hidden, or lost?"

She inhaled and plucked at her lower lip, then tapped the backs of her teeth with her tongue bar. A contemplative device, James thought. He wondered if she were married, or partnered, and believed such a mannerism could drive a person to tears.

"There's a suggestion," she began, "that the painting is cursed."

James smiled and rolled his eyes. "I believe in the power of persuasion," he said, gently touching one corner of the canvas. "I believe in coincidence. But curses? No…sounds a little Bill Stoneham to me."

"Stickling went mad. He sawed off his painting hand with a breadknife, then clambered onto the roof of his Buckinghamshire home—don't ask me how—and leapt to his death. This piece, along with other works, was purchased at auction in late 1953 by a collector from Edinburgh. He died of a brain hemorrhage two years later."

"Coincidence," James said. "Much like the fact that I'm from Buckinghamshire, too."

"Full disclosure, remember?" Angelique smiled and raised her eyebrows. "I don't want any blood on my hands."

"Continue."

"The painting was inherited by a family member. A nephew, I think. The dates are muddy, but let's say 1957. Within weeks he began hearing voices in his head. He claimed the painting—*this* painting—was talking to him. He was admitted into psychiatric care, and released in 1962. No sooner was he out than he killed three people with a screwdriver."

"I'm not convinced."

"He died in a high security hospital in 1964. *Typing the Canvas,* meanwhile, was in the possession of the nephew's ex-wife, who'd wrapped it in a blanket and put it in the attic. She didn't go mad or die of a brain hemorrhage, although she claimed her house was haunted—would often see shrouded figures standing in the hall. She made no association between the visitants and the painting in the attic. At least not until she got rid of the painting, and the visitants went away."

James smiled, shook his head, said nothing. He didn't believe in curses, and he certainly didn't believe in ghosts. He looked from Angelique to the painting, and was again drawn in by the subtle use of color. He may have stayed there, lost between the lines, had Angelique not resumed talking and pulled him out. There was a moment's discomposure, like waking from a vivid dream.

Something about those drips, he thought. *Those lines.*

"I found all this out through phone calls, trips to the library, and the wonder that is Google." Angelique linked her hands and looked at James. "And from the previous owner, of course, a collector from Harrow, who also experienced intense headaches and notable discomfort. He was more than happy to pass it along to me—at no cost."

"Very generous."

"Indeed." That smile again, which tweaked the corners of her mouth. "Now, I'm not saying I believe any of this; I'm something of a skeptic, too. But I should tell you that in the ten days this painting has been in my possession, I have also experienced quite awful headaches. Migraines, I'd say. And some terrible nightmares, too."

"The power of persuasion," James said.

"Probably…but sufficient for me to withdraw the painting from tonight's fundraiser. I felt it the proper thing to do. Even so, I'd rather *not* take it home with me."

"You won't have to." James pulled his checkbook from his pocket. "Did you have a number in mind?"

"There's one more thing."

"You're determined to make this difficult for me."

"This isn't acrylic, or enamel." She swirled one finger at the painting, indicating the nest of red lines. "It's blood. Human blood."

James faltered for the first time. He took an involuntary step backward and his mouth hung open, caught between saying something and remaining silent. The air between him and Angelique thickened. He could almost *see* it; tiny, damp crystals that sagged in the yellow light.

"Okay, that's…interesting." He ran a hand across his face. There was sweat on his upper lip and he smeared it away. "*His* blood? Stickling's?"

"No. Or at least not exclusively." She tapped her teeth again. "Tests have pulled four different blood types. There's no solid information as to where the blood came from. Perhaps volunteers or accident victims. One document—by no means reliable—suggests it was procured from cadavers."

"Delightful."

"With a mortician's consent."

"Which makes it entirely acceptable, of course." James rolled his eyes, then frowned and took a step closer to the painting. He'd noticed something—a smudge of sorts—in the lower right hand corner. "And what's this?"

It was a fingerprint, quite small, also in blood.

"You wanted depth," Angelique said.

"Stickling's fingerprint? A signature?"

"Doubtful," Angelique replied. "It's too small. Maybe his little finger. But he signed it in his customary way in the bottom left hand corner. And he never marked his other work with fingerprints. No, this is a unique touch. We don't know who it belonged to, or why it's there. We'll never know, either. Add it to the mystery."

James shook his head. "It's altogether fascinating."

"Isn't it?"

"Any more surprises?"

"I'm done."

"Good," James said. He smiled and opened his checkbook. "Now let me buy the wretched thing."

It had been a long evening. He'd shaken many hands and talked to many people. After buying *Typing the Canvas,* he'd returned to the hall where he was asked, as a parent directly affected by acute lymphoblastic leukemia, to make a speech. This he did, and without qualm. He never mentioned Stuart in his speech—how he'd faded like a bright color under too much sunlight. He never mentioned the days of useless prayer or the arguments with Annie. He talked, instead, about hope and possibility, love and support. When he'd finished, there were more hands to shake, and enough pitying expressions to make him want to run screaming into the night. He endured, though, and always with a smile. As a result, he was now incredibly tired and irritable. He had a headache, too.

A twenty-minute drive home that felt more like twenty hours. He hit every red light, and the speed cameras on the Bickford bypass meant that he never climbed above forty MPH. To compound his misery, his mobile phone chirruped less than three miles from home, and he answered it without screening—something he'd never do when more alert.

"James. Not too late, I hope?"

William, his older brother and former mainstay. William, who had shown indefatigable support during Stuart's illness, and indeed beyond. Annie, in particular, had found comfort in his attentions. Stuart was barely ashes in the wind when they'd discovered that solace was more rewarding with no clothes on. They lived together now in a four-bedroom detached in the Beeches. William drove an Aston Martin. Annie a Lexus. James drove a four-year-old Ford Fusion, and left them to their happiness.

He almost cut the call without speaking. How delightfully easy, to press a little red button and make his brother disappear. Such a shame all of life's annoyances couldn't be so conveniently deleted. Instead he sighed, and tiredly said:

"Not too late, but I'm driving and I have a headache. Let's make this quick."

"Ah, yes. The resentment. The sour grapes. Even now."

And always, James thought. He eyed the little red button, then his gaze flicked to the rearview mirror, where one corner of Stickling's painting was reflected from its place on the back seat. It was covered, but still it pulled.

"What do you want, William?"

"Annie left a box of photographs in the attic. *Your* attic. Old, family photographs. Her side. She'd rather like them back."

James—stopped at a red light—pressed a hand to his forehead. He felt the pain dissipate momentarily, then it blew back in…thicker, darker. It was like fanning smoke. The painting on the back seat urged him to look. He obliged, eyes to the rearview.

Green light. He drove.

"James?"

"In the attic?" he said. "I'll get them when I have time. Can I post them to you?"

"I'm in your neck of the woods on Friday," William said. "I may as well pick them up. Then it's done, right?"

"I suppose." The last thing James wanted was to see William. Three years had passed since he and Annie revealed their affair. It was still very raw. But it always would be. "Listen, I have to go."

"I'll see you Friday."

He cut the call and tossed his phone into the passenger seat. A mile from home now. The headlights of oncoming cars were like spears in his eyes and the streets buzzed in their pale electric glow. He clasped one hand to his brow as he drove—imagined a blood clot skittering spider-like along the sulci of his brain, looking for a place to settle. At last he arrived. He parked on the road outside his house and sat for a moment, both hands pressed to his temples. A single tear leaked from his left eye. He used his cuff to wipe it away.

In his dream he was in a cold and black space with but a single point of light in the distance. *Stuart,* he thought, and ran toward him. Short breaths snapped from his lungs. The darkness whispered to him and pushed its full body close. It touched him with fingers like seaweed. He heard screams and felt rain on his back.

"Stuart."

He ran into a room filled with boxes that towered and creaked. Blood on the floor. Faces in the window. They had lost eyes and pale skin, and were tethered to something unseen. *Typing the Canvas* was placed on an empty desk at the back of the room. Stuart stood before it, his back to James. Delicate shoulders. Small, bald head. James couldn't remember what he looked like with hair.

The faces pressed against the window. Their lost eyes looked everywhere.

Stuart reached out and touched the painting. The bottom right hand corner. The fingerprint.

"You didn't save me, Daddy," he said.

One of the faces screamed. Its black mouth smeared the glass.

Stuart turned around. He had no eyes. No mouth or nose. Where his beautiful face should have been—beautiful, even at the end—was a large red fingerprint.

James closed his eyes. He felt his son's hand on his face. It was cold.

"You didn't save me."

James left work early the next day. His headache had faded, but not disappeared. A pulsing behind the eyes that made concentrating on sales quota reports next to impossible. At no point did he entertain the idea that Stickling's painting was in some way affecting him.

He was tired. Hadn't slept well. A little stressed about his brother's imminent visit. Nothing more than that. Indeed, as soon as he got home, he loosened his tie, unbuttoned his shirt, and stood staring at the painting for almost six hours.

No…it wasn't affecting him at all.

Three AM. Awake on the sofa. Bad TV reflected in his eyes. He wasn't watching it. Too doped up for that. Painkillers—strong, wonderful painkillers—and lots of them. Too many, probably. His living room appeared *rounded,* somehow, all the corners and edges smoothed away. Same as the pain. His mind, too. Everything was just a little numb and that was fine. The painting called to him—it even said his name—and sometimes he looked at it, sometimes he didn't. "I'm too tired," he would say. "We'll talk later." And then he would laugh. Stupid painkillers. Playing their games. At one point he picked up the phone and spoke to nobody. At another he hugged a cushion close to his chest and wept.

Sleep, when it finally came, brought another terrible dream, one of swirling red drips and darkness. He woke up on the sofa. Mid-morning sunlight filled the room and the TV still played to no one. His mouth was dry and his head whirled. The nightmare didn't fade. It felt as if those red lines were wrapped around his brain.

He called the office to let them know he wouldn't be in. His partner, Harrington, assured him his timing was horrible. "The Brighton conference is next week," he said. "It's the big one, remember? Money to be made. This is not the time to fall ill." James told him to hold the fort and hung up, but that little dose of reality—hearing the anxiety in Harrington's voice—made him feel better. He ate a light breakfast, took two more painkillers, and showered.

His phone rang at lunchtime. It was William. He chose not to answer, but it reminded him that it was Friday, and his brother would soon be knocking on the door. It also reminded him that he needed to get Annie's photos from the attic. He had little inclination to do as such, but being able to hand William the photos as soon as he walked through the door would no doubt ensure the visit was brief. Thus, he fetched the stepladder from the spare bedroom (formerly Stuart's room) and positioned it beneath the hatch. He climbed up, pushed the hatch door to one side, and hoisted himself into the attic.

James knew that one day Annie would remember her photographs and ask for them back. He had hoped, to begin with, that he could use them for emotional leverage. Maybe he'd even get an apology from her. But where resentment had once turned to anger, it now turned to tiredness. Better to hand them over and do without the dispute. James was not without emotion, however; crouched in the attic beneath a dimly glowing bulb, he opened the box and flipped through his ex-wife's photographs. Most were of her family—her siblings, cousins, aunts and uncles…people who had faded from James's life since the divorce. So completely gone they might never have been there to begin with. There were a few Polaroids of Annie as a baby—all kiss-curls and smiles—and some of her as a teenager. There was even a photograph of the young woman James had fallen in love with, looking exactly as she had when they'd met at the Glastonbury music festival in 1994. Grungy, yet *together*, and with a fierce intellect that leapt from her expression. Seeing her like this again, even in a photograph, touched him inside, deeply and unexpectedly, and placed small, bright tears in his eyes. It passed through his headache and fatigue like an arrow, and stirred memories of a life before it had been so irrevocably ruptured.

His emotion was not tempered upon finding three photographs of Stuart. One at the beach, armed with bucket and spade. One with his Spider-Man outfit on. The third was taken at James's former place of work. He sat on James's knee with his big eyes shining and happy. Four years old, and only weeks from showing the initial symptoms of a disease that would kill him. James clearly remembered this picture being taken. He could feel the weight of his son on his knee, and smell that dusty office with the rickety desk, the old-fashioned rotary phone, and the marked map of South Buckinghamshire—there, it was even in the photograph—on the wall.

James lowered his head and wept in the dim light. It felt okay to cry in this tight space, where no one could see him. It was like holding his pain in cupped palms, like a bird with a broken wing, and waiting for the moment it would take flight.

❊

He kept the photographs of Stuart—put them on the dresser in his bedroom. Annie was not getting those. The rest he put in the box and took downstairs. He meant to place them on the telephone table in the hallway, but was halted in the living room by *Typing the Canvas*. He'd hung it on the north wall, because it was a dour space and it needed the color, but also because it was out of direct sunlight, where bleaching would be minimized. As James passed the painting, he felt it—actually *felt* it—reach out of the gloom, grab his shoulder, and drag him close.

"What do you want?" he said.

The bloody lines drew him in. He followed them, like pathways, with his heart pounding and sweat running into his eyes. He dropped the box of photographs. His head filled with a glassy ache. He moaned and covered his eyes, but the red lines were still there.

Something, he thought. *A key. A riddle. A puzzle.*

Blood leaked from his left nostril.

Something about those lines.

He slapped himself. Hard.

And that fingerprint.

Cold air swirled around him. He saw shapes in his periphery. They drifted across the living room and he wanted to look to see what—*who*—they were but couldn't drag his eyes from the painting. He felt them settle behind him and *loom*. He recalled Angelique Mayer's full disclosure. She'd used words like "cursed" and "visitants." Blood trickled onto his upper lip and he licked it away. She'd used the word "hemorrhage," too.

Tiredness. Stress. The power of persuasion.

What else could it be?

"WHAT DO YOU WANT FROM ME?"

He whirled on his heels but saw nothing. Nobody. The TV was still on, reflecting images onto the pale walls. He slapped himself again, then grabbed an empty vase from a nearby side table and threw it at the wall. The breaking sound was perfect.

He crouched for some time in the corner with his hands over his head, shivering, licking the blood from his upper lip. He imagined his mind like the vase...shattering. It made the same sound.

By the time William rang the doorbell, James's nosebleed had stopped and his headache abated—nothing more than a listless throb, at least. He sat in front of his own blank canvas, as he had many times over the last three years, charcoal stick in hand, waiting for something to say. But inspiration, as ever, proved difficult to attain.

He was shirtless. Dried blood caked his left nostril and he'd charcoaled a few doodles on his body. As such, he opened the door.

William, understandably, was taken aback.

"My God, man!"

"Welcome, brother." James grinned. "It's been a long time."

William hovered on the doorstep a moment before coming in. He followed James down the hallway, into the living room. James sat in front of his canvas and studied its emptiness. William gave him a wide berth, as if he were a stray dog. One that could bite.

"I thought you'd pulled yourself together," he said. "But obviously not. You look terrible."

"As endearing as ever, dear Bill."

"You think I enjoy seeing you this way?"

James sneered. "Annie's photographs are over there." He gestured to where they were strewn on the floor beneath Stickling's painting. He hadn't picked them up. "They...fell out of the box, I'm afraid."

"So I see." William's nostrils flared. He started across the room, but stopped when he noticed the broken vase. His gaze darted from the scattered pieces, to the photographs, and then to James. "Oh, I understand now."

"I doubt you do."

"You looked at the photographs." William nodded. His mouth was a thin, dry line. "Of course you did. And the memories came flooding back, didn't they? You became angry. Threw the photographs on the floor. Broke a vase. Your mind, too, I'd say."

"Such powers of deduction."

"Look at you." William shook his head. "It's suggestive of manic depressive behavior. Bipolar, even."

James drew two faces on his chest. One happy, one sad. He looked at William and shrugged.

"You need help, James."

"Indeed," James said.

William gathered the photographs while James leaned back in his seat and watched. They were physically alike—were often mistaken for twins: tall and slim, with dark hair turning gray at the temples, and that English countenance a foreigner might consider regal. James often wondered how unusual this was for Annie, even now, taking William into her arms, into her body. Did he kiss her in the same way? Did he hold her throat while they made love, and squeeze lightly?

Did she lay silently afterward, her hair spilling onto his pillow?

If they were to have a son, would he look like Stuart?

"My word!" William said. He had retrieved the last photograph, and on standing directly faced *Typing the Canvas*. James distinctly saw his legs wobble, and his upper body tilt forward, just a fraction, but enough to note.

"My new painting." James sprang from his chair and stood at his brother's side. "Isn't it delightful?"

"You did this?"

"No. I bought it." James indicated the signature in the bottom left hand corner. "It's an original Edward Stickling. Have you heard of him?"

"Of course not," William replied. "Abstract art isn't a passion, James. You know that."

"Yes, I suppose." He grinned. "Do you still have that wonderful print of *The Hay Wain* in your living room?"

William jerked his gaze from the painting. His posture realigned, shoulders square, and he regarded James with disdain. "You've no place for snobbery, James, looking like you do."

He turned away and James placed one hand on his upper arm. The charcoal on his fingers left gray smears on William's shirt.

"Is there anything…familiar about it?" James asked.

William looked at the painting again. He shook his head.

"Something in the pattern—in the placement of the lines?"

"Nothing." William leaned forward again. His eyes shone. "Should there be?"

"I don't know," James said. His hand fell from William's arm. "It just triggers something, and I can't think what."

"It's ghoulish." Again William pulled his gaze from the piece. "Looks like blood."

"Well—"

"Abstract nonsense." His upper lip curled, as if he had an unpleasant taste in his mouth. "But then, our tastes have always been different."

"Except in women, it would seem." James said.

"*Touché,* brother." William pushed past him. Their shoulders butted aggressively. He strode across the living room, but paused at James's easel and regarded the blank canvas with a bemused expression. "A potential masterpiece?"

"A work in progress."

He rolled his eyes. James led him into the hallway and showed him the door.

"Always a pleasure."

"You know," William said. "There was another reason for my coming here today, quite aside from collecting Annie's photographs."

"Oh?"

"I was hoping we'd begin to smooth things over. We're brothers, after all."

It was James's turn to sneer.

"We still have a long way to go, I see."

James pointed at the unhappy face on his chest.

"Get some help," William said, and left.

James slammed the door, then reeled back into the living room, sat in front of his canvas, and fell into its emptiness like a beaten man.

❋

He never made it to the conference in Brighton. The next thirteen days passed in a storm of pain, delusion, and despair. He spoke only to his partner—furious Harrington, who called him a condemnable bastard and slammed down the phone—and his doctor, who immediately arranged for tests at Bickford Hospital. James had every intention of going. The possibility of a tumor seemed suddenly very real. It perhaps being psychosomatic, caused by the power of persuasion, mattered not; the interminable headache and frequent nosebleeds could no longer be discounted, and demanded a more reliable diagnosis. James showered thoroughly—washing the crust of blood from his upper lip and the doodles from his body—and dressed in clean clothes. He faltered, however, when it came to leaving the house, getting only as far as the front door before collapsing in a fragile heap.

He burned through painkillers. Crunched them dry. Dozens every day. They masked the headache, but didn't eliminate it. He ordered more when his supply ran short and had them delivered to his house. The alcohol in his liquor cabinet took a hit, too, but coupled with the painkillers offered no relief—only a bleak, slumberous wave of hallucination. He saw faces at his living room window. Shadows without reason. A bloodstained dress draped over the shower rail. *None of this is real,* he thought, and sometimes just had to laugh—mad, whooping sounds. *Not real. Not at all.* Eventually, he took the bottles from his liquor cabinet and hurled them spectacularly against the wall.

Breaking things helped.

While James found the act of destruction satisfying, the breaking sounds—particularly when they matched the frequency of his mind—were altogether soothing. A long period of anxiety was lifted when he took a cricket bat to his television set. Smashing an antique lamp gave him a brief rush of optimism. His insecurity faded, albeit temporarily, when he shattered his collection of Waterford figurines. And feelings of worthlessness were suppressed when throwing crockery on the kitchen floor.

He also broke two mirrors, a coffee table, the shower door, the bathroom cabinet, six picture frames, three light bulbs, a mantel clock, and his entire CD collection.

Sleep brought no such relief, because of the nightmares. He tried staying awake, but always succumbed, often weeping. Into the cold…the darkness. His dreamscape was a desperate place, where sometimes his dead son stood alone, and always the red drips of Stickling's painting tried to lure him deeper. He followed—what else could he do?—but always woke up before the end, like those dreams of falling…never hitting the ground.

The little girl stood at the foot of his bed. Maybe ten years old. Long black hair and a bloodstained dress. Her face was a gaping hole. It looked like she had been broken with a hammer.

"Who are you?" James asked.

The details of his bedroom were exact. The stains on the walls. The sweat-stink of the sheets. Even the sounds outside his window: distant cars and rattling branches. If this was a nightmare, its realism was unsurpassed.

"Are you from the painting?"

She crossed to the dresser and picked up a photograph of Stuart—the one taken in James's old office. She looked at it with her empty face for a long time. James watched her a moment longer, then hid beneath the sheets. *Not real,* he decided, and by morning the little girl was gone but the photograph was on the pillow beside him.

"Simpatico Museum."

James heard her tongue bar tapping against her teeth.

He sat in the corner of his living room, among ruin, dressed only in underpants and a raggedy beard. Five weeks and three days since he'd bought *Typing the Canvas.* He knew this because he'd kept the receipt and could still count. That part of his brain hadn't yet leaked away. He couldn't remember when he'd last showered, though, or brushed his teeth. Judging from the dirt in the creases of his arms and neck, and the thickness of his tongue, it had probably been weeks. Not that it mattered. Time moved differently now. He'd broken all the clocks in his house. Night and day meant nothing. But the man on the radio said that the date was August the 15th, which meant that exactly five weeks and three days had passed since he'd bought that ungodly painting.

"Simpatico Museum."

Again with the tapping.

"James," he said. "Cloak."

"Mr. Cloak," she said, allowing a moment to place the name. "Yes. How are you?"

And he replied, "The painting is cursed."

Not that it had taken him five weeks and three days to realize this. And it wasn't so much the blinding headache (he was used to the pain now—couldn't imagine what his head would feel like without it, in fact) or the vivid nightmares. He could still—though barely—ascribe these anomalies to the power of persuasion. But the painting itself, the way it pulled him in and possessed him, went beyond explanation.

It was powerful, and it was destroying him.

Angelique Mayer tapped the backs of her teeth as she considered her reply. James imagined grabbing that silver piercing, yanking her tongue from her mouth, and snipping the tip of it off with a pair of sharp scissors.

"Are you," she began hesitantly, "experiencing some…?"

"*Everything*," he growled. "Headaches, nightmares, hallucinations. I'm losing my mind."

"With respect, Mr. Cloak, this is—"

"You can have it back," he said. "No charge. Just take it away. Get it out of my house—my *life*."

After a pause, she said. "Thank you, Mr. Cloak, but the Simpatico Museum has no interest in that piece."

He remembered the barcode tattooed on the back of her neck, and wondered—if he scanned it—what her value would be. Was she an August work of art, to be exhibited at the world's premier museums? Or a throwaway piece—all style and no substance—that nobody would miss?

"Just take it away," he said. "I don't care what you do with it."

"You might try another museum." Angelique's voice trembled. "Or you could simply destroy it."

"Simply," James said. He laughed, and the sound was just one degree from maniacal, perhaps two from a scream. "It *can't* be destroyed, Ms. Mayer. It can only be deciphered—an endeavor that is quite beyond me."

He had thought to destroy the painting on many occasions. A knife would surely do it. Several broad slashes across the canvas, until it was in ribbons. Or he could bury it, deface it, burn it. Throw it on the railway tracks or off the Romney Bridge. But first he needed to get close to the painting, and therein lay the problem. Every time he got to within a step or two, it curled red hands around his throat and dragged him in. It howled and screamed in multiple voices, and he rode the lines and tried—oh, how he *tried*—to untangle them.

He could burn his entire house to the ground. He wouldn't need to get close to the painting then. Not being able to leave, though, meant he'd go up in flames, too. A laudable sacrifice, perhaps...but losing his mind was marginally better than burning to death.

"I can't help you, Mr. Cloak," Angelique said.

"You *have* to."

"I gave you full disclosure."

"Please."

"I'm a curator, not a doctor."

Tap-tap went her piercing and again he imagined cutting off the tip of her tongue and perhaps eating it, feeling the little bar click and clack against his own teeth. Then he could drive the scissors into her eye and work them inside her skull, cutting little triangles—*snip-snip*—out of her brain.

"Do you have value?" he asked. His voice was full of broken pieces.

"What do you mean?"

"Will you be missed?"

She hung up. The sound of nothing was inexplicably loud in his mind. A great, tumbling emptiness that reminded him just how alone he was.

Stuart's voice on the radio.

"*Daddy...Daddy...*"

He found it in a sea of static, scrolling across the dial, trying to find a news or weather report—some shot of reality from beyond these walls.

"Stuart?" he gasped. Tears welled in his eyes. "Baby, is that you?"

"*Daddy...*"

The tears spilled down his face. He touched the radio with a trembling hand.

"Daddy's here...it's okay, baby."

"*Can you see them?*"

"Them?"

Static, like a sudden burst of rain hitting his window. He tweaked the dial and leaned closer to the speaker. From the midst of the white noise, he heard his son's voice.

"*They're dead like me,*" he said. "*And they want you.*"

Where was the line between nightmare and reality? Had everything he'd known, and all the things he feared, toppled into the same indistinct space, for him to pick among the farrago and decide what he could trust?

Early evening. Falling sunlight struck his living room window and painted a broad orange flag on the west-facing wall. James sat in a piss-stained armchair with the radio in his lap. Nothing but static. He hadn't heard from Stuart in days.

The sun dropped slowly. The flag turned from orange to violet.

He heard footsteps on the stairs.

Not real.

Thud and creak. Someone heavy, or hurting. More footsteps—these lighter—from directly overhead. Someone else in his bedroom.

James placed the radio on the floor and stood up. His eyes tracked from the ceiling to the open hallway door. He moved toward it, hearing Stuart's voice in his mind: *They're dead like me …And they want you.* Two steps into the hallway, until he could see up the stairs. And there, at the top, a stooped figure. He caught just a glimpse before it lurched out of sight. Black rag clothes and pale hands. A face smeared with blood and dirt.

He retreated into the living room, walking backward. More footsteps overhead. His heart slammed bitterly in his chest.

"Not real," he said, but his voice cracked with uncertainty. He stumbled over the radio, almost fell, then cranked the volume so that the static drowned all other sound. He crawled past the window and saw his shadow on the wall. A cowering thing, with a crown of wild hair and spidery limbs.

James covered his eyes and waited. He listened to the static and tried to fall into that nothing sound, that nowhere place, away from this cruel tangle of obscurity. When he looked again the light had faded, sweet pink now, like something from a romance novel.

There was a woman at the other end of the room. Her shape was crooked…broken. Her long hair swayed and she moved toward him—strange, gimp steps—until they were close enough to kiss. James saw the bruises on her ribcage and the puncture wounds in her stomach. There was a boot print on her chest. The left side of her face had been smashed open.

She brushed her fingers over his lips.

He fell.

And there was depth.

His fascination with art stemmed from a propensity for interpretation, to uncover by layers a truth within the frame. All art is story, and all story is life. To look beyond device and form, and to find the place where art breathes, was as close to divine as he would get this side of heaven.

He read the visitants in the same way. They came to him—man, woman, and child—silently, formed of layers, and he uncovered.

The woman had been a life model, in her early twenties, intelligent and passionate. James touched her hair and saw her ambition—the way she used to smile. In the shape of her eye he determined an infectious *joie de vivre*. She had modeled for Stickling, of course, and despite promises of fame had scorned his advances. The bruises on her ribs, and her crippled posture, described the artist's response. James moved his hand to the puncture holes in her stomach and saw a palette knife flash in a cool silver light. He touched the boot print on her chest and envisaged Stickling standing over her, crushing her ribcage with his weight. A tall man, with a scrawl of black hair and narrow shoulders. He carried a long-handled cross-peen hammer. James touched the collapsed side of the woman's face, and saw the hammer fall.

Her blood in a jar, alongside tubes of paint and used palette cups.

The man had come to him over many nights, and James did not cower, but rather embraced him. He'd been a transient, simpleminded, who had made the mistake of knocking on Stickling's door in search of work. James had touched his cheap clothes and sensed a heart that wanted only to achieve. His sunken cheeks told of hardship and desperation. James fell deeper. He stripped away the layers and saw Stickling fellating the man, followed by a rush of shame and disgust. The man's broken bones regaled the level of the artist's emotion. The hole in the back of his skull was the final, violent flourish.

A second jar of blood on the shelf.

And the child—the little girl in the bloodstained dress. She was, of all the visitants, the most disturbing by far. James cringed at her touch. He wanted none of her depth. But her layers were intricate and vibrant, and he fell into her hardest of all. She touched his face and he heard birdsong. He stroked her hair and saw that she'd been lost in the woods. A long, shadowy man had followed her, skulking between the trees: Stickling. He'd scooped her into his arms and taken her to his house. Her pale skin told James how frightened she'd been, and the bruises on her arms revealed her futile attempt at escape. James counted every tear and heard every scream. He touched the empty space where her face used to be. As hollow as a bowl. He saw that cross-peen hammer again. He saw it fall.

Three jars of blood. Three blood types. Stickling's made four. And that was when James realized that *Typing the Canvas* wasn't a painting at all.

It was a confession.

But there was more to it yet. A final layer. The puzzle. The key. Something about that fingerprint, and those lines. Those deliberate, wandering lines.

He never stopped looking. He *couldn't* stop looking.

And months passed.

"*WHAT AM I MISSING?*"

Then one day, and quite by accident, with his beard long and his ribs showing, James discovered what it was.

For three years James worked as campaign manager for the Chesham and Amersham Member of Parliament. One of his duties was to determine effective campaign routes within the constituency, where they could plant their proud blue placards, and go door-to-door where necessary. He bought a large map of South Buckinghamshire and used a red marker to highlight certain roads between key towns and villages. The result was a mesh of lines, looping and crisscrossing, that would appear arbitrary to anyone else, but which he knew as well as the lines on his palm. James had pinned that map to his office wall and looked at it every day for three years. Those red lines glowed in his mind even when he blinked, like the afterimage of a bright light.

That was a long time ago. Happier days, for sure, when he'd had a wife and son...a future. The photograph he'd found in the attic—the one taken in his office, with Stuart sitting on his knee—was a reminder of those days. James smiled in the photograph. Stuart smiled, too. The map was pinned to the wall behind them, its roadways colored in red.

James had looked at that photograph a thousand times and hadn't seen it. Perhaps he'd been too focused on Stuart. That was understandable. But even when he looked at the map, it wasn't immediately obvious. It was only when he happened to glance at the photograph via the broken mirror on his dresser that it finally fell into place. His heart had boomed, his eyes like moons. He remembered Angelique Mayer saying that Stickling had lived in Buckinghamshire, and the sound of the final layer being peeled away was like an earthquake.

He grabbed the photograph and a shard of mirror from where it clung to the dresser, and staggered down to the living room. He stood in front of *Typing the Canvas* (its pull had already diminished, he noted), then turned his back and viewed it via the mirror shard. With his heart still pounding, he held up the photograph. His eyes flicked from the red lines drawn on the map, to the inverted painting.

Stickling had added a lot of artistic subterfuge—random loops and swirls—but the darkest, broadest red lines, running diagonally across the canvas, precisely mirrored a network of roads in South Buckinghamshire.

Typing the Canvas was a confession. It was also a map. Which meant that the fingerprint, placed somewhere between Little Chalfont and Seer Green, was a location.

James lowered the mirror shard and smiled.

"Let's go for a drive," he said.

His car had sat idle for eight months. The battery was dead and it had a flat tire. A wonder it hadn't been towed away. James called the AA and within an hour they had it running like new. With *Typing the Canvas* on the backseat (the only way he could leave the house was to take it with him) and old clothes hanging off his emaciated body, he pulled away from the chaotic stink-hole he called a home, and drove east to Buckinghamshire.

He made one stop along the way: a hardware store on the out-skirts of town, where he bought a pickaxe and shovel.

It didn't take him long to find them.

They'd been buried in a small, wooded area known locally as Magpie Grove. He parked as close as he could—what would be the top edge of the fingerprint—and walked from there, painting under one arm, pickaxe and shovel on his shoulder. It was sunset. Clear tangerine light filled his eyes. The air was crisp and fresh. He crossed farmland, scattering sheep and cows, and reached Magpie Grove as the nightjars started singing. It was gloomy between the trees but the painting guided him. He stepped slowly and thought perhaps the visitants walked alongside him, but couldn't be sure. When he turned he saw only the shapes of trees, as black as charcoal sketches. At some point the painting lost its hold on him. He threw it to the ground and started digging.

It was soon too dark to see, but he dug a little deeper and then rested. He curled up in the shallow hole and slept. Stuart flew a blood-red kite through his dreams. James woke to the sound of bird-song. Dawn light slanted through the branches. A fox slept beside him, but was quickly startled awake by his movement and sprang away, tail bouncing.

James resumed digging. He went deep, his hands ragged, bleed-ing. Just when he began to believe he would find nothing, his shovel uncovered a wet patch of burlap. He worked faster and didn't stop until the job was done—the remains of three bodies dragged from the earth. Their cerements, mostly rotted, separated easily. He saw their shattered skulls, their broken bones.

He sat at the edge of the grave and lowered his face into torn hands.

The nightjars were singing again by the time he left Magpie Grove. The sky was beautiful copper. He walked straight and tall despite his fatigue, the pickaxe on his left shoulder, the shovel on his right. He had buried *Typing the Canvas* in the hole he'd dragged the bodies from. A fitting resting place, he thought. With each shovel full of earth he'd felt the uncomfortable edges pressing into his psyche gradually drawing away. The headache persisted, though. And the darkness, like a shadow at his shoulder.

He'd left the bodies uncovered. Crumbling skeletons like chalk marks in the leaves. They'd be discovered soon enough. Questions would be asked, and never answered. But that was okay, James thought, because in the end they'd be given a dignified burial. They, at least, would find peace.

Home by midnight. He ran a bath and washed the filth from his body, then crawled into his fleapit bed. Sleep didn't come easy. He tossed and turned for hours. His dreams were fragments, choked with shadow.

He spent most of the following day staring at the empty wall where Stickling's painting had hung. *That's my life,* he thought. *A bare and soulless space.* He had nothing. No job, no family, no friends. And soon—when his savings ran dry—no house.

He needed something, he realized. New color, new depth. Something to help fill the emptiness.

A creative outlet, perhaps…

"Hello, William."

"James. My goodness, what a surprise."

"Indeed."

James sat in his armchair, holding his phone in one hand and a piece of mirror in the other. His partial reflection fascinated him. As with all great art, it asked questions. One in particular: what lay beyond the broken glass?

"To what do I owe the pleasure?" William asked, and James imagined him sitting in his own armchair (his wouldn't be piss-stained), with the fat smell of Chesterfield furniture in the air, and a shot of fine cognac balanced on his palm. Annie would be there, rubbing his shoulders, perhaps, or selecting which of Debussy's compositions they should make love to.

"I thought you should know," James started, sneering into the mirror, "that I took your advice; I sought help."

"Splendid news," William replied.

"And in the interest of closure, I would very much like to invite both you and Annie to dinner."

He grinned as William deliberated. He could almost feel his brother's doubts fluttering across the line.

"Are you sure?"

"Absolutely," James said. "It's time to move on, wouldn't you say?"

"I would."

"Time…" His stained teeth flashed in the mirror. "…to bury the hatchet."

They ended the call, then James cleared a space in the living room and set up his easel. The blank canvas was like another mirror. He took a seat before it and smiled. It wouldn't be blank for long.

At last, he had something to say.

GPS

Rick Hautala

"Turn left onto Willow Creek Road," a voice said.

Mark had recently changed the voice on his GPS to this cold, commanding male voice. When he had first gotten the navigational device, he had—ironically, of course—programmed in the "nagging wife" voice. For a while, he found that relatively amusing; but before long, he realized how—subconsciously, no doubt—he had been trying to make light of how much Eileen had been getting on his nerves lately. Or maybe he chose it to mock her, demonstrating—to himself, at least, when he was driving in the privacy of his car—that she wasn't the only woman in his life who nagged him.

That had only lasted a few days.

Now, with this long drive from Maine to Florida ahead of him, keeping to back roads as much as possible, he didn't need any more "stressors" in his life.

Leaving Eileen had been the easy part, but letting go of Jeff—his six-year-old son—had been tough. But circumstances had forced his hand because he certainly hadn't wanted to leave his boy alone back there with that psycho-bitch.

"But a man's gotta do what a man's gotta do," as his father—now six years dead—used to say.

Shielding his eyes with his hand and squinting against the morning sunlight glinting off the hood of his car, he scanned the intersection left and right. The Virginia roadside was lush with spring growth. Down south, it was nothing like spring in Maine, which swung in with frozen slush and grit. He'd been driving with the car windows, front and back, open because of the stench in the car. Half-empty fast food containers, apple cores and banana skins, old coffee cups, cigar butts, and a host of other rotting smells filled the small space, but the sweet breeze that filled the car reminded him that spring had finally arrived…

Spring with so many new opportunities.

The directions from the GPS didn't feel right.

He was positive he was supposed to turn right onto the road, which would take him back to the main highway. Judging by the position of the sun and trusting his own navigational instincts, it just felt wrong. Unless the road drastically changed direction, he was convinced that turning left would head him east or—worse yet— back north.

Except for his car, the exit ramp was deserted this early in the morning, so he slowed down as he approached the fork in the road, not yet committing to either turn. He stopped the car at the fork in the road and sat there with the engine idling, expecting the GPS to correct itself and tell him to turn right after all.

"Turn left onto Willow Creek Road," the robotic voice repeated.

Mark scowled at it.

"You're sure 'bout that?" The graphic display clearly showed the road he was on with a thick, red arrow arcing to the left. "I dunno…"

He let out a startled cry when an eighteen-wheeler suddenly appeared in his rearview mirror, bearing down on him—fast. The sudden, sharp blast of the truck's air horn shattered the early morning stillness, the sound so loud it made Mark's teeth ache.

Muttering under his breath, he eased into the right-hand turn without bothering to snap on his turn indicator. The semi's driver gave him another quick, deafening blast of the air horn to express his appreciation for Mark's skillful driving. Mark resisted the urge to flip him off as he pulled out onto the road he was sure would take him back to the highway.

"Recalculating," the GPS unit said, and Mark shot it another scowl. Then he shifted his gaze to the rearview mirror to see the semi, so close to his rear bumper he could see only a portion of its shiny chrome grill grinning at him in the mirror.

"Back the fuck off, why don't yah?"

Just to make his point, Mark down-shifted because he could see, up ahead, that the driver wouldn't have an opportunity to pass him for a long stretch of road. The jerk needed to be taught some manners, trying to bully him like that.

Mark's grip on the steering wheel tightened and his teeth clenched as he drove. His jaw began to throb behind his ears.

It was obvious the truck driver wasn't going to be intimidated. He stayed right there on Mark's tail, the throaty rumble of the engine so loud and close it punched Mark's eardrums like the concussion of gunshots, drowning out everything else.

So much for a nice, pleasant drive this morning, he thought.

"Proceed one quarter mile to Casey Road and turn left," the GPS unit said mechanically.

"Up yours," Mark whispered, glaring at the GPS. And then faintly, just at the edge of hearing above the rumbling roar of the semi behind him, he thought he heard a voice say, "Watch your mouth."

Wondering if he had really heard it or only imagined it, he shifted his gaze to the truck's grill in his rearview and eased his foot off the accelerator to slow down just enough so the truck driver would know he shouldn't be fucking with him.

This earned him another, longer wailing blast of the air horn and a couple of quick flashes of the truck's high beams. Reflected in the rearview, the light stabbed his eyes like lasers, making him wince.

"You *really* don't wanna fuck with me," Mark muttered, shifting his eyes back and forth between the rearview mirror and the curving road that unspooled ahead down a steep incline. Even if this road didn't bring him back to the highway he was looking for, he was satisfied that he was at least headed south. Off to his left, range after range of mountains receded into a distant purple haze. The rising sun struggled to burn away the fogbank that hovered in the valley like a dense pall of smoke.

Mark eased back in the car seat and draped his right arm over the top of the seat, hoping the driver behind him would see just how casual and carefree he was. Lowering the driver's window all the way and with the backseat window halfway down, he let the slipstream of air tousle his hair and wash like warm water over his face. The fresh, smell of green growing things mixed with tinges of motor oil and burnt rubber that rose from the highway.

This is a good thing, Mark told himself.

Even with the windows down, the air in the car had been getting increasingly rank the further he drove into warmer climates. The fresh air rinsed the stench from the car.

The road weaved back and forth, curling around the mountainside like a huge, flattened snake in the morning sun. Mark wondered if he was foolish, playing games, irritating other drivers...especially a trucker responsible for a huge eighteen-wheeler. If something happened...if while trying to shut this asshole down he or the trucker made even a slight miscalculation, they both could end up skidding off the road and careening off a sheer cliff into the river valley below.

"Know what?" a voice asked.

It took Mark a heartbeat or two to realize it had been the voice of the GPS.

Perplexed, he glanced at it and said, "Umm… What?"

"That truck driver…?"

"Yeah? What about him?"

"He thinks you're an asshole."

The GPS's voice was thin and barely audible above the shrill sound of the wind whistling through the windows and the thundering of the truck behind him. Mark told himself he had to be imagining the voice and chalked it up to driving too long without a break. He should have paced his driving better, he told himself, and taken longer rest stops; but he was short of cash and hadn't wanted to spring for a motel, so he had been driving steadily day and night, taking only short breaks.

His knuckles went white as he gripped the steering wheel, guiding the car down the curving, sloping road, the car swaying gently from side to side. Still wondering if the GPS really had spoken to him, he kept flicking his glance at it while he navigated the road ahead.

"Did you really just…?" but that was all he could manage.

The eighteen-wheeler was still on his tail, impossibly large in the rearview mirror. It looked to be less than six feet from his tail. The wailing blast of its air horn thumped Mark's chest shudder like a series of punches.

"Are you talking to me?" Mark asked, but the GPS was silent.

He was stressed from the drive, he told himself, and had imagined…hallucinated the comments. He should pull over and take a nap before something worse happened.

He snapped himself back to reality, wondering if the truck might be a runaway. This high in the mountains, he'd noticed numerous emergency ramps angling off from the roads—long, straight dirt exit ramps that ran flat for a hundred yards or so and then ended with a sudden steep upgrade backed by ten-foot tall piles of sand to slow and stop runaway trucks.

What if this guy was having trouble with his brakes?

Maybe he's trying to warn Mark to get out of his way.

"Screw it," Mark said, gritting his teeth as he glanced at the grille in his rearview. "We'll know what's what if he slows down at the bottom this hill."

"He's laughing at you, you know."

The voice caught Mark off guard, but this time there was no denying that the GPS unit had spoken.

"Are you…? You're really talking to me?" Mark glanced at the curling red arrow on the digital view screen.

"No, asshole," the metallic voice replied. "I'm talking to your mother." After a lengthy pause, during which Mark wrestled with amazement and disbelief, the GPS unit added, "Of *course* I'm talking to you."

"How can you—? You're not programmed to…to—?"

Mark snapped his focus back to the winding road when he caught himself drifting into the opposite lane. Thankfully, there was no on-coming traffic, but the driver in the semi must have thought Mark was making room for him because he suddenly sped up and tried to pass him on the right. Realizing he was about to get squeezed out, Mark stomped down on the accelerator. His car sped ahead, pulling back into the travel lane mere inches from the semi's front bumper.

That earned him another ear-splitting blast from the horn, and Mark couldn't resist sticking his left hand out the window and flipping his middle finger at the driver. The wind tore at his hand.

The scenery was going by in a green blur as Mark negotiated the twists and turns, forgetting for the moment what had just happened with the GPS. Beads of sweat dotted his forehead, and he realized his stomach was tight and sour.

"He won't back off," the GPS unit said.

"Shut up!" Mark shouted, still only half believing he was really hearing this.

"He thinks you're a goddamned idiot. He's trying to run your ass off the road."

"Why would he do a thing like that?"

"Because he doesn't like you."

"Doesn't like me? How does he—" but Mark couldn't finish the question as he glanced at the GPS. With the wind whistling in his ears, he wanted to believe—he *had* to believe he was imagining all of this… Maybe his radio was on, tuned to some talk radio station that was fading in and out. When he looked at the radio, though, he saw that the dial was unlit. He twiddled the volume control back and forth a few times just to make sure the radio was silent.

"You're not real," Mark said, hearing the tremor in his voice. "You can't be."

His lips were suddenly as dry as paper. He licked them, but there was no moisture on his tongue. A sour taste, like vomit, filled the back of his throat. He felt around until he found the water bottle on the seat beside him, but when he shook it, he realized that it was empty. He had forgotten to buy another bottle at the last rest stop, and up here in the God-forsaken willy-whacks, who knew when he would find another gas station and convenience store?

"There's no water in hell," the GPS said.

"Will you *please* shut the fuck up?" Mark shouted, fighting the feeling that he was talking to himself, trying to shut of his own chattering thoughts.

"I'm just saying…" was all the GPS said, its robotic voice as emotionless as ever. But Mark was sure he had heard a mocking tone in the voice, nonetheless.

Negotiating the twists and turns of the down slope, Mark couldn't help but gaze at the damned thing, fighting the urge to tear it off its window mount and fling it out the window. If he did that, though, the truck driver could report him for littering and get him pulled over. Hell, he had probably already radioed ahead to the local police barracks to notify the Staties to be looking for him.

"He's laughing at you right now," the GPS said.

"Really?" Mark's grip on the steering wheel was so tight his wrists throbbed. "And how, exactly, do you know that? You're just supposed to give me turn-by-turn directions. I don't need any shi—"

"I told you back a ways to turn left, and you didn't listen to me."

"So you're doing this to—what? To get even with me? For ignoring you?"

The GPS unit was silent, and Mark concentrated on driving even as the big rig bore down on his ass, swaying back and forth, jockeying for an opportunity to pass.

"I don't need any crap from you…from you or…or anyone else," Mark said.

Nothing but silence.

"You hear me?" Mark shouted.

"No need to lose your temper, but we both know how you resolve your disagreements with people, now, don't we?"

"What the hell does *that* mean?" Mark asked, but he winced at the words, and the cold tingling in his wrists moved up his arms.

The GPS was silent.

The road leveled out into a straightaway. Off to the left, through a break in the woods, Mark caught a view of a wide, smooth-flowing stream that laced out across a meadow in wide curving arc that reflected the deep, blue sky. The painted lines on the road were broken, and up ahead Mark could see a rest stop. He considered yielding and allowing the semi to pass, but the thought of giving in sat like a lump of cold oatmeal in his gut. As the road leveled out into the straightaway, Mark stepped down on the accelerator, smiling wickedly when he heard the blubbering roar of backfiring exhaust as the truck driver also accelerated his vehicle.

"Aw'right, wise guy," Mark whispered, watching the truck swing heavily out into the passing lane. "Let's see what you got."

Tension blossomed in his stomach as he sped down the road, keeping his lead on the semi. Wind ripped through the opened windows, thumping loudly, sounding like huge fists were pummeling the car.

"How are you for gas?" the GPS asked, its sharp voice piercing Mark's ears like an electric drill.

Mark glanced at his fuel gauge and saw that he had less than a quarter tank of gas.

"How'd you—"

"I guess you'll have to stop at the next service station, huh?"

"No shit, Sherlock."

A heavy concussion smacked the air inside the car when Mark passed a car heading in the opposite direction. It appeared to be moving much slower than he and the semi, almost as if it was standing still. The trees and shrubs along the roadside whisked by in a dreamy haze of green and brown.

"If you pull into this gas station, he'll follow you."

"And?"

"And…he'll probably beat the shit out of you."

Mark couldn't deny the anxiety that twisted like a tangle of barbed wire in his stomach. He fixed his gaze on the GPS unit and said emphatically, "*He's* the one's causing trouble. Not *me!*"

"Uh-huh."

The voice sounded colder, now, accusing. A shiver ran up Mark's spine as he imagined a confrontation with the truck driver. No doubt he was a beefy son-of-a-bitch who would wail on him with a tire iron or baseball bat. The exit for the gas station was rapidly approaching.

Mark had to decide.

Finally resolved, he slowed down and even snapped on his turn signal a couple of hundred yards away from the rest stop exit. His shoulders tensed as he waited to see what the truck would do. He hoped he would swing out to the left and pass him by, but after a tense moment or two, he heard a thundering rumble of backfiring exhaust as the truck slowed to pull over.

"Fuck," Mark whispered.

"You're screwed, man," the GPS said. "When he catches up with you, he's gonna kick your ass from here to tomorrow."

"The hell he will."

Mark smiled when he saw the fork in the road ahead with large painted signs, indicating that passenger vehicles should exit to the left, and trucks should go to the right.

"Suck on this," Mark said as he slowed down and took the turn, but a lightning bolt of terror hit him when the truck driver, ignoring the signs, remained right there on his tail.

"Oh, boy. You're a dead man now," the GPS said.

"Will you *please* shut the fuck up?"

There weren't many vehicles in the parking lot, but Mark slowed down to ten miles per hour in case a pedestrian darted out in front of him. Through the opened window, he could hear the semi as the driver rapidly downshifted, its air brakes gasping like a laboring beast as he slowed down.

Why isn't there a cop around when you need one? Mark asked himself, looking around for a cruiser. He was certain—now—that the truck driver was going to stay on his tail no matter what.

"You're fucked twelve ways to Sunday," the GPS said, and this time Mark couldn't ignore the almost gleeful note in the machine's voice.

It's a damned machine, he reminded himself. *That's all it is.* If it really was talking to him, then someone at the factory must have messed with it, programming it to screw with him like this.

Mark slowed down, letting the truck close in on him, making as if he was going to pull into one of the vacant parking spots close to the front door of the convenience store. The truck rolled behind him silently now, blue exhaust spewing from its exhaust pipes and rising like smoke into the crisp morning sky.

"Aw'right, asshole," Mark said as he squeezed the steering wheel and slammed the accelerator down hard. His tires screeched on the asphalt, sending up plumes of black smoke and gravel behind him. The smell of burning rubber filled the car, making Mark nauseous, but he let out a whoop of joy as he sped toward the entrance ramp leading back onto the highway. Glancing at his rearview mirror, he saw that the truck had come to a full stop.

"I'll bet he calls the cops and reports you," the GPS said.

Mark glared at the GPS and said, "What the fuck do you know?"

"Oh, I know plenty," the GPS said.

"I've got enough gas to make it to the next rest stop," Mark said, but the truth was, he had no idea where that was.

"Next gas station in twenty-three point five miles," the GPS unit said and then, after a slight pause, added, "But if you ask me, I don't think you'll make it."

"Who asked you?"

Mark smiled grimly as he drove past a grove of red pine with a scattering of picnic tables before merging back onto the highway. There was no traffic in front or behind him, and his smile widened as he settled into the car seat, letting the steering wheel play loosely in his hands. It would take the eighteen-wheeler a long time to get back up to speed, and by then, Mark would be miles down the road. Just to be on the safe side, he figured he would take the first side road he saw, but he was now leery of leaving the main roads.

How could he trust his GPS unit?

Then again, he could always stop at the next gas station and pick up a map. Do it the old-fashioned way. He was in no real hurry to get to Florida, and now that it was behind him, he wondered why he had let that confrontation with the trucker get on his nerves so badly. He should have just let the fool pass when he first came up behind him. If he had, none of this would have happened.

For the time being, anyway, he was free and clear.

As he drove, he started whistling the old John Denver song "Take Me Home, County Roads." The day was warming up fast, and the piney woods smell that filled the car was intoxicating.

All of that changed when a black and white police cruiser came up the road heading in the opposite direction. Its lights weren't flashing, and its siren wasn't sounding, but the cop was speeding as if he had a definite purpose.

"You bet'cha he called the Staties, all right," the GPS said.

The suddenness of the mechanical voice broke the hypnotic road sounds, startling Mark who had all but forgotten that the damned thing had been talking to him.

"When this is all over," he said, "I intend to write a sternly word-ed letter to the company."

That was a quote from some damned movie or other. At the moment, Mark couldn't remember which one. Probably some dumb-ass flick Eileen had made him sit through. But Mark didn't have time to ponder that for long. He tensed as he watched the police cruiser pass by. And then his stomach dropped when, in his side-view mirror, he saw the cruiser's brake lights flicker. The police car pulled over to the side of the road and slowed. A second later, the emergency flashers came on, winking madly. Mark watched with steadily mounting horror as the cruiser cut across the median strip, bumping and bouncing in the grassy gully. Its tires spit up clumps of grass and roadside gravel. Then it started speeding up the road, heading in his direction.

"You're fucked now," the GPS said.

Mark glanced at his speedometer and saw that he was only doing about five miles per hour over the speed limit. He was tempted to speed up, but he'd never be able to outrun the cruiser; so he slowed down to a hair below the speed limit just in case the cop wasn't after him. The skin on the back of his neck tightened as the cruiser rapidly closed the distance between them, its red lights flashing in his rearview mirror like razor slashes.

"Kind of makes your ball sack shrivel up, doesn't it?"

Mark bit his lower lip and shook his head in frustration.

"Come on… Come on…" he whispered. "Just pass me by… Pass me by…" He narrowed his eyes as if in prayer, but the sudden sound of the siren—a short, single whoop—told him it was all over.

"Told you. You're fucked."

"*Shut* the *Christ* up!"

Mark released the tension in his arms and snapped on his right turn signal before pulling onto the shoulder of the road. The cruiser glided to a stop about twenty feet behind him, the front angled so it pointed back toward the highway. For what seemed entirely too long a time, Mark sat there, tense and staring at the patrolman, who remained in his cruiser. He held a radio microphone in one hand and was talking into it. Mark could see that the patrolman was wearing mirrored shades that—like his windshield—reflected a distorted silvery arc of the surrounding woods.

Mark waited patiently, trying his best to breathe even and swallow the sour, dry lump in his throat. His pulse was racing but, at last, the cruiser's door opened, and the patrolman stepped out onto the roadside. He tilted his head back and adjusted his utility belt.

In Mark's side-view, he looked to be better than six-feet tall. The window was already rolled down, so Mark just sat there, waiting. He looked up when the patrolman got to the window and leaned down to address him.

"Mornin'," the trooper said with a thick, Southern accent, but before Mark responded, he took a step away from the car and waved his hand in front of his face.

"Good morning," Mark managed to say, noting the pinched tone in his voice. He glanced at the GPS unit, ready for it to say something, but it remained silent. The display showed the icon representing Mark's car, stopped by the side of the road.

"Y'all have any idea why I pulled you over?" the officer asked.

"None whatsoever," Mark replied, suddenly conscious of how much he sounded like a Yankee. Was that going to work against him here?

"Could I see your license and registration, please. And proof of insurance."

Mark's hand was trembling almost out of control as he reached for the glove compartment and snapped it open. He took out the necessary papers and then hitched his hip to one side so he could fish his wallet out of his back pocket to get his license.

"You're fucked now," the GPS said, its robotic voice low and grating.

"You say something?" the patrolman asked as he waited patiently.

"Nothing at all," Mark said as he handed the papers to the officer, who scanned them with an expressionless face. Mark studied his own reflection in the policeman's mirrored shades, noticing how small and pitiful he looked. After a long, tense moment in which Mark hardly dared to breathe, the patrolman grunted and walked away.

Mark watched as he sat back inside the cruiser and used the radio again, obviously checking to see if there were any outstanding warrants on him. He wiped the sweat from his face with the flat of his hand and tried not to breathe the fetid air in the motionless car. Now that he was stopped, he realized how bad it was and told himself he would have to do something about it soon.

After what seemed like forever, the patrolman, still unsmiling, got out of the cruiser and walked back to Mark's car. His mirrored shades reflected the graveled roadside.

"You got a problem with your headlights," the officer said.

"I've got 'em on," Mark said, perhaps a bit defensively as he glanced at the switch to confirm they were on. "I know we're supposed to keep 'em on for this stretch of road."

"Your left light's burned out," the patrolman said, nodding to indicate the front of the car.

"Really? Son of a gun," Mark said, trying hard not to let his relief show.

Maybe the truck driver hadn't reported him after all. Maybe this was just a routine stop.

"You're from Maine, huh?"

"Yes, sir."

"Where you headed?"

"Florida," Mark said, terribly aware of the tightness in his voice. He tried to swallow but couldn't. "Going down to visit my…uh, my brother in—ahh, Melbourne. I—umm, you see, my wife and I split up, and I…I'm thinking of moving down south with my son to—you know, to get away from it all. Start over."

"I'm going to have to write you a warning," the patrolman said, indicating that he had zero interest in Mark's personal problems. "You'll want to have that headlight attended to as soon as you can… especially if you intend to drive at night in these parts."

"I will. For sure. Yes, sir. First chance I get."

"Wait here," the trooper said.

Mark realized he'd been talking too fast, and he couldn't catch his breath as he watched the patrolman walk back to his cruiser still holding his license and registration. After getting back into the cruiser, he set about writing something on a clipboard.

"You haven't fooled him, you know," the GPS said, its voice so soft and low and grating.

Still staring into the rearview, Mark hissed it to silence, but it didn't do any good.

"You don't think he's on to you? For fuck's sake! He knows all about you. He knows what you did. He's fucking with you."

Mark wanted to deny this, but his tongue was frozen to the roof of his mouth as he waited for the patrolman to return with his license and registration and the written warning. He tried not to think that, just like the truck driver, this cop was screwing with him. Both of them were busting his balls because they enjoyed watching him squirm.

"You'll never get away with it," the GPS said. "He knows. Everyone knows. Every car that's passed you by since you left Maine... every driver and every passenger knows *exactly* what you did."

"Will you *shut* the fuck *up?*" Mark said, his voice strangled as he stared into the rearview mirror, trying to look perfectly normal.

After what seemed like an hour but was really less than five minutes, the cruiser door opened again, and the patrolman sauntered back to Mark's car. He didn't smile when he handed the papers and the warning to Mark through the open window.

"I noticed you got a problem with your rear tire, too," the policeman said.

"A problem?" Mark's voice was an octave higher than normal.

"Looks like you've lost a lot of air. It's almost flat. Do you have a spare?"

Mark swallowed hard and nodded but was unable to speak.

"You might want to change it now. I'll stay behind you with my lights on so you'll be safe."

"I think I can make it—"

"I can't let you drive off with your tire in that condition, sir."

The officer leaned closer to the window, his shades reflecting the inside of Mark's car like a kaleidoscope. Mark's heart was pounding high and fast in his throat when he looked at the GPS unit. His ears started buzzing as he waited for it to say something that the patrolman would hear.

"If you don't do that right now, sir, I'll have to call a wrecker to come and remove your car from the highway."

Seeing no way out of this, Mark reached under the dashboard and popped the latch to release the trunk. The sudden snapping sound was like a kick to the gut, and Mark's left hand was greasy with sweat that slipped on the handle when he opened the driver's door.

"You're fucked for sure now," the GPS said, but its metallic voice was so low Mark could barely hear it. He knew the patrolman hadn't.

His legs felt like they were stuffed with straw as he walked to the back of the car. A sudden concussion slammed the air when an eighteen-wheeler—*the* eighteen wheeler—sped by followed by a long, trailing blast of its air horn.

Mark smiled wanly, convinced now that the GPS had been right. This cop *did* know!

So did the truck driver!

Everyone knew!

"All I have is one of them donut spare tires," Mark said, glancing at the expressionless face of the patrolman. The curvature of his mirror shades reflected the roadside and Mark and his car. "It ain't much."

"It'll get you to the next town. The exit's less than six miles from here. You can buy a new tire there."

Mark nodded but still was unable to move to the car trunk. He couldn't open it, not with this cop standing here; but he also couldn't avoid it or talk his way out of it. A sudden high-pitched buzzing filled his head like he'd stepped on a beehive. It took him a paralyzed moment to realize that it was the GPS unit, talking in the car. He couldn't make out anything it was saying, but the patrolman cocked his head to one side and listened. His expression remained perfectly fixed as the voice of the GPS filled Mark's head.

"Whatever you do, don't look in the trunk!" the GPS unit said.

Mark glanced at the patrolman and saw that he was staring at him, now, with a cold, downright mean expression.

"Go on," the cop said, his voice as toneless and merciless as the GPS's. "Open the trunk."

Mark swallowed once—hard—and then his fingers hooked under the metal edge of the trunk latch and pulled up. The trunk rose slowly on rusted hinges, and there on the floor of the trunk, lying in tight fetal positions, was the body of his son, Jeff. The stench of rotting flesh after four days arose like a noxious cloud. Jeff's abdomen was swollen with gas, looking like he had a huge beach ball tucked under his shirt. The skin around his mouth had turned purple, and his pale lips were pulled back, exposing his teeth in wide, gruesome grin. His eyes were closed as though he slept, but there was no peace in the expression on his face.

Mark had to turn away, but he could still see his dead son reflected in the patrolman's mirrored shades. The patrolman turned away, too, and let out a long, agonized moan from somewhere deep inside him. Then he leaned over, his hands braced on both knees, and vomited onto the side of the road.

"He's my son…" Mark said, his voice strangled with emotion. "They'll find her back at the house, but I…I couldn't leave him back there with her…not with that bitch!"

Room 8

Roberta Lannes

Six, seven…room *eight*. She stopped, her suitcase bumping her calf. The key felt cold in her hand.

The door was only slightly more familiar than the previous thirty-odd doors marked "8." Most were plain, without features. Most had a glossy coat of paint, with a raised metal numeral, sometimes the "8" falling halfway into a mocking infinity symbol. Exhausted from her seemingly never-ending quest, she was still compelled to open the door and risk the possibility that once again, she'd been wrong. Yet this one, the color of rotting pomegranates that complemented the carpeting at her feet, had to be right. The abstract pattern in the carpet made her dizzy, slightly nauseous. When had she last eaten?

She maneuvered the key into the doorknob, turned it, and held her breath. *Be inside, be here.* She pushed the door open, blinking into the late afternoon sun as it flared into the room through a wide window.

She adjusted to the glare and details began to take shape. With each object—the simple brass lamp by the bed, the shiny golden bedspread, oak veneered desk topped by a room service menu and *Sights of the City* guide—her memory was reinforced. And the crib was there, just below the window! Sunlight imbued the translucent drapery above it with a moiré haloed effect.

Her heart thudded with blows born of fear and rusty hope. She moved inside, allowing the door to slam shut behind her. She jumped, dropping her suitcase and handbag, but didn't turn. Her eyes were on the crib. She heard infant mewling sounds coming from the froth of baby blankets and she clasped her hands to her chest.

She whispered his name in a husky voice. *Joseph.*

She stepped toward the crib, her legs like foreign objects that she had to concentrate with all her might to move. They felt weak, stiff. Standing three feet away, she smelled him, that ripe, sweet baby smell, inexplicable and impossible to imitate. *Her son.* At last.

She exhaled, suddenly light-headed. She staggered, her high heels catching at the shag, nearly throwing her into the guard rail. She gripped it as if her legs might give way and peered in, taking in the small round head with its pale downy hair, recognizing that pudgy profile that was like no other child's. She listened for the faintest sound of breathing, wondering if the slightly bluish tinge of his skin was a result of the abrupt shift of light in the room. He was sleeping so soundly. How finicky a sleeper he was! She'd let him slumber on, though her body ached to hold him, let him suckle at her breast.

She stood staring down at him, rocking side-to-side, humming the song she'd sang to her growing belly her entire pregnancy. It always helped him sleep, calmed him. Tears dropped from her cheeks to her dress before she realized she was crying. That happened from time to time, and she wondered if they came because she'd finally found him, or for all that lost time when they were apart. At least she wasn't weeping, wailing with grief. That always woke him.

She knew she'd find him. After she ran off with her baby and her husband had found her, he took Joseph away, hid him from her, then locked her away. But he'd underestimated just how long and hard she'd search for her child. Men didn't understand the bond between a mother and child. Certainly, her husband hadn't, nor that cruel doctor he'd hired to watch her.

She reached out her hand, brushing lightly over the blanket, feeling the warmth of her boy. Satisfied, she turned away.

She plucked out cigarettes and lighter from her handbag. She kicked off her heels, and crawled across the satiny expanse of quilted gold sateen bedspread. The bed felt as hard as she remembered. She propped herself up with the pillows, pulling a heavy glass ashtray into her lap and she lit up. The nicotine relaxed her, slowed the slamming of her heart. With each breath, the bluish light warmed, and at last she could relish the end of her search.

Thinking back, she realized there had been clues to the *rightness* of this city. This train station *had* seemed more familiar than the others, with its seven sets of rails, the girders arching over the opening of the station, the green lacquered benches. At the previous train stations, she'd seen perhaps one recognizable landmark—the benches or the seven sets of rails—but not all the attributes together. As her train pulled into this station, she'd seen the large, rolling luggage carts with their oval signs, green on custard-yellow, and it was the last piece. She even felt, without a doubt, she knew which direction to exit to the street.

Farad, her taxi driver, treated her the same way the others had in all the cities prior. When she described the hotel (she didn't know the name, but it was old-fashioned, had a long lobby that ended in a wine-colored marble tile and mahogany desk, where the staff wore uniforms the color of bruised apples, or was it grape?) and asked to be taken there, said that she'd know the hotel when she got a glimpse of it, she saw in the rear view mirror that he rolled his eyes. They all rolled their eyes. He told her there were fifty hotels like that in the city, that he could drive her around but it would cost her. When she opened her purse and showed him a thick stack of bills, he warmed to the idea of a mid-morning drive, and to her. She was still beautiful, after all. He even winked at her before turning back to drive.

Her reverie was broken by the thought of her husband. Older, extremely wealthy, James Prescott was used to getting his way. It pleased him to have a gorgeous wife who had no interest in a career of her own, who wanted children, and would make him look good. With five former wives he'd discarded when they disappointed him, he thought he'd found someone young and sufficiently pliable to make into the perfect wife. He treated her with the same careful consideration he gave all his businesses; measured attention, just enough, and threw money at her as if coinage equaled affection. Then he sat back and expected a good return for his investment. Naïve and grateful, she was obediently pregnant eight months after they married.

In the beginning, she'd thought him the most attractive man she'd ever seen, powerful, yet generous and thoughtful. But within weeks of the lavish wedding he'd paid for, he began to browbeat her about her smoking and drinking, the pills she took for her *sensitivities*. He forbid her to see the friends she'd made before they started dating (They're beneath us!). When she was five months pregnant, he didn't want her seen in public (That belly!), and stopped having clients to the house (Once the baby's born, and you look good again, we'll have parties…lots of them!). Captive in her enormous bedroom suite with a television, telephone, and personal maid, her smoking, drinking and medications were all that kept her sane. The pregnancy was uneventful, but she looked forward to doctor's appointments because then, for a few hours, she escaped the gilded trappings.

She smiled at that last thought, then exhaustion stole her pleasure and she drifted into sleep. Dreamless, but restful, she slept for hours. When she woke, it was with the baby's cry.

The room was dark except for the dim glow of a streetlight a few dozen feet down the street. She glanced about, looking for the crib, heard pounding, expecting it to be beneath the window. Now it stood against the wall next to the door. When she saw the light puddled beneath the door, she wondered if someone had come in and moved the crib while she slept. The growing chill of dread spread in her gut.

Had he found her? Was he playing his games with her again? Or had she simply forgotten where the crib had been?

As she started toward the crib, the crying stopped. She crept up, tucked the blankets in around the slumbering form, and tip-toed back to the bed. She stripped off her suit, her hosiery and crawled into bed in her underwear, too tired to open her suitcase.

In the middle of the next day, she ordered breakfast. Room service delivered it and when the boy reached out for his tip, she held back, asking him why someone might come in during the night and move the crib from under the window. He'd looked at her oddly and told her that they never put cribs under the window. It was too cold there at night, and the sun baked in during daylight hours. They were always put where it was now. It made perfect sense to her. She handed him a dollar and he left.

The bacon, eggs, potatoes and buttery toast were delicious. She drank the entire pot of tea and then settled in to smoke a cigarette. The baby was quiet. She went to the window of the room and looked out. The windows were a bit dirty, she noticed, as if there had been spotty rain since the last time they were washed.

Below her, she saw the movement of traffic, strangers walking to or from their destinations. She wondered if they were tourists or lived in the city. It saddened her that as anonymous as she was to them, so were they to her. The loneliness of running, searching, got to her. The familiar warm ache in her throat signaled the onset of a weeping assault. She fought it, knowing she'd be useless if she indulged the emotional slide into sorrow. Joseph. He was all that mattered now.

Soon, the rhythm of the cars and purposefulness of the people dissolved her anguish. Cities fascinated and terrified her. That had been why she'd taken Joseph someplace her husband wouldn't have suspected; to a roiling city, not a small, quiet town like Buskirk, where she'd been raised. As she moved from one city to another, seeking the most unlikely place he'd look for them, everyone had been so solicitous to her and Joseph. He was only two months old, and she was traveling on her own. People suspected she was on the run from an abusive husband, she thought. After all, she had scads of cash, dressed well, wore a huge wedding ring, and had the kind of movie star looks that made others think they needed to be discreet about seeing her.

But he'd found her. He told her, "Nobody goes anywhere in this country without me knowing where, how and when. You want to disappear? Go to China." He'd laughed. "Good luck with that…you have a passport, darling?" Of course she hadn't. She didn't even have a driver's license. He wouldn't let her drive. He'd given her a chauffeured car. She still had the tiny gray card with her social security number on it, but she couldn't recall where.

The light in the room seemed to shift, go blue again. She felt grimy from traveling, but didn't dare take a bath and leave Joseph alone. She wasn't going to lose him again. Maybe it was her pills. She hadn't taken them when she got up.

She laid her suitcase on the bed, plied it open and sighed. Her two dresses, low-heeled shoes, and cloth case of toiletries barely filled the small piece of luggage. Her pills were lined up along the inside edge, tucked behind the silk ruched fabric. She took a pill from each vial and went into the bathroom to drink them down. The water from the faucet in the sink was cold and fresh.

She glanced at herself in the mirror and had one of her moments when she didn't recognize herself. The woman she saw was in her late sixties, with graying hair swept up in a loose spinster's bun. The deep blue eyes were ringed with dark skin, wrinkled and drooping. The lips were thin, colorless, and the smile, when it came, was yellowed to near brown, tar-stained. Sometimes the woman wore glasses that made her eyes seem larger. Not today.

Hurrying from the bathroom, she looked out into the room and didn't recognize it. Panic set in and her heart raced. She felt her face, the smooth unlined skin, and the lively auburn curls over her shoulders, and knew she was herself, but the room! It was dark. Hadn't it just been morning? The bed was under the window and the crib was beside it. The railing was down and she ran to see if Joseph was still there.

Gone! She felt around the crib for him, throwing off the blankets. The sheet was still warm. He'd just been there! Turning on the brass lamp by the bed, she could see her suitcase in the corner on the folding carrier, closed tight. She blinked as she swept the room, looking for signs of her son. The bed was unmade and she saw then that next to where she'd slept was the nest of pillows she'd set up to protect him from rolling off. There he was, on his back, his head turned to the side, his tiny fists against the curves of the pillows.

Once she saw he was all right, she lay beside him, staring at his perfect little face. Was he hungry? No, he'd be crying if he was. But her stomach growled. She reached for the phone and ordered a meal.

A different boy brought her a steak dinner, more a man than a boy. He stared at her, his eyes searching as if to identify an actress or celebrity, she thought. Hadn't strangers often asked her if she was famous? Thrown a movie star's name at her? But when she handed him the dollar, he told her they had to substitute the brand of baby formula for the one she'd ordered; they didn't make it anymore. She nodded, put her index finger over her lips to shush him, pointing to the empty crib, and told him her son was sleeping. He squinted over her shoulder, shrugged and turned away. She shut the door quietly behind him.

She felt as if it had been days since she'd last eaten. She filled herself with baked potato slathered in butter and chives, an enormous rib-eye, and vegetables topped with fried onions. Had she ordered the wine that gleamed in the glass on the table? How she loved white wine! The bottle was empty when she went to refill her glass. The alcohol mixed with her pills made her groggy. She had a cigarette, then put it out in the remains of her rib-eye. She threw herself onto the bed, careful of Joseph.

She dreamed. Nightmares really. Babies falling, bursting into flames or casting blood on sidewalks like water-filled balloons breaking, spewing water on hot cement. Her pills were gigantic, like dinner plates, trying to enter her belly through her cesarean section scar. As she flailed, she felt the pressure of a straitjacket reining her in until she couldn't move. She woke drenched in sweat, wrapped in the sheets.

The pillow nest was gone and the crib was again by the door. She sat up and noticed two ashtrays on the floor beside the crib, filled with a week's worth of cigarette butts. Three full bottles of infant formula stood in a row on the night stand. Empty wine bottles filled the waste basket, and crumpled chip packets littered the carpet around it. Outside, clouds obscured the sun, so the room had that blue quality she now associated with losing time. Her memory playing tricks.

As she got out of bed, she realized she had nothing on. It was the old woman again, her body with the sagging breasts, spotted skin, protruding hip bones. The baby's whimpering stopped her self-examination. She found her dress on the floor and pulled it over her head, ignoring her undergarments.

He seemed blissfully asleep, pink, and healthy. The railing was half way down so she raised it. She'd had no idea she could ever love anything or anyone more than Joseph. What a handsome boy!

When she was pregnant, toward the end, she had to go off her medications, and a depression settled into her bones. She'd not wanted him during that time, felt unprepared and unworthy to be a mother. What did she know about mothering? She was an only child, with a mother who was put away months after she was born. Her father had done his best, adoring her, giving everything his postman's salary allowed. But he was lonely. There were women in town who were attracted to her father. He was striking, with his dark auburn hair, clear blue eyes, and lean build. Many of them brought casseroles, took in his laundry, and sat next to him in church, but the only girl he fancied in his house, in his bed, was her. Her alone.

The night school course in secretarial skills saved her. She was good at shorthand and taking dictation and had the kind of personality her teacher said would be "Front office. Sparkling and warm." A friend of her teacher got her a job in the city at one of James Prescott's companies. It was the best time of her life; rooming with the girls in the hotel for employees, going out for drinks, meeting men, collecting their gifts that dotted her dresser like so many dew drops on a leaf. The quality of her clothes improved, as did her ability to afford the niceties such as manicures, and having her hair cut and styled. By the time she turned twenty-two, she was engaged to the CEO.

She'd fallen asleep again, this time on the carpet. The cry of the baby woke her. She rolled onto her side and glanced up at the door. The crib! Gone! Hadn't she put the desk and crib there to stop the maids and nosy bellboys from coming in? She looked around and saw that it had moved, against the wall across from the bed. Someone had gotten in again. It wasn't *him*. If it had been, Joseph would be gone.

It was raining. The sound against the window set her nerves on edge. She remembered her pills. Fumbling in her suitcase, she pulled the bottles from the lining and shook them. She was out of the mood stabilizers. She'd had a newly filled prescription when she left on her journey. That was only a few days ago! She took two each of the others into the bathroom. She avoided the mirror, went to the toilet. She sat there for a while, musing over her good fortune in finding Joseph at last. She shut her eyes, felt dizzy, opened them. She grabbed for the toilet roll dispenser beside her as she began to teeter off, fall. Her pills fell onto the marble floor. She needed a glass with water. She scooped up the pills, got herself up, let the bright bathroom settle from its wild orbit and went to the sink. She put the glass to her lips and sipped.

Every summer her father took her to her grandparents' house near a lake. She couldn't recall the name. The lake was large enough to take boats out and fish, but not so big that she couldn't swim across. She was a good swimmer. The smell of her skin turning brown, the algae at the water's edge, and the sweet taste of the lake water seemed so real. She expected to open her eyes and be there, under the sun, her father on the blanket beside her, watching her as she adjusted her swimsuit.

She turned out the light and hurried into the room. The crib remained as it had been. She sighed, relieved.

A sudden, fierce longing filled her. For the lake water? Her youth? Her innocence? She wobbled with her legs heavy and uncooperative. If she didn't get into bed as the pills hit her, she'd end up on the carpet again. Carpet burns dotted her knees, elbows, and shoulders. She couldn't remember how she got them.

She checked on Joseph. His eyes were open and his arms wide. She lifted him and took him to bed. Pulling the pillows into a tight circle ready to nestle him in, she embraced him, his tiny mouth going to her full breast to feed.

Just then, the door flung open, banging against the crib, waking her. She opened her eyes, dopey from her pills. Two men in uniforms stood beside a portly man in a suit. They filled the doorway, then spilled into the room. The man in the suit had a letter in his hand and waved it about as he instructed the men in uniforms to get her dressed.

In a shrill voice, he explained the hotel had put the crib in the room because she'd asked for one, as if one of the uniformed men had asked why the crib was there. They'd expected perhaps her granddaughter was coming to stay with her, but no one ever came. Three weeks! There was nothing left to do but call them.

The taller man in uniform began gathering up her clothes, shoving them into the battered, swanky suitcase while the other pulled a dress over her head, gently maneuvering her arms into the sleeves. Then he helped her to stand. She slid her feet into the low-heeled pumps at his insistence, and started pulling stray white hairs up into the flattened bunch of hair at the nape of her neck. He found her glasses on the night stand and slipped them onto her face. When he spoke, he had a deep, commanding voice, like her husband's. For a moment, panic pushed at her stupor. He said he thought she appeared lost. He wondered who she belonged to. She wanted to shout, "Joseph!", but all she managed was a grunt.

The man in the suit handed the letter to the taller man, noting it was the woman's bill, as the other held her by a scuffed elbow. He shook his head and exhaled. What a sad case.

Where was the baby? She felt her legs go out from under her. She went onto her hands and knees and retched. Nothing came of it. She looked up at her captors. The man in the suit seemed woeful to her, as if he'd discovered she couldn't pay. She'd never stiffed a hotel. *Never.*

She looked around to see if the baby was all right. But he was gone. One of them had taken Joseph. She was sure. But they underestimated her. She'd find him again. She always did.

Severance Package

Bev Vincent

Once upon a time, not so very long ago, it would have been much more difficult for Jerry to get what he needed. He would have had to venture into disreputable parts of town and associate with people who were assertive and shameless enough to expose—even flaunt—their predilections, as well as those who preyed on them.

Thanks to the internet, he didn't have to leave his house. His requirements could be fulfilled via any one of dozens of websites. It was almost as easy as ordering take-out, no matter what his craving. And it was all free—and fast, which was important because time was of the essence. Like so many who frequented these sites, Jerry's window of opportunity was narrow and his burning need had to be sated *now*.

With his browser in stealth mode, he refined his search by geography. He couldn't wait for someone to drive across the city. He sent emails to several potential candidates and, within minutes, had three responses. Two had photographs attached. Faces blurred, but nothing else left to the imagination. Jerry responded to the closest contact with his Skype ID, requesting a face-to-face before proceeding. There were a lot of whack jobs out there. Who could forget *Fatal Attraction*?

Jerry wore a cap that cast a shadow on his face. He and his first choice hit it off right away. They quickly got down to logistics and ground rules. Jerry hoped his eagerness didn't make *him* look like a whack job. However, Jerry's new friend was as enthusiastic as he was and could be at Jerry's place in less than fifteen minutes. Jerry said the front door would be unlocked. He'd be waiting in the bedroom at the top of the stairs.

He made a few last-minute preparations. Everything had to be absolutely perfect, and he had to be utterly discreet. As the vice president in charge of innovations (the VP of wacky ideas, some called him behind his back) for a major corporation, he had a reputation to consider.

Once everything was in place, he retreated to his bedroom and waited. The only light in the room came from a reading lamp beside the bed. His heart raced. Would this be his sole encounter with his visitor, or would they be seeing more of each other in the future? That was out of his hands. He had no way of knowing how things would turn out. He had everything mapped out in his head, but once another person entered the equation, all bets were off.

Ten minutes later, Jerry heard the distinctive sound of weather stripping gliding across the hardwood floor inside the front door. He grabbed his cell phone. After several seconds, the bottom stair creaked. His visitor was being drawn to the light at the top of the stairs like a moth to a flame. Just before the other person reached the upstairs landing, Jerry turned off the ringer and stowed the phone in his nightstand.

The bedroom door creaked open. "Hey?" the man said. He had a mustache and black hair, swept back. He was wearing a muscle shirt and tight jeans. "You said to just come in."

"Yes," Jerry said.

"Got a safe word?"

"Perfidy."

The man frowned. "The fuck's that?"

"Doesn't matter. Will you recognize it if you hear it again?"

"Purr-fiddy," the man said. "Like perfectly. Way you look, all sprawled out."

"Aren't you a flirt," Jerry said. "There's rope on the nightstand."

"Brought these," the man said, producing two sets of handcuffs from his pants pocket. "You're still dressed."

"Yes," Jerry said. "I want you to tear my clothes off. After I'm cuffed."

The man's eyes gleamed. "I'm down with that. Get on your stomach."

This was the point of no return. Either Jerry went with the fantasy or he called the whole thing off. He looked at the man—the stranger—and complied. What other choice did he have?

"Spread your arms." The man's voice was raspy. When Jerry was slow to respond, the man tugged his right arm into position. His grip was strong enough to leave marks. He clicked the cuff around Jerry's wrist and connected the other end to a rung on the bedpost. Just like that, Jerry was a prisoner in his own home. Safe word or no safe word, he was at this man's mercy.

His visitor repeated the process with Jerry's left hand, then yanked Jerry's legs straight before climbing on the bed and straddling him. His weight pressed Jerry's hips into the mattress. Jerry smelled the man's heavy cologne and felt his rough face abrade his ear. Then came a hoarse whisper. "Relax, you little girl. Enjoy it."

The man grabbed Jerry's shirt by the neck and pulled. A few buttons tore loose, but the material proved too strong. Before Jerry could say anything, the man grabbed something off the nightstand. The knife he had left with the coil of rope.

The cold metal blade brushed along Jerry's cheek. His heart seized. The room grew deadly quiet. Had he underestimated the man? Would he feel the point of the knife push between his ribs, or its razor-sharp edge slice into his vulnerable throat?

The man chuckled before grabbing Jerry's shirt by the neck and slashing it to shreds so he could tear it off. The ruined garment whispered to the floor. Cool air rushed across Jerry's back, chilling the sweat that had formed on his shoulders and pooled in the small of his back. The man ran his hands across Jerry's bare skin. His touch was warm, his palms rough and calloused, his fingernails untrimmed. "Make you my bitch," the man said. "That what you want? Be my bitch?"

"Yes," Jerry said. "Make me your bitch."

"Minute I saw you I thought—this candy ass needs a real man to show him what's what." He pushed his hands under Jerry's waist and caressed him. "Hmm," he muttered. "Soon fix that."

He grabbed the coil of rope, cut a couple of lengths, and affixed Jerry's ankles to the corner posts at the foot of the bed. Then he forced his hands under Jerry's waist and fumbled with his belt.

Trussed up like a turkey, Jerry's arms and shoulders stretched uncomfortably, but he couldn't complain. He had ceded all control.

Once the belt was undone and pulled free of its loops. Jerry felt the man's weight shift. A second later, the belt whipped across his bare shoulders with a resounding crack. It stung, but only a little. He cried out, though, playing along. Three more thrashes guaranteed to leave angry welts on Jerry's back, and the man dropped the belt.

The stranger fumbled with the top button on Jerry's pants, then with his zipper. He reached in and caressed Jerry intimately and seemed satisfied by the response. He grabbed Jerry's pants by the waist and tugged. Jerry's shoulders felt like they were about to pop from the sockets, but then his pants slid down over his hips as far as they could go with his legs spread and bound as they were. His briefs followed a second later, and he was exposed.

His breath came in short, rapid pants. He was close to hyperventilating. This was where things got dicey. He could utter his safe word and hope the man would be as cooperative as he'd seemed before Jerry was restrained and helpless. However, if he got the timing wrong, everything would be ruined. He had to grin and bear whatever was about to happen.

Another whisper of material as the man's shirt fell to the floor atop Jerry's. Another rattle of a belt buckle. The mattress rose and fell like a ship on rough waters when the man got off the bed. Jerry watched him shuck his shoes, jeans and underwear. The man noticed Jerry watching, but said nothing. He merely grinned and stroked himself. His girth was impressive. Fearsome. Jerry's stomach clenched. He closed his eyes and took a deep breath, holding it for several seconds.

The mattress shifted again as the man crawled back on and positioned himself between Jerry's legs. Jerry cringed at the intimate contact. The man's naked body radiated heat like an oven broiler. He picked up the knife again and started working on one leg of Jerry's pants.

Jerry heard a creak. A male voice rumbled up the staircase like thunder. "Hello? Anyone here?"

"Who's that?" the man hissed.

Jerry's shackles prevented him from looking at the man. He twisted his head as far as he could and said. "I thought you might like some company." His heart was pounding. Would the stranger go along?

The man slapped Jerry's buttock with his free hand. "Threesome, eh? You naughty bitch. Gonna have fun with you. You gonna walk funny for days."

"This guy..."

"What?"

"He likes to dress up. Might be a fireman or a clown."

"Ha!" The man's hand was between Jerry's legs, exploring, stroking. "I can roll with that."

"Sir? Mr. Wallace? Are you here? We received a call."

A man in a cop's uniform appeared at the door. He had a flashlight in one hand and a gun in the other.

"Play along, okay?" Jerry whispered.

The man snorted. "Come in, officer," he said in a jaunty voice. "Get out of that uniform and join me."

The other man's eyes widened. The gun wavered in his hand as he glanced over his shoulder. "Drop the weapon, sir."

"Just interrogating a naughty witness," the man said. "Wanna be bad cop?"

"Sir. I said, drop the weapon. Kramer, get over here."

"Help," Jerry cried in a weak, strangled voice. "He's going to kill me."

"Shut your face, pussy," the man said, poking his shoulder with the tip of the knife. "You got the right to remain silent."

"Help," Jerry croaked again. His body trembled.

"I'm not going to tell you again. Drop the knife."

"The second I'm done here. We all on the same page, ain't we precious?" He slashed Jerry's pants.

A single gunshot emptied the room of air and replaced it with an echoing percussion. The man gurgled and spasmed. The knife scraped against Jerry's hip as it dropped to the mattress. The man swayed and toppled off the bed on the side farthest from the door.

By now, another cop had appeared. Both men aimed their weapons into the room. The first officer flicked on the light switch and made a beeline for the bed. He grabbed the knife and tossed it in the corner, then circled the foot of the bed. He knelt and extended his arm. A few seconds later, he shook his head. "Call it in," he told his partner. Then he looked at Jerry. "It's all right, sir. He's not going to hurt you any more. Let's get you out of those cuffs."

After that, things got busy, especially when the cops found the body in the living room.

Jerry spent the rest of the night repeating his story, first in the kitchen with a blanket around his shoulders while crime scene investigators collected evidence. A technician photographed the marks on his arms and back. Then they let him get dressed and transported him to a tiny, grim room at the police station.

No, he'd never seen the killer before. No, he didn't know why his attacker had targeted his house. Maybe because the lights were on in the living room? Yes, he might have forgotten to lock the front door after Todd arrived with pizza and beer to watch a ball game. The man had burst in without knocking, waving a knife and demanding money. He looked like a lunatic. Jerry had wanted to give the guy whatever he wanted but Todd went after him. Knocked him to the floor. They struggled. Jerry's cell phone was in his bedroom, so he ran upstairs to call 911. Maybe he should have stayed to help, but the other guy was so big and acting crazy. And that knife. They both might have ended up dead.

No, he didn't mind if they searched his house. No, he didn't want to consult a lawyer. He was just so thankful that the police arrived when they did. Another couple of minutes and there was no telling what that maniac would have done to him. He shuddered at the thought.

Sometimes he told the whole story from beginning to end. Other times they asked him questions out of order, as if they were trying to trip him up. It was a simple story, though, and he stuck to it. Most of it was true. Todd *had* come over that night with beer and pizza. They *had* watched part of a ball game before it happened. He didn't even have to pretend to be devastated that Todd was dead—they'd been friends for years.

However, the baseball game had been a pretext, and the pizza and beer was a peace offering. Things were getting tight at work, Todd had told him. They had to cut expenses, so he had decided to eliminate Jerry's division. Nothing personal, but they could no longer afford to finance projects that weren't going anywhere. It had been a while since any of Jerry's ideas had turned into something profitable, hadn't it? He understood, didn't he?

"You'll get a generous severance package, of course," Todd said. "And a glowing recommendation." He shrugged. "It won't be a golden parachute, but you'll land on your feet, I'm sure."

The more Todd talked, the louder the buzzing in Jerry's head grew. His vision clouded and, before he knew what he was doing, he had plunged a knife—used to divide the last piece of pizza in half—into his friend's chest. It felt so satisfying that he did it again.

The buzzing stopped. His vision cleared. Sanity returned. He went straight into crisis prevention mode. If he didn't want to spend the rest of his life in prison, he had to think—and fast. They might call him the VP of wacky ideas, but every now and then he came up with a good one. This one, spawned under tremendous pressure, was among his best.

He couldn't dispose of the body. Too risky. Todd probably told someone where he was going, which would lead the police to Jerry's door once he was reported missing. No matter how careful he was, he was bound to leave behind evidence. Besides, there were cameras everywhere these days and too much of a chance that someone would report suspicious activity.

The best solution was to *bring* the police here, but make it seem like someone else had killed Todd. Even better, he would turn himself into a victim, too. The best case scenario had the cops killing his patsy, though there was a strong possibility they would end up merely arresting the guy if he didn't play along according to Jerry's plan. It was a gamble, but it would be the stranger's word against Jerry's if that happened. Given the circumstances, Jerry knew who the police would believe. It would be a mess, but a manageable one.

Prepping the scene had been absurdly easy. There had been very little blood, and Jerry was sure that none of it had gotten on him or his clothes. There was nothing else damning for the investigators to turn up. It had been a crime of passion, so there was no trail to cover. The handcuffs—an unexpected bonus-- belonged to his attacker. His prints would be all over them, and Jerry hadn't touched them. Besides, he couldn't have cuffed and roped himself to the bed. The knife was a stray, not part of a set. Jerry had wiped it on Todd's shirt, leaving only traces of blood the stranger wouldn't notice in the dimly lit bedroom. The man's prints were all over it, too, and the cops had seen it in his hand. Had seen him threatening Jerry with it.

So, Jerry didn't have to make up anything. He only had to gloss over a few details. He could tell the story backwards, forward and inside out. Everything supported his version of events. Nothing contradicted it. Dead men tell no tales.

A squad car took Jerry home shortly before dawn. Later that afternoon, a detective came by to brief him. The perp's prints were in the system. He told Jerry the guy's name, but Jerry couldn't remember it five minutes later. The perp had been arrested several times for bar fights and had a history of hooking up with submissive men to dominate them. So far, they had no evidence he'd injured any of his partners before, but one guy they'd interviewed said he felt uneasy around the man. Such was the power of suggestion, Jerry thought.

The detective thought they might find something in the toxicology report to explain his erratic behavior. Even if they didn't, Jerry was in the clear. Internal Affairs were calling it a good shoot. As far as everyone was concerned, the case was closed.

As an added bonus, after Jerry returned to work upper management promoted him into Todd's position. It was on a trial basis, but Jerry was certain he could make it permanent.

He had landed on his feet after all.

One night, two months after a stranger invaded Jerry's house, killed his best friend, and was about to commit unspeakable violence upon Jerry himself—for that was how he now remembered the evening—Jerry awoke to feel a terrible pressure in his chest. He had trouble catching his breath. He couldn't move. At first he thought he was having a heart attack. He was naked, spread-eagled, the covers pushed down to the foot of the bed.

He took several deep breaths. Forced himself to relax.

Then he saw Todd perched on the edge of the bed. He looked much better than the last time Jerry had seen him, dead on the floor beside the living room sofa. He was wearing a dress shirt and slacks. His hair was neatly groomed and his face clean-shaven. Jerry could almost smell cologne. I'm dreaming, he thought, but the vision was too clear to be a reverie.

"Time for me to move on, old buddy. Just wanted to drop in to say goodbye first."

Jerry tried to sit up, but he couldn't. It was as if his hands and ankles were bound to the bedposts. Again. His version of that terrible evening pushed into his mind, but he fought it off. "Move on? Where?"

Todd shrugged. "All I know is that I'm done here. Paid my dues. Atoned for my sins. I got off lucky. I lived a pretty clean life. I hurt a few women—sometimes without realizing it—and damaged a few people doing business, but all in all, I did not do too bad."

"But you're dead."

"I know, Jerry. You are the one who killed me, after all."

"Not me. Him. The robber. He killed you and he was going to rape me."

"Come on, Jerry. It's just you and me here. We can get past all that silly stuff you've been telling everyone. Even yourself, I guess." In the moonlight, his grin looked demonic. "We both know that Victor was an innocent victim. You remember him, right? Victor Quezada?"

Jerry didn't answer.

"I'm not here to forgive you for killing me, though. That's your burden, not mine. I just wanted to let you know what you have in store. Maybe that's cruel, but since nothing prevented me from being here, I guess it's all right."

"You're...a ghost?"

"I suppose. Know why people don't see ghosts all the time?"

Jerry shook his head. This is a dream, he kept telling himself. Must be.

"The dead can only contact a living person who's about to die. Anyone who says otherwise is making it up. Or imagining things. People can convince themselves of just about anything. Like the way you persuaded yourself you had nothing to do my death or Victor's. You think you're a victim, too." Todd shook his head.

Jerry blinked. "I'm not about to die. I'm in perfect shape."

Todd smiled. It wasn't pleasant. "I don't make the rules. Anyhow, I wanted you to know what to expect. After you die, you end up in— well, let's call it purgatory. Your life doesn't flash in front of your eyes *before* you die. That happens later, and it isn't a flash. You see it all in slow motion. It's excruciating. You see the ripples. The tentacles." He spread his hands in the air. "Cause and effect. The consequences of everything you did. It can be quite humbling."

Jerry struggled against his invisible restraints. He needed to sit up, catch his breath. Figure out what the hell was going on.

"Then you get to go time traveling. That's the cool part. Forward as far as you need to, until you meet all the people you've wronged. Even your worst enemies are ready to make peace when they know they're about to die. Usually." He leaned forward. "One catch: You can't go backwards. You can't apologize to the dead. They've already passed on. Do you get that, Jerry? It's too late. You'll never get to apologize to Victor and me for what you did."

He straightened his shoulders and put his hands on his knees. "I suspect your purgatory is going to last a long, long time. I can't say that disappoints me." He looked at his wrist. "Time to be on my way, Jerry. Goodbye."

With that he vanished. There was no sound. No pop of air rushing in to fill a void. No rattling of chains or whisper of breath. One moment he was there, the next: nothing.

Jerry tried to move his arms again, sure that his restraints would have vanished, too, but he still couldn't move. He dropped his head back onto the pillow and expelled a burst of air. He felt the mattress shift and dip. A dark figure materialized before him.

"Todd? You forget something?"

The man's face loomed in front of his. The stranger. The man the police had shot. What was his name? Victor something. He was naked. A bullet wound in his chest oozed blood. He was, Jerry noted with dismay, erect.

"Why you do me like that? Thought you was nice. Thought we'd have fun. Setting me up for offing your friend? Not cool. Know what that did to my family? Ruined them. You didn't just mess me up, you messed up a lot of people. And your friend? Fuck, dude. That was harsh. People get fired, know what I'm saying?"

Jerry tried to look away, but he couldn't.

"When you die, you can learn just about anything you want. Fucking safe word. Thought you were being cute. Wrapping up your tricks in a fancy word you knew I wouldn't get. Rubbing it in my face. Fucker."

Jerry struggled to get a few words out. His chest felt tighter. "Why are you here?"

"I done a few bad things in my time. It's gonna take me a while to put everything right. Do my twelve-step program—that's what I call it. But you know what?"

He waited for an answer. Jerry couldn't even shrug.

"I don't fucking care what comes next. I can go wherever I want. Shit, *whenever* I want. So I came here. The place you lured me to. Us all set to have a good time, and you tricked them into shooting me." His hand went to the bullet wound in his chest and came away bloody. He shook his head. "Fucker. So, here's what's going to happen, dude. I'm going to finish what I came here for that night. Have myself a good old time. No rush. Time don't mean much to me any more. Don't care what it does to my moral balance, either. If I have to spend eternity making up for it, that's a-okay. Now let's roll you over and get this show on the road."

The official cause of death was a heart attack, but the officers sent to check Jerry's house when he didn't show up for work and didn't answer his phone were struck by the look on his face.

"Ever wonder what you see when you die?" one officer asked the other.

The other shook his head. "Too deep for me, brother. I just hope I don't see whatever this guy did. Looks like he saw something evil."

As She Lay There Dying

Brian James Freeman

The roads were wet from another morning of April showers, and the co-ed freshman lying on the pavement was missing part of her head. Her legs were twisted awkwardly under her body and there was blood on the sidewalk. One of her tattered running shoes had landed on the other side of the street, knocked clear of the scene of the accident. A broken iPod lay just beyond her hand.

The dying girl wore mesh shorts and a pink shirt featuring the Haverton Field Hockey logo. She was sprawled next to the curb at the entrance to the school's grounds, directly in front of the big stone wall with the sign proclaiming "Welcome to Haverton College."

"Oh shit," Sam whispered, turning to the bushes and vomiting. The English professor wasn't alone in his horror.

A secretary named Marge Wilson held the girl's hand. At the time of the accident Marge had been walking to the pizza parlor just off campus to pick-up lunch for her co-workers, and a wad of cash was still in her left hand, forgotten. She had seen everything.

Students on their way to one o'clock classes gathered around the dying girl. Some held their hands to their faces while others texted their friends.

The dying girl moaned. Her disfigured head rolled loosely on her rubbery neck and blood spit from her broken mouth. Her teeth were red.

She turned her face blindly toward Sam and she whispered in clipped breaths: "Sammy, we can't run anymore."

Sam blinked, startled by the sound of his name. He stared into the girl's glassy eyes. He didn't recognize her, but no one called him Sammy, especially not students. The only person who ever called him that had been dead for six months.

Then Sam heard the artificial click and whirl as a camera phone snapped a photo.

"Get out of here, you ass," Sam said, turning and shoving the young man with a backpack slung over his shoulder. The student stumbled backwards and then just stood there, off balance and stunned. Sam yelled and shoved him again, right up against the stone wall with the school's name.

Next came more shouting, but the rest was a blur as the campus police arrived and then the ambulance—the girl was dead by then—and the questioning began.

According to one of the department secretaries gossiping in the third floor hallway of McGrove Hall, the dead girl's name was Lauren Redman, a first year Math Ed major from the other side of the state who came to the school on a field hockey scholarship.

Sam listened as he posted a note on his office door, canceling his classes for the rest of the week. He couldn't stand the idea of facing the slack jawed students while their obvious boredom burned a hole right through him.

Not today.

Walking home to his cozy neighborhood outside the small college town, Sam took a side street to avoid the main entrance to the school. The girl's blood would still be there.

What am I going to do? Sam thought, not for the first time.

As far as he could remember, the dead girl hadn't taken his mandatory Intro course, but the thousands of names and faces had blurred together over the years, so he couldn't be sure.

Actually, everything was a little blurry these days. Sam's shoving match with the cell phone voyeur felt like a distant memory of something he only witnessed. He didn't know what had come over him, but maybe it was a knee-jerk reaction to someone disrespecting the dying.

If that student had been there and photographed Julie when she died, Sam probably wouldn't have stopped with a shove. But his wife had died alone, with no one to hold her hand and comfort her. Sam hadn't even known she was dead until an hour later.

Did Lauren Redman really say, *Sammy, we can't run anymore*, as she lay there dying on the pavement?

Those words disturbed Sam, but he didn't know why. The poor girl was dead. Why was he so bothered by her last words? She probably had a boyfriend named Sammy. Or a brother. It was a common name. Just because *he* was standing there didn't mean she was speaking to him. She probably had no idea where she was, let alone that she was dying.

The words didn't mean *anything*. They were just a result of the last firing synapses as what remained of her brain shut down. Some fragment of a memory.

This conclusion should have comforted Sam, but it didn't. He just kept hearing the words over and over in the dead girl's halting voice:

Sammy, we can't run anymore.

Sam entered the foyer of the house he had shared with his wife until her sudden death and he stopped in the doorway.

Like always, he vividly recalled every detail of the day he arrived home from a run and discovered he was a widower.

He closed his eyes and relived it again for the hundredth time. And why not? What else was he going to do tonight?

On the morning Julie died, Sam was soaked from head to toe in sweat, his feet ached, and his legs moved like they were made of marble as he paced the driveway to cool down and keep his muscles from tightening up. The winter air clung to his exposed flesh and steam rose from his clothes. Two hours of running had never felt better than it did in these moments when the pain and the joy were still fresh.

If there was anything wrong inside the house, he didn't know it yet. His mind was just starting to come down from his runner's high, the rush of endorphins that washed away all of the pains, distractions, and annoyances of the real world.

No matter how badly his legs hurt when he finished a run, his mind was always clear and ready to face new challenges. Julie had taught him this trick not long after they first met on a blind date. She called running her secret weapon for a long and happy life.

This particular morning, though, after Sam completed his cooldown routine, he tried to open the front door and found something had been pushed up against it from the inside.

He had to shove the door open to discover Julie lying at the bottom of the steps, a tiny pool of blood next to her head. Her iPod was still clutched in her hand like a talisman and her arms were twisted under her body, as if she had fallen down the steps.

She was dressed in her purple jogging suit with her top still zipped. That meant she hadn't made it out the door for *her* morning run, which usually started an hour after Sam's most Sundays. She ran for speed, her husband ran for distance.

Sam stared at his wife's motionless body, then he knelt and very gently touched her wrist.

"You love your melodramatic English Department bullcrap," Julie said to Sam one evening early in their marriage while she helped him out of his suit at the end of a long day. This was a few months after they moved into the house and nothing was really unpacked yet.

Sam had just finished telling her about the latest crisis in his department. Was that the time the janitorial service cut back to only emptying the office trashcans every other day? It was hard to keep all of the crap straight, year after year, and he still couldn't believe how much bitching and moaning his well-paid colleagues with seventeen-hour work weeks could muster about such trivial matters and perceived slights.

"What do you mean?" he asked.

"If everyone in your department wasn't a little insane, you'd be bored to tears and you know it," Julie said, slipping her fingers into the elastic band around his waist.

Sam couldn't deny the truth in her statement, especially considering his underwear came off before he could reply and they spent the rest of the evening in the bedroom.

That was one of the many good times they had shared in their ten years of marriage, and there were so many good times he couldn't even count them, but he didn't think it was fair those moments were done and gone forever.

Their ten years of marriage had been wonderful, but he had been promised a lifetime.

Upon finding his wife's dead body and touching her cool wrist, Sam whispered, "This isn't melodramatic English Department bull-crap," for reasons he still didn't understand.

Julie might have been able to explain it to him. She saw things differently than he did, after all, and that was what made them perfect for each other.

Then, with his hand still on Julie's wrist, Sam asked the quiet house: "What am I going to do?"

Every time Sam opened the front door of his home, he expected Julie to be there, dead again, but she never was, of course.

Julie was buried in the Haverton Community Cemetery on the far side of town, and Sam walked to her grave three or four times a week during his lunch break to discuss the latest news and drama with her, just like the old days.

Today Sam had wanted Julie's input on his big decision: whether to take a year's sabbatical and use it to pursue some other career.

Like always, he had sat on the ground and ate the peanut butter and jelly sandwich he brought from home, leaning against her granite marker and picking at the grass around the base, keeping everything neat and tidy. The day was overcast and forlorn. Sometimes he felt like the funeral had never ended.

To his credit, Sam never actually heard Julie reply to any of his questions or observations, but he liked the idea that maybe she was out there somewhere, listening. He didn't really buy into the whole afterlife concept, but if it were possible for Julie to still somehow exist on some other level of the universe, Sam would gladly change his beliefs in a heartbeat.

She probably would have the answers he needed, too. What to do with the rest of his life was a pressing decision for Sam. He had to request the sabbatical by Friday if the paperwork was to be approved in time for the fall schedule.

Sam understood he wasn't doing the students any good right now. He had cancelled more classes than he had attended this semester. At any other job he would have been fired, but he had tenure and the union wouldn't let anything happen to his position, of course.

Sam's livelihood wasn't in any danger. He could just put himself on cruise control and retire with full benefits at the age of sixty. Plenty of his colleagues were already on the thirty-and-out plan, after all. It was practically tradition.

But what would he do with all of the years to follow? Would he sit around the house writing reams of so-so poetry and watching television? Would he go to his desk and read old syllabi and pretend he missed his glory days? What kind of life would that be?

Besides, putzing along at work for a couple of decades without giving a crap wasn't the way Sam wanted to live. He wanted to really be *alive*.

Of course, he also wanted Julie by his side to carry out their plans—the fixer-upper in the country, the beach house, the second honeymoon to Bermuda, the babies, all the beautiful babies—but that was the most impossible dream he still clung to with a quiet desperation.

No one seemed to be holding Sam's inattentiveness at work against him, at least. Most people understood the grief of the unexpected death of the person who made your life feel so complete and full of purpose.

Who could blame Sam for not wanting to discuss Colonial Period American Literature while he was still attempting to comprehend how his beautiful bride, who was in better shape than him, could have been felled by an aneurysm while coming down the steps for her morning run, her brain shutting off before she even landed on the cold linoleum floor?

As far as Sam could tell, no one cared that his classes were falling so far behind, least of all the students.

Standing there in the foyer again, Sam wondered if the parents of Lauren Redman had been notified yet.

They were probably driving across the state right now to visit her in the morgue, to confirm her identity.

Sam believed the only thing worse than finding your beloved dead on the foyer floor was getting that dreaded phone call and making that drive, half your heart wanting to believe it would just turn out to be a terrible misunderstanding.

With Julie, Sam knew his wife was dead the moment he found her. There was no mistaken identity. There was no hoping for a miracle.

He guessed he should be grateful for that, but he wasn't. Julie was still dead, either way.

After Julie's death, Sam developed a condition that reminded him of a phenomenon he heard about all the time in his field. The symptoms snuck up on him from out of nowhere and he was deep in the affliction before he realized what was happening. He blamed the grief.

Truman Capote, Ralph Ellison, Harper Lee, Samuel Taylor Coleridge, Arundhati Roy, Gabriel Garcia Márquez, and Arthur Rimbaud all knew variations of the condition quite well, even if some of them suffered from it before the phrase was officially coined: writer's block.

Only Sam's problem wasn't with his writing. He continued to churn out poetry at his normal rate and he had updated his notes and syllabi for next semester without issue, just in case he felt a renewed vigor for teaching or simply couldn't pull the trigger on the sabbatical.

Sam didn't have *writer's* block. He had *runner's* block.

The last time he even tried to run—maybe a month after Julie's death when he desperately needed to escape from the world—was so dreadful that he held no ambition to make another attempt, not if he lived to be a hundred years old.

Like most people with a block, Sam understood what he wanted to do, but his mind wouldn't let him, which created a little cycle of hell for him to experience again and again. He needed to run so badly some days, but even the thought of wearing his running clothes could push him to tears.

The last time Sam had tried to go for a run, he sat on the edge of the bed and tied his running shoes, convinced this time would be different. He loved running. The act of getting out there and attacking the road was the only thing he had left in life that could truly make him feel good—and this time everything would be okay, he just knew it.

Sam stood, stretched, and then headed down the stairs, his mind clear and his heart full of confidence, but he never even made it outside.

When he reached the last step, he tripped and fell, landing hard on the linoleum floor, sending a dull ache through his bones. He found himself in a position strikingly similar to Julie's death pose, and he cried for over an hour, his entire body shaking uncontrollably.

He hadn't put on those shoes since.

❉

Sam had never realized grief could run so deep and be so all consuming, but these days he truly understood the misery of knowing you'd never be able to have the one thing you needed most to fill a gaping emptiness in your world.

The love of his life was gone, he couldn't run, and he didn't want to teach anymore... so what was the point of riding the Earth around the sun year after year after year?

That was the question his mind would get stuck on in his darkest hours. He knew there was an easy answer to that question, and the ease with which he sometimes contemplated that answer scared him badly.

As darkness settled across the land, ending yet another lonely day, Sam couldn't help but think of Lauren Redman's final words again: *Sammy, we can't run anymore.*

A few hours later, Sam was dreaming, and in this dream he was running, following the trail around campus.

His legs had never felt better and there was no pain. He could go a hundred miles if he wanted. Maybe more.

Sam was calm and collected as the campus rolled past him like a groovy Technicolor background. The sun was shining brightly through the trees and everything was incredibly vivid and alive. Birds were singing. A breeze cooled his sweaty skin.

Sam couldn't remember spring ever being this beautiful and he never wanted this run to end, but as he neared a small wooden bridge over a stream, he saw two women jogging in his direction.

This wasn't unusual considering how many students frequented the trail, except for one important detail: both of these women were dead.

They were running side by side and they were smiling, showing off their bloody teeth. Julie's hair was maroon from the small pool of blood she had died in. The top of Lauren's head was missing and bits of gray matter were speckled across her pink field hockey shirt.

Sam tripped and stumbled to his knees as all of the color drained from the dream.

Then he screamed.

The two dead women looked at him, startled, and screamed back.

Their mouths were open so wide.

Their teeth were caked in dirt and blood... and then they shielded their faces with bruised and broken fingers.

They had clawed their way out of their graves.

Sam fell out of bed, soaked in sweat, his heart racing.

He crawled across the bedroom floor and into the master bathroom, where he lay in the dark and sobbed.

Until now he hadn't experienced a single bad dream after Julie's death, but this one was like a thunderbolt through his head.

Sleep was the one place he could escape after each long, painful day, but now his peaceful slumber had been stolen from him.

He was cold and lonelier than he had ever felt in his entire life. He really wasn't prone to melodrama like some of the prima donnas in his department, but he was completely overwhelmed and exhausted and disoriented by the nightmare. Every moving shadow made him cringe in terror.

This was all too much.

What was he going to do?

He couldn't live with nightmares like that.

He simply couldn't.

He couldn't run, he couldn't sleep, and his wife was dead.

What am I going to do, Sam thought. *What am I going to do?*

What could he possibly do?

Sam closed his eyes and sobbed, and he hated the answer that came to mind again and again and again.

A few hours later, Sam opened his eyes.

Sunlight had slipped between the curtains and into his bedroom, washing over him where he lay on the cold bathroom tiles.

Next to him were the running shoes he had given up when he realized his days of pounding the pavement were probably over.

He had no memory of retrieving them from the closet where he had tossed them with a mixture of sadness and disgust.

Sam looked at the shoes, caked in dirt and grass stains.

He heard the dying student whisper: *Sammy, we can't run anymore.*

Sam didn't believe in messages from beyond the grave, yet those dying words were true for both Julie and Lauren, weren't they?

Neither of them could run anymore... but Sam could still run. What the hell was runner's block anyway? He hadn't run in almost six months and why? Because his mind was somehow stopping him?

"What a load of melodramatic bullcrap," Sam whispered.

He put on his running shorts, a gray t-shirt with the Havertown College logo, and his running socks with the extra padding on the heels.

Finally, Sam laced up the shoes. They felt just right.

He took the stairs slowly, his hand on the railing the entire way, careful to avoid a repeat of what happened the last time he tried to run.

When he reached the foyer, Sam opened the front door without stopping to second-guess his decision.

A few minutes later, he was jogging toward town and he didn't look back, not even once.

Sam understood where he was headed as soon as he made it out the front door: the trail around campus.

He passed by the entrance to the school where Lauren Redman died in a puddle of blood, probably not even aware that her run had come to a tragic end.

He locked his eyes on the road ahead of him and he ran even harder.

When Sam reached the start of the trail, his heart was pounding, but he couldn't slow down, not yet.

His legs were thundering under him like he was charging into battle.

Sam certainly wasn't expecting to see Julie and Lauren crossing the bridge in the woods, but he had to run across the bridge for himself.

They wouldn't be there. He knew that. He was certain of that. It simply wasn't possible for a million different reasons.

And when Sam reached the bridge, the dead women were nowhere to be seen... but for a man who didn't expect to see anyone, Sam was maybe a little too relieved.

Ten minutes later, Sam arrived at the bottom of the hill in the Haverton Community Cemetery. His clothing was soaked in sweat, his heart was pounding like a jackhammer, his lungs were tight, and he hadn't felt this good in a long time. It was as if an enormous weight had been lifted from his shoulders.

The sun was blazing brightly above the mountains to the east and the world was more beautiful than Sam ever remembered it being, even in the early days of his marriage when *everything* was picturesque and perfect. Every blade of grass shimmered in the sunlight. Every birdcall was a love song.

Sam had never felt relief like this. The darkness smothering him had been stronger and deeper than he ever realized.

This experience was more than his usual runner's high that lifted him away from the pains and displeasures of the real world. This was the cure to end all cures.

Julie had been right, as she always was. Running really was the secret to a long and happy life.

Today Sam wasn't running from despair and loneliness, he was running toward a bright and welcoming future.

But as he reached the hill where Julie was buried, Sam slowed to take in his surroundings. There was a change in the air. His vision and his senses were still clouded from the runner's high, but when he really concentrated, he could hear shoes pounding the pavement behind him.

He stopped, frozen by the sound. Those shoes were the only thing he could hear and they were suddenly so loud. No wind, no rustling of grasses, no birds in the sky. Other than those shoes, he was deaf.

The land grew dark again and Sam couldn't force himself to look back and see who might be coming. His newfound colorful world was being drained of light and life and he was terrified.

There were now heavy, rapid-fire breaths behind Sam as the person got closer and closer. The impacts of the shoes echoed around Sam as if he was locked inside some kind of vault.

Inside his ears, a voice whispered: *Sammy, we can't run anymore.*

Sam stumbled forward in the direction of Julie's grave.

There was someone standing at the top of the hill.

The person was merely a silhouette against the gray sun. She raised her arms, reaching out toward Sam.

He ran and the world grew bright again, full of colors and sounds that were wonderful and overwhelming.

Sam basked in the light and all of his pain melted away, returning him to that comfortable place, the place he never wanted to leave again.

He understood he had to keep running if he wanted this beautiful day to continue. He dug deep inside himself and ran even harder, the dark figure growing ever closer.

Sam prepared to embrace whatever he found at the top of the hill.

Weeds

Stephen King

Jordy Verrill's place was out on Bluebird Creek, and he was alone when the meteor traced low fire across the sky and hit on the creek's east bank. It was twilight, the sky still light in the west, purple overhead, and dark in the east where Venus glowed in the sky like a two-penny sparkler. It was the Fourth of July, and Jordy had been planning to go into town for the real fireworks show when he finished splitting and banding this last smidge of sugar maple.

But the meteor was even better than the two-pound whizzers they set off at the end of the town show. It slashed across the sky in a sullen red splutter, the head afire. When it hit the ground he felt the thump in his feet. Jordy started toward Bluebird Creek on the dead run, knowing what it was immediately, even before the flash of white light from over the hill. A by-God-meteor, and some of those fellows from the college might pay a good piece of change for it.

He paused at the top of the rise, his small house with its two out-buildings behind him and the meandering, sunset-colored course of the Bluebird ahead of him. And close to its bank, where the punkies and cattails grew in the soft marshy ground, earth had been flung back from a crater-shaped depression four feet across. The grass on the slope was afire.

Jordy whirled and ran back to his shed. He got a big bucket and an old broom. A faucet jutted out from the side of the shed at the end of a rusty pipe; the ground underneath was the only place grass would grow in Jordy's dooryard, which was otherwise bald and littered with old auto parts.

He filled the bucket and ran back toward the creek, thinking it was good the twilight was so still. Otherwise he might have had bad trouble. Might even have had to call the volunteer fire department. But good luck came in batches. The fire was gaining slowly with no wind to help it. It moved out from the crater in a semi-circle, drawing a crescent of black on the summer-green bank.

Moving slowly, with no wasted motion—he had fought grass fires before—Jordy dipped his broom in the water and beat the flames with it. He worked one end of the fire-front and then the other, narrowing the burn zone to twenty feet, ten, nothing. Panting a little, soot on his thin cheeks like beardshadow, he turned around and saw four or five burning circles that had been lit by sparks. He went to each and slapped them out with his wet broom.

Now for that meteor. He walked down to the crater, leather boots sending up little puffs of ash, and hunkered down. It was in there all right, and it was the size of a volleyball. It was glowing red-white-molten, and Jordy thanked his lucky stars that it had landed here, where it was marshy, and not in the middle of his hayfield.

He poked it with his boot, a roundish hunk of rock melted jagged in places by its superhot ride from the reaches of the universe all the way into Jordy Verrill's New Hampshire farmstead on the Fourth of July.

He picked up his bucket again and doused the meteor with the water that remained. There was a baleful hiss and a cloud of steam. When it cleared away and Jordy saw what had happened, he dropped the bucket and slapped his forehead.

"There, you done it now, Jordy, you lunkhead."

The meteor had broken neatly in two. And there was something inside.

Jordy bent forward. White stuff had fallen out of a central hollow, white flaky stuff that looked like Quaker Oats.

"Well beat my ass," Jordy muttered. He got down on his knees and poked at the white stuff.

"Yeee-*ouch*!"

He snatched his fingers away and sucked them, his eyes watering. He was going to have a crop of blisters, just as sure as shit grows under a privy.

A series of thunderclaps went off behind him and Jordy leaped to his feet, looking wildly at the sky. Then he relaxed. It was just the one-pound crackers they always started the fireworks show with. He hunkered down again, never minding the green starbursts spreading in the sky behind him. He had his own fireworks to worry about.

Jordy wasn't bright; he had a potato face, large, blocky hands that were as apt to hoe up the carrots as the weeds that grew between them, and he got along as best he could. He fixed cars and sold wood and in the winter he drove Christmas trees down to Boston. Thinking was hard work for him. Thinking hurt, because there was a dead short somewhere inside, and keeping at it for long made him want to take a nap or beat his meat and forget the whole thing.

For Jordy there were three types of thinking: plain thinking, like what you were going to have for supper or the best way to pull a motor with his old and balky chain-fall; work thinking; and Big Thinking. Big Thinking was like when all the cows died and he was trying to figure if Mr. Warren down at the bank would give him an extension on his loan. Like when you had to decide which bills to pay at the end of the month. Like what he was going to do about this meteor.

He decided the best way to start would be to have some pictures. He went back to the house, got his Kodak, went back to the creek, and took two flash photos of the thing, laying there cracked open like an egg with Quaker Oats coming out of it instead of yolk. It was still too hot to touch.

That was all right. He would just leave her lay. If he took it up to the college in a towsack, maybe they would say Jordy Verrill, look what you done, you fuckin' lunkhead. You picked her up and bust her all to hell. Yes, leave her lay, that was the ticket. It was on his land. If any of those college professors tried to take his meteor, he'd sick the county sheriff on them. If they wanted to cart it off and take pictures of it and measure it and feed little pieces of it to their guinea pigs, they'd have to pay him for the privilege.

"Twenty-five bucks or no meteor!" Jordy said. He stood to his full height. He listened. He shoved his chest up against the air. "You heard me! Twenty-five bucks! Cash on the nail!"

Huge, shattering thunderclaps in the sky.

He turned around. Lights glared in the sky over town, each one followed by a cannon report that echoed and vaulted off the hills.

These were followed by sprays of iridescent color in fractured star-burst patterns. It was the grand finale of the fireworks show, and the first time he'd missed seeing it on the town common, with a hotdog in one hand and a cone of spun sugar in the other, in over fifteen years.

"It don't matter!" Jordy shouted at the sky. "I got the biggest damn firework Cleaves Mills ever seen! *And it's on my land!*"

Jordy went back to the house and was preparing to go into town when he remembered the drugstore would be closed because of the holiday. There was no way he could start getting his film developed until tomorrow. It seemed like there was nothing to do tonight but go to bed. That thought made him feel discontented and somehow sure that his luck hadn't changed after all; the gods of chance had been amused to haul him up by the scruff of the neck and show him twenty-five dollars and had then jammed him right back down in the dirt. After all, Verrill luck was Verrill luck, and you spelled that B-A-D. It had always been that way, why should it change? Jordy decided to go back out and look at his meteor, half convinced that it had probably disappeared by now.

The meteor was still there, but the heat seemed to have turned the Quaker Oats stuff to a runny liquid that looked like flour paste with too much water added in. It was seeping into the ground, and it must have been some kind of hot, too, because steam was rising out of the burned crescent of ground beside the creek in little banners.

He decided to take the meteor halves back to the house after all, then changed his mind back again. He told himself he was afraid he'd break it into still more pieces, being as clumsy as he was, and he told himself that it might stay hot for a long time; it might melt right through whatever he put it in and put the house afire while he was sleeping. But that wasn't it. The truth was that he just didn't like it. Nasty goddam thing, no telling where it had been or what that white stuff had been, that meteor shit inside it.

As Jordy pulled off his boots and got ready to go to bed, he winced at the pain in his fingers. They hurt like hell, and they had blistered up pretty much the way he had expected. Well, he wasn't going to let this get away, that was all.

He'd take those pictures in to get developed tomorrow and then he'd think about who might know someone at the college. Mr. Warren the banker probably did, except he still owed Mr. Warren seven hundred dollars and he'd probably take anything Jordy made as payment on his bill. Well, somebody else then. He'd think it over in the morning.

He unbuttoned his shirt, doing it with his left hand because his right was such a misery, and hung it up. He took off his pants and his thermal underwear, which he wore year-round, and then went into the bathroom and took the Cornhusker's Lotion out of the medicine cabinet. He spread some of the pearly-colored fluid on the blisters that had raised up on his right fingers and then turned out the lights and went to bed. He tossed and turned for a long time and when sleep finally did come, it was thin and uneasy.

He woke at dawn, feeling sick and feverish, his throat as dry as an old chip, his head throbbing. His eyes kept wanting to see two of everything.

"God almighty damn," he muttered, and swung his feet over onto the floor. It felt like he had the grippe. Good thing he had plenty of Bacardi rum and Vicks ointment. He would smear his chest up with Vicks and put a rag around his throat and stay in. Watch TV and drink Bacardi and just sweat her out.

"That's the ticket," Jordy said. "That's—"

He saw his fingers.

The next few minutes were hysteria, and he didn't come back to his wits until he was downstairs with the phone in his hand, listening to that answering service tell him Doc Condon wouldn't be back until tomorrow afternoon. He hung up numbly. He looked down at his fingers again.

Green stuff was growing out of them.

They didn't hurt anymore; they itched. The blisters had broken in the night, leaving raw-looking depressions in the pads of his fingers and there was this green stuff growing in there like moss. Fuzzy short tendrils, not pale green like grass when it first comes up, but a darker, more vigorous green.

It came from touching that meteor, he thought. "I wisht I never saw it," he said. "I wish it come down on somebody else's property."

But wish in one hand, spit in the other, as his daddy would have said. Things were what they were, and he was just going to have to sit down and do some Big Thinking about it. He would—

God, he had been rubbing his eyes!

That was the first thing he did every morning when he woke up, rubbed the sleepy seeds out of his eyes. It was the first thing *anybody* did, as far as he knew. You wiped your left eye with your left hand and your right eye with…with…

Jordy bolted for the living room, where there was a mirror bolted on the back of the closet door. He stared into his eyes. He looked for a long time, even going so far as to pull the lids away from the eyeballs. He did it with his left hand.

They were okay.

A little bloodshot, and scared for damn sure, but otherwise they were just Jordy Verrill's blue forty-six-year-old peepers, a little near-sighted now so he had to wear specs when he read the seed catalogue or one of his Louis L'Amour westerns or one of the dirty books he kept in the drawer of his night-table.

Uttering a long sigh, he went back upstairs. He used half a package of Red Cross cotton carefully bandaging his fingers. It took him quite awhile, working only with his left hand, which was his dumb hand.

When he was done he knew it was time to sit down for a spell of Big Thinking, but he couldn't face that yet so he went out to look at his meteor.

He groaned when he saw it; he couldn't help it.

The white stuff was all gone. The steam was gone. So was the burned crescent of ground. Where the burn had been there was now a fresh growth of dark green tendrils, already as high as clipped grass. It had begun to rain in the night, and the rain had brought it along fast.

Jordy shuddered just looking at it. The fingers of his right hand itched insanely, making him want to turn around and run back to the shed and turn on the faucet and rip off the cotton and stick his fingers under its cooling flow…

But that would make it worse. Look what just a little rain had done to this here.

He crept a little closer to the clear line of demarcation between yellow hay stubble and new green growth. He hunkered down and looked at it. He had never seen any plant that grew so thick, not even clover. Even with your nose practically touching the stuff you couldn't see the ground. It was the exact color of a flourishing, well-tended lawn, but the plants weren't blades. They were round instead of flat, and tiny tendrils sprouted from each stalk like branches from the bole of a tree. Except that they were more limber than branches. What they really reminded him of were arms…horrible boneless green arms.

Then Jordy's breath stopped in his throat. If anyone had been close enough to see him, they would have been reminded of that old saying, *he had his ear to the ground*. In this case it was literally true.

He could hear the stuff growing.

Very faintly the earth was groaning, as if in a sleep filled with pain. He could hear it being pulled apart and riddled by the strong thrust of this thing's root system. Pebbles clunked against pebbles. Clods crumbled into loose particles. And woven through these sounds was another: the rubbing of each tiny round stalk pushing itself up a little further and a little further. A grinding, squealing sound.

"Christ have mercy!" Jordy whined, and scrambled to his feet. He backed away. It wasn't the sound of plant growth that frightened him, exactly; once, long ago in his youth, he had heard the corn making. Nowadays the smartasses said that was just a story the rubes told each other, like holding frogs would bring on warts and stump-liquor would charm them off. But when the summer was just right, hot every day and heavy showers at night, you could hear it. In August you could hear it for maybe two nights. Jordy's father had fetched him out of bed and they had stood on the back porch of the old place not even breathing, and sure enough, Jordy had heard that low, grinding rumble from their cornpatch.

He could remember the low, red-swollen moon casting dim fire on the broad green leaves, the jumbled scarecrow that fluttered and dangled on the fence like a horrid and grinning Halloween treasure, the sound of crickets. And that…that other sound. It had scared him then, although his daddy said it was perfectly natural. It had scared him plenty. But it hadn't scared him like this.

This sound was like an earthquake whispering deep down in the earth, working itself up through bedrock, shunting boulders aside, moving the ground, getting ready to make plates waltz off their shelves and coffee cups tap-dance from counters to shatter on the linoleum. It was at the same time the smallest and the biggest sound he had ever heard.

Jordy turned and ran back to his house.

Now you can explain why a smart man will do something, because a smart man goes by the facts. If a smart man gets car trouble, he goes to a service station. If he gets wasps in his house, he calls the exterminator. And if a smart man gets sick somehow, he calls the doctor.

Jordy Verrill wasn't a smart man. He wasn't feeble or retarded, but he sure wasn't going to win any Quiz Kid award, either. When God hands out the smart pills, he gives some people placebos, and Jordy was one of those. And you can't predict what a man will do in a given situation after he reaches a certain degree of dumbness, because the man himself doesn't know if he's going to shit or put his fingers in the fan.

Jordy didn't call another doctor, not even after lunch when he looked into the mirror on the back of the closet door and saw the green stuff growing out of his right eye.

There was another doctor in Cleaves Mills besides Dr. Condon. But Jordy had never been to Dr. Oakley because he had heard that Dr. Oakley was a son of a bitch. Dr. Condon never acted that way, and Jordy like him. Also, Oakley was reputed to be fond of giving shots, and Jordy still retained his childhood fear of being injected. Doc Condon was more of a pill man, and usually he would give you the pills free, from samples. Paying up, that was another thing. Jordy had heard that Doc Oakley had a little sign on his waiting room wall that said IT IS CUSTOMARY TO PAY CASH UNLESS AR-RANGEMENTS HAVE BEEN MADE IN ADVANCE. That was hard scripture for an odd job man like Jordy Verrill, especially with the hay as poor as it had been this year. But Doc Condon only sent out bills when he remembered to, which was rarely.

None of these are smart reasons for not going to the doctor, but Jordy had one other, so deep he could never say it in words. He didn't really want to go to see *any* doctor, because he was afraid to find out what was wrong with him. And what if it was so bad that Doc Oakley decided to stick him in the hospital? He was deadly afraid of that place, because when you went in it was only a matter of time before they lugged you out in a canvas bag.

Still he might have gone to Doc Oakley if the answering service had said Doc Condon wasn't going to be back for a week. But just until tomorrow, that wasn't so bad. He could call Doc Condon tomorrow and get him to come out *here*, and not have to sit in anybody's waiting room where everyone could see that revolting green stuff growing out of his eye.

"That's the ticket," he whispered to himself. "That's what to do."

He went back to the TV, a glass of rum in a water glass by his hand. Tiny green fuzz was visible, growing on the white of his right eye like moss on a stone. Limber tendrils hung over the lower lid. It itched something dreadful.

And so the eye, of course, resorted to its old tried-and-true method of cleansing itself, and that's why Jordy, had he been a smart man, would have gotten over to Doc Oakley's office just as fast as his old Dodge pickup could travel.

His right eye was watering. A regular little sprinkling can.

He fell asleep halfway through the afternoon soap operas. When he woke up at five o'clock he was blind in his right eye. He looked in the mirror and moaned. His faded-blue right eye was gone. What was in the socket now was a waving green jungle of weeds, and some of the little creepers hung halfway down his cheek.

He put one hand up to his face before he could stop himself. He couldn't just rip the stuff out, the way you would hoe up the witchgrass in your tomato sets. He couldn't do that because his eye was still in there someplace.

Wasn't it?

Jordy screamed.

The scream echoed through his house, but there was no one to hear it because he was alone. He had never been so dreadfully alone in his life. It was eight o'clock in the evening and he had drunk the whole bottle of Bacardi and he still wasn't schnockered. He wished he *was* schnockered. He had never wanted so badly to be out of sobriety.

He had gone into the bathroom to piss off some of the rum, and that green stuff was growing out of his penis. Of course it was. It was wet down there, wasn't it? Almost always a little bit wet.

Jordy went just the same but it itched and hurt so much that he couldn't tell which was worse. And maybe next time he wouldn't be able to go at all.

That wasn't what had made him scream. The thought of having that stuff *inside* him, that had made him scream. It was a million times worse than the time he had gotten the bat caught in his hair while he was insulating old Missus Carver's attic. Somehow the green plants had picked the two best parts of him, his eyes and his pecker. It wasn't fair, it wasn't fair at all. It seemed like Jordy's luck was always in, and you spelled that kind of luck B-A-D.

He started to cry and made himself stop because that would only make it grow the faster.

He had no more hard liquor but there was half a bottle of Ripple in the ice box so he filled his tumbler with that and sat down again, dully watching the TV with his good eye. He glanced down at his right hand and saw green tendrils had wriggled out from underneath the cotton…and some stalks had pushed right up through it.

"I'm growin," he said emptily, and moaned again.

The wine made Jordy sleepy and he dozed off. When he woke up it was ten-thirty and at first he was so muzzy from everything he had drunk that he didn't remember what had happened to him. All he was sure of was that his mouth tasted funny, as if he had been chewing grass. Awful taste. It was like—

Jordy bolted for the mirror. Ran his tongue out. And screamed again.

His tongue was covered with the fuzzy green growth, the insides of his cheeks were downy with it, and even his teeth looked greenish, as if they were rotting.

And he itched. Itched like fire, all over. He remembered once when he had been deer-hunting and he had to take a squat right that minute, or else. And he had gone and done it right in a patch of poison sumac—Jordy's luck was always in. That had been a bad itch, the rash he had gotten from that, but this was worse. This was a nightmare. His fingers, his eye, his pecker, and now his mouth.

Cold water!

The thought was so focused, so steely, that it didn't seem like his own at all. Commanding, it came again: *cold water!*

He had a vision of filling up the old clawfoot bathtub upstairs with cold water, then ripping off all his clothes and jumping in, drowning the itch forever.

Madness. If he did that it would grow all over him, he would come out looking like a swamp-log covered with moss. And yet the thought of cold water wouldn't go away, it was crazy, all right, but it would be so *good*, so *good* to just soak in cold water until the itch was all gone.

He started back to his chair and stopped.

Green stuff was sprouting from its overstuffed right arm. It was all over the worn and stringy brown fabric. On the table beside it, where there had been a ring of moisture from his glass, there was now a ring of green stalks and tendrils.

He went out into the kitchen and looked into the trash-bag. More of the green stuff was growing all over the Bacardi bottle he had dropped in earlier. And a Del Monte pineapple chunks can next to the Bacardi bottle. And an empty Heinz catsup bottle next to the Del Monte can. Even his garbage was being overrun.

Jordy ran for the phone, picked it up, then banged it back down. Who could he call? Did he really want anyone to see him like this?

He looked at his arms and saw that his own sweat-glands were betraying him. Among the reddish-gold hairs on his forearms, a new growth was sprouting. It was green.

"I'm turnin' into a weed," he said distractedly, and looked around as if the walls would tell him what to do. They didn't and he sat down in front of the TV again.

It was his eye—what had been his eye—that finally broke him down. The itching just seemed to be going deeper and deeper into his head, and creeping down his nose at the same time.

"I can't help it," he groaned, "Oh my Jesus, I can't!"

He went upstairs, a grotesque, shambling figure with green arms and a forest growing out of one eye socket. He lurched into the bathroom, jammed the plug into the bathtub drain, and turned the cold water faucet on full. His jury-rigged plumbing thumped and groaned and clanked. The sound of cool water splashing into the tub made him tremble all over with eagerness. He tore his shirt off and was not much revolted by the new growth sprouting from his navel. He kicked his boots off, shoved his pants and thermals and skivvies down all at once. His upper thighs were forested with the growth and his pubic hair was twined with the limber green tendrils that sprouted from the plants' central stalks. When the tub was three-quarters full, Jordy could no longer control himself. He jumped in.

It was heaven.

He rolled and flopped in the tub like some clumsy, greenish porpoise, sending water sheeting onto the floor. He ducked his head and sloshed water over the back of his neck. He shoved his face under and came up blowing water.

And he could feel the new growth-spurt, could feel the weeds that had taken root in his body moving forward with amazing, terrifying speed.

Shortly after midnight, a slumped, slowly moving figure topped the rise between Jordy Verrill's farm and Bluebird Creek. It stood looking down at the place where a meteor had impacted less than thirty hours before.

Jordy's east pasture was a sea of growing green weeds. The hay was gone for a distance of a hundred and sixty yards in every direction. Already the growth nearest the creek was over a foot and a half high, and the tendrils that sprouted from the stalks moved with a twisting, writhing movement that was almost sentient. At one point the Bluebird itself was gone; it flowed into a green marsh and came out four feet further downstream. A peninsula of green had already marched ten feet up the bank of Arlen McGinty's land.

The figure that stood looking down on this was really not Jordy Verrill anymore. It was hard to say what it might be. It was vaguely humanoid, the way a snowman that had begun to melt is humanoid. The shoulders were rounded. The head was a fuzzy green ball with no sign of a neck between it and the shoulders. Deep down in all that green, one faded-blue iris gleamed like a pale sapphire.

In the field, tendrils suddenly waved in the air like a thousand snakes coming out of a thousand Hindu fakirs' baskets, and pointed, trembling, at the figure standing on the knoll. And on the figure, tendrils suddenly pointed back. Momentarily Jordy had a semblance of humanity again: he looked like a man with his hair standing on end.

Jordy, his thoughts dimming with the tide of greenness that now grew from the very meat of his brain, understood that a kind of telepathy was going on.

Is the food good?

Yes, very good. Rich.

Is he the only food?

No, much food. His thoughts say so.

Does the food have a name?

Two names. Sometimes it is called Jordy-food. Sometimes it is called Cleaves Mills-food.

Jordy-food. Cleaves Mills-food. Rich. Good.

His thoughts say he wants to bang. Can he do that?

What bang?

Don't know. Some Jordy-thing.

Good. Rich. Let him do what he wants.

The figure, like a badly controlled puppet on frayed strings, turned and lurched back toward the house.

In the glow of the kitchen light, Jordy was a monster. A monster in the true sense, nearly as ludicrous as it was terrifying. He looked like a walking privet hedge.

The hedge was crying.

It had no tears to cry, because the growth was mercilessly absorbing every bit of moisture that Jordy's failing systems could produce.

But it cried just the same, in its fashion, as it pulled the .410 Remington from its hooks over the shed door.

It put the gun to what had been Jordy Verrill's head. It could not pull the trigger by itself but the tendrils helped, perhaps curious to see if the bang would make the Jordy-food more tasty. They curled around the trigger and tightened until the hammer dropped.

A dry click.

Jordy's luck was always in.

Somehow it got the shells from the desk drawer in the living room. The tendrils curled around one of them, lifted it, dropped it into the chamber, and closed the slide mechanism. Again they helped to pull the trigger.

The gun banged. And Jordy Verrill's last thought was: *Oh thank God, lucky at last!*

The weeds reached the edge of the highway by dawn and began to grow around a signpost that said CLEAVES MILLS, TWO MILES. The round stalks whispered and rubbed against each other in a light dawn breeze. There was a heavy dew and the weeds sucked it up greedily.

Jordy-food.

A fine planet, a wet planet. A ripe planet.

Cleaves Mills-food.

The weeds began to grow toward town.